EXPLICIT DETAIL

SCARLETT FINN

Also by Scarlett Finn

GO NOVELS
GO WITH IT
GO IT ALONE
GO ALL OUT
GO ALL IN
GO FULL CIRCLE

EXILE
HIDE & SEEK
KISS CHASE

WRECK & RUIN
RUIN ME
RUIN HIM

**THE BRANDED
SERIES**
BRANDED
SCARRED
MARKED

**FORBIDDEN
PREQUEL DUET**
ALL. ONLY.
ONLY YOURS

TO DIE FOR...
TO DIE FOR TRUTH
TO DIE FOR HONOR
TO DIE FOR VIRTUE
TO DIE FOR DUTY
TO DIE FOR LOVE

**LOVE AGAINST THE ODDS
STANDALONE COLLECTION**
SWEET SEAS
HEIR'S AFFAIR
RESCUED
MAESTRO'S MUSE
GETTING TRICKY
THIRTEEN
REMEMBER WHEN...
RELUCTANT SUSPICION
XY FACTOR

NOTHING TO...
NOTHING TO HIDE
NOTHING TO LOSE
NOTHING TO DECLARE
NOTHING TO US
NOTHING TO SAY
NOTHING TO GAIN
NOTHING TO YOU
NOTHING TO THIS

THE FORBIDDEN NOVELS
FORBIDDEN DESIRE
FORBIDDEN WANT
FORBIDDEN WISH
FORBIDDEN NEED

KINDRED SERIES
RAVEN
SWALLOW
CUCKOO
SWIFT
FALCON
FINCH

THE EXPLICIT SERIES
EXPLICIT INSTRUCTION
EXPLICIT DETAIL
EXPLICIT MEMORY

MISTAKE DUET
MISTAKE ME NOT
SLEIGHT MISTAKE

**RISQUÉ & HARROW
INTERTWINED**
TAKE A RISK
FIGHTING FATE
RISK IT ALL
FIGHTING BACK
GAME OF RISK

LOST & FOUND
LOST
FOUND

ONE

"WOULD YOU RELAX?"

"No."

"Ask a stupid question…" Flick muttered to herself, pushing her shoulders back against the poolside chair to tilt her chin toward the blazing sun.

Rushe's eyes narrowed further. She opted to ignore him. "You're doing that on purpose," he growled. "We're all aware of your tits. You don't have to put them on show."

"Rushe, baby, I love you, but we came out to the pool to relax."

"No, Kitten," he said. "You came here to relax."

"You didn't have to come with me."

"You're wearing a bikini," he said, as though it required no further explanation, and actually… it didn't.

"If you thought I was the type to run around on you, you'd have dumped me three months ago. You'd have walked out of my studio apartment with Jansen. I wouldn't have seen you for dust."

"If I thought you were that type, I'd have chained

you to the wall weeks ago."

"You have… once or twice." Oversized shades concealed her eyes, but she let her head roll toward him anyway. "You could've at least brought a bathing suit… do you own a bathing suit?"

"We didn't come here to swim. We came here 'cause you like baiting me."

"You didn't have to—"

"You're wearing a bikini."

She twisted as she sat to set her feet on the ground between their parallel chairs. Theirs were just two of forty similar loungers arranged around the glistening outdoor pool.

When she tried to glare, the intensity of his burning eyes distracted her. Her love's concession of the day was removing his tee-shirt. That was a big concession coming from him. One which gave her an up close reminder of how capable he was, how he possessed her… and of how his body lured hers.

"You're here to protect my virtue from other sexual predators." Rushe did his own sexual stalking of her on a daily basis. "But when you look at me like that… I'm the only person here."

"I'm looking at you," he said. "But I'm aware of exactly where the other thirty-seven men are."

"You counted them," she said on a sigh. "Of course you counted them. There must be fifty women here."

"That I hadn't noticed."

Rushe never tried to romance her. Sweet nothings definitely did not feature in his repertoire of skills. But he could charm her. Unintentionally. Somehow, that made it all the more potent… not something she should be aroused by while people surrounded them.

"I'm going to get a drink," she said, sashaying

away from their seats without giving him a chance to retort.

She weaved through various groups of people to reach her aim. As she progressed, she was most conscious of one constant, Rushe's eyes burning into her spine. His stare was so intense, and already being protected by it was second nature to her.

At the refreshment stand, she ordered for herself and Rushe too. As the vendor disappeared to fill the order, she drummed her fingernails on the counter.

"Let me buy that for you."

Uh oh. She didn't want to turn around and give face to the words. One thing was for sure, they hadn't come from Rushe's mouth.

"No, thanks," she said, leaning over the counter seeking the drinks guy, silently pleading with him to hurry up.

"A beautiful thing like you shouldn't be buying her own drinks."

"I'm not," she said. "My boyfriend opened a tab when we arrived."

"Is that your standard response? You must get hit on a lot."

"Not so much recently, if I'm honest."

These days she was aware of drawing men's attention. Partly because her more recently found vigilance made her look around. The other part? Rushe. He went on high alert when men looked at her.

"I'll change that if you turn around and talk to me," he said.

"No, actually, that's not a good idea."

"What do you mean—"

"Problem?"

Yep. They definitely had one now.

"No problem," she sang, cursing her need for hydration.

"I wasn't asking you," Rushe said.

She spun to see him looming over the man who'd spoken to her. "Said boyfriend," she said by way of explanation. "I did try to warn you."

Rushe hadn't been having fun… until he had this hapless victim in his sights. He would remind her it was impossible to be a hundred percent sure of someone's intentions. This guy didn't pose an obvious threat, but her love had been bored, now he had sport.

This couldn't end well. At least it couldn't end well for the guy who didn't have a shred of a tan left. His pallor likely had more to do with the invisible pressure Rushe exerted than the lack of sunlight.

"Maybe we should go," she said.

Though her words were vague, the intent of her intonation was to convey her adamance.

"You're having fun," Rushe said, without taking his attention from the shrinking man.

"I was having fun," she said.

Though sitting by the pool hadn't been fun so much as foreplay.

Rushe was commanding in the bedroom at the best of times. But subtle actions on her part could push him closer to the edge. Her love took what he wanted, when he wanted it, and she didn't make a habit of refusing him. In fact, she could count on one hand the number of times she had.

The stranger spoke up, "Man, I didn't mean anything by it. She's a good looking woman and—"

"Trust me, you're only making things worse," she said, coiling her fingers around Rushe's wrist. "I want to go home now."

"I'm busy," Rushe grumbled, in that way when his lips didn't move.

"Ignore him, he intimidates for a living," she said.

Rushe didn't say anything. As the guy shrank even further back, her nails dug deeper into her love.

"He's good at it," the guy stuttered.

"I want to have sex," she said.

"I don't," Rushe replied.

"Yes, you do. You're just being ornery."

"And you're trying to distract me."

"Even so," she said. "You get sex out of the deal."

"If I want sex, I get sex. I say when."

Rushe knew how to take control and liked to imply sex was for his pleasure above all else. But when his pleasure came from controlling her orgasms time and again, she was okay with the illusion.

"I want sex now, and if you won't supply…"

She released his wrist but didn't get two inches away before Rushe's hand snapped up to seize her wrist.

"You want me to hurt people?"

"No," she said. "Hurting them is your choice. All I'm looking for is a little attention… topless sunbathing is allowed around here, isn't it?"

Rushe's growl wasn't audible, but she felt it all the same. Her smile spread. She'd achieved her goal… both of them knew it.

"I'll get the car."

He turned and hooked her hand into his back jean's pocket. She laid her smile briefly on Rushe's stricken almost-victim while trotting along behind her love. Judging by the strength and the breadth of his gait, he was sufficiently tormented to make every second of their next joining count.

TWO

NO ONE WOULD MISS that Rushe was dangerous. Her first encounter with him had been in voice only. Back then, the deep resonance of his tone stopped her in her tracks. Just a shame she hadn't heeded the instruction his words gave.

Although if she had, she wouldn't be with him now. Funny what she'd had to endure to find the most important thing in her world. Every second was worth it. He was worth it.

Walking into that bar, in spite of Rushe's warning, threw her into the path of criminal depravity. Much to her shock and confusion, Rushe protected her. Until it was safe to free her from the criminals' hideout, he'd kept her under his wing. When the time was right, he'd cast her out. His harsh behavior saved her life. Except the evil brought her back, twice. Each time Rushe protected her, to his own detriment, until…

By then, they were both in deep and at the penultimate play had confessed their love. The truth was revealed when there was no way out. When they thought losing their lives was guaranteed.

To that day, she wasn't sure how they'd made it out alive. The odds had been stacked against them. Liberating Rushe from his confines had ensured she and Jansen, the undercover cop working with her, came out on top.

With most of the criminals dead or behind bars, she'd had a choice. Remain in her mediocre life, with a sub-par job, without friends to trust, and estranged from her family, or she could be with the man she loved.

The decision wasn't difficult.

Rushe was a man with a checkered past, a vagrant lifestyle, and some serious trust issues. He wasn't on any system; the system had failed him from almost the moment he was born. He'd never known his parents, never had family, and always relied on himself.

One tragic episode in Rushe's pre-teen years shaped the path of his life. A woman he'd barely known was tortured and killed. Though he'd witnessed the attackers carry the woman away, he'd been powerless to stop them.

To look at the man he was now, it was difficult to believe he could ever be powerless. That was because he'd spent his life ensuring he never would be again.

She stretched her toes in her sandals and wiggled them while peeking at his solid form in the driver's seat. He hadn't said a word since he'd powered out of the pool parking lot. But they were nearly home, and she struggled to keep her eager anticipation in check.

During the mission that brought her and Rushe together, she'd been held for a ransom that Rushe paid. After, he'd told her that the job paid well and he knew people, whatever that meant.

His bank balance was healthy, but he lived modestly. His car wasn't new, his apartment decent. Rushe didn't care where they lived or about things. She'd asked why a boy raised with nothing wouldn't take full advantage of his improved means. His response had broken her heart.

"*It doesn't pay to get attached to anything,*" he'd said. "*Attachment is another word for weakness.*"

Men like him didn't get attached. No matter how many times Rushe said those words to her, he hadn't been able to resist their bond. He'd told her he resented their love, but he didn't really. The contempt wasn't resentment, it was fear, and men like Rushe didn't experience fear.

Having her, accepting their union, was a risk, and he tried to minimize those. Now that they had each other, Rushe's emotional issues flared up. He feared trusting her, and their feelings for each other, because losing her, or letting her down, was his biggest burden.

A button on the dash opened the shutters for their underground parking lot. Rushe drove down the ramp to park in their usual spot.

"So, Lover…" she said into the ether. "What now?"

"Sex."

There was the monosyllabic man she loved and adored. As he slammed out of the car, she dawdled over unfastening her seatbelt. As she predicted, her side door was wrenched open, and he hauled her out without finesse.

The moment he pressed the elevator call button, the doors opened, as though the carriage was intimidated by Rushe's mood too. A few seconds later, a ding declared them on their floor, and he pulled her down the hall to their door.

The apartment was spacious, with half the external wall made up of windows from the ceiling down. To the left upon entering was a solid partition, hiding the otherwise open-plan kitchen from the rest of the living space.

He dragged her past the dividing kitchen countertop to the alcove hallway, which led to the other rooms: a family bathroom and two bedrooms. The second bedroom was presently half study, half gym. The latter was a necessity for a guy like Rushe.

He hung a right into their corner master suite. They had a wall of built-in storage, and their private shower room was accessible at the other side of the bed.

In the bedroom, Rushe relaxed, and with a generous nudge he sent her stumbling onto the bed. Before she could steady herself, he grabbed her hips to pull them up, getting an eyeful of her ass.

His grunt of satisfaction made her smile, and while his hand skimmed her curves, she straightened her arms to prop herself up on all fours. Describing Rushe's skills as a lover never did them justice. He'd told her she was the only woman he'd made love to in his entire life, and she believed it. This man, her man, didn't do soft, not at first. Her patience paid dividends.

Rushe's fingers traveled over her bathing suit down, between her legs, until they found her opening.

With slight pressure, he began to circle it. "You think you're smart, don't you, Kitten? You think you're a bad girl. You think you're tough… Playing games with me is dangerous, Kitten, very dangerous."

Curling one finger around the crotch of her suit, he pulled it aside to plunge two fingers into her. Yes. Oh, yes, she pushed back to meet them.

"Oh," Rushe said with that dry, sinister amusement he utilized so well. "I know you like that, Kitten. I know just what you want. You're my horny little slut, pleasure on demand, that's what you are to me…"

His fingers withdrew, but the bite of disappointment didn't last. He dragged her suit down her thighs, just enough to reveal her most intimate corner, then he stopped. Everything stopped.

"Are you going to fuck me?" she asked, trying hard not to beg or show impatience despite the rising heat of blood rushing through her veins.

"Maybe."

"Maybe?"

She hadn't meant to sound quite so indignant.

His heavy hand smacked her ass in immediate punishment. "You been screwing around?"

"What?" she barked, astounded by the insane question.

"Your little boyfriend might like the attitude but don't forget your place here. You get it when I give it, and you'll be grateful for it."

She always was.

Always.

She would never have imagined her life looking like this. Could never have imagined playing their games or that she'd enjoy them so much.

"Up," he commanded. She jumped off the bed, tugging up her suit, finding herself right up close to the bearer of those arousing words. "You got something to say?"

"Sorry," she said. His head tilted a few degrees. "Sorry, sir."

"Strip."

She was almost as close to naked as someone could get without going all the way. But she did as told, taking careful time to untie each knot, the one behind her neck, the one on her left hip...

Rushe bared his teeth in familiar frustration. While he gave the orders, she held the power. The control... Almost. Before she reached the next knot, his thick, muscular arm came around her waist to haul her body against his. It took a few seconds to register his damp, devouring lips and the slick heat of his tongue invading her mouth.

When they'd met, Rushe hadn't been a kisser. That changed after they made love for the first time. He gave her so much, more of himself than he'd ever given anyone.

Coiling her arms around his neck, she prepared for their mouths to battle it out a while. So when in the next breath, he thrust her away, she reeled.

"Let's see those cans."

Rushe loved her breasts. Then again, he loved every part of her.

Twisting her arms around to her back, she untied the top and let it flutter to the floor. Her love said nothing. His gaze gobbled her breasts as though this was their first encounter.

Rushe didn't have to move closer, he lifted his arms and cupped a breast in each hand, testing their weight, their texture, their responsiveness. She'd never been a fan of the large breasts that dominated her meagre five three stature… not until Rushe laid his eyes, and his hands, on them.

"You've got a body made for sin, whore," Rushe said, rolling her nipples then caressing their very tips in the way he knew drove her wild.

"Rushe," she sighed, relaxing into his hold.

"You talk when I tell you to."

She could only nod. Her eyes closed, anticipating his mouth, yearning for it. With his skill, he could torment her for hours playing with her breasts, her figure. His entitlement over her was enthralling, his ownership gave her an intoxicating power. She wanted him to be entitled, to possess her body and her pleasure.

"Naked." With his one stern word, she untied the last knot, finally presenting herself for him, bare, without barriers. "Just my insignificant plaything."

Her eyes remained closed, reveling in the wonder

of his voice. Each of them lived in awe of the other. In amazement they would choose to love and live with each other.

She opened her eyes to his and moved her hand slightly toward his fly. "Can I...?"

Rushe shook his head. "On your knees."

A shimmer of arousal quaked her and he didn't miss it. He hadn't bothered putting his tee-shirt back on, it still hung tucked in at the back of his jeans. So close to his sculpted form, it was difficult to resist the urge to touch, to taste, but he'd just given her implicit access to his most valuable asset... or the physical one she valued most in moments like this anyway.

Taking his order, she descended to her knees, her attention trained on his all the way. Sometimes she was meant to retrieve him, and sometimes he took the lead. She awaited further instruction and after eight seconds, his hand moved to the top of her head.

"You like to show off your stacked little body, Kitten. You like playing with me. You think you can push my buttons? Speak."

"No," she said.

In the moment it appeared he meant to respond, he was distracted by her tongue moistening her lips. "You lying to me?" he asked eventually. "Are you allowed to do that? Speak."

"No."

"You think you can push my buttons?"

Either her lungs had shrunk or the air in there was thinning, because her chest pulsed with the desperate shallow breaths that were all she could muster. "Yes."

THREE

SHE WAS RIGHT, though he didn't acknowledge or deny it. Unbuckling his belt, she sucked her lips in around her teeth ready to consume him. Like a starving animal, she shuffled forward a few inches.

"You dirty little skank," Rushe muttered. With a tug, he loosened the buttons on his jeans. Running his fingers through her hair from forehead to crown, he coiled them into a tight fist. "You want it? You wanna suck my cock? Do you? Speak."

"Yes."

"You hungry for it? You gonna suck the spunk from my balls? You want it? Speak."

"Yes."

On that syllable, he opened his jeans to liberate the heavy organ. It jutted up, hard, long, insistent. It might be daunting, sure was in their early days, but she didn't fear it, not anymore. Over the last few months, her technique had improved, and Rushe had no issue with her getting in as much practice as possible.

Guiding her toward his groin, Rushe shifted

forward a step and took himself in his other hand to touch the tip of his bulging head to her sealed lips.

"You're my whore, open."

Unlocking her jaw, her sticky lips parted as he yanked her forward and plunged in deep. The blunt top of his cock hit the back of her throat. Sliding out, he painted her lips with his pre-seed and urged himself into her cheek, undulating back and forth, reminding her of his mass. She tried to reposition, to direct him to the back of her mouth again, but his grip in her hair bit deeper, locking her in position.

"You're a greedy little slut," Rushe grumbled. "This isn't for your pleasure."

No, maybe not, but she loved it all the same. He surged into her throat, catching her off guard, so she didn't have the time to inhale. Rushe held for a couple of seconds then moved out and back in, stretching the confines of her throat half a dozen times, each advance slower than the last.

Retreating, he left her mouth entirely and bumped her aside. The taste of him on her lips gave her a craving for more. She flopped against the edge of the mattress, tucking her feet underneath herself.

Rushe sat on the edge of the bed, his denim clad thigh only a few inches from her head. He bent to unlace his boots, as if he had all the time in the world.

"Rushe," she sighed, angling her cheek to gaze up at him.

"You like it when I fuck that sweet little mouth of yours. You get what I give you. It's not feeding time yet."

He stood to shirk his jeans. As soon as he was naked, he took hold of her hair again, this time lifting his cock to ease her closer. She licked her lips and kissed the base of him before sucking on his balls. Yes, he knew how to pleasure her, but she knew how to return the favor. Using gentle pressure, she clasped and bounced them. She didn't hear his groan, it vibrated through him and into her.

The hand on the top of her head shifted until both were on the back of her skull. That was her invitation to take control. She parted her lips and took him into her mouth again. With a long suck, she held position. Releasing the vacuum of suction, she slurped him in and out. Exploring the ridges and grooves of his member again, she toyed with his testicles, placed kisses where she could, then pulled him into her throat again, sucking him in and letting her hand follow him out.

With another push his hands balled tight in her hair to increase her pace, forcing himself deeper until all she could do was breathe.

Extending her arms up between them, she dug her nails into his torso, scratching her way down to his groin until with a roar of possession, he surged into her throat and his thick, salty milk flowed into her belly.

His fast, shallow breathing was a thrill. Sometimes it still amazed her that she could do it for him. Long after she'd swallowed him, he stayed in her mouth. Maybe he'd forgotten. When she swallowed again, he twitched, and withdrew.

"On the bed," he said. "On your back."

She climbed up and landed on her back. Bringing her bare heels up to her rear, her knees fell apart, just how he liked her to present. Then, she waited.

"That snug little cunt of yours hungry?" he asked. She nodded. "If you weren't such a greedy little whore, I'd be fucking you right now. You want me to fuck you? Do you?" She nodded. "Speak."

"Yes."

His dirty talk got her deep every time. With just a few words, he could take her close to the edge. Now that they were together, he played it up, pushing further each time. Their deep-rooted trust allowed their sexual play to become almost like theatre. Each knew their roles, both worked hard to get the other riled more every time. It was a game. A saucy, sexy exchange that stirred them into a stimulated, lustful frenzy.

"You liked showing off those hot titties today? You're a little whore, out parading for those pretty boys… Those tits are mine. Your pussy is mine. Your body belongs to me. You do with it what I tell you. Speak."

"Yes, sir."

He opened his hand. "Ankle."

She stretched her leg toward him, he grabbed her ankle and thrust it up, yanking her closer to the edge of the bed. He bit the ball of her foot, then kissed it. He kissed her instep, her heel, her ankle. Crouching lower, he rested her calf on his shoulder and put a knee to the mattress between hers.

The anticipation prickled her skin.

His rough hand skimmed down her leg to the back of her knee, and she sighed at the delicate magic touch that trailed electricity in its wake. He'd found a soft spot there on the back of her knee that poured heavy embers into her abdomen, every hair on her body responded in salute.

"You don't deserve to be fucked, not after that stunt today."

"I'm sorry, Lover, I—"

"No," he said, slapping his other hand on her still bent knee. "You're gonna learn that playing with me has consequences."

Falling to his knees on the floor beside the bed, she was surprised when Rushe hooked her other leg over his shoulder and yanked her butt to the edge of the bed. He kissed her clit and ran his tongue down the seam of her body to push into her vacant passage. Her eyes sank shut as she wriggled against his advance. When his tongue retreated from within, he directed his attention back to her clit, flicking it repeatedly, he sucked it between his teeth and salved it with his tongue.

His arms came around her thighs and each of his thumbs pushed down the inside of her outer labia, narrowing the space his tongue played in, concentrating her pleasure.

"Rushe," she whimpered.

"You're dirty, Kitten. Dirty and desperate, you're fucking drenched. I'm drinking you down in mouthfuls. What's in your head now?"

"I'm thinking about your mouth, about your tongue, your hands, how you torment me."

Instantly, his mouth abandoned its post. She lifted her head to see his frowning eyes over her pubis.

"I torment you?"

"You know how you do," she said, crossing her legs at the back of his neck. "You know how much I want you." She constricted her legs slightly. "How much I love you."

She tightened further, but he got a hold of her ankles and ducked out of her vice.

"You're gonna pay for that manipulation," he said, rising to full height before her. "Maybe I leave you without."

Until then, he'd never left her sexually unsatisfied, but he wasn't the type to make false promises. Skimming her palms over her breasts, she stroked and squeezed, watching his eyes light and flare. She knew how to get her guy.

He shook his head. "Hands off. I didn't say you could play with my toys."

With force, he grabbed her knees and shunted her to the center of the bed then came down upon her. Taking a breast in each hand, he mimicked her squeeze and rolled her nipples. Dipping his head, he pinged one with his tongue, but the pampering didn't last long.

His face appeared above hers again. "Sex. The only thing a man thinks when he looks at you is sex. You weren't teasing them today; in his head, each one of those guys nailed you good. They were thinking about your body, what they'd do to your hot, tight ass."

Sweeping his arms under her, he took a butt cheek in each hand and adjusted her angle. His thickness took up residence in his tongue's playground, in a delectable, pleasurable torture.

"You belong to me, Kitten. You do what I tell you. No other man will ever touch you. If I see it again… if I have to watch one more man approach and threaten my property, I'll kill him, Felicity. I don't want any man near you."

"He didn't threaten me." Her love despised being out of control, but until that moment she hadn't realized how much that day riled him. "Lover…?"

"You're gonna see one day…"

"See what?"

"You're gonna see what I'm capable of."

"I know what you're capable of," she said. "I've been with you, we've been through it together."

"That was nothing."

There was more to his words than the physical. Something was going on in his head. "You've got something to lose now," she said, her fingers running into his hair. "That's what you're afraid of."

"I'm not afraid of nothing."

"You don't work alone anymore, Rushe. I stand by that. There isn't anything—"

"You don't know what you're talking about, Kitten. You think it's over. You think this is it. You think we're past the danger."

"We are."

"Danger is what I do," he said, with a shake of his head. "I've turned down a couple of dozen jobs these last three months because…"

"Because?"

"Nothing."

Just because they did it every day didn't mean it ever got boring. His hips rose and he thrust into her, forging a path of familiar union.

Familiar, but unexpected. "Oh, God, Rushe," she inhaled in surprise.

He withdrew and advanced, his lazy frequency crossed her eyes and moved her hips.

"That feel better?" he asked, grazing his nose down hers and licking her lower lip before he sucked it into his mouth. "You forget all about your troubles, my predictable little slut. I'll take care of everything. You think about my cock, Kitten. Think about it every second of the day. You keep my dick happy, and you'll have everything you could ever want… You thinking about my dick?" This time he held himself steady, half-in, half-out. "What do you want? Ask me."

"I want you to fuck me, Rushe," she breathed, opening her eyes to meet his.

"Yeah?" he asked, pulling back further. "I'm not convinced."

"Please," she said, locking her ankles at his lower back in hope of bringing him deeper.

"You're not stronger than me," he said, fully aware of what she was trying to do. "You get it when I give it."

"Please fuck me, Rushe. Please!"

"You learned your lesson?" She nodded. The very corner of his mouth twitched in amusement. "I fucking doubt it."

Pushing in, he filled all of her making it impossible to resist the urge to squeeze herself around him. When he froze, she curled her legs higher, tighter.

"More, please, sir… fuck me."

"Felicity Hughes," he murmured. "You're gonna fucking kill me one day."

She didn't like the statement, and wasn't sure of the sentiment, but he wiped away her worries by driving in fast. He picked up the pace until the knots in her stomach clamped tight. She was up for another ride to remember.

FOUR

MANY, MANY HOURS LATER, she yawned into the darkness and stretched herself out on the body she called her bed each night. The opportune lump in her mattress tempted her to wriggle south.

Rushe's chest fell in a regular pattern that betrayed he was still sleeping. Running her hands the width of his shoulders to his neck, she stroked the stubble on his jaw, and pressed on his chest as she slithered south.

Her intention had been to pleasure him awake, but her pussy kissed the rod she'd slept on, the temptation was too much to resist. She sat up, keeping him steady in one hand to spear herself deep. Still in the half-mist of sleep, she wriggled, side to side, in small circles, in a figure of eight.

Before Rushe, only one man had been inside her. All other sexual encounters had ended prematurely. Even after kissing and rolling around with other men, she'd never felt the urge to go all the way… then there was Rushe.

So despite being in her late twenties, she was still learning what to do sexually. What she liked, what Rushe did, what got each of them off, what worked.

Continuing her assault, she leaned back a little and nudged the head of his cock against a sensitive spot inside her. Resting her hands on his thighs, she lifted slightly. At this angle, she got him to the optimum ecstasy point and kept on rocking and writhing. She was almost lost to it when she heard a rapping noise.

Her body tensed. Her senses went on alert. She strained to listen and see if she could hear it again. The rapid knock was insistent. Only a couple of seconds later, it came again.

"Rushe," she whispered, slapping her hands to his chest. "Rushe."

On a grumpy mutter, he sucked in a breath.

Even though he didn't open his eyes, he spoke. "Sex."

"No," she said, unsure if he was awake. "I mean yes, we're having sex, but—"

The knock came again, and Rushe's eyes instantly opened. In an involuntary but flattering act, he observed her naked figure straddling him and his embedded member pulsed in satisfaction.

"Can't get you off my cock, can I?"

The knock sounded again, and he sat up.

"Is this it?" she asked. "The danger coming to us?"

The drawer in the nightstand on Rushe's side began to buzz. He reached past her to open it and retrieved a small black pager she'd never seen before. She also couldn't see the glowing screen he now read.

The knock distracted her again. "Should I get dressed? Do I need a weapon?"

"You don't need to do anything," Rushe said. With an arm around her waist for support, he dipped her back to kiss each of her nipples. "Don't touch. I'll finish you off when I get back."

He lifted her body away from his, but she snatched his neck. "Back? You're not going anywhere without me. What's going on?"

"No time to explain, Kitten."

"But—"

"No," he said without humor, so she let him remove her hands from his body.

Still with the pager in one hand, he grabbed his jeans from the floor to put them on.

She sat alone and naked in the middle of the mattress, feeling hollow now that he no longer occupied her body or her bed. "I love you," she said as he clipped the pager onto his belt.

His eyes flicked to hers. "I'm not gonna die. I'm going into the living room, that's it."

She snatched the corner of their sheet to her chest. "You're inviting them in here?"

The knocking continued. Either the person didn't know not to piss off Rushe by hurrying him, or they were frantic.

When he observed her action and her position his brows clamped down. "You think I would let anyone hurt you?" He approached the bed again. "Do you think I would let anyone into our home who'd hurt you?" He stole the sheet from her hands and tossed it off the end of the bed.

"I—"

"Up!" Rushe demanded.

"But—"

"Up!"

She rose to her knees and walked on them to the side where he stood. "They're still out there."

"They'll wait," he growled, without moving his lips. "This…" he grabbed her breasts, "is mine."

"I know."

One hand began to work her nipple, while the other glided down her sensitive waist to her hip and descended to cup between her legs.

"No one touches what's mine. You'll always be safe here."

"I know," she said, hooking her hands into his jeans pockets to rest her weight on him. "But I still love you."

"I know." At the same time she kissed his jaw, one of his fingers jabbed into her up to his knuckle, taking her by surprise. "I'll wake you when I'm done."

As he departed, he took his invading finger into his mouth to clean her taste from his digit.

FIVE

SHE TRUSTED RUSHE'S instinct. He regularly gave her commands to obey... though, if they weren't sex related, it was hit or miss whether she'd comply with them.

They'd known each other for less than half a year, but with the gravity of what they'd experienced together, they understood each other's essence. Again, not something she'd say to him. But that night reminded her she didn't know all of what he was or everything about him.

She'd trust Rushe with her life and had done so in the past. Still, questions zoomed through her mind just like they hung in Rushe's aura. But she wouldn't push, not with a potential threat in the next room.

This was the part she struggled with the most. Not so much the being left out, though she didn't like that, more the temptation of information just out of reach. Her curiosity grew. Lying there in their bed, alone, listening to the distant murmur of voices drifting through, she felt helpless and didn't like it. He'd spoken about them working together, but so far, hadn't had the whisper of work. At least that was what she'd believed until his declaration he'd been turning jobs down.

Rushe was selective. In describing what he did, he'd told her he was "…*the guy people come to when every other avenue has been exhausted.*" More curiosity. Being with him gave her confidence. He provided a security she'd never had in her life before. In return, Rushe got acceptance from her. She'd never tried to change him, and never would.

But he'd been out in their living room for an hour with whomever had been battering down their front door. She wouldn't sleep with them out there. Strangers, and unknowns, weren't conducive to slumber. Telling her he'd wake her was wishful thinking on Rushe's part. It was also his way of telling her to stay out of it. Another thing he should know better about her.

Sick of lying there wondering, she punched the mattress to sit up. Being there helped no one, and she didn't want to be out of the loop. Rushe would take care of her from a distance forever if she let him, but she didn't want to be treated like glass. From the moment they'd met, he treated her as a woman, he didn't handle her with kid gloves. Just because she didn't want him to change didn't mean he hadn't.

Decision made, she tiptoed out of the bed and swept his tee-shirt up from the floor. After tucking her head and arms into the fabric, she opened the bedroom door a fraction.

The bass of Rushe's voice carried to her immediately. "What do you want me to do about it?" he asked.

She crept out the narrow gap and pulled the door almost closed behind her. Staying in the shallow hallway, she pressed her back to the wall and skimmed along it.

"You going into retirement?" an unknown male

asked.

"Maybe," Rushe said.

"I don't believe it."

"I don't give a fuck."

Who was that guy? Rushe didn't have friends. In their time living together, the only person to come to their door was the pizza guy. Her love didn't even own a phone, though, apparently, he owned a pager.

"Rushe, you're the guy for this… the only guy."

Inching closer, she turned to press her chest to the wall and peeked around the edge. Three men sat in their living room. Rushe was closest, with his back to her. One man sat opposite him on another couch. At the top of the coffee table, in the armchair with its back to the window, was a second unknown man.

"You haven't—"

The man opposite Rushe stopped talking, prompting the guy in the armchair to look up and ask, "What?"

"You got company?" the couch man asked. The guy in the armchair followed his attention, and she ducked back to hide again. "This about some whore? You want us out so you get your money's worth? Shit, what did you pay her? I'll give you double to get the fuck out of here, darlin'!"

The last sentence was for her. Any shame at being caught spying evaporated into outrage.

"I beg your pardon!" she retorted, leaving her hiding spot to march toward them.

"You shut up," Rushe said, getting to his feet faster than she'd seen him move in a while.

"I'm not a whore!"

"Yeah, you are," Rushe said.

She'd thought her love was telling the couch guy to shut up. When he skirted the furniture making a beeline for her, she re-thought that assumption.

"What is going on here?" she asked.

"Bedroom," Rushe commanded.

"No," she replied, looking him in the eye when he bore down upon her.

"Now."

That snarl and those bullet black eyes were familiar. The thunder that emanated around him had flared in the past too. She had seen it intimidate men into humiliation… she was immune.

"I'm not—"

"Now!"

Rushe got hold of her. When she tried to resist, he hooked an arm around her stomach and swung her up into his arms. She fought, because she always did, but she kept her mouth shut until he got them back into the bedroom and tossed her on the bed.

As the bedroom door slammed, she scrambled up to her knees. Her intention was to get back on her feet, but Rushe closed the space between them and blocked her from leaving the bed.

"When the fuck are you gonna do what you're told?" he roared.

"Did you hear what he said? He thinks I'm a hooker!"

"Good!"

That took her aback. "You love me. You're happy with him disrespecting—"

"First off…" Rushe started, "there's nothing fucking shameful 'bout being a hooker. I know some damn fine hookers, some do it by choice. Others are forced into it, but… it doesn't fucking matter."

"You've slept with hookers?"

From the way his expression relaxed, it was obvious her naivety entertained him. "Yes."

She smacked his chest. "Why?"

"A guy has needs, Kitten. The only thing better

than a good fuck is a woman who doesn't ask questions. Hookers don't fall in love with their clients. They don't give a fuck who you are or what you're doing. They fuck and run, perfect for guys like me."

"You paid for sex?"

"Sometimes yes, sometimes no."

"I'm learning there are few absolutes where you're concerned. You had relationships with these women?"

"We don't have time for this," Rushe said. "When I tell you to stay, you stay."

"I don't," she said. "When have I ever done what I'm told?" His attention flitted to the bed. "Apart from in bed."

"If I tell you it's a sex game, will you stay?"

She wasn't convinced and hoped her blank expression conveyed that. "It arouses you to have me out of the loop?"

"It arouses me to have you safe," he said, all teasing over. "If you're dead, who's gonna screw with me every chance they get?"

"I do not!"

Rushe snagged her hands and stuffed them in his jeans pockets. "If they think you're a whore, they won't look twice. It's nothing to have a hooker in my bed. But if they think… I don't have relationships. I sure don't have long-term commitments."

Conceding some, she formed fists in his pockets and leaned forward, tucking her head under his jaw. "I'd be expensive."

The single bob of his chest released one low bassy note of a laugh. "Yeah, Kitten, I pay for you every day."

He wasn't talking money. She pressed her cheek closer, turning her face to kiss his chest. While still kissing him, her fists relaxed just enough to find the length of him, still imprisoned in denim. He was already hard, because of her actions, or just because of her presence?

Kissing up to his throat, she was surprised when he lowered his chin to urge her away enough to meet her mouth. His hands cradled her face to control the merging of their lips in a calm but insistent kiss.

Rushe had to be aware of the men in the living room; to be doing this now he had to trust them. If they had sex with others in the apartment, they'd be vulnerable. But this wasn't a sex kiss, or rather it wasn't a regular sex kiss. His devotion encompassed her and increased when his hands slid around and down her back. As he lifted her, she took her hands from his pockets and wrapped her legs around his hips.

"Rushe," she whispered when he trailed kisses to her throat.

The heat of bliss circled her brain, making her heavy, her head fell back under its own weight, giving Rushe a larger area to work with. He laid her on the bed, his weight still in control of hers when they landed in the soft cocoon of their nest.

Once again, his mouth kissed its way up to hers, and with the sweep of his tongue on her lip she opened wide. Torn between snatching his hair to keep him in place, and freeing him from his jeans, she didn't notice one of his hands leaving her body as the other snaked under her tee-shirt to fumble with her breast. Arching into the caress she craved, his belt buckle won out.

He caught her hand, delaying its journey, she expected him to direct it to exactly where he wanted it. She tightened her legs around him and let her love stretch her arm above her head. His other hand took her wrist, something cold and metallic touched her skin.

Her eyes opened, but it was too late. On the familiar grating snick, she tried to tug her hands free, but they stayed put. He'd locked the handcuffs to her wrists around one of the metal bars of the headboard.

"Rushe!"

The rogue told her she tormented him and then had the audacity to do this. Fastened in place, bound, kept prisoner, in what had become her own bed!

He conveyed no apology just pulled her legs away from his hips. When he sat up, he raised her tee-shirt to expose her body and kissed one nipple then the other.

"Stop that!" she said.

He continued to tease her breasts with his mouth, burying his face in her cleavage. "You gave me a free pass, Kitten."

She couldn't argue because she had done exactly that, just as he had. Their open consent was the reason she took the liberty of using his erection without asking for permission when he was still asleep.

Rushe made such a huge deal of consent when they started sleeping together. Even after they'd been having sex for quite a while, he still asked her for consent every time. So she'd made an exaggerated plea of granting him full and permanent access. Consent was important to him, and she knew why. But after a long discussion, and constant reassurance on her part, they'd agreed consent would be presumed. They even established a safe word to use if they wanted the other to stop what they were doing.

Showing him the truth of the trust she had in him, a trust she'd never experienced with anyone else, was crucial. It meant everything to him, he cherished it. Even if he didn't say it aloud, it was obvious in his uncertainty. Giving him that faith somehow translated to a responsibility he took seriously. He didn't want to let her down.

Her responsibility to him was as valuable to her.

When he claimed her as his, it gave her a sense of completeness. She wanted to be owned by him. Maybe later, in the course of what he did, he'd have to rent out his body to be away from her. Wherever he was, he belonged to her just as much as she did to him, even if neither of them said it regularly.

"This is not okay," she said but didn't use the safe word. Neither of them ever had. Probably never would. "I'm not having sex with you for a month."

"Seems like that's up to me," he said, slipping a finger inside her, following it with another.

"You're going to leave me here and go back out there," she said, gritting her teeth, fighting to ignore the warmth of his mouth on the underside of her breast, and the pressure building around his fingers in her pussy.

"You're safe in here," Rushe said, licking his way up to her nipple.

"I'm safe in any room you're in."

The curl of his lips around her breast was so gratifying, she sighed. Rushe never smiled. He just didn't. Well, he did, and she'd seen it around the apartment on a somewhat regular basis. But outside, or in situations with others, it was gone, locked away in a place she hadn't found yet.

"Good girl." Rushe pressed her clit, massaging it while drawing her nipple deeper into his mouth.

His other hand squeezed her neglected breast and a yelp of bliss escaped her. The slope of orgasm was long; her lover kept working his mouth and hands until he'd coaxed her through every aftershock.

Then, in a snap, his body leaped from hers and he was on his feet by the bed like he hadn't just completely undone her.

She panted through the endorphin haze marring her vision. "You're a real bastard."

"I know."

"Who are those people?"

"Don't worry about it," Rushe said, perusing her exposed figure.

"You expect me to trust you?"

"Yes."

"When you don't trust me?"

His perusal halted. "Explain."

"If you don't let me in… you don't trust me to understand or you don't trust me to accept it. Has to be one of the two."

"You don't need to know."

"No," she said, her body sank into the bed as every part of her deflated in dejection. "A whore is only good for one thing."

"Kitten—"

"Go to work," she said.

Rushe was a man of few words. Though he carried frustration in his gaze, he departed the bedroom, closing the door, leaving her alone, restrained, exactly where he wanted her.

He'd been putting off work to avoid this. She realized that now. Jobs meant questions he didn't want to answer. Understanding his work meant sacrifice was one thing, but if he expected her to let him walk out the door and disappear for months, he had another thing coming. Yes, he'd worked alone for years, when he didn't have a choice. What he didn't understand yet was that he had no choice now either.

She hadn't signed on to this life expecting to sit at home and be the dutiful little woman. What if he needed back up out there? Wasn't like she'd never helped him out of a jam before. Both of them had almost lost their lives; their unity was the only thing that saved them.

All her life, she'd been an information gatherer. Her work in the National Library research department whetted her appetite for investigation. When she left her previous life be with Rushe, she did it to be of help. Of course, they loved each other, but she had told him straight she wouldn't simply be a female for him to fuck. She wasn't going to be a hooker: live off his money and be around to service him when he demanded it.

The last three months had been spent talking and learning each other… and a lot of sex, a helluva lot of sex. Some laughs too. Rushe might not be a smiler, but he occasionally let her make him laugh; his ultra-dry sense of humor had often left her in stitches. She'd asked him to show her some fighting techniques, but he'd insisted she would never need them. After a lot of persuasion, he had shown her a couple of moves, but it quickly became a naked workout session on the gym mat… which was probably his plan all along. At the time, she hadn't cared enough to push the issue.

They lived deep in the city, ideal for Rushe because he liked to blend in, or at the very least be invisible in the jumble. On various occasions, she told him he'd never be invisible. From his perspective, all they needed to do was be still, there were enough distractions elsewhere. At the time, she'd rolled her eyes and told him that being "still" didn't make him invisible. But, to his credit, he got where he was by mastering it.

Lying there, in their bed, she cursed herself. She should have realized as soon as he started with the seduction that he had an ulterior motive. Rushe wasn't soft; he took what he wanted. If he'd wanted sex while they had company, it would have been quick and messy.

While she was still learning a lot about sex, Rushe was still learning a lot about love. Sex he was great at. The relationship part was a mystery, and a wonder, to him. After what they'd been through, a break from life and reality was needed. Getting lost in sex was a vacation for them both.

But Rushe was getting restless. She'd noticed it

more and more. So much so that he was working out like a machine. He was running at least fifteen miles a day while she busied herself at the Public Library. It wasn't as large as the National Library where she'd previously worked, but it was on the city and college network and was housed behind City Hall.

Every day for a month she'd woken up and gone there, familiarizing herself with the layout and immersing herself in topics of interest she'd never had the time to investigate.

Liam Hutten, the IT support manager from the complex, had become a friend who often helped her out with technological issues. They'd met when he directed her to the new software lab in a corner of the basement level, which had more up to date systems.

Whoever the men in the living room were, one thing was clear: Rushe would be going back to work. Something had to have piqued his interest to have the men here this long.

Knowing Rushe as she did, if he'd heard enough, he wouldn't have let them in at all. This could be a chance for him to return to his normality. She'd encourage him to get back out there, if he didn't do it now, he never would. One day, he'd resent her for that.

Still, with a sigh, in that moment she was useless. Again, she was restricted in Rushe's bed and there wasn't a damn thing she could do about it until he chose to come free her.

SIX

ANOTHER HOUR PASSED, and she was just slipping toward slumber when the noise of movement awakened her. Though it was dark, she sensed Rushe in the space so braced herself for whatever would come next.

His jeans hit the floor, the bed moved, and his fingers curled around her calf to part it from the other. He scooped her body under his, the bulk of his dick sliding up her inner thigh.

"I'm gonna fuck you."

"I'm pissed off," she said.

"When are you not?" he grumbled. "Are you gonna give me shit?"

"Yes," she said but sighed. "After we have sex."

"You're easy, Kitten."

"Are you going to fuck me, or are we going to lie here all night shooting the breeze?"

"You gonna do what you're told?"

"No, probably not," she said. "Who were those guys?"

"We're gonna have another conversation about

your obedience."

"I don't see why—" With one thrust, he surged up into her. The sudden intrusion expelled the oxygen from her fast. "Oh, Rushe!"

"You love it when he takes you by surprise," he said, groping one breast, then the other. "The girls approve."

"Don't make me laugh," she said.

"You're wet… What were you doing in here?"

"I can't touch myself," she said, remembering belatedly that she was still cuffed. "Are you going to release me?"

"I'm feeling nostalgic."

"Do you remember the first time we had sex?"

"I remember what came before it," he said.

To get her into his preferred position, for his maximum gratification, he hooked an arm under her to stuff a pillow beneath her waist. Driving into her half a dozen times, he coated himself with her nectar. When he dipped his head to suck each nipple, he slid out of her, taking his languorous time containing one peak in his teeth and orbiting it with his tongue. One then the other, then back again.

Her sense of purpose was circling the drain. What had she been mad about again?

"I remember what came after it," she said. "I thought you used me."

"I did," he said, still with his mouth full.

"You still don't let yourself believe it, do you? I love you."

"Enough talking," he said.

Sitting up, he took the neck of her tee-shirt and, with little effort, ripped it apart. Shredding the fabric from her torso, he left it tangled around her restricted arms.

"Did you take the job?" she asked.

"What did I just say?"

Seeing him through the shadows of the room was difficult. The blinds over the windows blacked out light and noise from the street a dozen floors below.

"Rushe—"

"Enough!"

It had been a while since she'd seen this Rushe. The black-eyed, soulless man who'd thrown her to the ground and told her he felt nothing. Thus far, they'd avoided having anything more than the odd superficial argument. But it was easy to get along when they expected nothing from each other.

This Rushe was the one she'd met and was under no illusions about his capabilities. This Rushe was numb to everything, he cared about nothing. This Rushe could detach and hold himself away from anything.

Seeing what she could of him there, in that moment, instinct betrayed he'd distanced himself from her. What that meant, she didn't know. Perhaps he had taken the job, so the role of this blank, emotionless person was, in his view, necessary. Or maybe Rushe hadn't taken the job at all, and in turning it down realized what he'd sacrificed to be with her.

"What do you want?" she whispered.

Rising to his knees, he took his time looking her over, her legs spread around his form, her center swollen and damp.

"I'm gonna fuck your tits," he said.

It had been a couple of weeks since he'd done that.

"Okay," she responded.

"And your face, and your pussy, and anywhere else I fucking want."

"Okay."

"You comply," he snarled. "Every fucking time, you are a fucking whore."

"I thought you were done talking."

She didn't see it in his eyes but did feel the spasm of his body tensing. "You're in my bed. You're my thing. My possession. I do with you anything I damn well want."

"Right now you're doing nothing. You've got the words but not the balls."

"Flick."

That rumble was so low she knew his lips were static, his chest was still, and his teeth were clenched in his frozen jaw.

"I'll push as hard as I want," she said, hearing his warning without him voicing it. Lifting a foot, she shoved his shoulder, and with her other she kicked at his waist. "You man enough to check me?"

With a few more shoves and prods, he snatched both her ankles and pinned her feet to the bed. "You're crazy," he hissed.

"Yeah, what you gonna do about it? Huh? You think I'm scared of you? Do your worst, Lover, I dare you."

Rushe roared forward, thrusting her legs up and apart, he forced them against her torso and plunged into her. The pillow underneath her made the position more awkward but gave him primo position to fuck her hard. His depth and angle hit her everywhere all at once. She called out, trying to arch into him but he kept her in place proving he made the rules.

When he did release her legs, it was only to grab her breasts. He squeezed, embossing his fingerprints into her skin. It wasn't enough; she wanted more. Calling out his name, taunting and begging, her words only jeered him on. When he shoved in deep and climax consumed her, she opened to scream, but his hand came over her mouth, sealing her voice inside.

He withdrew and slung her legs out of the way to

rise and straddle her chest, keeping his weight off her. Still in the darkness, it was difficult to see anything except his outline, but she felt his cock in her cleavage. He really loved her breasts and having his dick right there between them.

"Open your mouth."

He wasn't there to play with her breasts. His hand left her mouth, and she did exactly as told. This was how he made sense of the world. So many of his emotions came out in sex, and she was there to help him work through things in whatever way he needed to.

His cock stabbed between her lips, feeding her the taste of herself, which made her suck hard.

"That's what your mouth is for," he growled. "It's for my cock, nothing else, you understand me? You're gonna do what you're told. You're gonna suck it all better." Shoving a second pillow behind her head, he slid in and out between her lips. "You taste your pussy? How wet you are for me? You didn't even like me when I walked in here and your pussy was dripping. That all you want? Sex? It's all you're for, your body knows it. You crave it, don't you? You're desperate to be fucked good and hard."

His words trailed into a roaring groan. He snatched the top rail of the headboard, pulling the bed down as he pushed forward. As he spurted his release, he drew back, leaving a trail of liquid from her throat to her incisors.

She swallowed him down and closed her lips around his head. With a slurping kiss, she took the last of him.

Rushe climbed off her, but he didn't leave the bed. "Do you think you could go back?"

The question was so… normal. Yeah, the pant of sex was still in his voice, but it wasn't a growl, wasn't a command. "To where?"

"To your life."

"This is my life, Rushe," she said. "You can't get rid of me."

"Right."

With a huff, he leaned over her to release the cuffs, and tossed them into his drawer.

She stretched her arms, circling her wrists. "Did you expect me to say yes?"

"No," he said. "That's exactly what I thought you'd say."

He lay down and plucked her body up to spread her over him, just like they always slept. But his hand squirmed between them to massage her clit, so they weren't quite ready for sleep yet. He'd play with whatever was in his mind, but he'd bring it to her eventually. She trusted him; it was just a shame he didn't trust her yet.

SEVEN

DURING THE NEXT new day, she'd been preoccupied. Waking up alone wasn't unusual, but Rushe had a weight on his shoulders that day, one he didn't share with her, that he wouldn't share.

Long nights filled with deep emotional discussions and heart to hearts would never be a part of their relationship. But she would always know Rushe's feelings. He conveyed them in the way he touched her. Their sexual escapades clued her in to what was behind the mask he cultivated.

Fully aware Rushe would go for an extended run then spend hours at the gym, she whiled away her time at the library. He got a pass for the day. That night, when she got him, she'd pin him down.

Stuffing her books back into her bag, she tossed the strap over her head, adjusting it between her breasts.

Liam Hutten, IT wonder, appeared beside her desk. "Heading out?"

"Yeah. You haven't been around today."

"There was a freak out with the new systems in

Life Sciences."

"Sure." She smiled. "Fix it?"

"I did," he said. "Think I'm ready for my superhero cape now."

Liam stood at five eleven, had mucky brown hair, glowing blue eyes, and an easy smile that put her, and everyone else, at ease. Liam was everyone's friend, warm and funny, he was the most approachable person she'd ever met.

"Glad you've had a productive day," she said, "and that the casualties were minimal."

"Was touch and go for a while."

"But you only use your powers for good, right?"

"During daylight, sure," he said, propping himself against the desk. "Got time for dinner?"

"If my boyfriend heard you ask that—"

"Big and scary, you told me already. We have lunch together all the time, no biggie. I've got a coupon for buy one get one free at The Grill. It's right across the street."

"No, thanks," she said. "I have to get home."

"Everything okay? You're a fan of The Grill, not that I get your obsession myself."

"Says the guy who ate three cheeseburgers last Tuesday."

"I lost the bet," Liam said.

"You lost the bet on purpose. You knew I would get the IP in less than twenty minutes; it took me less than five."

"You're a quick study, and I'm an excellent teacher," he said. "You want to tell me about the off-the-book questions on information access yet?"

"No," she said. "I told you, I'm writing a book."

"Sure you are. Anyway, dinner?"

"I have to get home, but thanks."

Liam accepted her rejection with a nod. She

patted his shoulder as she passed and went straight for the stairs.

The sky was dark, meaning it was later than she thought. Rushe didn't have a cellphone, and she didn't communicate with her family, so she had never gotten around to replacing hers. Just meant no one was keeping tabs on her, which was fine, no matter what happened, Rushe would always find her.

Setting up a free email account at the library had been sufficient to send her family an email to let them know she was alive. They'd been estranged for more than a year. She had only been back to the Hughes family home when Rushe dumped her there. Sometimes she thought about getting in touch with them again, but she hadn't gotten around to it.

Rushe would have noticed her lengthy absence; he noticed everything. It hadn't been her wish or intention to worry him. She didn't want him to think she was playing reckless games. Sex was the only time games were welcome between them. Since they'd been imprisoned together, and confessed the truth of their feelings, she'd been honest. They'd been honest with each other. But last night shook the foundations of what they'd built. Would their openness continue beyond that night? Only time would tell.

She'd run down the library stairs, got across the busy stretch of road, and to the corner where The Grill was situated, when a man ran up beside her.

"You know him," the guy said.

She kept walking. "What?"

"I saw you come out of his building this morning. Scott told me you were with him last night."

"I don't know what you're talking about. Excuse me."

She tried to pick up the pace, except the stranger grabbed her arm, pulling her to a stop. She wrenched her arm free, but he snatched for the other one.

"Please, I don't mean you any harm. I need you to listen."

"Listen to what?" she demanded. "If you keep hassling—"

"Rushe. I need Rushe." The guy was about five eight, blond, and very obviously desperate. "Eric, he spoke to Rushe last night. When he came out, Eric said Rushe wasn't taking the case."

"Whatever," she said, trying to round the assailant, but he got in front of her. "Get out of my way."

"It's my sister! She's in trouble! I need help! What the fuck does this guy want? Is it money?"

"No—"

"I've tried everything! I've been everywhere. She's nineteen, she's a kid, she's in over her head, please."

"Why do you think I can help? Why would I?"

"You know Rushe," the guy said. "We were watching this morning, Scott and me, when you came out of his building. Scott told me not to come near you, but... You were there. You know Rushe. You were sleeping with him—"

"That's none of your business."

Rushe had been right about people knowing they had a relationship. If she'd been a faceless hooker, neither of the men last night would have noticed her.

"Do you know how long it took me to find someone who could help? Eric and Scott found me; they said they knew someone who could help. I gave them a fortune, a finder's fee. They said they would get him on board. But he said no, why did he say no?"

"I have no idea," she said, attempting to side-step, but she was thwarted again.

"What's it going to take? What does he want? What does he need? What does he care about?"

She froze, absorbing that question for a second before responding. "You better be careful talking like that. Rushe—"

"You do know him," he begged, "you can help, please."

"I can't help you."

"Listen to me! All you have to do is listen."

"I really can't—"

"My sister got this job, in a bar at the Waterside Casino Private Lounge, she lied about her age. It's a private, exclusive, members-only deal. I can't get in! God knows what they… She got mixed up with this guy… have you heard of the King Club?"

"What?"

"She got… she thinks she's in love with him. They took her in, and she vanished. Please, she's my baby sister. My family is devastated. How can you…? She's young. That gang swallow people up. They devour them from the inside. She could be on drugs or tied to a mattress. God knows what! It took me weeks to get this far! A month ago I hadn't heard of the King Club, and now… I'm scared for her life."

"I'm sure there are other people who can help—"

"We went to the cops, they did nothing. I went private, trailed the streets myself but no one can find her, least they don't tell me anything. Someone gave me one name, then I got another! One name I got, Joey Galante, his family is tied to the Club, but… I can't even get into the Lounge. I can't find anyone in the King Club! I don't know what I'm doing! I was out of hope, out of… When Eric and Scott said they knew someone… he was my last hope. Then they tell me he won't take the case."

"He's very particular about—"

"Anything he wants, I'll pay anything, do anything, I'll work it off. Please, I need help." He grabbed her arm again. "Think about what she could be going through. She's just a kid, think about what they might be doing to her, can you imagine that?"

Yes, she could imagine because she'd witnessed some horrors in her time.

"What's your name?" she asked.

"Michael Lewis, my sister is Lisa."

She pointed back at the orange sign above The Grill on the corner. "Do you see The Grill?"

"Yeah."

"Meet me there tomorrow at ten," she said. "They open for brunch."

"But—"

"I make no promises. I'll have a conversation with him."

"With him, with Rushe? Take me with you, I—"

"No," she said. "My conversations with Rushe are private, and to be honest, you don't want to be within twenty city blocks when he finds out you approached me like this. He'll kill you… no exaggeration. That wouldn't be beneficial for your sister, would it?"

She left his side and continued down the street, unsure if Michael would follow. At the next corner, she paused to look back over her shoulder. No sign of a stalker. Just on the chance she might be mistaken, she altered her route, taking a longer, more convoluted way home. Though if Michael had seen her exit their building that morning, he already knew where she and Rushe lived.

Her new course toward home would delay her arrival, she needed the extra time to plan her approach. Rushe would go through the roof when he heard about her day.

EIGHT

AFTER ARRIVING BACK at the apartment, she tossed her keys into her bag and threw everything into the closet beside the front door. The melodious murmur of the radio came from the direction of the gym. No food cooking in the kitchen, which meant take out again.

If Rushe had come home from the fitness club just to spend time in his home gym, he was either very worried about her, or he was still unsettled about last night. If it had been the former, he would have come looking. The first place Rushe would check if trying to locate her was the library, so he'd have found her. Which meant his activity was down to door number two.

To give Rushe the time to come to her if he wanted to, she carefully unbuckled her heels. The noise remained constant and unchanged. She progressed into the gym doorway. On pushing it aside, she saw Rushe lifting weights. If he raised his head he would see her, but he didn't. There was no way he wasn't aware of her. The radio was just a hum in the background, a distraction, it wasn't there for entertainment purposes.

"Hungry?" she asked.

"No."

For three months, she'd been spoiled with his attention. She'd taken that devotion for granted and had almost forgotten how difficult it was to extract information from this man. When he was being distant, the best way she'd found to deal with it was not to skirt the issue.

"What's the King Club?"

The dumbbell in his hand lowered slowly, at the same rate, his chin came up until he looked her straight in the eye. "I'm gonna kill him."

He tossed the dumbbell aside like it weighed nothing and snatched a nearby towel to wipe the sweat from his head and chest.

"Kill who?" She stayed in the doorway and held out her hands in an attempt to soothe him remotely. "It was my question, answer me."

"Who was it?" he asked. "Scott? That manipulative little fucker would do anything for... Did he touch you?"

"No one touched me," she said, still braced in the doorway when he reached her.

"Move."

"No!"

Grabbing her arm, he yanked her out of the doorway, removing the obstacle from his path. She got hold of his wrist, but he jerked it away, and stormed into the bedroom. All she could do was follow. Already he was out of his shorts and retrieving clothes from the closet.

"Rushe," she pleaded. "You can't shut me out of this. Why did you turn the job down?"

"I'm gonna make it slow," he growled, baring his teeth as he jerked up his jeans and buttoned them. Dropping to the bed, he tugged on clean socks. "I'm gonna make him cry. I'm gonna make him beg—"

"No! You're not! You're going to talk to me! Me, Rushe! Do you remember who I am?"

He flew off the bed and closed the space between them in a heartbeat. "You are my woman! There are consequences for anyone who hurts you."

"Do I look hurt?" she asked, holding open her palms. "The only thing hurting me right now is you!"

He faltered. "What?"

"We're a team, Rushe! If you turn down a job, I deserve to know why. You shouldn't have a problem giving me your reasons, if they're valid."

"Valid?"

"Why aren't we working?"

"We?"

"I knew what you were when I told you I was coming with you," she said. "Remember, in my apartment? You gave me a choice. You told me what this life would be. I didn't want you to change. But you have, why?"

He took one step backward, then another. "I haven't changed."

"Yes, you have," she said. "And you know exactly why, it's because of me. The only thing I can't figure out is if you're worried about my safety… or if you're worried about your own."

"I don't give a fuck about me."

"I know," she said, crossing to sit on the bed, taking his arm to bring him down to sit at her side. "But if something happens to you out there, who'll be here for me?"

And when his eyes met hers, she knew she'd hit the nail on the head.

"You're reckless," he said.

"You'd do anything for me, I know that. Why don't you believe I'd do the same for you?"

Still, he didn't have words, so he got up to pace away from her. "Who was it?" he asked, lifting his head without turning to face her.

"I'm going to assume Eric and Scott are the men who were here last night, and it was neither of them."

Surprised, Rushe turned. "So how…?"

"He's worried about his sister, Rushe. She's nineteen and the police are doing nothing. He needs help. He's desperate."

"The brother?" Rushe asked. "Coming to you was a risk. Scott would've told him that."

"Why do you believe it was Scott?"

"He doesn't like me," he said. "He'd be happy to see me in a jail cell."

"If he doesn't like you, and you don't trust him, why did you let him in here?"

"He doesn't like me, but he's had my back in the past, and he knows I'm useful for him. Work isn't personal between guys like us."

"He makes a fortune from referrals," she said, recalling what Michael had said about a finder's fee.

"Yeah," Rushe said. "His girl went missing a while back."

"You found her?"

"She left him."

"Because of you?"

"No," Rushe said, actually affronted. "I don't have women on the job, I told you."

"But you did have sex."

"I didn't fuck his woman. Turns out she was… they weren't happy, he had debts needing settled… it's complicated."

"I've heard that before. She wasn't happy?"

Rushe shook his head. "Not that I blame her. As soon as he got her back… she walked out. He's never gotten over it."

"And he blames you by association?"

"Maybe," he said. "He didn't like me before that either."

"You don't make friends easily, do you, Lover?"

"Never needed friends, never wanted them. You start to care about something and…"

Another reminder of how she'd changed his world. "We can't live in a bubble forever. You take cases in defense of women for a reason. There aren't enough men like you out there. You need to do this because no one else will. You worked alone because you didn't trust anyone. Do you trust me?"

She held her breath in anticipation of his response.

"I'd kill any man who touched you."

"That's not what I meant," she said, aware he knew exactly why she'd asked. "No games, Rushe. Do you trust me?"

"I don't know if I trust myself."

"You feel responsible for me," she said. "You care about me, just like you cared about…"

"I didn't tell you about that so you could bring it up at every opportunity," he snarked. "And you're different, you're not like that."

"Rushe, we're going to do this. I'm going to do it… I'm asking you to help me."

"You'd go against me?"

"What else is new?" she asked and smiled.

He didn't see the funny side. "You don't know what you're doing out there. You'll get hurt."

"Maybe. I got hurt the last time I got drawn in. But we did the job. I rescued your ass, remember?"

"This isn't a game."

"If we don't do this, she'll be lost," she said. "Maybe they'll kill her. Maybe she's hooked on some drug. The family don't know, and they deserve to know.

Since when do you let scum like that get away with the store?"

"You've made your point."

"What do we do next?"

Rushe, in his hesitation, still wouldn't look at her. "Focus on the details. Check the brother, the family, get the real story."

"Okay," she said. "Michael Lewis is going to be at The Grill, opposite the library, at ten tomorrow morning."

Rushe shook his head. "I don't want to meet him."

"But—"

"Eric will tell him I'm on the case. I'm not interested in listening to the sniveling. He won't tell me anything relevant."

"How do you know that?" she asked.

"He has a stake in this, an interest, which means he's biased. I'll check things out for myself. If I need to talk to the brother after that, I will."

"Okay, I'll meet him alone."

His eyes cut to her. "You won't. I'll tell Eric to meet him."

"But—"

"There are three positions in a case like this. The family is the pursuer. The defender is the group in possession of the target. Then there is us, the investigators. We don't give a fuck about the pursuer."

"Why not?"

"Because if you care too much and fail in the mission it can be…"

"Your sense of responsibility," she said. "Okay, you don't want to disappoint them. You keep yourself at a distance."

"Right."

"So we care about the defender?"

"Not really," he said. "We have a target to obtain. After checking out all the parties, we need an eyeball. We need to know where she is."

She nodded. "Lisa has a relationship with Joey Galante who has ties to the King Club."

"Yeah," he said.

"Do you think he loves her?" she asked. His features relaxed. "What? What's funny?"

"You have to resist the urge to…"

"To what?"

"Treat every couple like they're in some Shakespeare tragedy," he said. "I don't think he loves her. I'd be surprised if he was still fucking her."

"You don't know that."

"No, I don't, but I will. I'll know everything there is to know about everyone involved before I go near any of them."

"What is the King Club?"

"A consortium," he said. "They've been around a couple of hundred years."

"They're a cult? A secret society?"

"I suppose you could look at it that way, but you're doing it again, romanticizing it. These are men who want money. They're involved in a bunch of illegal shit, but I don't know the details yet."

"You've dealt with them before?"

"Not directly," Rushe said. "But I've had contact with some of their people a couple of times."

"Will that cause problems?"

"I don't know yet," he said. "It's a far-reaching group."

"Okay. So we check everyone out?"

"I'll pull up what I can on the system here, but I'll need a wider—"

"I can do that," she said. "You want to know about the family? I can go to the records at City Hall tomorrow and research them from the software lab too. I can access official records, credit reports, newspaper articles."

His chest expanded with the depth of his inhale as he leaned back against the closet door. "I'm not sure about this."

"You don't trust me to—"

"I trust you," he said. "You're great with the paper stuff, the computer. I've seen you at the desk here but…"

"But…? A computer search isn't going to hurt me."

"You told me you didn't want me to change," he said. "I can handle this. But if you research these people, look into their lives and their history… you're going to get invested, Kitten. You're going to care."

"I can switch it off," she said. "I've seen you do it enough times."

"You'll get yourself hurt," he said. "I don't want you to make a stupid decision based on your emotions."

"Like I did with you?" she asked. "I came back for you."

"Because I'd have come back for you."

"Because I love you."

He shook his head. "I don't want you doing that again. We were lucky last time. Pure dumb luck got us through."

"That and my superior powers of manipulation," she teased.

"Of me, Jansen, or Skeeve?"

"All of the above."

"We're gonna take this one step at a time," he said. "I can't tell you what's gonna happen. I can't tell you what to expect."

"I'll wow you with my research powers."

"You do that, Kitten," he said. "But we have to

get one thing straight."

"What's that?"

"I'm in charge."

A grin burst to her face. "Okay."

"I mean it, Flick. This isn't poolside, or some loser in a coffeeshop. If I tell you to do something—"

"I'll act in our best interest," she said, taking off her top as she stood. "That's the only thing I'll promise."

She unzipped her skirt to wriggle out of it and her underwear too.

Her lover's eyes descended to her bare breasts. "Did I tell you to do that?" he asked, his blood diverting south.

From his tone, he really wasn't sure of the answer.

"No, but you need a shower. Consider me your human loofah."

She didn't wait for him to react again and bounded up onto the bed to run over it and jump down at the other side by their bathroom. Things would start to change now they had a job. How easy would they find the transition?

NINE

RUSHE ARRANGED FOR ERIC to talk to Michael at The Grill, so she didn't need to go. That gave her the chance to immerse herself in her task at the library.

That morning, Rushe woke her up before he left the apartment. It was early, maybe around five a.m. He never usually woke her. But he had that day. He'd stroked her awake, in a way that made her certain it was a prelude to morning sex. She was wrong. He'd kissed her, then left her alone to get to work himself.

After that, sleep wasn't easy to find again. She'd gone to the computer in their office slash gym to compile a list of questions that needed answers.

Using the home computer made her uneasy. She'd learned just how simple it could be to trace someone. Their computer had internet, but she wasn't sure of the protection on it. Rather than take any risks, she got ready and went to the library.

Liam had interrupted a couple of times but finally got the message she was busy and left her alone. She worked tirelessly, surprised by just how much information existed. Every time she tugged on one string, a dozen others came loose.

The library was open until midnight for use by the college students, but she decided to head home at around seven p.m. At home, she worked on getting the information she had into files, into an order that might be useful. Rushe hadn't told her exactly what they would need. He'd said they would take this one step at a time, she'd learn as they went along.

She cooked for them but hadn't eaten under the assumption they would eat together. As it turned out, when the front door did eventually open, hailing his return, it was almost midnight.

Her impulse was to leap to her feet, to run to him, but she resisted. He hadn't given her any hint his day might be dangerous. Still, sitting there that night, with minutes slipping by, her anxiety level had increased.

While he dumped stuff in the closet with a thud, she stayed at the dinner table, in front of the counter that separated the kitchen from the rest of the living room. Still with a pen in her teeth, when he approached the table, she turned to observe him.

He didn't say anything, and her patience broke first.

The pen dropped from her mouth. "Good day?"

"You've been productive," he said, nodding at the half dozen files strewn across the table.

"Yes, I found out quite a lot actually. Joseph is a family name, the grandfather Joseph Eugene Galante the second was tied to the King Club when the Rosebud Ballroom burned down in nineteen thirty-one. That's the first record of a Galante being associated with the King Club. I have to say though that it's only listed as rumor. No one was ever charged with the arson."

"Who profited?"

"The ballroom," she said, flicking through some

copies in one file, "was insured by the Johnson-Davis Company. They owned a dozen clubs around the city then. They cashed in the insurance."

"You really did your homework. I'm impressed."

"That's just the tip of the iceberg. What did you find out?"

"That Michael Lewis is as pathetic as I imagined," he sneered.

"You're angry?" she asked.

He sat at the table. "Damn right, the man should've stepped up."

"Not everyone's as happy to take charge as you are, Lover."

He picked up her file of biographies and read without expression. "You've got everything."

"Everyone I could find associated with the King Club. No one talks about it directly, but it pops up now and again in a police or newspaper report."

"It would've taken me weeks to get this far."

"Because you don't like paper, you like action. And because you can't be in two places at once. We're going to make a good team, Rushe."

When his eyes rose over the top of the file, she could tell he still wasn't convinced. "Do they still own nightclubs now?"

"Yes," she said, picking up another file to hand it over. "They go by the moniker the JD Group now, but yeah."

"Four clubs in the city."

"Joseph Galante the third, Joey's father, owns a casino on the waterfront. It's part of the Waterside Hotel complex, though the hotel itself is owned by Evan Whyte... He has a financial stake in a couple of the JD Group clubs too, but..."

"What?" Rushe asked, lowering the file.

"Forgive the pun but... Whyte is white. Whiter

than white. I came across dozens of newspaper articles and press releases about his altruism. And he's never appeared in a police report. He's thirty-two, Joey Junior's contemporary. I found their yearbook, they went to school together."

"You found the yearbook?"

"The high school has them archived online," she said on a shrug. "The boys were in the same year. There are pictures of them together at events. They knew each other."

"So?"

"If Lisa ran away with Joey… I can't see how… I mean, if Joseph Senior owns a casino in Whyte's complex, and the boys knew each other at school, it's a long-term friendship. Whyte has to know something."

"So you think we rock up to Evan Whyte and ask about Lisa Lewis?"

She shrugged again. "Why not? At the very worst he'll tell us he doesn't know anything."

"You think that's the worst that can happen?"

"You don't?"

"I think we don't know enough yet," he said. "People who go to great lengths to be seen as respectable are usually the most crooked."

"So what next?"

"Sex."

The turnaround gave her whiplash. "But what about—"

"Take off your clothes."

"But—"

"Kitten."

He would always keep her guessing. Though she stood, she didn't move. What she'd forgotten about for half a second was Rushe's infinite patience. No one would win a staring contest against him.

So instead, she used the strongest weapon in her

arsenal to entice him. One button at a time, she unfastened her shirt. With each of her deliberate movements, she watched him grind his teeth.

Eventually parting the fabric, she revealed her satin covered breasts. Her love growled aloud and thrust to his feet, grabbing the corner of the dining table to throw it out of the way, removing the barrier from between them with a deafening crash.

The violent action sent her libido into overdrive, but she didn't have time to do anything. In two strides, he was upon her, tearing the cups of her bra from her body to expose her flesh. He took her in handfuls and pushed her backward until she hit the wall by the kitchen. His mouth closed over her breast as he twisted the other nipple in the joint of his thumb, then she was up, off her feet, off the floor.

"You don't play with me," he snapped. "You're a cocky little kitten; let's see how much cock you can take."

Forcing her to her knees, he opened his jeans and pushed himself into her mouth. After the abrupt move he pulled back, and flattened his hands to the wall, letting her control the pace.

"Look at me!" he demanded. She cast her eyes upward while sucking him off. "Feel clever now, do you? You want to gimme crap now?"

Withdrawing, he wrenched her back to her feet.

"Rushe—"

"Quiet!"

He crouched to hook her knees over his arms and straightened, boosting her up against the wall. A long time ago, he'd held her like this, open to him, exposed, at that shack before they'd been intimate. As her lover tried to hold onto his ferocity, she rested a gentle palm on his cheek. The soothing action was enough to infuriate him again, and he stabbed his cock into her.

"Rushe!"

"Quiet!" he demanded again. "I'm gonna fuck your pussy raw."

She squeezed her lips together, holding in the carnal noises attempting to erupt from within. Wriggling forward, she slanted her hips to ensure her clit made contact with his groin when he pounded against her.

"You like that? Did I tell you to enjoy yourself? You think I want you coming on my cock? Do you? Speak."

"Yes."

"Good girl. You love my cock, don't you?" he panted, his words as hot as his breath on her skin. "Love it when I fuck that tight cunt of yours. You're my whore. Speak."

"Yes," she said. "Yes, I'm your whore."

He pulled out and rammed back into her, his grasp on her hips ensuring every plunge smacked them together. In the ecstasy that exploded within and around, she called out for him, unable to catch a breath. She couldn't see. Couldn't feel. This was intense, this was like the old days, when everything was so uncertain. Back then, he couldn't know the way out, just as he couldn't now. That was what tormented him.

The true cause of this wildness was his quest for order. He wanted to be in control, felt he had to be in control. But he couldn't control everything, as the last job demonstrated.

Having a long-term partner had never featured in his plans, yet there they were. Some part of him had to feel his life was spiraling downward. Because of her. Because of them. And this was him fighting to regain the reins.

His mind had an ability to see half a dozen moves ahead. At least he had been capable of that before her. In so many ways, she was an unknown variable. She stood up to him, she didn't cower, and he admired that. What he didn't realize was that the confidence in her came from him.

Rushe gave her the right, the arrogance, the ability to stand up for herself, and for what she cared about. He needed a strong woman, and right then, as she matched him thrust for thrust, their eyes met. With crushing force, his pelvis slammed her into the wall, and he called out. His feral roar shivered through her. This wasn't his usual call of climax. Something was different. Fear cooled her heart, in a profound way that was new, a way she didn't like.

He panted short wet breaths against her temple. He didn't back off and kept her sandwiched there, without enough room to take a deep breath.

"I love you, Kitten," he murmured eventually.

"Tell me what's different," she said, sensing the danger ahead. "You're different, something's different. Something's about to change, isn't it? What is it?"

"I'm leaving."

She heard what he said, but it took her a dozen seconds to react. "No, you're not."

"Just for a day or two, could be a week… maybe longer."

"No," she said, trying to wriggle free, but he didn't give her an inch. "I'm going with you."

"No, you're not," he said. "I'll come back."

"No. Where are you going?"

"It's deep background."

"Take me with you."

"It's not gonna happen," he said. "You're gonna stay here. Keep poking around."

"I don't want you to go," she said. "How will I get in touch with you? What if something happens? What if you need back up?"

"I won't," he said. "I have to establish cover—"

"A minute ago it was deep background," she argued. "Would you please move? It feels uncivilized to argue while your cock is still inside me." At the reminder, he grew hard again. "No. No more sex. Not until you promise to stay."

"There was a time you tried to tempt me to stay using sex."

"It didn't work then," she said. "You can get pussy anywhere."

"True."

One word and she froze.

Her hands fell from his shoulders to hang at her sides, useless and pathetic, just like the rest of her. "You're going now, aren't you?"

"I came back to fuck you."

"You came back to be a bastard, because somewhere in that complex mind of yours, you think hurting me is going to make this easier on us."

"I don't give a fuck about easier," he snapped.

"You're creating distance," she said. "Is that in case something goes wrong? Do you think if you get killed, I'll get over it faster if the last time we spoke you were a prick?"

"Trust a bitch to overreact."

"Do you want me to dislike you? Is that the goal here? You certainly didn't come back to prepare me for your death. You're so pragmatic that you've already told me about the safe deposit box with the money. You gave me my own key," she said. "You explained about the hidden car key and the essentials pack in the trunk. Maybe I'll just run off with all of it while you're not here."

"Would give me less of the earache."

"You're so frustrating!" He glared and dropped her back to the floor. It took her a few seconds to catch her balance before noticing he'd turned away to button his jeans. "You tell me you love me and then... is this about getting into character?"

He whirled to face her. "Character?"

"I know you need to be detached; I've seen how easily you put on that mask."

With a huff, he took one stride toward her, bringing her back up against the wall they'd just screwed against. "I haven't been on a job this last three months. You sure made for an interesting vacation."

"You're not going to convince me this meant nothing, that I mean nothing. I know you love me."

"Yeah," he hissed. The anger in his eyes fell to her mouth, then her breasts. "Why the fuck did I have to fall for you?"

His life would be easier if he didn't love her, he'd told her as much straight out. Lashing out, this anger, his demanding sexual nature, was his go-to place. This was the man he'd been all his life, the man he still was. In truth, the man who'd been patient with her, who had communicated and made love with her, he was the new man, he was the man she created.

"Will you make love to me?"

His attention snapped upward. The despondency in her heart would be written all over her face. Her breathing hadn't returned to normal yet, but the longer he remained silent, the more her breaths grew shorter, sharper, more panicked. It wasn't until she blinked and moisture scored her cheeks that she realized she was crying.

"Don't do that," he exhaled.

The only thing Rushe hated more than being out of control was seeing her cry. Maybe it was every woman, she wasn't sure. But every time she cried, he got this look of pain and discomfort on his face.

"Will you?"

His hand came up between them, the back of his fingers drifted toward her face. For half a beat, the water on her skin mesmerized him. But as quickly as it was there, it vanished. His brow came down, his anger snapped into place, and his hand fell away.

"No."

"But—"

"I don't have time to screw you again," he said.

Though what they'd just done wasn't making love, and they both knew that. She wouldn't ask him a second time. Everything about their sex life had been amazing, they'd shared everything in equal measure, it had been just right, until now.

What might be on the horizon scared her, and her words betrayed that fear, which would be exactly why he refused her. Rushe knew her emotions; he was so perceptive of them. If he conceded to a long, slow show of dedication with their bodies, he'd be conceding that she had a reason to be afraid.

Neither of them spoke for a few seconds. With his eyes darting between hers, he nodded once, and turned his back on her. He disappeared into the bedroom and came back less than a minute later with a duffel bag in hand.

She knew that duffel, she'd seen it before.

"Finish yourself off when I'm gone," he said, grabbing up the files from the floor and then marching straight past her. He dumped the duffel at the door to retrieve his leather jacket from the closet. "Play with yourself as much as you want. I don't know how long I'll be gone. The last thing I want to come back to is a clingy, randy slut."

She stayed against the wall, numb to his words. The man she loved was leaving her to go out into the unknown. Distance was what he wanted because isolation was what he knew. The possibility of them being separated on jobs had always existed, but she'd hoped for more notice.

"The condoms are in the second drawer of your nightstand," she said, staring out into the empty room. "Don't forget them."

The closet door slammed with a dull thud. She could picture his hands spread out flat on it.

"Thanks," came the deep reply. "But I'll get more."

"Wouldn't want you bringing anything back to the family bed."

"Goddamnit, Flick!"

The pound of his fist bursting wood startled her, but she kept her place. "Lock the door on your way out. I've got to go and shower you from my body."

Resignation weighed heavily in her soul. Saying goodbye had never hurt like this. Part of her hoped he'd follow. When she crossed the bedroom threshold, she paused. For a few seconds, there was nothing. Was he considering it?

But the front door opened, she heard the lock drop, and then the door was closed. Just like that. He'd gone. He'd left her.

More tears fell, but she swiped them away and shook her head. She was not going to fall apart just because he was gone. Rushe was going to do a job. This was her chance to show she could pull her weight on the team. He'd told her to poke around and that was exactly what she planned to do.

TEN

INSOMNIA TURNED OUT to be a side effect of occupying their bed alone. In the period they'd been living together, the only time she slept alone was if Rushe left her in bed in the morning. On the third night of suffering, she took a sleeping pill to knock herself out.

The man she loved could be in trouble. Who knew what danger he was facing? Yes, he could take care of himself… Somehow, that didn't ease her worry.

His body in her bed wasn't the only thing she missed.

During their last encounter, she'd been cruel. She still had to learn, apparently, it wasn't necessary to respond to him in kind. They could bring out the worst in each other. By the same sentiment, they brought out the best too… didn't they?

The morning after he left, she'd gone back to the library to collate her work. By chance, while looking through the day's newspapers, a job vacancy for cocktail waitresses at the Waterside Casino's Private Lounge caught her eye. Joseph Galante Senior's casino. The

Lounge was the same one Michael Lewis had mentioned in reference to his sister's employment.

The adjoining casino and hotel buildings held the answers. Originally, it had been her plan to reserve a stay in the Waterside Hotel in hope proximity would lead to revelations. But getting a job in the Lounge would afford her the perfect opportunity to walk in Lisa's shoes and maybe get close to the teen.

Ignoring her apprehension, she called the advertised number from the public phone in the library and arranged an interview for the following day.

The interviewer, a broad black man named Ray, didn't care that she'd never worked in a bar because she wouldn't be pouring the drinks, only serving them. Never once did he look her in the eye. The most important part of the interview seemed to be what she thought of the uniform, or rather what she looked like in it.

The uniform? Black patent stilettos with a platform sole, seamed stockings with a suspender belt, and a micro-mini red dress with black lace trim that left half of her ass on show. This was a job in the Lounge. Apparently, she made the cut, because he told her Marv ran the bar and to show up the following night for her first shift.

So she did exactly that. Per instructions, she pulled her hair up high on her head and fastened it with the provided black satin bow on elastic. Then she'd donned her uniform and looked at herself in the mirror.

The dress struggled to cover her decency. The trouble with a dress tailored for a shorter woman was it never took account of her generous chest. The off-shoulder neckline struggled to keep her unbound breasts in place. People on the street didn't need to see her like that, so she covered herself with a knee-length wool coat and ran out of the apartment to catch a cab.

One solace was her familiarity of walking in such high heels. In that area, she was, in fact, a pro, having done it all her life. The dress was restrictive, but she'd scored the jackpot in acquiring the job. No one paid any attention to the staff serving the drinks. While working the same job, Lisa caught someone's eye. Now she had the chance to find out whose eye that was, or maybe find the teen herself.

The uniform was designed to put on a good show, or as Rushe would put it: for the art. Men liked to have semi-nude women hanging around. To make progress in the investigation, she would happily shirk her inhibitions. When Rushe returned, she wanted to have something to report.

Walking Lisa's path would get her so much further than digging at the library. There, lost in text and pictures, she was digging blind, putting in a lot of work without knowing what, or who, was relevant. Nothing could substitute primary experience. The goal of the mission was to locate Lisa Lewis, and to do that she needed to know the players firsthand.

The cab stopped at the end of the alley Ray told her to use. She paid the driver and walked down the broad unlit space adjacent to the imposing monolith of the thirty-story hotel that blanketed the whole area in intimidating murk. Any time she felt fear, she reminded herself who she went to bed with. She could do it. If she could tame Rushe enough to make him smile, she could face down a threat… right?

The narrow staff entrance opened onto a stairwell that led downward. At the bottom, another door opened before she could reach it.

A man on the other side blocked her path. "You Flick?" the bass-baritone asked.

She nodded and he backed away, pointing to one of two doors in the small dark hallway, she accepted the direction with another nod. Something had to be said for a place that had a doorman guarding the bowels of the complex. If someone tried to come in around there and caused trouble, no one would hear, or see, any altercation.

She walked into a room that made her think of a theatre dressing room. A row of mirrors took up one wall, perpendicular was a closed door with a small security scanner attached. Restroom in the corner, and a metal rail with rows and rows of clothes. She peeked around that rail to see another... not just clothes on that one, it was packed with lingerie.

Wary, her chin rose. The entrance door crashed into her, giving her no time to panic or flee.

Three women came in laughing.

"You the new girl?" the first blonde asked. "I'm Kimberly, and that's Rosa Vallario, our queen bee."

Rosa was brunette and the oldest of the women, though not by much, she couldn't be more than a couple of years older than her. The woman's dress was black with red lace trim, her shoes red, her contrast of inverted uniform colors marked her out as different.

"I'm not sure what I just walked in to," Flick said.

Kimberly cackled out a laugh. "You saw the underwear and freaked!"

"Don't worry about that," Rosa said, taking Flick's hand to lead her to a station in the furthest corner. "You can set up here."

"Set up?" she asked, allowing herself to be turned as Rosa took her from her coat.

"Don't be freaked," Kimberly said. "Nancy here got freaked by it too."

Nancy was the other blonde? The young woman's eyes darted one way and then the other, but she didn't speak. Her legs were long and her figure slight, until the breasts on her body, much like Flick's, except

Nancy's were very definitely of the silicone variety.

"I just started last week," Nancy said. "The women here are really nice."

Rushe had told her about listening more to what people didn't say than what they did. The "women" were nice, but Nancy didn't say a thing about the men.

"What's the underwear for?" she asked.

Rosa and Kimberly were adjusting themselves, admiring their figures and their make-up in the mirror next to hers. There were six stations in all, but only four women. More people were coming or there were other vacant positions to fill.

"Not for you to worry about," Rosa said. Recognition hit her when Rosa straightened up. Something about her was familiar, but she couldn't put her finger on what. "Marv won't like us being late. We'll show you what to do." Kimberly and Nancy went out first. Rosa took Flick's hand and led her out too. "You'll be on Thursday to Sunday night shifts. Tips are great on the weekend. My best piece of advice is to keep smiling."

"Smiling?"

Their gaggle moved through another door into The Lounge. It was larger than she anticipated. The room was long and rectangular with a sunken bar of the same shape in the center. Heavy armchairs stood at one side of the bar, as it was low enough to act as a table for patrons.

Her initial confusion about why they would have a sunken bar was cleared up when Nancy teetered up at its side and bent to pick up a tray while talking to the bar tender. Now the thong underwear made sense too.

"The men in here gamble big, they drink big, and they talk serious. Learn to be invisible until they want to see you," Rosa said and released her hand when they got to the bar.

Rosa's words weren't far off Rushe's. Except

Rushe would tell her she didn't ever want to be seen. In this outfit, in this job, she doubted that was possible.

"Where should I start?" Flick asked.

A couple of poker tables were positioned beside a roulette wheel on one side of the bar. An unlit stage dominated the head of the room. On the side of the bar where they were, broad leather couches were arranged around large, low tables.

Patrons were scattered around the place. Being the newest server, she drew the attention of more than a few of them. Just because she hadn't made eye contact didn't mean she wasn't aware of their gazes. Appearing meek and unsure on her first night played into what she wanted them to see. Coy. Unthreatening. Benign.

She didn't want anyone to think her vigilant. She wanted them to look their fill and then forget her. The uniform had one major upside, such a revealing costume would ensure that the customers would likely forget her face and anything she said… if they even heard it in the first place.

"Stick with me tonight," Rosa said. "I'll show you around. Ten 'til three is a good shift."

That night was about learning the ropes and remembering every possible detail. She would learn the job until she belonged there. Rushe did the undercover thing; he'd done it for years. She had ground to gain in experience but was determined to pull her weight. Her love would be happy to have her with him. She had to make him proud. After everything they'd already been through, this would be a walk in the park.

ELEVEN

THE WALK WAS GOING to be longer than anticipated. After four nights working at the Lounge, there was still a lot to learn. Marv, the bartender, was the sort of head guy. The croupiers were male too, but they answered to him. Security remained outside the room. Marv, in turn, answered to Rosa.

Rosa, Nancy, and Kimberly worked the ten to three shifts, Thursday to Sunday night, just like her. She'd met a few other women in passing during the shift change, but none matched Lisa's description. None of the women seemed to be under duress either.

At three a.m. each night, women swathed in lingerie came into the Lounge. Their purpose was obvious, but they didn't appear upset about it.

What was she missing?

Details. What did she know? The Lounge had three access points, the staff entrance, the casino access, and the most frequently used door led to the hotel. Men came and went. Some of the three a.m. women left with male patrons, sometimes only a few minutes after their shift started. Given it happened so quickly, it had to be a pre-arranged or regular agreement. She'd witnessed some drug use, but nothing that caused significant alarm. The men were rich, and the women willing.

There had to be something else.

On Sunday night, she was beginning to wonder if her undercover gig would ever reap results. Then, the hotel access door opened and through it walked three men.

Straight away, she recognized one of them as Joseph Galante Senior. The man in the center, she didn't recognize, but the third was Evan Whyte. She was almost positive. If she was right, this was a coup. Results were right there in front of her.

She served the drinks from her tray, reminding herself not to stare, and hurried back to the bar at Rosa's side.

"That there is Joseph Galante, the shorter one with the dark hair," Rosa said without prompting. "In the middle, with the paunch, is Richard Davis. His family is old money."

"Who is the other one?" Flick asked, trying not to gawp in the same way as Nancy.

At least the interest of the other waitress gave Flick cover to look her fill. These men were probably used to attracting attention. No doubt they coveted it. Especially that of young women who would probably be impressed by the tiniest display of wealth and flattered by the slightest show of admiration.

The affluence meant nothing to Flick, not just because Rushe took care of their finances but because her family were money, probably older than Davis's. Her upbringing gave her an advantage. She sized up the shallow men in an instant. Those men, like her father's cohorts, were superior sons of bitches. Worship was what they wanted; they were the type to believe being idolized and envied was their right.

The three men took up residence in the corner, seating themselves in the leather couches. Not one of them detracted from the debate they were engaged in, despite the interest they were drawing.

"You want to serve them?" Rosa asked.

It took Flick a dozen seconds to realize Rosa was talking to her. "Me?"

"Kimberly and I know them. Nancy shakes when she serves the dealers on their breaks, and they're no one. You've got a head on your shoulders."

"But I've never—"

"Marv has the order," Rosa said. "Just take it over."

"Should I introduce myself?"

"If they ask… Mr. Whyte likes to get to know the girls in here."

So she'd been right about the identity of the third man. "Okay."

Marv put the last glass on the tray and tapped the counter, in the way he did when orders were ready to go. Rosa widened her smile and Flick set her eyes on the table, her destination. Bending at the waist, she lifted the tray, and began to move across the room. This was the reason she was there; she couldn't lose her nerve now.

Power didn't intimidate her, neither did physical size. But her love wasn't there, and without the net he provided, she was nervous. Why hadn't he come home? She hadn't heard a word. More was the point, her fear wasn't that Rushe wasn't there, but that he didn't know her location.

Being there wasn't enough to get her into trouble. She had a job, a right to be there. No one knew her ulterior motive. So pasting on a smile, she strode toward them and bent to slide the tray onto the table.

"You're wrong. He'll be valuable," Joseph

Galante said, but no one responded.

Peeping up through her long lashes, she noticed all three men staring at her. The angle of her body gave them optimum viewing pleasure. They might remember her cleavage, her face wouldn't be as memorable.

"I'm sorry," she said in a small voice that wasn't nervous, it was… innocent. Until she opened her mouth, she hadn't realized that she was going to play it coy. "I'm new, I don't… I'm not sure who drinks what."

"Don't you worry about that," Davis said, taking his own glass, then pushing his two cronies their respective drinks. "Aren't you a cute thing."

"Thank you," she said, taking her tray from the table. "I'm sorry I interrupted."

"Stay a while," Davis said, sliding along the couch to create space.

"Don't do the smarmy thing with my girls, Davis, please," Whyte chimed in. "I'm sorry."

She accepted Whyte's apology as sincere. The men sat in perfectly pressed business suits. Galante was shifty and Davis was smarmy, Whyte seemed the most genuine of the three. Through her research, she knew the history of each man. Now that she'd looked them each in the eye, it felt dishonest to be so familiar with their lives.

Whyte held her stare, his smile was comforting. It didn't matter how well someone played the game, everybody needed reassurance. She had approached full of confidence but spoke with none. Nancy's anxious manner was starting to make more sense.

"You started this week?" Whyte asked. She nodded and blinked her eyes five or six times. The coy thing seemed to be working. "What's your name?"

"Flick."

Davis laughed. "I love it. Is that really your name or just your name at work?"

"She's not a stripper," Whyte said to Davis. "Please ignore my associate, he has issues in communicating with those on a higher plane than he is."

"God complex," Galante muttered, and buried his mouth in his glass.

The words reminded her of a dead man. "It's okay," she said. "Everyone has been very nice."

"I'm glad to hear it, I'm Evan Whyte. If you have any trouble you come to me, okay?"

She let her smile twist reluctantly. "Thank you, but I..."

"What is it? Whyte asked.

"I don't think I'm allowed to just drop by your office. I haven't seen anything of the place outside this room."

He seemed to appreciate her reluctant humor because his smile briefly widened. "Really? You haven't seen the hotel?" She shook her head, keeping her eyes trained to his. "That's a travesty. How do you feel about having dinner with me?"

"Oh no, I... I don't think I'm supposed to—"

"You're off tomorrow night, right? That's how the shifts work."

"Well yes, but..."

"I'll show you around. I might even show you my office."

His office? How to react? Spending time with Whyte would show her his true persona. If she was right about him maybe he'd help her locate Lisa Lewis. Except if Rushe was right... It was a risk she'd have to take and hope that her love would be home to advise her before she found herself in any compromising positions.

"I'd love to."

TWELVE

SHE CONTINUED TO SERVE drinks throughout the rest of the evening. A few times, she caught Whyte watching her work. Since he'd declared his interest, the other two men ignored her. Apparently, she was no longer relevant to them.

According to the research, Whyte was single. Although pictures of him with different women existed, she didn't get the impression he was a womanizer. Having dinner with him was safe. In her opinion, the risk had to be minimal, and she was determined. Getting closer to this man would be useful to the case and insulate her from others. Davis seemed like the type to get handsy after a few alcoholic drinks and she could do without that complication.

At three a.m. precisely, two women came in wearing lingerie. The provided call girls. Neither of them went anywhere near the Whyte table. But that table didn't flinch at the sight either.

On returning her tray to the bar, she noticed a woman come through the hotel access and go straight to the Whyte table. The newest blonde wasn't like the escorts. She went to the table and waited to be acknowledged by Davis. Words were exchanged, and then the woman with the refined features went back to the hotel alone.

"You don't want Davis to catch you looking at him like that," Rosa said. "Stick with Whyte."

News of their meeting tomorrow night had spread like wildfire. Already, she was committed.

"It's nothing," she said. "He's just being nice."

"Men like that don't have to be nice," Rosa said. "Don't tell me I have to explain it to you. You don't strike me as the naïve type."

Maybe a few months ago she would have. She hadn't carried her innocent act with the men onto her colleagues. "I know he's rich. I know he could have his pick of women. Do you think he just wants sex?"

"If it was just sex, he could have one of the girls provided for that… or a bunch of them. They pay the hookers through a third party, so it's all legit. Course we pass on the cost to the john, with a little extra on top."

"Do they work elsewhere in the complex?"

"The Lounge here is the only place anyone is allowed to pay for sex or sell their body. It wouldn't be tolerated anywhere else. All the girls are checked out before they're allowed to transact in here."

Her focus landed on Rosa. "Checked out? Does that mean blackmailed?"

"No," Rosa said on a laugh. "Nothing like that. These girls are the high-class type, not your regular crack whores. They do this because they want to, and they get paid damn well for it too."

Any man using a prostitute was open to blackmail himself, especially if he wanted to brand himself as squeaky clean.

"So what is it Whyte wants from me?"

"I've worked here for years, and I've seen him take an interest in a few girls. A couple of them spent his money, then he set them loose. Three or four had their hearts broken. One even broke his heart."

"How did she do that?"

"Screwed around on him we thought, don't know exactly. We saw her once after they split. She didn't tell us anything, just disappeared after that."

"Gone?"

"Moved back west, we think. She came from Vegas, plenty of work out there for a girl in our trade… or in theirs."

Rosa let her interest drift to another corner where one of the call girls was leading a well- lubed patron across the room toward the hotel access. That particular customer had come in from the casino; it was unlikely he had a hotel room reserved.

He groped as the escort teased. On that kind of promise, it wouldn't take the guy long to get a room, perhaps their most expensive suite available. The elite escort would be used to deluxe standards.

Busting a place like this wide open would be a vice detective's dream. But she hadn't seen any indication of undercover activity, or of the place being under any kind of surveillance. Maybe the establishment was legit, and she was coming at this from the wrong angle.

If she discovered that to be the case, she could quit and walk away. But she wasn't ready to do that yet. Lisa Lewis had worked there and gotten herself mixed up with someone. Could be that someone was Whyte and he would reveal himself, or it wasn't Whyte and he could help her establish what happened.

When Rushe got home, she'd explain her findings and suspicions. Their argument still dogged her. Her love didn't intend to screw around. But sending him out the apartment angry meant he was alert, in the frame of mind he had to be to do whatever was necessary. It hadn't been her aim, but she also hoped it would make him more eager to return to her.

They weren't mushy. as far as she was concerned, couples who insisted on "not parting angry" had to be insecure. She missed Rushe, craved his presence, his body, and his voice. She could wax lyrical, but there was no need. It came down to one simple point: she loved him, and he loved her.

But going on a date with another man… might take some explaining.

THIRTEEN

SHE HAD STARTED the next day full of gusto, by lunchtime the enthusiasm had waned. By the evening, she was anxious. In the past, it hadn't mattered if dates were enjoyable, but this date had to be a success. She needed to strike a balance between showing interest in order to maintain his and not appearing too easy. If Whyte got the wrong idea, there would be trouble.

Her choice of wardrobe was important. She went with a V-neck white silk dress that hung to her knee and blue accessories. Looking at herself in the mirrored panel on the sliding door of the closet in their bedroom, all she could think about was Rushe.

For a week, she'd waited for word, and received none. Thoughts of trying to find or communicate with Eric or Scott had occurred to her. Except Rushe had been adamant about those men not understanding their connection.

She'd give her love a little more time, and then all bets were off. If he didn't want her poking around in his life, he should have provided a way for her to get in touch with him.

Trying to focus, she brought her thoughts back to the evening. Whyte had told her to meet him in the hotel lobby at eight. Good. The idea of another man at Rushe's door wasn't a good one.

Rather than the back alley, her taxi drove to the front of the building. A novelty. She paid the driver and exited the cab to enter the hotel.

The Waterside Hotel should have impressed her, except her family frequented places like it. She'd been in and out of many high-class, luxury venues throughout her life. Her first impulse on entering the vast marble lobby was to stifle a yawn.

Everything glittered; the rumble of conversation in the lobby bar was low and distinguished. The elevator doors opened, and the rattle of wheels crossing its threshold revealed the bellhop directing a gold suitcase trolley. The scent of vanilla permeated, and every single person stood tall, believing themselves to be important.

She didn't see Whyte straightaway. For a moment, she wasn't sure how to proceed. Then another elevator opened, and Whyte appeared, as though their arrivals had been timed to coincide. He didn't stop to seek her out. He walked straight toward her, again, like it had been orchestrated.

In a gray suit and blue shirt, Whyte did look every inch the man she expected him to be. Men like him had all the confidence in the world. Maybe it was the money, or the success, or the adoration, but men like Evan Whyte expected perfection. They entered every space like their coming had been expected, desired, needed to somehow make the event perfect.

Whyte was about Liam's height of five eleven and wore a smile that reminded her of the library IT engineer. Whyte was everybody's buddy.

"You found us," Whyte said as he came up in

front of her.

It wasn't exactly a miracle. After all, she worked in the basement. "Yes," she said, quickly understanding her role was to take his lead. "It's very beautiful."

She ensured to exude awe. Like just being there was a treat.

"This is just the beginning," Whyte said, pointing upward to the fully aglow gold light fixture. "Do you like the chandelier?"

"Yes, it's beautiful."

"You can have it. We're having a new one installed next month."

"I don't think it would fit in my apartment," she said, laughing along, "but thanks anyway."

"We'll get you a bigger apartment."

Whyte took her hand and tucked it into his elbow to sweep her around in a semi-circle to lead her toward the back of the lobby, behind the elevator banks. His sense of entitlement mirrored that of the men she'd dated in her early twenties.

In those days, she was every inch the socialite her family expected her to be, calm, quiet, and compliant. With her family, in her life with them, she was always out of place. After refusing to marry the suitor her father chose, she left the family. She could not fall in line as her older sisters had.

On leaving them, she lived for a year trying to carve out a life for herself. Surviving on her own for that year had been tough, lonely, she'd had to learn how to take care of herself. Then there was Rushe, hailing the beginning of the life she felt she was meant to live. This one was for keeps.

"The building is amazing," she said.

"I thought we would eat here, then go upstairs to the bar for a drink," Whyte said. "Is that acceptable?"

"Yes."

Entering through the colored glass art deco frontage of the restaurant, Whyte directed them toward a window, and the only set table. Beyond was a quiet, external courtyard. A bottle of Cristal sat in a high-hat next to the meal laid out under silver. Of course. The setup was probably supposed to separate her from her panties.

"I'd have expected a place like this to be busy," she said, allowing Whyte to pull out her chair and slide it in under her as she sat.

"There are three restaurants in the complex," he said. "This one is my favorite. I wanted us to have our privacy."

"You are a man who knows how to impress."

Whyte picked up the champagne to fill their flutes. "Are you asking if I do this often?"

"Do you?"

"No, I don't," he said. "But you have no reason to believe that, not yet."

"Yet?"

Putting the champagne away, he lifted the covers from their meals. "You're not a vegetarian, are you?"

"No."

"Good," he said. "Pigeon with warm foie gras sorbet, it's delicious."

Funny, she thought that particular nerve in her had died. Apparently not. If she needed a reminder why she turned her back on her first life, this was it. Whyte seemed like a decent enough person; he would probably impress most women. She had to literally bite her tongue.

Not only had he poured her drink without confirming champagne was what she wanted, but he had pre-ordered food, relieving her of that choice too. The cherry on the cake was him telling her in advance how she would enjoy it, she would find it delicious, before a single piece of cutlery had been lifted. The most Rushe would do was order pizza or slam something in the microwave, but if she didn't want to eat it, she wouldn't. If he had a problem with that, he'd fuck her down off her high horse.

She missed her love so much.

"Everything okay?" Whyte asked, poised to begin eating.

"Oh, yes, sorry, this is just so… wonderful."

"You'll love it," he said, gesturing with his fork.

Maintaining her smile, she began to eat. With a reminder of her purpose, she hoped to make it through the meal without throwing something at him.

FOURTEEN

WHYTE LIKED TO TALK about himself, and she let him. Most of his conversation didn't seem relevant, but she tried to stow away the details. Evan Whyte was a self-made billionaire. He'd had a good start, his parents lived a respectable life, but Whyte hadn't been content with mediocrity, as he put it. At thirty-two he'd hit a billion, three years ahead of his target.

The wait staff remained scarce, appearing only to clear or serve. By the end of the meal, nausea roiled. The food was rich and the champagne bubbly.

"Do you have many friends in the area?" she asked. "A man like you must spend a lot of time globe-trotting."

"I'm setting up resorts across Europe at the moment, so, yes, I spend a fair amount of time abroad."

"Last night, in the Lounge, was it a social occasion?"

"Davis and I have been in business together for years. We own nightclubs across the city." Her date sat forward twisting the stem of his champagne flute between his thumb and forefinger. "I say we own them, but actually I've had to bail him out a couple of times."

"What kind of nightclubs?"

"Oh, nothing like this. They are standard music venues frequented by the young and the reckless. Not your type of place at all."

"I don't know," she said. "I like to dance."

"I'm glad to hear it. Are you ready for that drink now?"

Despite already consuming two glasses of champagne, she nodded in agreement. They were starting to get somewhere. She couldn't give up now.

"Sure."

Whyte escorted her from the table, out through the lobby and to the elevator. He opened a small gold panel and put a card into a slot. Where were they going? Below the slot, he keyed in a four-digit code on a horizontal keypad then closed the panel.

It would be strange to drink in the Lounge, if that was their intended destination. Though none of her usual colleagues should be working that night.

"What about the other man?" she asked of the Lounge drinking buddy Whyte hadn't mentioned yet. "Are you in business with him too?"

"Joseph Galante owns the casino next door." Whyte put an arm around her shoulders.

"I think he's afraid of you."

"Nonsense," was Whyte's reply, but she read satisfaction in the curl at the corner of his lips.

The elevator came to a stop, and the bell rang as the doors slid open. A lush red carpet stretched ten feet toward a single white door. The Lounge door was black.

Whyte's arm remained over her shoulders as he directed her out of the elevator.

"This isn't the Lounge," she said.

"No."

He opened the door to guide her into a room with rounded walls and curved floor to ceiling windows that presented a silent view of the glowing city lights. They had to be twenty floors up.

"You had the bar closed too?"

"In a manner of speaking," Whyte said.

Muted cove lighting drew her attention to a small bar on their right. This wasn't a commercial bar; at least it wasn't a public one.

"Where are we?" she asked.

The perimeter floor was raised like a flat doughnut. In the lowered round center were two deep semi-circular couches with a low glass table in the center.

"This is my personal lounge. What would you like to drink?"

Whyte took her to the bar, sat her on a leather stool, and went to the other side.

"I'm not sure—"

"More champagne?"

"No," she said. "I'd be happy with a mineral water."

"Nonsense," he said and bent to retrieve something from under the bar. "I have cranberry vodka, just shipped in, it's delicious."

Why bother to ask if he was going to ignore her answer?

Biting her tongue again, she smiled along. "This is an incredible room," she said. "You truly are an impressive man."

"There is more to come," he said, pouring the vodka.

Vodka had never been her thing. Still, she took the proffered glass and touched it to Whyte's. They both sipped. Rather she let the liquid reach her lips but not pass them.

"Do you have a stake in the casino next door

too?" she asked, as though just carrying on the conversation from earlier.

"The two buildings were designed and built together by me, but the business of the casino belongs to, and is run by, Galante. Do you enjoy gambling? I can arrange to—"

A low ringing sound interrupted him, and the ease left his person for a second. That glimmer was curious. All night he'd been reasonable and attentive, but that expression wasn't either.

"I apologize, excuse me," Whyte said, and went to a phone by the couch.

Her aim to eavesdrop for salacious details was thwarted. The call was over after a couple of brief mumbles. He slammed down the phone. Oh, he was pissed.

She could see him trying to re-establish his composure as he returned to her, but the anger didn't leave him.

"I apologize," he said, taking her hand from her glass. "I specifically requested no interruptions tonight."

"I understand," she said, fluttering her eyes as she had frequently through the evening. "A man as important as you must be very busy. I've taken up too much of your time already."

She didn't want to walk out on the conversation when they were making headway, but she'd be happy to walk out of the situation. Taking advantage of the out was just smart. The low lighting and complete isolation set her on edge.

"No," he said, lifting her hand to his lips. "I'm enjoying our date. We'll just have to stomach a minor interruption. A colleague wishes to speak to me with regards to a time-sensitive issue. Can you endure a short wait?"

Again she made herself smile and nod. What the

hell else was she supposed to do?

"Good."

Whyte kissed her hand again. Thankfully, there was a knock on the door, forcing him from her side. She struggled to restrain the urge to wipe away the residue of moisture he'd left on her skin.

"Enter!" Whyte called out like a high school principal.

The door opened. At that moment, she was only paying partial attention while also trying to locate a sink to pour her drink down.

One tall broad man dressed in black entered. The second man was Marv. Curious, she sat up straighter, now much more interested in proceedings. For a split second anyway, because another man entered at Marv's back, a man dressed in black too. A man she knew… intimately.

She winced… on the inside anyway. Despite her surprise at seeing her lover there, he didn't share the sentiment. In fact, those stern black eyes of his were positively evil when they landed on her without a hint of hesitation. Rushe had known she was there. Somehow, he'd known.

He'd lied to her. What an asshole. She'd thought he was out there, lost and alone somewhere. What if she'd done something stupid in pursuit of him? All the while he'd been within ten miles of their apartment.

Forgetting their place, she slid off the stool and opened her mouth ready to reprimand him. Before any words could escape, Rushe switched his view to Whyte and Marv mumbling at each other, reminding her of where they were.

Rushe was doing remarkably well to stand there quietly by the door with his cohort flanking the other side. When his eyes snapped back to her, she bristled, more than happy to match his anger with her own.

"Excuse me, just for a moment," Whyte said.

Without waiting for her response, Whyte nodded to the other man, and the three vanished into a side room. The door clicked shut behind the trio. She immediately drew breath to talk.

Rushe got there first. "At home," he threatened through his teeth, in a tone so deep it was only bass, no voice.

"You must be confusing me with someone else," she hissed in a whisper. "I live alone."

The fury he pinned on her made her physically recoil. Rushe bared his teeth on an inhale. Damn. She wasn't sure if she wanted to hide from this man or hump him.

Whyte returned with the others. "I'm sorry," he said. "We have to cut our evening short, Flick. Something has come up."

"That's not a problem," she said, quashing her visceral urge to run. "I understand."

"I'll have a hotel driver take you home," Whyte said, meeting her mid-way to the door, only a few feet from Rushe.

Whyte was spared from looking at her lover spitting silent psychic wrath, cataloging every minute movement of the other man on his turf. His eyes narrowed further when Whyte touched her upper arm.

"There's no need," she said.

"I insist. If you leave a contact number—"

"I don't have a phone," she said honestly.

That startled him. "At all? Whatever I'm paying you, it's obviously not enough."

She laughed at the joke, irking Rushe further. "I'll be at work on Thursday."

"I won't wait that long to make this inconvenience up to you," Whyte said. "I'll have someone courier a phone to you in the morning."

"That's really not necessary. There is no inconvenience."

"There certainly has been on my part."

"It would make me uncomfortable to accept a gift like that."

Whyte didn't seem to expect that response; it left an awkward silence in the air. Most probably the billionaire wasn't accustomed to being refused in front of his men.

"Very well," he said eventually. "Then I expect you to return. Come to the hotel on Wednesday, same time. I'll meet you again."

She couldn't think of a reason to say no, other than the fact that Rushe knew how to kill a man with his bare hands. Her reason for accepting Whyte's invitation in the first place was valid, he hadn't fulfilled his purpose. Why should she say no? She nodded.

Rushe already looked set to explode, so when Whyte moved to kiss her cheek, she stepped out of the way, conveying the coy nature Whyte expected.

Marv came toward her. As she wasn't sure how long their silence would hold, she chose not to look at Rushe again. Her escort took her down to the sidewalk and waited until a car arrived.

All that occupied her mind on the journey home was Rushe. His lie made her angry, but his presence settled her apprehension. His words in the suite implied he'd come home. She couldn't have him back a minute too soon.

FIFTEEN

AFTER A QUICK SHOWER, she slipped on a camisole and waited. When it became clear Rushe was in no hurry to return, she tried to read, then she tried to watch TV. Nothing held her interest. For a long time, she stared out across the city as though she could will him to arrive with the sheer power of her emotion.

At two a.m., she went to bed. By two thirty, she was on her feet again. Anger had become agony. The last time she and Rushe had been apart for this long, she was terrified he'd lost his life. That old anxiety met that moment.

She was drinking water at the kitchen sink a few minutes after three when she heard a key in the lock. The scrap of satin that she wore offered no heat, but the temperature wasn't what made her shiver. She cast aside the highball glass and wiped her mouth with the back of her hand.

Rushing around the kitchen counter, the cold water she'd just consumed flooded to her fingers and toes, splintering them with ice.

The door slammed and she stopped, holding her breath. He dumped something, then with three daunting footfalls he was there, fifteen feet from her, in the unlit apartment.

She should have put something on her feet. Sharing the open space with his tall, broad form, she felt puny. The fireworks of emotion she'd endured struck her dumb, leaving her unsure where to start, what to say.

He didn't speak either. He shrugged his leather jacket from his shoulders and tossed it in the direction of the door. All the while he observed her, scrutinized her figure that he knew so well.

"Take it off." His words rumbled through the walls, vibrating her every atom.

There were things to say, things to ask, but this wasn't a Rushe to be reasoned with. Right then, the power of speech had vacated her anyway. Raising her hands to her shoulders, she trailed the fine spaghetti straps of her camisole off and let the pale fabric shimmer away from her body.

He looked at every inch of her, slowly. His eyes traveled across her figure and settled on the apex of her thighs.

"Turn around."

She did as told. His words were rough, but they skimmed over her, cool and refreshing on a body filled with searing sand. Already her breasts ached, her core was swelling. She longed to be reminded of the power he held, the protection he enveloped her in.

"Bend over the table."

The dining table was solid oak and heavy. With four place settings, two at each side, the top and bottom were clear.

Placing her hands shoulder width apart, she bent over as instructed, but Rushe wasn't happy. His heavy boots stamped toward her, and he kicked her feet further apart. Without giving any warning, he reached over her to grab her arms, locking her wrists in one hand at her lower back. His other hand landed between her shoulder blades with a weight that pressed her face to the table.

"You've been naughty, Little Kitten," he growled. "Did you think you'd get away with screwing around on me?"

"I didn—"

"Ah," he said, spanking her ass, keeping her wrists restrained. "You're my whore. You don't screw around on me. Did your pussy forget who feeds it? Is it hungry, Kitten? You fucking skank, this body belongs to me! You're for my pleasure alone!" He spanked her again, harder, then squeezed her butt cheek, sending a burning ache throbbing through her body, pleasure shimmered to her apex.

"I'm gonna fuck you, Kitten. I'm gonna fuck your pussy 'til my spunk's dripping out of you. I'm gonna fill you full, fuck your mouth 'til your belly's got no room for more, you hear me? Speak!"

"Yes," she croaked.

His hand slid from her ass to her pussy, his fingers roamed every inch of her but didn't probe inside. He circled her clit, pressed it, rubbed it faster and faster until the embrace of climax compressed her gut. The moment she whimpered, his caress disappeared.

"Second thoughts, maybe I don't want my dick in you. Where you been? Tell me."

On that, he snatched her hips. Flipping her over, he dropped her onto the table, grabbing her thighs to haul her to the edge. With his fingers biting into her flesh, he used his strength to hold her legs against the table, her center on open show, laid out for him.

"You got a hot cunt, how many men you let play with my pussy? You're my toy, Kitten, mine, only mine."

She tried to move her legs, she tried to touch him

with her feet, anything to reassure him, but he didn't let her move. When she tried to sit up, he snatched her breasts and pushed her down again. He didn't caress, he didn't kiss, he didn't make eye contact.

When her hands moved over his on her breasts, he hissed away.

"Rushe," she whispered.

"Quiet!"

Seizing her wrists again, he planted them at the sides of her head, pinning her body down with his. Her chance to embrace him came now; she wrapped her legs around him. On the contact, he gritted his teeth, his jaw tensing.

She couldn't get into his head, didn't know what he was thinking, or even if he believed what he was saying.

Sliding her hands up the table, he locked her wrists above her head in one solid grip, giving him the opportunity to reach between them. He almost always tested her with his fingers before he entered. This time, he didn't touch her, he opened his jeans and the heavy weight of his rock-hard cock collided with her folds, Still, he didn't enter. Though she frowned, she didn't speak. What was wrong? What was the delay? She needed to know what was in his head.

His next words brought her moistening eyes to his.

"Consent," he murmured.

Her heart turned to stone, the fire in her chest extinguished by the notion they'd lost ground, gone back a stage. Tears seeped from her eyes, running down each temple, dripping to her ears.

His grip on her wrists loosened, and a look of horror crossed his usually set expression. He hadn't believed his words; he hadn't questioned her loyalty. Not until she hesitated to consent.

"Yes, Rushe," she yelped. "Yes. I am only for you."

The grip above her head tightened fast as the weight of his body left hers just enough to grant him access to finally invade her core. The conquering impact wrought a scream of climax from deep within her.

Rushe was hammering forward, pounding into her thrust after thrust with such an intensity that he had to link their fingers palm to palm above her shoulders to keep her in place. He bent over her, slowing his actions enough to nudge her head out of his way and suck her neck, high up near her hairline, a fingers length behind her ear.

The marking of her, the physical sign of possession, clamped her internal muscles around him in place with a spasm so fierce he couldn't immediately withdraw.

He swore on plunging forward and grabbed her hips, hauling them off the table so he could stand upright while pouring his seed into her.

When his release subsided, he dropped her back down, obliging his slaked member to slither from her body. Tucking himself back into his jeans, he did a couple of buttons then grabbed her arm to pull her off the table. She stumbled to the floor, but he picked her up under one arm and carried her to the bedroom.

He sat on the closest side of the bed, his own side, and flung her down behind him. While still holding her in place with one hand, the other opened his middle drawer.

"No," she said at the same time he retrieved what he was looking for. "Rushe, Lover, you don't have to…"

He got the cuff on her wrist without delay despite her struggling. She couldn't get away when he locked the cuff to one of the horizontal bars of their bedframe. She rattled it but there was no way to fight the metal.

"You did it again," he said, sitting back.

"Me?" she asked, her body going limp. "I seem to remember you're the one with the habit of attaching me to the furniture. I've never chained you up anywhere!"

"It's my fault, I forgot…" He ran his hand up her shin, but she pulled it away causing him to land a glare on her. "You want me to let you go to him?"

"Don't be ridiculous."

"Is that what you want?" He pounced forward, diving over her. His body covered hers, his arms stretched up the length of hers, enclosing their faces together in a private cocoon. "Is that what turns you on, Kitten?" He ran his parted lips down her nose, after grazing her mouth, they carried on back up her jaw to her ear.

"You want a rich boy? A respectable guy you can take back to daddy? But he doesn't know you, does he? Not like I do, no one knows how down and dirty you like it. You enjoy being a slut, don't you? My slut… you like it when I fuck you every second of every day, don't you, Kitten? Speak."

"Yes."

"You want to open your legs for me, on my command, don't you? Speak."

"Yes," she exhaled.

"You'll do exactly what I tell you, 'cause that's all you're good for, isn't it? That's all you're good at, following my orders like a dumb little lamb?" he asked. "Speak."

"Yes, sir."

"You love my cock, say it."

"I love your cock," she said, trying to catch his mouth with hers.

He pulled away. "I say when you get it, think I'm gonna kiss your mouth before I fuck it? You can't be with a prick like Whyte, couldn't be with Robert, couldn't be with any pretty boy. You can't even hack it with a regular joe." He stopped in the fog of their merged breath to lift his head and look her in the eye. "Why not?"

"Because I love your cock," she responded

When she smiled, his expression relaxed. Yes. Good sign.

"Good girl."

This time he did let his mouth close over hers. His tongue delved into her, seeking out its mate, and it wasn't lost for long. She moaned her soul into this union, into him… until she recalled his question on the dining table. The warmth in her eyes joined her stinging sinus. His hand slid up her inner thigh, so she took the lead to wrap it around his broad thigh.

He flicked her upper lip with his tongue, then kissed her cheek, her jaw, all the way to the shell of her ear.

"I love you, Kitten," he whispered.

The only time or place he was comfortable being so emotionally open with her was there, alone, whispering into her ear.

"I missed you," she responded, lifting her head to caress his stubble-covered cheek with her smooth one.

Something startled him because their intimacy was shattered when he sat up. Catching her leg on his kept him upright on his knees.

He smudged his fingers to her face. "Explain."

"You didn't hurt me," she said, knowing physical trauma was always his default concern.

"I was faithful, if you think—"

"No, I know you were. I trust you."

Using his open palm, he wiped her face with all the finesse of a soldier smudging on war paint. "So explain," he said.

"You asked for my consent, back in the living

room. We talked about that. It's like we went backwards."

"I couldn't judge your mood. I don't like miscommunication."

"I know," she said. "How long have you been working for Whyte?"

"I could ask you the same question."

"You knew I was there, when you walked in, you looked at me. How did you know?"

"I saw you at dinner," Rushe said. "I knew Whyte had a date, didn't know it was you until you walked in."

"You were there?"

"I watched those elevator doors close and…"

He struggled to process tender emotion because it was so alien to him. Sex was a physical manifestation of the feelings in him he still battled. He used the physical to deal with the things he otherwise didn't know how to handle.

"You were scared for me," she said, and noted he was as angry with her for saying it, as he was with himself for feeling it.

"Didn't expect you to go to his bedroom."

"That wasn't his bedroom."

"It's his suite, where he lives," Rushe said. "He took you upstairs to fuck you."

"He did not!"

"Did you ask him?"

"Over dinner? No, I didn't ask him. Whyte isn't that kind of man."

His eyes descended to her breasts. "One thing on his mind when he's looking at your jugs."

"You mean yours," she said, happy to remind him of his declaration of ownership.

"Right."

"Did you think I was going to have sex with him? Is that why you were angry?"

"I'm pissed you went to the effort."

"The dress?"

"You're fucking hot," he said, disentangling himself from her limbs to leave the bed.

"Thank you. But I don't think the compliment was your point."

"What the fuck are you thinking going places alone with a guy?"

"Any guy?"

"You learned nothing," he said, dropping his hands to the horizontal bar at the end of the bedframe.

"I was trying to help! If you and your friends hadn't interrupted—"

"Sorry to bust up the party," he retorted. "I could've blown my cover making excuses to get up there!"

"Excuses?"

"You think the interruption was coincidence? Who do you think created the situation?"

"You?" she asked.

"I'm not gonna watch my woman…" he fumed. "What was your exit strategy?"

"I…" she began. "I thought he was taking me to a public bar."

"You know what Rohypnol is? GHB?"

"Rushe!"

"He wanted to fuck you!"

"I doubt that he's—"

"But you don't know," he barked.

"That girl is still in there, somewhere."

"You told me to find her," he said. "You pulled the lever, Kitten, you started this."

"Yes, and I was trying to help. You told me to keep poking around."

"In your computer!"

"Don't shout at me! You're the liar! You told me

you were leaving."

"And I did," he snarled, remaining steadfast and unapologetic, he wasn't the apologetic type.

"I didn't realize you meant just a few blocks over!"

"I left the city," he said. "But I got the chance to come back and get close; you don't fuck around with a chance like that."

"This was about shutting me out. All the time I've been here, I thought there was progress. I thought we were on the same team!"

"We share a bed, Kitten. You're too reckless to be in on the action."

He started for the door, and she sprang up to a crouch. Being tethered again brought back old memories.

"Where are you going?" she asked.

"I'm thirsty."

"We're talking."

"I don't argue with women."

She cursed him, but he carried on out of the room leaving her there anyway. Calling out or shouting wouldn't hurry him, and she wouldn't give him the satisfaction. So she lay there, right in the middle of the bed, and closed her eyes.

Something close to twenty minutes passed by the time he sauntered back in. She maintained her facade of sleep, but her curiosity was awakened when Rushe dropped something. There was a zip, he muttered, and then there was the flutter of pages. She wouldn't give in though. Sure enough, less than a minute later she heard the tell-tale sounds of him getting undressed.

It had been more than a week. She was spread out there, naked, going nowhere, and they were alone. He had to be a starving dog. Usually, they had sex several times a day, but they'd just gone cold turkey.

The bed shifted; he'd seated himself beside her. His hot palm covered the breast furthest from his position; he squeezed and massaged the flesh, pinching her nipple several times until it was in a painfully tight peak.

Her breast closest to him was treated to his mouth. He slapped the other breast a couple of times and kept working her nipple between his thumb and forefinger. He sucked on her neglected nipple, tugging it between his teeth to flicker his tongue over it. Breathing out her pleasure, of its own volition her body gently arched into his mouth.

Taking his attention to her other breast, he lapped his tongue across the pebble he'd created, and blew slow circles to it. Her lover would claim not to know what making love was, this kind of glorious attention was inadvertent on his part. He could play with her breasts for hours and still not realize how his devotion indulged her.

"Release me," she whispered, though she still hadn't opened her eyes.

"Not a chance," he hummed, suckling her again.

"Please, Lover."

"You're not getting your greedy hands on my dick."

She sighed. "He likes me."

"Yeah."

To her disappointment, his mouth disappeared. She opened her eyes to see him lie down at her side. His erection, in so desperate want of attention, poked her thigh.

"Let me kiss him," she said. "We've been separated for so long."

"Yeah, less than an hour."

"That, in the living room, doesn't count," she said, biting her lip when his mouth returned to her chest.

"That can't have sated him… that can't have sated you, can it? Have you had your fill of me?"

His scorching breath met her cleavage when he let a pulse of laughter escape. "Kitten, you're not getting any sleep tonight, or tomorrow." His head rose. "I've got you tied down and you're not going anywhere… you're my prisoner, just the way I like it."

SIXTEEN

HE HADN'T BEEN LYING. Her body shook, and her muscles screamed. Standing there in the shower they shared, she let the water run over her face and pushed her hair back. Her love stood behind her; the dual stall had a shower at each end. Her steadying hand descended to turn off the water, but Rushe caught it, and pressed her palm to the tile.

His chin stopped on her head, then he crouched to rub his face in her wet hair. A moment later, his hand replaced his face, and he stroked downward, smoothing her hair again.

As though none of that had happened, he shut off the water and slid open the stall to leave her alone in the puddle that still trickled toward the drain.

He took no time at all to get himself back together after a shower. As women did, she went through her routine and blasted her hair with the blow dryer. Her natural color mesmerized Rushe, for no reason she could understand. He had a preoccupation with her dirty-blonde hair, which was darker than she remembered.

Then again, it had been close to a decade since she'd seen it. Rushe's hair was a deep brown that she likened to the color of expensive dark chocolate.

Leaving the towel, and any thought of clothes, behind in the bathroom, she entered the bedroom to see that Rushe had changed all the bed linen.

"You're not usually so domesticated," she said. "What's the occasion?"

"We need to re-group," he said, capturing her wrist to pull her onto the bed.

Her guess? It was mid-way through Tuesday, maybe as late as dinnertime, but her love apparently wasn't finished with the sex. Except when her butt hit the bed, something clicked, and she was dumbfounded. He'd cuffed her to the headboard again.

"This is ridiculous!"

"You're not dating other men," Rushe said, lying down to spread out.

"I'm not actually dating him. I got a job—"

"In the Lounge, I got the skinny on you last night."

"You asked about me?" She rolled toward him, leaning on her restrained right arm. "Wasn't that suspicious?"

"Suspicious not to," he said, groping her breast. "Man, you've got great tits."

"You asked about my breasts?"

"It's what men notice."

As he liked to tell her on a regular basis. And she'd be lying if she denied using that nugget of information to her advantage. She now knew how to make sure her face was forgettable.

"Breasts you've been very intimate with, you know them better than I do."

"Those bastards don't know that," he said.

She poked her chin into the pressure point of his

shoulder. He didn't react much, his attention remained on the ceiling. His arm came around her to tuck her body closer.

Being tactile wasn't a natural urge for Rushe, but he had become accustomed to her body being against his. The impulse to seek her form was subconscious. Maybe it was an act of protection, or maybe it was a sex thing. She didn't much care about the why. They were a normal extension of each other. Meaning that without him near, she felt almost unreal.

His fingers lost themselves in her hair where they played, and stroked, twisted and twined. That he wasn't conscious of doing it only made it more endearing.

"Next time you lie to me I'm going to schedule a breast reduction," she teased. "And I'll be paying for it with your money, see how you like that."

The diagonal slope of his smile was vague. "You try it, and when the doc puts you under, I'll triple his fee to make them bigger."

Her jaw fell as she sat up, away from his hair-frolicking hand. "You wouldn't!"

"Sure about that?"

How did he always know just what to say and do? If shouting and stomping was required, he was more than capable. Equally, like just now, he could plant a seed in her mind that would take root.

"You don't mess with my girls," he said, pulling her body onto his.

Shoving her cuffed hand past his face, he settled her back on his chest, so he could grope her breasts as if they were on his body.

"They won't be yours again until there are no restraints."

"I've told you to trash the underwear," he said, closing his fingers over her.

"Not that restraint," she said, rattling the cuff.

"This."

"You can't go back to work there," Rushe said.

"Yes, I can, and I will. There are other women there, it's safe."

"It's anything but safe. They have a job ad in the paper every week. The staff turnover is suspicious."

"I got the job hoping I would find Lisa still working there."

"She hasn't worked in the Lounge for weeks. But Lisa is in the hotel."

"How do you know that?" she asked.

"I haven't just been sitting on my ass."

"Tell me more. Who is she in a relationship with?"

"Joey, but you don't need to know—"

"Lover," she said, clamping her hand on his to still its movement on her breast. "Tell me about the best sex you ever had."

"What?"

"You heard me, what was her name?"

"What the fuck do—"

"We're a team, Rushe. I came with you to be part of the team. You trust me, or you don't. You know I'm strong enough to handle this. You fell in love with a fighter. Why do you expect me to roll over and play dead now?"

Rushe squeezed. "You never do as you're told."

She turned her face toward his arm. "If I'd done what you told me to, I wouldn't be with you now."

"You'd be safe."

"I'd be unhappy," she said, but chose to lighten the mood by joking with him. "We're going to learn how to do this together... If you can't adjust, I'll demand you get a nine to five that requires you to wear a suit to the office every day, then we'll have to get married... and I'll have to start squeezing out the kids and—"

"Okay," he griped. "You've made your point."

"You better make me happy, or I'll make you miserable," she teased. "Whatever we do from here, we do together."

A forgotten fantasy zipped her senses. The zap of it straightened her spine, at least as best it could, she sat up, only getting to forty-five degrees because of the cuffs.

"What is it?" Rushe asked.

"Nothing, I was just reminded of…"

"What?"

"That morning, in the shack… when you woke up and I was…"

"Sucking me off," he said, relaxing while she remained seated on his abdomen. "If it'll make you feel better you can—"

"No," she said, bringing her legs around, sitting side-saddle so she could see him. "It's me. I'm the woman."

"What woman?"

She wasn't making much sense. A knock at the front door interrupted her chance to explain. The bedroom might be as dark as night, but it wasn't night outside.

"Did you order pizza?" she asked.

"Order pizza then come in to fuck you?"

"That sounds exactly like you, yes," she said, aware of his proclivity for forethought. He reached to open the nightstand drawer without moving the rest of his body. "Your buddies?"

"No," he said, finding and checking the pager. "Wait here."

He shunted her body away and swiped his jeans from the floor.

"What if it's people come to kill you?" she said, desperate to be at his side in case he needed help. "I'm tied to your bed naked; they could do anything to me."

"I could do with a good fight."

He pinched her nipple and moved away before she could catch him. All she could do was watch as he left her alone in the bedroom, again. She expected her love to get rid of the interruption and didn't expect to hear shouting, especially from an unfamiliar voice. Flesh hit flesh, something crashed, and the yelling stopped abruptly.

She pulled at the cuff, twisting her body to get her feet against the headboard. Trying to pry the bed bars loose was useless, so she fought to squeeze her hand out of the cuff. The pressure on her bones was excruciating, pain quaked through her, but she didn't let up. She had to get free, she had to get out there. The man she loved could be hurt, in need, but she couldn't even take the risk of calling out. She couldn't make any intruders aware that she—

The bedroom door swung open, ricocheting off the closet in the wall. Her pounding heart overwhelmed her breath, panic seized her until she recognized her own personal thunder filling the entrance.

"Rushe!" With two strides, he was at her side, unlocking the cuffs. In her moment of freedom, she flung her arms around his neck and locked her ankles at his back. "I was scared, I thought they hurt you!"

"How many guys you had around here?" Rushe asked.

She didn't care about him heckling her, but to shut him up, she clashed her mouth onto his. He hadn't touched her; his hands remained loose at his sides. She just couldn't help herself.

"Smallest hint of danger makes you horny, Kitten," he said, tipping his head back to separate his mouth from hers.

Her body slid down his until her center met the

tell-tale mass of his equivalent arousal. "Why do you think you turn me on so much?"

"No," he said, taking hold of her hips to bounce her back onto the bed. "Put your clothes on."

"What happened?"

"I knocked him out."

"Who?" she asked and was up off the bed in a flash. He caught her wrist and swung her around against his body to prevent her from exiting the bedroom. "What?"

"Clothes."

Being naked in their apartment had sort of become second nature, so much so that her nudity hadn't registered. Dragging open one of Rushe's drawer's, because it was the closest, she grabbed a tee-shirt to put on as she left the bedroom.

"Who is it?" she called over her shoulder to Rushe before reaching the person. The body was hidden by the kitchen wall so she could only see a pair of prone legs.

"Michael Lewis," Rushe responded, sauntering out of the bedroom.

She got to the legs in time to make the ID for herself. "If you knew that, why did you hit him?"

"He approached you in the street," Rushe said.

"He approached me in the street," she muttered, tucking a hand into Rushe's jeans pocket when he joined her. Personal space was nothing to Rushe where she was concerned. "So that earned him a concussion?"

"He's lucky that's all he got."

Michael groaned.

She hopped over his leg to crouch at Michael's side. "Michael, can you hear me?" she asked. "Rushe, go get an ice pack."

"Not a chance," Rushe said, and began to move away.

"You did this," she shouted after her lover.

"Which is why I ain't undoing it."

Michael groaned again and rolled to his side.

She forgot Rushe. "Are you okay?" she asked Michael when he tried to sit. "Take your time."

"What happened?" he asked, clutching his head, finally managing to sit up.

"What are you doing here?" she asked, deliberately ignoring Michael's question.

He took a few seconds to survey his surroundings, to get his bearings, and then a flash of understanding seized his features.

"Rushe," Michael said, attempting to stand.

"You don't want to talk to Rushe right now," she said, unsure where her lover was but hoping he would stay there.

"I do. I do! Where's my sister? It's been a week! It's been…" Rushe reappeared, and Michael trailed off. "You hit me… Are you Rushe?"

"Your sister is in deep," Rushe said. "But not unhappy about it."

Once again, she second guessed prioritizing sex over talking.

"No," Michael said. "No, she's a kid. She doesn't know what she's doing."

"She's doing Joey and his father."

Rushe was a helluva calm while delivering such shocking news. But he had been doing this type of work for a long time.

"How do you know that?" she and Michael asked in unison.

"I've seen her."

"Having sex?" she asked her love. "With both of them?"

"No," Rushe said.

"My sister is a good, kind person," Michael said.

With her assistance, he managed to get to his feet.

"So?"

"She's not a slut."

"Nothing wrong with being a slut," Rushe said, scanning her figure in an unusually detached way. "You don't know what your sister is."

"Where did you see her?" she asked.

"In the Lounge," Rushe answered.

"That's impossible." She shook her head. "I—"

"Last night."

While she was on a date with Whyte?

"What did she say?" Michael asked. "Did she look well? Were they making her take drugs? Why didn't you bring her home?"

"You asked me to locate her, not extract her, that's extra."

"You want more money?" Michael asked.

She was as surprised as him.

"We're no charity, and this is serious shit," Rushe said.

"Serious, how?"

"You're talking about messing with a crime syndicate. These kinda guys don't give up shit for nothing."

"I want her back, we'll pay, whatever—"

"You've got dick," Rushe said. "It'll take you a lifetime to pay off what you owe us already."

"How do you know about my finances?" Michael asked. "You can't walk away, you can't leave her there. You said yourself it's dangerous."

"It is."

"If you won't help, I'll find somebody else who can."

"Great," Rushe said. "Now beat it."

Michael had no other options, he'd said as much

to her on the street. Rushe remained apathetic while Michael lingered.

"We'll get her back," she said. "We wouldn't leave an innocent person in harm's way."

"She's no innocent," Rushe muttered.

"Michael, you have our word that we will get her back for you. But you can't come here like this, it's unsafe… for all of us. Please, go, now, we'll be in touch when we have something positive to report."

"You'll get her back?"

"Yes," she said, directing him to the door. "Don't come back here."

She opened the door for him.

"Thank you," Michael said.

She pushed him out, closed the door, then spun on Rushe. "What was that?"

"I don't like him."

"So…? What has that got to do with it?" she said and had to hurry to catch him when he began to walk away. "You don't like anyone."

"I make my own rules."

"I'm going to help them," she said and stopped at the end of the dinner table. "Are you going to leave me out there alone?"

"Why do you care?" Rushe asked, spinning around.

That required a second of thought, but the truth was so clear for her. "Because I know what it's like to be alone. I know what it is to be desperate, to need help, and to have no one to turn to."

On a nasal inhale, his face went up and his shoulders went back. "Fine."

"That was… easier than I thought it would be."

"Are you ready to walk away?" he asked, coming toward her, disregarding her previous words.

"I've already told you I'm not—"

"Not from me," he said. "In this game things can go wrong fast. If I tell you we're leaving, do not hesitate. You understand me?"

"But—"

"No," he said. "When your game is fucking people over, you get paranoid."

"We're not fucking anybody over."

"Not us," Rushe said. "Them. If these guys get clued in, about us, about our questions or our connection, they will pull the trigger." She nodded and was surprised to feel his fingers thread between hers. "I will pull the trigger."

"What do you—?"

"I don't know how involved the King Club are in this. We do not want to make enemies of them, that's serious trouble."

"As opposed to what we've dealt with in the past," she asked.

"I'm telling you that I'll do what I need to do."

"I haven't forgotten who you are. I know that you're capable of doing what needs to be done. I won't let you down." Rushe nodded, but she could tell he was unconvinced. "What now?"

"Sex."

"Stupid question," she said and let Rushe lead her back through to the bedroom to continue with their spree.

Each had a lot to get out of their system. Things were more intense, rather than regret, she felt strong. Rushe was with her. He trusted her. She could rely on him. Now she needed Rushe to realize the same in return.

SEVENTEEN

TUESDAY NIGHT WAS GREAT. Rushe couldn't cook to save his life, so she made them a meal. In a show of appreciation, he ate her for dessert right there on the living room floor. Yeah, maybe they should be talking, but when she tried to bring the subject up, he screwed her curiosity out of her on the promise they'd talk about it on Wednesday.

Having the following day together gave them a chance to get back to them, she even heard him laugh with ease.

His repose was surprising given she had a date with another man that Wednesday night. Subsequent to their afternoon having sex, she got into the shower alone, surprising in itself. She got out, went through her routine, and entered the bedroom to change her clothes.

Rushe came up beside her as she perused her wardrobe. He kissed her neck, arousing and enlivening her, fondled her breasts, and told her just what he wanted to do to her. When he picked her up off the floor and, in an oddly romantic gesture, laid her down on the bed.

Reality struck at the same moment the cuffs were attached to her wrist.

She should have known he would never let her date another man. Whyte wouldn't appreciate being stood up, but her love was adamant. Something in the possessive nature of her love was actually flattering. Fighting with the man who would always remain between her and danger was fruitless.

She sulked for a while, not that it made an iota of difference, Rushe would not let her leave their safe haven to walk into the unknown alone. That was how he put it. Rather than danger, his opposition was more about the other man she was going to, and what ideas said man might have in relation to her. That was what she believed anyway.

She woke on Thursday to find herself already loose, alone, and with a note from Rushe saying that he'd gone to the gym. She doubted the veracity of that and promised herself when Rushe got back she would push to find out everything.

Turned out she had to wait a while, until nine p.m., for him to return.

"Where have you been?" she asked, on the pulse of the front door closing behind him, as if she was the typical nagging housewife.

"Out." As Rushe maneuvered his way around her, she took a deep breath. "Why? You horny?"

"Yes," she said. "Yes, the only reason I could possibly be interested in your whereabouts is if I want to have sex with you."

Rushe was in the kitchen, at the sink filling a glass with water when she rested her hands on the counter between the rooms. "Then take off your clothes."

"I'm not actually horny," she said, knowing very well he knew it too. "We have to talk about the case. I have to be at work in less than an hour."

"I know," he said, observing her already done hair and make-up.

"If you saw Lisa on the other shift, I have to get myself switched to that shift. I can get close to her—"

"No," Rushe said, pouring the remaining water down the drain and shoving the glass aside. "She wasn't working, it was social."

"She was out with Joey?" Rushe nodded. "Okay…" She considered that. "Then I have to get Whyte to take me to the Lounge on my off-day."

"No." Rushe came to the opposite side of the kitchen counter to slam his own hands down. "You are not going out with him."

"I can't show up alone," she said. "And if I go with another man it will look like game playing. I have no reason to take a date to that Lounge other than to show up Whyte, or to flaunt my match in front of the other girls.

"I'm not close enough to any of my colleagues to consider them friends I might want to visit. Dating Whyte is the only choice. He has to know about Lisa, he has to know about her relationship with Joey. Whyte must have met Lisa when she worked in the Lounge, for all we know he's the man. Michael said there was someone else, another name involved." Could be that just meant Joey's father, everything was supposition at this point. "We need to keep investigating."

"How far you gonna go?" Rushe asked, with an upward bob of his head. "First base? Second? Third?"

"Rushe, I am not going to be intimate with him. You know that. You said it yourself, it's your cock I love."

Her attempt to be playful fell on deaf ears.

"Do you get how easy it would be?" Rushe asked. How easy what would be? He rounded the counter, grabbed her off her feet and threw her body against the perpendicular wall the counter was attached to. "You've got a pretty dress on."

Pushing his weight on his forearm to her chest, he kept her in place and crouched down to shove aside her skirt and underwear to stick two fingers into her.

"Rushe," she whispered, grabbing the arm he held against her body.

"Could've been my dick, Kitten. You're nothing. You don't understand how insignificant you are. Your weight, your build, they're nothing to a guy who wants to fuck you. If he wants it, he'll take it."

Rushe didn't trust anyone. She'd seen this thunder around him before. On baring his teeth, his fingers slid out of her and back in. Then in a rush of movement, he had her face down on the kitchen counter, bent over, his arm now pinning down her shoulder blades. Grabbing her skirt in the other hand, he tossed it up out the way then tore her underwear away from her body.

"Show me how you'd stop him," Rushe rumbled.

His feet came to the inside of hers and he shunted them further apart, forcing her legs open.

His chest came down on her back, freeing up his arms, and he rubbed his face in her hair.

"Rushe," she said, turning her cheek down against the granite.

His palms slid down her outer thighs then around to the inside. Proceeding on up, his thumbs pushed to her clit, slid through her intimately and advanced on to caress her rear.

"If I'm not there, I can't stop it," he mumbled into her hair. "I won't have you unsafe. I won't. No one touches you, no one violates you, and it's my job to keep you safe."

Her love was brutish, but he'd made his point and shown his own vulnerability. Yes, maybe he was jealous, maybe the threat was small, but he had a habit of pushing what he thought best for her onto her. Although she wouldn't admit it out loud, most of the time Rushe was right.

"Not every man is a sexual threat."

"Not every man can be trusted," Rushe replied.

She tilted her hips, pushing into his stroking hand. "I won't be alone with him," she said in compromise. "He gives us the cover I need, and we have to know what he knows.… I don't want another man to touch me for as long as I live. No one touches your stuff."

Rushe growled aloud, his two fingers started to move in her, then three. "Kitten," he hissed out.

"Fuck me, Rushe."

"No reward for disobeying me."

"Please," she said, trying to wriggle back, but he forced his pelvis to hers. While it locked her in place, it also betrayed his own arousal. Except the teasing mass of him, pressing against her ass, only made her want to wriggle more. "Mark me, own me."

"You belong to me."

"Yes," she pleaded. "Put your cock in me, please. Fuck me hard, teach me a lesson."

"You never learn," he said. "I've tried fucking sense into that pretty little head of yours. You're reckless."

"I want you. I want your dick inside me, please."

"You begging for it, Kitten? Begging me to fuck you?"

"Yes, please!"

"No."

Just like that, he was gone, his body separated from hers. What just happened? She tried to comprehend it and came up empty. Standing up while overcoming the adrenaline high made her wobble, and when she turned, he was leaning back against the high scroll back of a dining table chair.

"Go put your uniform on," he said.

His cool detachment reminded her of how he'd scanned her figure when Lewis had been there.

"But I—"

"Now."

She had to walk out the front door in less than half an hour. As confusing as his request was, she had no reason not to comply. So she went into the bedroom and changed into the get-up required for the Lounge: thong underwear, suspender belt and all.

The last thing she did was slip her feet into the platform stilettos. Rushe hadn't come into the bedroom; he hadn't made a sound. Was that a positive sign or not?

His potential reaction to the outfit had been in the forefront of her mind when she'd first put it on. Part of him would have to be turned on to see her trussed up like this. But he was always turned on, around her anyway. He'd never required or requested any special packaging. He accepted her body, her mind, her soul. All of her. No bravado or stipulations necessary.

As she stood there in their bedroom looking at herself in the full-length mirror, a glimmer of fear, like from the old days, trembled in her stomach. She feared him. Not physically, or sexually, she could never fear him in those ways. Emotionally, Rushe adored her. In his own way, he proved his devotion to her time and again, the words didn't matter. But she feared his reaction to this.

If he'd been in the Lounge, he had to know how the women dressed. But he'd never seen his woman like this, on show for other men, exposed, vulnerable. If he flew into a jealous rage, the job would be finished, except she couldn't stay hidden in the bedroom forever.

Steeling herself, she opened the bedroom door

and strode back into the living room, with confidence. Rushe was where she'd left him. She paused to let him scrutinize her. His gaze started at her feet and worked up, then back down. He continued to look at her for at least a minute, but he was so stoic that reading his mind was impossible.

"What do you think?" she asked when she couldn't stand the silence anymore.

"You look better naked," he said, seemingly stuck with his attention on her legs.

"Do you want me to change?"

Only now, after her joke, did his eyes meet hers, the truth of his agony rippled through them. "I had to see you, Flick. I had to see you here, like this… if I had walked into that Lounge and…"

It made sense. Once again, his presence of mind amazed her. "You had to see me like this, alone, so you don't overreact in the Lounge."

"Overreact?" he asked, checking her out again. "You're selling sex, you don't even know it."

"I know what this outfit—"

"Not the outfit, the Lounge," he said. "Things are going on there."

"Like what?"

"We don't have time to talk about it now. You're gonna see me tonight."

"Thanks for the warning," she said. "Will you be alone?"

"Don't know."

She didn't want to ask the question but had no other choice. "Is there…?"

"What?"

"Another woman?" she asked.

"I'm not gonna bring a date to your doorstep if I can help it, Kitten."

That wasn't actually an answer to her question.

"So Whyte will be there? If you're working for him—"

"I don't work for Whyte."

"But I thought… he said security and—"

"You see me standing quietly in the corner?" Rushe asked.

"Yes."

"Jumping in to save a dick like Whyte?"

"No," she said. "You don't jump into action."

Her love worked calmly and efficiently. Also, Whyte had touched her, only on the arm as far as Rushe knew, but that was enough. She'd never let her lover know Whyte had kissed her hand, that knowledge would be liable to induce homicide.

"I'm working with Galante."

On her journey toward him, his fixation stayed on her legs. "Senior?" she asked.

"Yeah," he murmured, as she tucked her hand into his jeans pocket. "Look at you away up here." He touched the top of her head. In spite of the towering shoes, he could still tuck her under his chin. "Those shoes make your tits pop. How do they do that?"

High heels hadn't been prominent on the agenda since they'd got together. Even her highest ones didn't make a dent in their height differential, so they seemed pointless. That and she spent a lot of time indoors… without clothes.

Still propped on the edge of the table, Rushe crouched further. His arm circled her and with full entitlement, his large hand went under the scrap of lace to cup her butt cheek. Her smile curled signaling their disagreement, and the tension, were forgotten.

She hadn't expected him to scoop her up, so whooped when he did. Directing her legs to straddle his lap, he slid back into a seated position on the table. Then resting her weight on one arm, he tipped her back and dragged his teeth down the swell of her breast to take a bite of her, though not with enough pressure to mark her.

"What are you doing with Galante?" she asked, resting her elbows on his shoulders.

"Thinking about investing," Rushe said. "Right now he's trying to impress me."

"What happened on Monday? What was the issue?"

"Don't have time to talk about it."

"You always say that."

"You have to get to work," he said, and gave her ass another squeeze as he stood up, sending her back to her feet.

She kept her body on his and didn't move away. "I will see you tonight?"

"I'll fuck you to sleep, Kitten—"

"I'll see you at the Lounge?"

"Yeah."

She nodded. "We will be stronger together, I will be an asset to you, I will."

EIGHTEEN

GETTING TO WORK on time, she was so preoccupied by thoughts of her lover that she almost forgot the mission. After serving her first tray to a leery group in the corner, she was back on track.

Rosa returned to the bar at the same time as her, so she took the chance.

"Nancy has a night off?" Flick asked of her co-worker, who hadn't arrived for work.

"She wasn't working out… she got a better job at the Rich Room, I think."

One of Richard Davis's nightclubs. Was the connection coincidental?

With small talk out of the way, she got to the point. "Who can I talk to about a shift change?" she asked.

Rosa put her tray next to the others and began to wipe them all down. "You want to change your hours? Lounge is open ten p.m. to six a.m. What shift were you thinking?"

"The hours are fine, it's the days I want to

change."

Rosa left her job of cleaning the trays. "Get the best tips on the weekend. It's busier, more customers. You were looking to cut down?"

"I was thinking about the start of the week, Monday, maybe."

Rosa shook her head. "Don't need anyone Monday."

"Do you make the schedule? Maybe I could ask one of those girls to switch?"

"I don't think so," Rosa said, returning to her task of cleaning the trays, except this time she worked faster, using more of a scrubbing motion.

"Why not? I don't think—"

"You've been here a week, Flick," Rosa snapped. "The job doesn't suit you, don't let the door hit you…"

The hostess spread a welcoming smile and opened her arms to join a group entering from the casino.

Rosa had always been happy and easy going, but the woman she'd just spoken to was neither. Something smelled off.

ALL NIGHT she awaited Rushe's arrival. At one a.m. the hotel entrance opened, and she held her breath to see who would arrive. It was Whyte. Yeah, hmm, this encounter wasn't one she looked forward to. Sure enough, the mogul came straight to her.

"Sit with me."

The statement came in time with Whyte taking her arm to lead her to a couch in the darkest corner of the Lounge. It apparently didn't matter that she was waiting for Marv to fill an order. No doubt one of the other girls would deliver it.

"I'm sorry about last night," she said on sitting

down.

Whyte landed next to her, thigh to thigh. "I presume you have an excellent explanation."

Standing men up on dates was becoming a habit, not that it was ever her fault.

"I had no way to get in touch with you, and—"

"You could have called the hotel," Whyte said. "Whatever the problem—"

"Like I said, I don't have a phone."

"Tell me what happened."

For most of the night, she'd been trying to come up with a good excuse he wouldn't be able to argue with.

"I can't," she said, fidgeting with the lace on her dress.

"Why not? You stood me up, that should warrant some explanation. I am entitled to—"

"You scared me."

That shut him up. "What?"

"I've never been out with a man so…" Playing coy and innocent had captured his interest in the first place, why not capitalize on that? "You're so successful and sophisticated, you're just… I enjoyed our date so much, but I couldn't… in front of those other men in your bar… I couldn't tell you how overwhelmed and intimidated I was by the power you have."

If she said something like that to Rushe, his eyebrow would slope and he'd un-intimidate her by eating her pussy or encouraging her to be on top.

Whyte took a breath and settled back against the couch. "I scared you, of course, I'm sorry." Typical that he would accept the explanation so easily. "I should have realized. I was concerned you were upset about how our evening ended. I should have known you would not be so… high maintenance." Whyte took her hand. "We can go upstairs now, finish the evening properly."

"I'm working."

"Don't worry about that. Rosa and the others can handle the Lounge."

"Is this about sex?" she asked when he tried to stand and take her with him.

He paused. "You believe my proposition was to take you upstairs and have sex with you?"

"Was it?"

"You're a very attractive woman, Flick, I'm sure you know that," he said. "However, my interest in you is not purely physical."

"You believe we could have a relationship?"

"Yes," he said and took something from his pocket to give her: a cellphone. "So we can keep in touch."

"This is a huge gesture, and after only one date…"

"I enjoyed our conversation," he said. "I look forward to sharing more meals with you, and more drinks." His hand touched her knee and slid up her stocking to the flesh exposed by her suspender.

"You want us to be alone," she said, aware she'd promised Rushe that wouldn't happen.

Rushe was never far from her mind. The casino door opened and closed, causing a blast of noise from the frenetic outer space. A few seconds later, Rushe came into her periphery; he and Galante were moving past to sit on another couch. Both men looked at Whyte and ignored her.

"You have nothing to fear," Whyte said, doing his own staring back at Rushe and Galante, but eventually his attention settled back on her.

She had to think fast on her feet, Rushe had been right, she sensed it now. If she didn't come up with something, she'd be ducking and weaving Whyte's sexual advances until this was over. It might work for a while, but he'd grow suspicious, and perhaps more aggressive, over time.

"I don't fear you," she said, wracking her mind for a safety net. "But you're such a powerful and attractive man, you could have any woman you want."

"I want you."

And from the way he touched the clasp of the suspender, it was clear he wanted a more thorough apology for the previous night's humiliation.

"But—"

"Perhaps after your shift tonight we could—"

"I'm a virgin," she said, stalling Whyte mid-word and stroke.

Her own frown sought Rushe's profile, though he was deep in discussion with Galante.

"Oh."

She hadn't meant to say that, except now she had, the words made sense, and would explain her reluctance to be alone, or get physical, with him.

"I can't believe I just blurted that out," she said, clutching her face.

The flaming in her cheeks would be understandable, and good cover. But her mortification was really for the man in the room aware of her without looking. Rushe could come over there, pluck her up and fuck her, and they'd come up with a reason why for the rest of the room.

On the other hand, if a man other than Rushe was to touch her and her love was to spot it, he'd drag her out, barricade the doors, and set the whole building on fire, consequences be damned. At the reminder of his primitive nature, her thighs clamped together. Rushe actually could turn her on from across the room. Impressive.

"I hadn't realized," Whyte said, after taking the time to process her revelation.

"It changes things, doesn't it?" she said in such a

way that if he agreed, he'd come off as a bastard. "I wanted to be honest but didn't want to say it. I wouldn't want to tease you, or have you think I'd be easy… please say something."

Though she hadn't really given him time.

"I didn't think they still existed," he said, looking into her eyes, letting his smile stretch. "It's refreshing and endearing. I knew you were special from the first second I saw you." Whyte touched her face. "Your first time will be special too. I promise you."

NINETEEN

"SPIT IT OUT."

"What?" she asked Rushe's reflection in the bathroom mirror the following afternoon.

Working the night shift had flipped their traditional routine. She put her toothbrush away and wiped her mouth.

"Something's been tickling your snatch all night, what is it?"

"Are you going to tell me about your night with Galante?"

"You bartering?"

She had to tell him anyway, whether he conceded or not, and it was never smart to lay a challenge at Rushe's feet.

"You saw me talking to Whyte last night?"

"Yeah."

She turned to face him. "I told him I was a virgin."

She'd never seen him smile so spontaneously. Usually there was some build up, some teasing or joking, but not today.

"Well, sweetheart, you should've told me that last night, I wouldn't have fucked you 'til you were unconscious."

"I'm glad you find it funny."

"Did I hurt you? I'm a big guy for a woman to swallow first time. You're a pro, sweetheart."

She glared at him, but the expert of the expression was unmoved. Giving up, she tried to shove past him, but he caught her in the doorway and urged her back against the frame.

"He'll want to break you in."

"He can want all he likes," she said.

"Did I make your first time special?"

Apparently, he wasn't finished mocking her, but he delivered the line so believably with his dry wit.

"I seem to remember your way of putting me at ease our first time was asking if I wanted you to eat me out before you fucked me."

"I'm that kinda guy, Kitten," he said with a stoic strut.

"Tell me what's going on with you and Galante."

Initially, he said nothing. She glued on her facial expression and undid one button on his jeans, then another, until she could gain access to slide her hand inside where she took gentle hold of his balls. Triumph came when he spoke.

"He wants to open a second casino; it's a great way to clean money."

"Clean money?"

"Make it legit."

"Laundering," she said. "And you want to invest in the new casino? Why would he need money? The consortium—"

"I'm in the market for a membership."

"To the King Club? No."

"No?"

"It's too dangerous," she said, shifting her hands flat into his pockets. "That would involve you meeting with them all. If they find out—"

"What? Find out what, Kit? We're not cops. We're not collecting evidence or trying to bust the group."

"Do you think they'll see it like that?"

"You don't see the world in the right way to be in this game."

"What does that mean?" she asked.

"They're into serious shit," he said. "Pissing them off could be suicide, but if we allied ourselves…"

"But they're bad people… criminals."

"What do you think I am?"

"You want to work with them?" she asked.

"Might be lucrative."

Her initial indignation waned when she realized he was watching her, not looking or checking her out, Rushe was watching. The master of forethought was assessing her.

"You want me to see the world in neutral terms. We're not on a crusade to save the world, but we're not willing to step on anyone to better our own ends." Rushe remained silent and static. "You don't want to be a member of the King Club, you're a loner. The fewer ties the better. You're testing me, to see how I react to the prospect of criminality."

"The heat's mine, Kitten."

"Talk to me, where's Lisa?"

"Staying in the hotel, best I can tell," he said. "Galante Senior and his son Joey live there, Whyte too."

"Why can't we just walk up to her room and—"

"Michael tried to pull her out that way," he said. "Lisa is being protected from the inside. They're not giving her up."

"Why not?"

"Don't know," Rushe said. "I get in with Galante, I get close to Joey, and then I talk to Lisa."

"That simple?"

"It's not simple at all. We can't trust Lisa. If she wants to stay with Joey and rats us out, the lid's blown off."

"So we have to gain her trust," she said, considering the new information.

"Fuck trust." His brash response interrupted her thoughts. "We have to know the dynamic. If Lisa doesn't want to be there, getting her out is easy."

"She's not being held against her will. You've already discounted that."

"How do you know?"

"Because I do," she said, enjoying being under his scrutiny once more. "I know you, Rushe. I know when you're testing me."

"She likes the money, the lifestyle."

"She likes screwing the boss?"

"Galante is the boss," Rushe said. "From what I can tell daddy and son don't get along."

"So she was screwing Joey, saw daddy had more sway, and shifted focus?"

"I assumed the same, but I have no proof yet."

"Why do you need proof?" she asked.

"Because if it's power she likes, we have to tempt her with more power. If it's danger, if it's money…"

She nodded because what he said made sense, except… "You plan to tempt her, don't you? There isn't a man more powerful or dangerous than you. And there's plenty of money in the bank for you to shower her with diamonds."

His hands rose to the top of her head, and he stroked down her hair. "You're dating another guy, got to even the score."

"She's nineteen."

"Yeah, that age usually costs more."

The very idea of Rushe so much as touching another woman made her nauseous, but she heard his imperceptible teasing. He'd never cheat on her; his loyalty to her was bone deep.

"Are you seeing him tonight?" she asked.

"Who?"

"Galante or Joey?"

"Joey and Lisa have been locked in their room," Rushe said. "Last anyone saw them was Monday."

"Monday? It's Friday, what have they been doing all week?"

Rushe rested a hand on the doorframe above her head and slid it up so his body loomed over hers. "Now that I've taken you for a test drive, maybe I'll show you."

She groaned and nudged her weight on his to gain entry to the bedroom again. "Do you want me to cook?"

"No."

She put her arms in the sleeves of his red and black check shirt, now her shirt. "Are you going to take me out to dinner?"

Rushe didn't wine and dine her. The nicest establishment he'd taken her to was a sports bar. Not that he'd been intending to take her there, not until she pestered him all the way down the street and into the place.

"I've got plans," he said.

"You have to tell me what's going on with Galante," she said, buttoning the last of the shirt. "Are you planning to give him money?"

"Not until I'm sure it's a good investment. He'll show me how the place works. We're meeting Whyte tonight. When is your next date?"

"Monday," she said.

"Where are you going?"

"The casino."

"Good," Rushe said. "It's crowded. I can keep an eye on you."

She wanted to remind him she didn't need to be watched, but the prompt would be futile. So she made her way out of the bedroom and into the kitchen, thinking about what to cook. Opening a cabinet, she took out the pasta and put it on the counter.

In the next breath, Rushe's form materialized behind her, stalling a gasp in her throat. "Don't do that," she whispered over her shoulder. "You scared me."

"Good," he mumbled. "Keep you on your toes. You're getting too comfortable."

Gathering her hair into his fist, he pulled her head back to land on his chest, and he rasped his stubble against her forehead. "He gave you a phone?" he asked. She nodded. "Do you know why I don't have a phone?" She struggled to shake her head. "They're traceable."

"I don't—"

"If they choose to look... we can't both keep coming back here every night. I've been complacent."

"But—"

"It's your tits," he said.

Releasing one fist from her hair, his thick arm came around her to take the shirt where the buttons met. Ripping his hand downward, the buttons shot out in all directions as plastic shrapnel.

"Hey! I love—" His hand clamped over her mouth.

Scratching his chin downward, it stopped at her temple. "That shirt... you were so goddamn vulnerable. You're gonna get us both killed."

She tried to move, but his strength held her skull against the wall of his chest. Her attempt at speech only made her squeak, and his pressure increased.

"I'm going to stay at the hotel. I won't be back until this is over," he grumbled. "Don't open the door to anyone."

Frantic to have a say, to make an impact, all she could do was fumble behind herself. Catching the corner of his jeans pockets, she tried to pull but only succeeded in squeaking again.

This had to have been in his head all day. He'd known this was his plan but left her in the dark. Sometimes she forgot his mind was always constant. If she had sat down to think about it for a second, she would have seen it herself.

Both of them coming back there was dangerous. Galante could be curious about Rushe, maybe he didn't trust him. Rushe could spot a tail, but she wouldn't. She hadn't even been looking, not properly.

In addition, this address was on her employment form. She hadn't had any other option but to put it down. Now that Whyte had given her a phone, which Rushe wouldn't trust to be legitimate, it could be traced too. But she didn't want her love to go.

Still he kept one hand over her mouth, but the other found her breasts. The span of his hand played with one, then the other.

"I'm gonna watch you, Kitten," he said, rubbing his face in her hair as his touch thrummed down her abdomen. "You be a good girl, keep your guard up, and don't trust anything. Don't trust Whyte, you hear me?" She nodded. "I'm gonna let you go, but I don't want you to speak. Words won't change my decision, I don't want to hear how you feel, and crying is only gonna piss me off."

His hand left her mouth. From his crouched position, his other arm locked around her waist so as he straightened his stature, he took her off her feet. Carrying her through into the living room, he sat her on the dining table and pulled out a chair away from the table. As Rushe sat, he unbuttoned his jeans and kept his butt at the edge of the seat.

"Sit on it," he said, holding his dick in one hand.

She was still thinking about what he'd said and only managed to look at it. Rushe reached forward to grab her wrist. Yanking her to him, he parted her legs with his feet so she stood astride him on the chair.

"You're gonna get your tight cunt on my cock now, understand? You're gonna sit right there in my lap and fuck yourself. I want to see those tits bounce, you get it? You gonna be a good little kitten? Speak."

"Yes," she managed to say.

"You do what I tell you. Your cunt's gonna fuck the jizz right out of me. She's hungry, and I might not feed her again for a while. Sit!"

Lowering herself down, Rushe kept himself in place to seek her opening. When he slid inside, she let her weight go and sank down onto him, taking him deep. Her inner muscles clenched around his throbbing organ.

"Good," Rushe said without emotion and shoved the shirt from her shoulders, sending it down to the floor. "Now fuck your pussy on it."

With her feet on the floor, she had good leverage and straightened in the squat, then descended again. Her hands fell to his shoulders, but Rushe smacked her arms away.

"Put them behind your back, on your ass."

The position would be awkward, but she didn't deny him. When her arms went back, her shoulders followed, forcing her breasts out and up. Rushe took them and squeezed them together. Licking the length of her cleavage he pinched each nipple and gave both of them a shake.

"Move faster," he said, giving her breasts a slap.

As he commanded, Flick picked up the pace. The

glitter in Rushe's feral eyes sharpened when her breasts bounced in time with her motion. Snatching her waist, he pulled her body against his, letting her breasts ricochet against him. Rushe turned his face down into them, and the scratch of his stubble seared into the sensitive flesh.

Taking him deep each time, pressure teetered within her. She wanted more and tried to angle her clit closer.

Rushe still had a hold of her waist, he was calling the shots. "Stop!" he demanded and shoved her hips down so his dick slammed up inside her. "Close your eyes."

Why? His preoccupation with her breasts kept his gaze away from hers, exactly what his new request succeeded in doing too.

"You're the perfect whore," he whispered when she complied.

Both were used to him occupying this passage within her, but he felt heavier now, fatter, somehow, larger than he had been.

"Straighten your legs," he said, and his hands swept around her ass to her thighs, forcing her legs straight without disturbing the position of their connection. She yelped and her eyes opened. Now he really was bigger, or rather she was smaller. Her internal walls squeezed around him, trying to force out this alien invader while simultaneously trying to keep him locked in place.

"Close your eyes," he said again, impatient by her reaction to this maneuver. "I don't want you to touch yourself while I'm gone."

A contradiction to what he'd said the last time he left her. He cradled a breast in each hand and suckled her nipples in turn.

The tremor of pleasure shook her diaphragm and traveled through her ribs. The combination of him stretching her and his warm tongue swirling her nipple relaxed her arms. She wanted to touch him, but she didn't want him to stop.

Except he did stop. He must have figured out her shoulder muscles had loosened from the way her breasts shifted. He grabbed her elbows and forced them behind her back until they almost touched.

"Do you want me to bind you? To keep you tied up until you prove to me you can be trusted to do what you're told? Nothing but my sex toy? Would you like that, Kitten? Like to be another piece of gym equipment, maybe I'll let you suck me off while I work out, maybe live on a diet of spunk and water.

"You're here for me Kitten, for what I want. You better learn how to do what you're told."

The angle of his breath moved from her face to her breasts. Though his strength kept her arms back, his mouth drew a nipple in again. Him digging his teeth into the stinging flesh made her jerk, which served to remind her of his member still solid within her enflamed center.

Keeping her arms in place, he shifted his hold to guide her hands to the opposite elbow; forcing her to keep the position he'd arranged her in. When she expected him to fondle her breasts again, she was disappointed... for a few seconds.

Scooping a forearm around her lower back, Rushe clamped her hips in place, then the digits from his other hand found their way between them to massage her clit. She sighed and took his invitation to rest her weight on his supporting arm, giving him more access.

His fingers slid through the juices between them and traced an arc around where his dick impaled her. She wriggled against that union as he went through the motion again.

But the next time instead of leaving her clit, they stayed in place. He rubbed her clit, and it was only when he started to move in and out of her again that she noticed he'd lifted them slightly off the chair. Still he steadied her weight, swiped her clit, and took control over fucking her.

She said his name, over and over, her volume building with the heat of pressure within her abdomen. On the spasm of her womb, she flung her arms around his neck. Rushe, it seemed, was beyond caring about the game because he had them on the floor. He pumped in and out of her. At the second and third crescendo, she braced her nails in the back of his neck and screamed out in time with his growl.

Their eyes joined with the last remnants of orgasm washing over them, but her love didn't stay long. He got to his feet and put his dick back in his jeans.

He needed a shower after that for sure, but he didn't seem to be heading in that direction.

"Be good," he muttered, then stepped over her and went to the front door.

When it slammed into its frame, Flick jumped. Still on the floor, her heart hammering in her chest, it thumped between the emptiness of the home and the hard wooden floor at her back. Again, she was alone. Again, Rushe believed it was in her best interest. And again, she'd had no say in the matter whatsoever.

TWENTY

COUNTING DOWN the last thirty minutes of her Sunday night shift, she didn't relish the idea of going home to no one. She hadn't seen Rushe or Whyte in the Lounge. Tomorrow she'd have to get herself all prettied up like a doll to tease a billionaire she had no intention of letting anywhere near her body.

Feeling useless was bad enough. So far as she could tell, working there hadn't helped the case at all. Then, as though by magic, the hotel door opened, and a man walked in alone. Joey Galante Junior. Until that moment all she'd heard were stories of this man, there she laid eyes on him. Granted, she had seen his yearbook picture, and his mug shot from his solicitation bust, daddy had to have loved that.

Even without seeing those pictures, she would have known he was Joseph Galante Junior. He was his father's son, his spitting image. Both had black hair, Joey's was longer and ruffled in a devil-may-care fashion. With sharp eyes and olive skin, Joey had four inches on his father's height, putting him at about six feet.

"That is Joey." Kimberly came up beside her gawping self. Wasn't very professional, so she averted her attention. "He's usually down here all the time. But his girlfriend's all high maintenance. Don't know what she bitches at him about, he throws money around like it's water. Not that you'll hear me complaining. She used to work down here, well for like a week."

During her co-worker's speech, Joey talked to every person he passed. He stopped at every table to pat shoulders and shake hands. From how flummoxed some people were, it was obvious not everyone knew him. But Joey kept that broad, shining smile in place and traversed the distance like a movie star.

Once he finished with the last patron, he switched his focus to her and Kimberly at the bar. Kimberly he knew, but his perusal of her figure felt no more than polite. When she became the object in his sights, he took extra care to examine her figure. After mentally noting her measurements, he landed the smile on her. Despite actually wanting to smack him in the head with a tray, she smiled back.

"Hello," Joey said, stopping directly in front of her, opening a hand to shake. "I'm Joey."

"She knows who you are," Kimberly said. "Everyone around here knows who you are."

"Hey, Kimmy," Joey said, though he remained intent on her, the new girl. Kimberly disappeared toward a group of beckoning customers. "You're a sweet little package."

"Thank you," she said. Her height, coupled with the flawless complexion she got from her mother, made her look around Lisa's age. In this situation, that could be an advantage. "You own the casino next door."

"Heir apparent," he said, taking her hand to his mouth.

"You're very kind," she said, ensuring to bat her

eyelashes in a way she minimized outside Whyte's company.

"Happy employees are productive employees," he said, leaning closer. "What can I do to make you happy?"

Men with money and position could be arrogant. They could be superior S.O.Bs who expected the world. But the men in this place took things a step further.

Davis had eyed her with intent until Whyte stepped in. Whyte had been forward in asking her out so quickly and making all the decisions about their date without knowing a thing about her. Now Joey was there, clearly expecting her to drop her panties and bend over the nearest solid structure.

"What can we do for you, Joey?" Rosa asked, joining them, not a moment too soon, though the Lothario still hadn't given her hand back.

"Maybe I'm just thirsty," he said, kissing her knuckles again.

"You don't come down here to drink alone. There's alcohol stocked in the suite you live in upstairs," Rosa said, confirming he lived in the hotel. "Where's Lisa?"

Joey dropped her hand and stepped back, landing a furious stare on Rosa.

"Your girlfriend?" Flick said, all innocence. "Kimberly told me she used to work here."

"Briefly," Rosa said, watching the playboy.

"I'm sick of the sight of her," Joey griped, and nodded past Flick at Marv.

"Trouble in paradise?" Rosa asked. "Tell me, do you two ever get along?"

"No."

"Must make for dynamite sex," Kimberly said, joining the group and passing an order to Marv as the barman gave Joey his drink.

Joey's glint reappeared. "You ever want me to show you again, Kimmy…"

He left the question open… lingering…

Rosa just glared at Joey.

The waitress smiled. "I think I learned my lesson," Kimberly said.

So screwing the waitresses was a regular pastime for Joey. That may not bode well for her. As could be predicted, Joey, again, openly perused her figure.

"Don't get any ideas about that one," Rosa said. "She's taken."

"Boyfriend?"

Flick started, "Well I—"

"I can work around him," Joey said, in a faux joke.

Maybe it was faux. Her mind stuck on the idea of anyone trying to circumvent Rushe.

"She's dating Evan," Rosa said.

"Whyte?" Joey smirked. "They never last long with him."

"Joey and Evan have known each other for years," Rosa said.

Flick pricked her ears, interested but not too interested. Kimberly's order was ready, so her colleague took the tray away from the bar.

"They went to school together," Rosa continued. "After that, Evan went on to work hard, make money, and become successful. Joey spent his father's money and developed addictions to drugs and sex."

"Wouldn't trade a day," Joey said, trying to shrug off Rosa's words as teasing, but it was clear they grated on him.

"You two must know each other very well," Flick said to Rosa and Joey.

"Sure," Joey said. "She's been banging the old man for more than ten years. Still, she sits in this damp, dark little hole pouring the drinks for the clients."

Rosa seethed, with a sharp inhale, she spun around and marched away, at which time Joey declared victory by standing taller and bringing all focus back to his newest prey.

"I can work around Whyte too," Joey said, retrieving her hand from her side. "I often have to keep his women happy because he fails to."

"You've slept with your best friend's girlfriends?"

His chin angled an inch closer. "Who said he was my best friend?"

"You went to school together and—"

"He's closer to my old man than me. We don't enjoy the same… pursuits."

If Joey was into women and drugs during the time Whyte built his business empire, she wasn't surprised they'd lost patience with, and interest in, each other.

"Won't your girlfriend worry about you?"

"It'll do her good to wonder," Joey said. "Are you working tomorrow night?"

She shook her head. "I'm Thursday to Sunday."

"Ah," Joey said. "Might explain why we've never met. I frequent Mondays."

"Are Mondays special?"

"Oh yeah," Joey said, bringing his body even closer to hers. In that space, with the bar behind them, she couldn't wriggle away. "Could I interest you in a shift change?"

"I asked for a shift change," she said. "Rosa said it wasn't possible."

"Leave it to me," Joey said.

"You can switch me on to a Monday? Won't that upset Rosa?"

"Rosa's always upset. She's been working this bar

since it was built; she's been here longer than the furniture."

"Why does she stay?"

"The girl…" Joey trailed off, seemingly searching for an explanation. "Can't stay away I guess."

She didn't know Galante Senior, but stringing Rosa along all these years was reprehensible. Joey had come into this place like a king, he spoke with entitlement, and obviously felt that extended to the employees.

"She must love your father very much," she said.

"Yeah," Joey said with a smile that humored her naivety, but it quickly vanished. "I have to clear something up with her. Don't go anywhere, I'll be back."

Joey disappeared from her line of sight presumably to seek out Rosa. One of her tables needed service, guess it was back to work. She wanted to go home and had no intention of being anywhere near Joey again tonight or ever again if she could help it.

TWENTY-ONE

SLEEPING WAS DIFFICULT without Rushe. It was ridiculous and corny that she needed his frame under hers in order to get a stable night's sleep, but she did. Rushe gave her a workout, sleeping came naturally after their sexual exploits. If she was unsettled, she could play with his body, or have him play with hers, until she was tired enough to sleep.

So instead of sleeping, she stayed up, sewing the buttons back on her adopted shirt. The shirt was the very first thing Rushe had given her. He'd given her it to keep her safe, to comfort her, even if that hadn't been clear at the time. Sewing wasn't her strong suit. Growing up with a silver spoon in her mouth meant many household tasks took practice. When she decided to strike out on her own, strike out she did, repeatedly. Like with the cooking and the cleaning, and public transport, she kept on. She persevered, and now those tasks were part of her life.

By the time she was finished, it was clear that the job wasn't professional, but it held together. It had character, and another memory woven within its fabric.

The task had exhausted her enough to sleep for a couple of hours before she had to prepare for her date with Whyte.

Whether she saw Rushe that night or not, she was confident he would be loitering around somewhere. His surveillance offered contradictory comfort and anxiety.

If she appeared to lower her guard, Rushe would fume. If Whyte got too close or did something Rushe deemed over the line, then she wouldn't see him coming. Whyte would be nothing but a stain on the wall.

Before leaving the bedroom, she couldn't look at herself in the mirror. She couldn't look at the kitchen, or the dining table, or anywhere, as she moved through the apartment. Rushe was everywhere, but he was nowhere. Her life was empty without his form near hers. So she ran from the place, bolted the door, and got to the street as fast as she could.

Nestling herself in the back of the cab, she tried to psyche herself up. She was going out to learn what she could about Lisa. She might get more information from Whyte on the issue now that she had met Joey. Once Whyte talked himself out, she would tell him about her encounter with the heir apparent.

If Rosa was adamant about her not changing shifts, she may have spoken with Galante about it. In turn, Galante Senior may have spoken to Whyte. Maybe he'd start the conversation for her.

Before she could worry about extracting information from Whyte, she had to meet him at the casino. Quicker than she would have liked, her request was granted. Walking through the broad entrance under its broad awning, she forced herself to smile. Whyte wanted to impress her. He thought she was innocent. She had a role to play and would have to get good at this game quickly; Rushe might depend on her.

Whyte was there to greet her, probably doubting she'd appear at all. "You made it," he said, sweeping her hand up in both of his to kiss her knuckles.

"Yes," she said. "It's wonderful."

For her initial interview, she'd been hurried into a side office and hadn't experienced the full impact of the casino. The whole floor was alive with activity. The Lounge didn't have numbers like this. Hundreds of people were in the labyrinth of a space. Music blared from a nearby speaker, slot machines clicked and beeped, their noise signaling to the masses how each game was progressing. The clatter of chips occasionally broke through and grew louder when Whyte drew her further through the cavern of flashing lights and rich, sweet scents. She paused, trying to identify the smell.

Whyte kept hold of her. "Come with me."

"Where are we going?"

Whyte moved them around the periphery of the room, past the clamoring masses. "Private event."

She'd fallen for that one before and wrenched her hand free of his to stop. "Oh no, I don't think we should be alone when—"

"We won't be alone. There are some people I would like you to meet."

"Meet?" she asked. Whyte tried to take her hand again, but she kept it out of reach. "How many people are at this event?"

"Eight or ten," he said, without much consideration. "If you don't enjoy yourself, we can leave. You've met Joseph Galante and Richard Davis already. They were with me the night you and I met. Joseph's son will be there, and his girlfriend. They're all people who live here at the hotel, people I consider close friends."

She'd been sold on hearing the first name, but she maintained her timid demeanor and eventually nodded. "Okay, a few minutes couldn't hurt."

Whyte took her hand to keep her on his heel and strode on with intent. At the very back of the room, they passed an elevator bank, and approached a door marked private. A casino security guard had stepped aside. Whyte made a show of opening the door for her while nodding at the guard, reminding her of just how much power he had there. Whyte took her hand again and led them down a wide corridor.

"This place is huge," she said.

"You'll find your way around quickly enough," Whyte said, guiding her to a large door simply marked with a shining brass A.

He opened it and swept her inside, tucking her body close to his when he came in at her back. Okay, well, there were more than eight people. It was more like fifteen or twenty, but there were two distinct groups: the males and the females.

"We've held public events here before, but mostly we use it ourselves," Whyte said, slipping a hand around her waist. "There's private access up to the hotel in the back corner."

That wasn't reassuring, and neither was the sight of Richard Davis behind the bar pouring a drink. There were no staff present. No witnesses. No watchful eyes.

Four of the men broke ranks with the other men. At their action, four women left their group too. This group of eight then moved down the room. She didn't see where they went, a tingling in her gut distracted her.

Whyte urged her forward at the same moment the tingling thudded to a halt. Somehow, her eyes just found his: Rushe. He was in the men's group, concealed from open view by the pillar that held up the bar. But he was there, and he was watching her.

Damn the game. Right now she was sharing space with the man she loved and missed so much, and there wasn't a thing she could do to acknowledge it.

"So this is the girl," one of the women said.

She hadn't seen the women join the men, the two groups merged into one. Now there were only four women in the room, including her. The woman in the center of the group was young and looked just like her picture.

"This is Lisa," Whyte said, bringing them into the group, keeping his hand flat on the small of her back. "She is—"

"Joey's girlfriend," she said, broadening her smile.

"You know Joey?" Whyte asked.

The question increased Joey's swagger. "We met last night," Joey said and winked at her.

Please God don't let Rushe have seen that.

"You remember Joey's father, Joseph Galante?" Whyte asked, gesturing to the man on the other side of Lisa, who now stood between father and son.

Who was the third woman? That question was answered by Whyte when Davis came back to the group and handed her a drink, taking his place next to her.

"That's Davis's wife, Eleanor."

"It's very nice to meet you," she said to the married couple, while wondering if Eleanor knew her husband was a sleaze.

With the awkward introductions over, she absorbed the room. Joey was leering and Lisa was sulking. Galante couldn't have been less interested in any of them.

"This guy is new, we don't know much about him yet," Whyte said.

It took a few seconds to realize her date was introducing her to her lover.

Apparently, Whyte forgot she and Rushe had spent time alone in his suite on the night of their first date, further highlighting his narcissism. It was quite a feat not to notice a man like Rushe when he entered the room.

"Oh."

"No woman on his arm tonight," Whyte said. "We're still figuring him out. This is Rushe."

"Rushe," she exhaled.

All the time she'd spent breaking down barriers between them evaporated. Still, she had to sledgehammer down walls over the simplest thing, like holding his hand or going out to a movie. She knew next to nothing about Rushe's past, but she wriggled closer every chance she got. Now, standing there in front of him, her love's cold, detached eyes dragged over her body as if they were strangers.

"Doesn't she have the most incredible voice?" Whyte said.

Rushe's unimpressed eyes settled on her breasts for a few seconds, then he lifted his glass to his mouth and sipped. Clear liquid. Vodka? She'd never seen him drink vodka. But this wasn't the man she shared a home with. This man had never seen her before in his life. Despite knowing it was part of the game, part of the process, she hated it.

"Where did you come up with this one?" Eleanor asked Whyte.

"They met in the Lounge," Davis answered his wife.

"Oh," Eleanor said and cast an eye over her, then over Lisa. "That place is turning into—"

"Eleanor," Davis warned.

Ever the dutiful wife, she stopped talking.

"I'll get you a drink," Whyte whispered, and left her side.

Lisa hissed at Joey, who then turned his back on the group to retort. She let herself look at Rushe again. Not that he was looking at her, not her face anyway, he was examining her legs. Hadn't he done that in the apartment too? How many times had he looked at her body? She thought about the things he'd done to it, and the things she had done to his.

He glanced toward the bar. A scratch marred the side of his neck. A smile sloped to her face. She'd made that mark, there in their living room, on that floor, when he came inside her, filling her with his come as she screamed out his name in her own release.

"Here."

She had to snap out of that memory fast. Whyte arrived back at her side and handed her a glass. With a sniff, she identified the liquid as vodka. Not her favorite... actually, she'd never elect to drink vodka if given a choice.

"Excuse us," Galante said, grabbing his son and Lisa to drag them away.

The couple and Galante were arguing... it seemed the father was disciplining the children. That would take courage and imagination on Galante's part given he was apparently sleeping with Lisa too.

Sex was on the menu there, with anyone of the opposite sex, and loyalty seemed to be nothing. What about Rosa? What did the hostess think of Galante bringing a date to the event? She had to know about Galante's affair with his own son's girlfriend as well. Rosa must have on some heavy-duty blinkers to be able to see the best in a man like that, especially after all these years.

"Have you seen the Hart exhibition?" Davis asked Whyte. "She has pieces in the auction at the end of the month."

"No," Whyte said. "Do you have the catalog?"

"Yes," Davis said, guiding his wife away.

Whyte followed on, Galante's date wasn't too far behind. The other three were arguing in a darkened corner, a curtain blocking her view of them.

Without following, she observed them walk into a long thin part of the room she hadn't seen initially. The room was actually L-shaped.

With a sigh, she brought her glass to her mouth. Just as it met her lip, it disappeared. Rushe had taken the glass so quickly she hadn't seen it go. Another glass was thrust into her hands. His glass. He didn't pause. He tossed her drink into a plant on the bar and shoved the glass aside before he strode off after Davis and Whyte. Whatever was in it, or he suspected was in it, wasn't there anymore.

She sipped what he'd given her, then squinted. It wasn't vodka at all, it was water.

TWENTY-TWO

AFTER GALANTE and son re-joined the group with Lisa, Galante dismissed his date and the men poured over the auction items. They discussed what they believed each was worth, and whom they thought would be interested in purchasing certain individual lots. Then there was a brief discussion and a phone call was made.

"This is when the pissing contest starts," Eleanor said, coming up beside her.

"Sorry?" Flick asked.

"Poker," Lisa said, joining them. "They get a dealer in, and they set up the table. They say it's all in good fun, but…"

"They're all good friends, aren't they?" Flick asked.

Lisa scoffed. "Is there a single man in here who can stomach the others?"

Eleanor took a knowing but resigned breath. "I don't know why they bother. They do this frequently. None of them feel any better at the end of it."

"I don't know," Lisa said. The women watched

the men seat themselves at the table the dealer was prepping. There were no extra chairs. Clearly, the women weren't allowed to play. "Rushe is new."

"Yes, and they'll all feel so much better if the new man wins and embarrasses them… We should just get a ruler out and have them line their penises up on the table, and we could be done with this for good."

Lisa laughed.

How many drinks had Eleanor consumed?

"I'm game if you are," Lisa said. "I'd be very interested to know how Rushe measures up."

Thank God she hadn't been drinking or she might have choked. "Should I call for a cab?"

"Don't let Lisa distress you, Flick," Eleanor said, directing her to a nearby table with Lisa joining them. "She's young and preoccupied with sex. Though, forgive me, you must be around her age."

"Am I?" she said, proud of herself for acting the innocent. "I'm twenty-seven."

"Oh, you're nowhere close," Eleanor said. "Lisa is twenty-one."

Lisa took a drink. Eleanor drew her eyes toward the men's table. No one was fooling anyone, but no one spoke the truth aloud either.

"How long have you been married?" Flick asked Eleanor.

"Fifteen years," she said. "I was young and idealistic."

"Is that a reason or a regret?" Flick asked with a smile.

Eleanor's eyes left the poker table to smile back. "Maybe both."

"Davis is great," Lisa said. "He always gets you a drink. Joey never gets me a drink."

Young was right. Then again, her own boyfriend hadn't got her a drink either, more thrust one into her hands in replacement for the sustenance offered by another predator.

It would probably be quicker and easier just to have him piss on her in the shower… not that they would be sharing a shower any time soon.

She examined Lisa, sitting tall and alert at the table, eager for something to happen. Yes, she was the type out looking for adventure.

"Do you have any family, Lisa?" Flick asked.

From how the blonde's attention snapped down, it was possible the question was too heavy handed.

"What does that matter?"

"It doesn't," Flick said. "Eleanor has Davis, so I wondered if…"

"Wedding bells are not in their future," Eleanor said.

"I wouldn't marry Joey if you paid me to," Lisa said.

As soon as the young woman uttered the words, Flick saw her consider them. No, they probably wouldn't marry given she'd been intimate with the father of the groom. How would they explain that one to the kids?

"You're young," Flick said. "It's okay to have some fun."

"Some," Eleanor said, with a note of displeasure.

"Joey and I have a lot of fun, and the sex is great, like really, really great."

"That's… good," Flick said, reminding herself that she was a virgin. "I hope you weren't too worried about him last night."

"I guessed he was in the Lounge," Lisa said. "He was so crazy mad that he would miss it tonight. I mean big deal, we'll just go later."

"He said he frequented the Lounge on a Monday," Flick said. "He said it was special and might be able to change my shift for me."

Both women moved with equal recognition. Something about that meant something to them. What was it? Why was her changing shifts significant?

"He said what to you?" Lisa said, a woman on a ramp up to indignation and anger.

"I asked Rosa and she said no, but—"

"Rosa runs that ship," Eleanor said. "Joey won't get her to move."

"Rosa is a shrew. Who knows what my brother ever saw in her," Lisa said to Eleanor, slapping her hand down on the table. "Why the hell is Joey saying that to her?"

Being spoken about as if she weren't there was disconcerting, but Lisa's mention of her brother was interesting. Michael hadn't said anything about being acquainted with Rosa. Thankfully, Eleanor seemed interested in quieting the youngster.

"Not now, Lisa."

"Why not?" Lisa snapped. "We all tiptoe around, but if my boyfriend is propositioning other women—"

"Joey propositions every woman," Eleanor said. "And you encourage it."

"Uh, she's here," Lisa said, pointing over the table at Flick without looking at her. "It's different in the Lounge, but here it's... that shit's not allowed."

Lisa shoved away from the table and started across the room toward the poker table. Heads were beginning to turn.

"Oh my goodness," Eleanor sighed out.

"Do you want to have sex with her!" Lisa hollered at Joey, before she'd reached the table.

"God, bitch," Joey said. "Sit on your fucking ass and shut up!"

"No!" Lisa said, stopping at the head of the table with her hands on her hips. "I want to know if you paid for sex last night, did you? Is that where you were? Did you fuck her?"

Try though she did to convince herself that Lisa wasn't talking about her, the young woman clarified any misunderstanding.

"Flick!" Lisa shouted. "Come over here. Tell me what the fuck you two did last night."

"Oh my goodness," Flick breathed out, in much the same way Eleanor had not long before her.

Eleanor patted her hand, but that did nothing to alleviate the embarrassment. The woman actually made things worse when she picked up Flick's hand to take them both to their feet. The last thing she wanted was to get up, or face this audacity but Eleanor was taking her across the room.

"Son, you must control your—"

"This has nothing to do with you," Lisa snapped at Galante, cutting him off. "Joey, I want to know if you fucked her. Why won't you answer me? Did you? Did you fuck her?"

"Yeah, I did," Joey said, kicking his own chair out of the way when he leaped to his feet.

All of the heads around the table came up, including Rushe's, and usually nothing affected him.

"No, you didn't," Flick said.

"Sure you did," Lisa said, glaring at her and then at Joey. "You think you're going to be clever, to talk your way out of this? I don't think so, Joe. I've had enough."

"You know where the door is," Davis said.

No one acknowledged him.

"Lisa, you need to calm down," Whyte said, leaving the poker table.

"I don't need to do anything," Lisa said. "I'm not one of your little bitches anymore. She's fucked you, she's fucked Joey, how many guys you fucking, Flick?"

"I didn't—"

"Hmm? Have you fucked them all? Fucked your

way around the table? Bet Eleanor would like to know that. You fucked Davis too?"

"I've not had sex with anyone here," she said, briefly forgetting Rushe was present.

They hadn't declared their relationship; the lie was necessary. Of course, that didn't stop her eyes from pinging to his. But the guy at the table wasn't her Rushe, he was a guy watching the drama unfold from his unscrutinized position.

A part of her was awed by his ability to hold himself away from everything. Somewhere inside Rushe was a button. Once he pressed it, everything went off.

In their time together, he'd convinced her of many things by putting on that mask. When he was that person, he was cold and cruel, and completely unaffected. Though the experience of their imprisonment had been traumatizing, she was glad they had been together. If they hadn't been through that, Rushe may never have confessed the depth of his feelings for her.

"I don't believe her," Lisa said. "Do you guys want to raise your hands?"

"What the fuck do you care about them?" Joey asked. "Who cares if she's fucked every guy at the table. She'd only be a couple ahead of you, wouldn't she?"

"This is inappropriate," Whyte said.

"He knows the rules," Lisa shouted. "You want to fuck another woman, you bring her to our bed, our bed, not you on your own in some shitty restroom, is that what you did? Is it? Where did you take her?"

"I didn't take her anywhere, you crazy bitch," Joey said, picking up his chair to sit at the table again, but the game was long forgotten. "You make up this shit in your head."

"You trying to tell me you didn't fuck her?" Lisa asked.

"No! I didn't fuck her!" Joey said, tossing his cards away. "Fuck this, I'm going downstairs."

"No, you're not," Lisa said, galloping after Joey when he tried to make a break for it. "You're not going down there, not tonight, not alone!"

The shouting followed the couple out of the room until the door closed with a concluding click. No one said anything. The room remained silent. So silent that she could hear the tick of someone's watch.

She was afraid to move. The whole dynamic had changed. Thank God she hadn't tried to gain Lisa's trust, the woman was unhinged. Though if Joey messed with her head, it wasn't all Lisa's fault. Then again, she had slept with her boyfriend's father. Oh, and they apparently had threesomes too. The sex had to be interesting, if nothing else. Fingers crossed the threesomes and father thing didn't overlap.

"I'm going home," Flick said and headed straight for the door.

Enough time had passed that Lisa and Joey would have cleared the corridor. Given her level of need, she was confident of finding her own way out. The trauma of the drama remained clenched around her heart, compounded by her foolish desire to go to Rushe.

She felt compelled to go to him and wanted to curl in his lap, just like she did at home when he watched sports, or late-night movies. She would curl up in his lap to sleep while he fondled whichever part of her body he fancied.

But that night he wouldn't be at home because he was in the room she'd just fled. Rushe was her rock and her salvation. If anything ever went wrong in her life, he would be the one to fix it. It was time to face the truth, she didn't know how to do the job. Rushe had been right all along. She had run into it headlong without checking the road was clear. Her love knew the obstacles, and he'd tried to warn her. Why had she believed she could help? Believed she knew best?

"Flick!"

At the sound of her name on masculine lips, she sped up. She got through the door with the security guard and onto the casino floor. The noise was disorienting, she looked one way then the other. It all looked the same. Which way was out? None of the walls had signs to indicate the location of the exit.

Striding into the swell of money and machine, all she wanted was to get out. She wanted to be free and didn't want to be a part of this anymore. She just wanted to go home and read a book, or to sit at her computer, or make love with the man she adored.

"Flick."

Again her name was on those lips, closer this time, close enough that when her arm was grasped and she was whirled around, she knew to expect Whyte.

Rushe had watched her embarrassed and upset, and he'd let her go without a word or action. Rushe had seen the truth of this. She had been hurt, just like he told her she would be. How he did it, she would never know. Her questions were about learning how to fight, how to defend herself, but she hadn't been able to comprehend the necessary emotional detachment.

For years, Rushe lived this way. He had the practice behind him, she didn't. That was how he'd been able to see her hurt and do nothing. She couldn't imagine seeing Rushe hurt and being able to walk away from him, or to watch him walk away. Walking away was a skill he'd perfected. He did it in their living room both times he left her.

She had to be stronger, to accept this was the job, and she needed to get better at it.

"I'm sorry about that," Whyte said, guiding her to the side of the room. "Lisa is an emotional person, she's young and—"

"Either Joey loves her or he doesn't," Flick said. "If he doesn't, he should let her go. They should both move on with their lives."

"You're upset," Whyte said, leading her onto a nearby couch. "I feel terrible about this. I should have known that… they're volatile. The pair of them together are ridiculous, but apart they're just as bad. I am sorry that you were forced to endure that."

"It wasn't your fault," she said.

"No, but our first date was cut short because of my employee's incompetence. Now our second date has been ruined as well. You must think terrible things about me."

"No," she said, feeling it necessary to soothe him. "It wasn't your fault. I'm not hurt, not physically. Embarrassed perhaps, but there was no harm done."

"I disagree. Let me get you a drink."

"No, I shouldn't drink."

"You're shaken up," Whyte said. "I understand that. Given your sexual position… I mean… well I didn't mean—"

"I know what you meant." She smiled and took his hand from her arm. "You have been kind to me, but I do think I should go home now."

"Given what you've heard about their sexual proclivities, I imagine you've been discouraged."

"Not exactly," she said, not ready to confess she'd never intended to encourage Whyte in the first place.

As for proclivities, plenty of men went upstairs with the lingerie-clad women in the Lounge after having paid for company. Coupling that with what she'd heard about Monday nights, a person had to wonder if the two were linked.

"Let me accompany you home."

"No," Flick said, startling Whyte. She hadn't meant to be quite so vehement. "I'll be fine."

"I insist. I wouldn't dream of pursuing you this evening, but I do feel responsible for what happened. I want to know you're safe, that you're okay."

"I am," she said. "Like I said, I'm not hurt."

"Let me get you a room. A room here, in the hotel."

"A room?"

"A suite. The best we have available."

"Oh no, I couldn't possibly…"

"You're not like other women," he said. "Your chastity may have been unexpected, but I've seen the way you carry yourself, the way you speak, your posture, there's something… refined about you. We don't have many women of your… class, around here."

Her mother would be proud Whyte had noticed her breeding, but she panicked. If he pressed for information, she had no idea what story to tell. If she told the truth, he could investigate her, but if she lied and he did that anyway…

"Thank you," she said, rising to her feet. "I should go."

"Please," he said, not releasing her hand. "Let me pamper you."

"I don't need to be pampered."

"I would feel terrible to see you going home alone while you're distressed. What is one night in a hotel? One night of room service, and a morning in the spa? No strings attached, I'll leave you completely alone, I promise."

"Why would you do that?"

"Not everyone is out for themselves," he said. "Your chastity proves you're a rare soul. You're sophisticated. Let me show you I can be the same. I can treat you to a night under my roof with no expectation.

I want to do something nice for you, to show what I can offer, in a way I haven't managed to do yet."

She pondered the offer for only a few seconds. "Okay."

WHYTE STAYED TRUE to his word. After making the arrangements, he escorted her to the door, handed her the key, and gave her his private extension number. In case she needed anything. She could read between the lines on that one.

The suite was beautiful; it included a large lounge area with thick drapes and a broad couch. The minibar was an actual bar, and the bathroom was about the same size as her and Rushe's bedroom. If Rushe knew she was under this roof, he would go postal.

Nevertheless, she admitted into the quiet night around her that he was the reason she'd stayed. Rushe was under this roof too. It didn't matter that she didn't know which room was his. Actually, it worked out for the best that she didn't know. If she did, she'd be tempted to visit him.

Rushe was there and she felt safer, more comforted, to know he was close by. Home wasn't home without him. There, in the hotel, she wasn't used to having him. She showered using the complimentary toiletries and changed into the complimentary nightgown before sinking into the sumptuous bed.

That night she closed her eyes ready to sleep soundly. Somewhere, not too far away, her love's heart was beating. That was enough to soothe her to sleep.

TWENTY-THREE

SHE HADN'T FOUND her senses before answering the ringing phone that woke her. The voice asked her what she wanted for breakfast. Breakfast? She declined the offer, but the voice informed her Mr. Whyte was seated in the members' breakfast room, awaiting her arrival.

The man had ordered dinner without her input, she shouldn't be surprised. This was clearly his way of gaining her company. Turned out there was a string after all, and that string was breakfast.

She went down and sped through breakfast on the claim she had things to do on her day off. Joey coming into the breakfast room with his father got her even more desperate to get out. Just as she thought she might have a clear shot and be home free... the door opened again, and Rushe entered.

Rushe didn't like people or care about three square meals. There would be no reason for him to come down to breakfast, except that he wanted more information. His role was to get into the lives and heads of these people.

When he spotted her, his eyes narrowed, and in the shame of the moment, hers fell. As soon as they did, she realized the act probably conveyed guilt, so she looked back up at him. But her love was already perusing the fruit, seemingly, she was forgotten. Again, he'd detached himself from her so easily.

"Tomorrow night," Whyte said when they exited the breakfast room. "Come to the hotel, at ten thirty. I want to show you something."

"I don't know," Flick said.

"You reacted last night with such grace and discretion; I feel confident sharing our secret with you."

"This just… it seems like it's never going to get off the ground."

"It will get off the ground tomorrow night, Flick. Please, give me one more chance. I'll show you all that I can be for you, all that we can be."

"The hotel?" she asked, trying to appear unsure while fluttering her eyelashes.

Little did he know, his talk of a secret had reeled her in.

"Yes. Come to the hotel. It's very important."

She nodded. She'd rather be at the hotel with the possibility of seeing Rushe than away from it wondering what he was doing.

Her day would be dedicated to the library and digging deeper. Rosa hadn't been an original figure of interest. That had changed. Understanding her connection to all this, and Michael's too, could change their perspective. Lisa's brother had duped her, but Rushe's instincts had been right on the money.

THE LIBRARY WAS a great distraction. Immersing herself in the investigation was vital. She needed to get back on course now that she'd met the players. Studying the Lounge led to her examining the architectural plans, something she struggled to scrutinize with all structures associated with the mission. The venue space was on the original blueprint, but its purpose was unspecified.

Years after initial construction, there was a refurbishment. From what she could tell, the room had gotten smaller. The plans were confusing, she couldn't read them properly but didn't know a professional who could assist her understanding.

The librarian literally had to ask her to leave. She hadn't intended to work until midnight but had gotten so much done. Glad that the day was over, she tucked everything into her oversized messenger bag and flung the strap up over her head to lay it across her body. The security guard escorted her out and locked the door at her back.

She ran down the stairs and crossed the road without seeing a single vehicle, in contrast, during the day, it could take ten minutes to get a clear shot.

Slowing her pace when she passed The Grill, she rounded the corner. How could she get in touch with Rushe? She couldn't call the hotel and ask for him. That would be too suspicious, and he would be angry with her for taking the risk.

Halfway down the block, she stuck her hands in the pockets of her button-down dress, wishing for a coat. It had been warm when she left the apartment that morning after going home to gather her things for the library and change her clothes.

Suddenly, someone grabbed her from behind, lifting her off her feet. A gloved hand smothered her mouth. Although she kicked and tried to scream, she could do nothing as the assailant carried her down the blackened alley and up a step into the deep entryway of a boarded-up doorway.

Bundled into the corner, the weight of her aggressor pinned her in place. The ominous size of the molesting body clenched her chest with utter terror. Her body was solid with the tension, she tried to struggle, to scream again, but her muffled sounds would alert no one.

Though his hand stayed on her mouth, he spun her around. On blinking her eyes upward, she half expected to see Satan himself. When her eyes met the attacker's, her whole body sagged back.

"What's a dirty little Kitten like you doing out alone so late?"

His hand relaxed but didn't drop.

Still, she had enough space to sigh out. "You scared me, Rushe," she hissed, swatting at him. "If anyone saw you grab me off the street—"

"No one saw," he said. "No one cares."

She'd heard that before and let her head fall back against the wall. His hands found her breasts like they were drawn there.

Their time together could be short. Despite it being obvious his mind wasn't on the job, she had to take this opportunity. "Can you read architectural plans?"

"Maybe," he said. "Where are they?"

She fumbled her way to the pocket of her bag to retrieve a USB memory stick. "On here."

He took it and slid it into his jacket pocket. "Dump the bag." He gave her just enough space to do that and no more. "You've been in the library all day."

"Have you been waiting all day?" she asked. "You didn't seem to care about me when you saw me this morning… with another man."

Her love paused in unbuttoning her dress. Probably didn't matter, he'd already exposed her bra-protected breasts.

"Do you think I didn't know that he got you a room?" he asked. "I knew exactly where you were all night."

"And you were okay with that?"

"Never got any sleep," he grumbled.

She'd thought he hadn't cared she was hurt, or that it appeared she'd spent the night with another man, when all the time he was monitoring her. Rushe didn't know it, but in his own way, he'd just romanced her again.

"What panties you got on?" he asked, crouching to lift the hem of her dress and grope underneath.

"I was going home to bed," she said as he pulled down her underwear. When he got them all the way to the ground, she stepped out of them. "You know bed? I have a really great bed. It's also known as *our* bed. If you wanted sex…"

"I can't go back there," he said, tucking her panties in his leather jacket pocket then shirking out of it.

He pulled her forward and tucked his jacket around her.

"What are you doing?" she asked.

"Put your arms in the sleeves or it will come off."

She complied. "I'm cold, but you can't go back to the hotel without your jacket."

"Don't plan to," he said.

Undoing a couple more of her dress buttons, he took the strip of material between her breasts that held the bra cups together. With one tug, he ripped it.

"Rushe!"

"Shut it," he said, rubbing his thumbs over her nipples.

"I seem to recall telling you once that a dirty alley was out of the question."

"A car's too conspicuous… and it can be traced."

"Is that supposed to persuade me?"

He crouched to kiss one breast and ducked to

grasp her ass, under the skirt, to lift her off her feet. "I gave you the jacket. The wall won't mark you or make you dirty… I'll take care of those things on my own."

Despite knowing she shouldn't encourage him, her smile was involuntary. "You think of everything, don't you?"

He had known she would object so covered his bases. What her love didn't understand was that she'd been as desperate for him as he had apparently been for her. Right then, she'd have sex with him anywhere.

Taking her own initiative, she unbuckled his belt. Already the bulk of him tried to insist its way around the denim barrier impeding it. She took hold of him and ran her thumb over his head, smearing the moisture seeping from him.

"He missed me," she said, tightening her grip and drawing her fist up and down around him.

"Don't do that."

"I've missed him too. I'm thinking I might want to slide down there and wrap my mouth—"

"Some virgin you are," he snarled, snatching himself from her hold.

He lifted her higher and stabbed himself into her pussy. Flat against the wall, she could do nothing but take his thrusts as he pounded into her, right up to the hilt every time. Leaning in against her, he got hold of her pelvis to tilt her up and yank her in against every deep plunge.

"Rushe," she sighed.

He growled. "That's my pussy… You in that dress… you got yourself all gussied up for that sack of shit." Forward, higher, faster, she struggled to get enough oxygen. "You like that, you're dripping, Kitten, getting that sweet juice all on my dick, letting me slide in nice and easy. You want it in you, you been dreaming about this? Thinking about my cock inside you? Speak."

"Yes," she moaned out through gritted teeth.

"You been a good girl? You been playing with my toy? Pampering my girls?"

"No, God, Rushe!"

She bucked into his grip when the explosion of pleasure tore through her. Just at that, he stopped moving. As she panted through the shimmering web glittering throughout her, she opened her eyes to see him staring down at her.

"Last night, when you walked in that room… with him…"

He didn't finish.

Though her breathing rhythm hadn't got back to normal, she covered his cheeks with her palms. "What?" she asked. "Lover, what is it?"

"I couldn't stop it."

She wasn't used to Rushe making so little sense. That was usually her role. "Stop what?"

"My cock smelled you or something; you weren't even in the room and…"

"You got hard?" she asked, wearing a wistful smile.

"Don't smile," he snapped. "You keep your guard up. You should be aware of everyone in the room, and all I could… it was the dumbest thing…"

He shook his head to the side as if trying to rid water from his ear.

"What?" she asked, not discouraged, or willing to relinquish her hold on his face just yet. "What was it?"

"Your shampoo," he said. "I never knew your shampoo was so fucking… I lost my senses, Kit. I couldn't see straight, then when you came over and… you used my soap, didn't you?" She nodded. "My scent on my woman and that fucker—"

"Hey," she said. His jaw clenched; rage clouded him. "Your woman is right here in your arms. Your woman loves you and misses you so much. I didn't go home last night because… I can't sleep there without you."

"I'm addicted to your body," he said. "I've never… I've had the choice in the past, drugs, women, money… I thought guys who got hooked on shit like that were… Last night, I couldn't remember why I was there or what I was doing…"

While all the time, she'd thought he was unaffected. She should have known better. Rushe could hide behind his solid, unaffected exterior.

"We still have each other," she said. "When this is over…"

He shook his head. "There's more going on here than you know."

"More?" she asked. "I know about Lisa and Galante. I know about Rosa's relationship with Galante too, and about Rosa's relationship with Michael Lewis. Joey came to the Lounge on Sunday night, he and Lisa were fighting I think."

"He's got a thing for you," he said. "You've got them all by the balls."

"I belong to you, Rushe. I've been around rich influential men all my life. I couldn't care less about the superficiality."

"I'm not worried about them, but my girl…" pride crept into his tone, "you were such a scared little thing, but that strength… You never cowered from me, not from any of them. You're strong, Flick, and I don't always give you credit for that."

As much as he meant emotional strength, she had to smile when he drew his hips back then advanced, exploring their point of unity. Just as she began to doubt herself, he displayed his faith in her. It had been a while since they'd made love, though this wasn't the best place or time to be considering that.

Fast and frenzied suited this situation; he'd started with such fervor and then stopped. His body was sturdy enough to handle the physical exertion, and he hadn't kissed her as he did when they mated slowly. His eyes burned into hers. She saw him try and fail to lift the shutter over his demeanor.

"You don't want to leave me," she whispered, figuring out why he'd stalled. "You're going to come in me and leave, aren't you?"

"I've been shooting my load into you for months."

"But you don't leave me after it…" He picked up his pace, but she wasn't satisfied. "You've left me before. Twice in the last month you've walked away from me, why is this different?"

His brow snapped down, shading his already sinister eyes. "Stop talking," he barked.

He hauled her up and smashed into her. Out and in, his force was so inflexible that her back began to bruise despite the jacket. His potency swirled in the vigor of his virility. With bruising force, he gripped her ass and battered on until he spilled himself into her cervix without care for her assaulted muscles.

"Rushe," she whispered through his huffed breaths. "Lover."

This time when she reached for his face, he stepped away, leaving her to slide down the wall to the concrete step. Her legs were not yet stable enough to take her weight.

"Go home. I don't want you out this late again."

Snatching the collar of his jacket, he whipped it from her body and walked away into the night that had birthed him. His actions didn't offend her, but she was curious. Her love was hiding something. This might not be a new phenomenon, but the guilt was new.

In the past when he'd had guilt over her safety,

he thought he had compromised it so wanted to make amends. That wasn't the case tonight. If it was, he would never have left her there like this.

He'd said that something else was going on. Rushe would always know more than she did, but this went deeper than dates and names. Speculating did nothing to illuminate any details, and she had no idea when she would see him again.

TWENTY-FOUR

SHE DIDN'T HANG around in the alley. In the past, trouble tended to find her; it wouldn't be wise to tempt fate.

Her encounter with Rushe vibrated through her on the trek back to their building. As she rode up in their elevator, Rushe was on his way back to the Waterside. Was he thinking of her? Mad that they couldn't spend the night together? Maybe a little sad?

The smile on her face and the warmth around her heart chilled when the elevator doors opened. At the end of the hall was their apartment door… ajar.

Creeping forward, there wasn't time to consider her options. Not that she had many. Rushe wasn't there, she had to go in, alone.

The corridor had never seemed so long. Eventually, she got to the door and gave it a push to peek inside. Nothing was out of place, except from that angle most of the space was hidden by the kitchen wall.

"Hello!" she shouted, hoping if it was just a gang of kids, or a regular intruder, they would flee in fear of being caught.

Unsurprisingly, no one shouted back. Turning on the lights didn't get a response either. With one step and then another, she crept inside. The coat closet behind the front door was open. Some of its contents were scattered, but she wasn't going to inspect the mess for details and turn her back on anyone who might still be there.

From the living room she had a clear shot out the door. From the bedrooms, it wouldn't be so certain. Her escape route could be cut off if someone snuck up on her.

As her view of the rest of the apartment expanded, her heart sank. The drawers in the unit under the wall-mounted TV were out and upside down. The kitchen was trashed. Whoever had done this was looking for something or hoping to cause as much carnage as possible.

She took the time to get a knife from the butcher's block in the kitchen, which was currently in the middle of the floor with only half its contents. The rest of the blades were lost somewhere in the mess.

With the long knife at her side, she took a deep breath and focused on the bedroom doors. It was unlikely anyone would be in the bathroom, but she opened the door to find the room largely undisturbed. Neither she nor Rushe used it with any regularity, so there was nothing in the room to tamper with.

The second bedroom had been wrecked. The gym equipment could offer cover. The desk, on its four metal legs, couldn't. No one was there. The computer was gone, the gym mats slashed, and the desk drawer was empty except for a couple of sheets of paper.

She picked up the papers without looking at them and turned to leave the room. The intruders had had plenty of time to flee if they wanted to. If Rushe had been there, he wouldn't have wanted them to escape. She was no coward but being alone, her defenses likely wouldn't hold up to an ambush. They'd be nothing in comparison to Rushe's punishment if he was around.

Her fear tipped beyond the physical when she entered the bedroom. Tears sprang to her eyes. Their beautiful room was in disarray. The place they shared their love was covered in torn clothes and ripped bed linen. Nothing was where it should be. The nightstands were tipped over, the sliding doors of the closet pulled from their runners. Condoms were strewn around the room too, like some sort of mocking symbol for what had, or hadn't, gone on in there.

Confident that whoever had done this was no longer there, she went into their bathroom more upset than afraid. She found more of the same disorder. On a long sigh, she turned in circles looking at the mess, and then took another journey through the apartment.

Her instinct to call the cops dissolved as quickly as she established it. Rushe wouldn't call the cops, and this was his place. She wasn't sure if he had insurance either, so a crime report reference was irrelevant. Rushe would rather go after the perpetrators alone. If they were serious people, she didn't want her love to get hurt. If they were small time, Rushe might hurt them and get himself in trouble.

But this didn't feel coincidental. For one thing, the culprits had to pass many other apartments to get to this one. The building was decent, and the area respectable enough, that anything noticeably shady would be reported. The television was there, the computer wasn't. Rushe's pager was gone, but her jewelry hadn't been taken.

In the bedroom, trying to figure out what to do, she dropped onto the corner of the split-open mattress and hooked her arm around the bedpost. For some reason, she was still holding the papers from the office drawer. She'd never seen Rushe deal with paperwork, and she hadn't gone looking, but it would be worth knowing if what they'd left behind was important.

The more she read, the deeper her frown became. It was a lease, a property lease, for this apartment. She had assumed Rushe owned the apartment, but that wasn't the most concerning detail. The lease was in the name of Jimmy Jones, and it was dated… the day before she arrived there. Either Rushe's real name was Jimmy Jones, or…

"He doesn't live here," she whispered.

When Rushe had made her pack up her things and given her the choice to come with him or not, she'd assumed they were going to his house, his home, wherever he lived. This apartment was where he'd brought her, and she hadn't questioned him. Why would she? She'd believed that they were embarking on a new and honest life with each other.

Rushe would have his reasons for misleading her and, as was always the case with Rushe, those reasons would make sense. But the reasons weren't as concerning as his motive. Only one of two things could be going on here: either Rushe wanted to protect her, or he didn't plan for them being together for very long.

While she desperately hoped the latter wasn't true, she struggled to come up with reasons for the former. Nothing came to mind. If by not telling her the truth he was trying to protect her, then he had to be protecting her from something about his own life, his real life. All these months she'd shared his bed and thought they were getting closer, and all the time Rushe knew their existence together was a fabrication.

Trust didn't come easily to Rushe. Still, this development, the new information, hurt. But she reminded herself Rushe always acted in her best interest.

With no other choice, she had to trust him. They weren't able to communicate, so she couldn't question him, unless he planned to pick her off another street in the middle of the night.

Conjecture wouldn't solve the new mystery, and neither would just sitting there on the bed. So she picked through the chaos and stuffed everything salvageable into her torn suitcase. She had a date tomorrow and a work shift the following night, though she'd have to request a new uniform.

Closing the door at her back, she made a mental note to phone a locksmith in the morning. Then she went back to the street, and back to the hotel she'd vacated that morning.

TWENTY-FIVE

RESERVING HER ROOM at the hotel had been easy. No one recognized her, so she had the night and the day to herself. Nothing she'd recovered from the apartment was date suitable. After she had supervised the locksmith as he fitted new locks, she took her credit card for a walk. The retail experience wasn't exactly therapy, it didn't make her feel any better.

By the time she got to the lobby for her date with Whyte, she was pissed off, seriously pissed off. That was what a day of obsessing about Rushe's deception did to her.

"Good evening."

The proximity of Whyte's voice alarmed her. She hadn't even seen him coming. "Hello."

"You were in a daze, I'm sorry, did I startle you?"

"No," she said as he kissed her hand. "No, sorry."

"Is everything okay?"

His look of concern was curious, she reminded herself to smile. "Yes, of course. Where are we going tonight? What did you want to show me?”

“I don’t want to put you off. But there’s openness in you, and I want to be honest. I want us to be honest with each other.”

“Yes, of course.”

Whyte guided her toward the elevator. “You asked about changing your shift at the Lounge.”

“Yes,” she said, when he pressed the button for the elevator.

“I know you must be curious about Rosa’s reaction to your request, and about Joey’s fondness for the place on a Monday specifically.”

“Well, yes.”

She wasn’t going to lie, and Whyte was giving her the chance to learn more. Typical that as it became apparent her own real relationship was based on a lie, this false relationship was all about honesty… on Whyte’s part at least.

“I’m going to take you down,” he said, guiding them onto the elevator. He pressed the lowest button and took hold of both her hands. “I want you to see what the Lounge offers on these three days, Monday through Wednesday. If you become uncomfortable at any time, we can leave.”

She nodded. Going to the Lounge didn’t negate her promise to Rushe that she and Whyte wouldn’t be alone. On reaching their floor, Whyte took her to a tall black door.

“Just take your time to look around, okay?”

She nodded again and smiled, bringing out Whyte’s smile. He ushered her inside, then they stopped, giving her a chance to absorb the new features. If Whyte hadn’t warned her in advance that this was her workplace, she wouldn’t have recognized it.

Music with a heavy bass line pumped into the air. The stage was lit up, spotlighting a nude woman dancing.

Two topless women danced on the bar with a metal pole that she'd thought was structural.

Whyte leaned in close to her ear. "Welcome to the X-Lounge. What do you think?"

She remained captivated by it all. The number of patrons hadn't increased, and the betting tables were still in play, but she couldn't see the armchairs usually next to the bar. They continued deeper into the space. The couch area had lower voltage lighting, and she could just distinguish the shapes of the armchairs scattered there too. No details. That area was shrouded in mystery.

More men were in that section, no doubt drawn by the women dancing on some of the low center tables. In the shadows, there were three females giving private dances.

Whyte took her hand to lead her toward a table. she struggled to take her eyes away from the vision of the dancing women and eager men.

Rosa intercepted them. "What is she doing here?"

"I thought it was time she knew," Whyte said, switching Flick's hand between his to move her body in front of his. "We have nothing to hide here, Rosa."

Certainly, Rosa had nothing to hide. The uniform was still black and red but consisted of a push up bra, hot pants, and hold up stockings with garters instead of suspenders.

"You want me to switch her?" Rosa asked, with a thread of doubt.

Flick was still drinking in the thumping music and constant movement of the women, while the slobbering men devoured each nuance.

"It's her decision."

Whyte didn't wait to say more to Rosa and left her behind to take Flick across the room to sit down.

Drawn in by the music, her smile was

involuntary. "This place is amazing," Flick said.

Whyte relished watching her enjoying herself. "I wasn't sure how you would react," he said. "I'm glad you like it."

"I do…" She laughed. "When I think of some of the things I dreamed up."

"What were we doing down here? Drugs den? Human slave trade, what?"

"All of the above," she said, though those weren't exactly what she'd imagined.

"I have nothing to hide, Flick," Whyte said, opening his arms to the venue. "This is what the customers want, and they're always right. In the twenty-first century, competition for business is fierce. If we don't evolve, we die."

"This is evolving," Flick said, watching the people, the movement, the joy of the place, infused with a thrumming sexual energy.

Men craved the women who taunted them with what they couldn't have. Music raised the energy, the women raised the blood pressure, and she was sure every man in the place had risen too.

"I'll get you a drink," Whyte said, taking her hand and kissing it again as he left the table.

She was barely aware of him, and not alert enough to remember that this place, her place of employment, offered table service.

"Hi."

She glanced over her shoulder in the direction of the voice she recognized. Rushe. Right there at her shoulder.

"Whyte will be back in a minute," she said.

"We met night before last, we know each other now. I'm saying hello."

His tone was about as happy as she felt. All enjoyment of the environment was gone, and she was tempted to throw her elbow up into his gonads.

"Hello. Now go away."

"What are you doing here?" Rushe growled.

"I don't see how that's any of your business."

He swung around to sit on the seat perpendicular to hers, thus blocking everything else from view. His hand remained on the back of her chair, he kept her in the arched enclosure of his arm, though it didn't actually touch her.

"You're in a joint selling sex with a guy who wants to fuck your cunt, which belongs to me—"

"Don't take a tone with me," she whispered, leaning closer to conceal her expression from onlookers. "Your sex talk's not going to work, Lover. Go as caveman as you like, it's not going to work with me, you lying sack of shit."

So much for giving him the benefit of the doubt. Her trust in him might be intact, that didn't mean she wasn't angry.

"What the—"

"Our place got tossed last night," she said. "They took the computer, your pager, trashed every—"

"What?" Rushe asked, his own brow crashing down over his eyes. "You were there?"

"No."

"Last night when we were…"

"Maybe," she said. "Now that you mention it, was that your role? To keep me busy?"

"Eric watched you go into the building, but he didn't—"

"You've got your sleazy friends following me?"

"I told you I'd be watching."

"I'm not surprised," she said. "Let's just add that deception onto the list with your other ones, shall we? Jimmy?"

"What the fuck are you—"

"Rushe, good evening!"

She sat back, her broad smile fixed in place when Whyte returned to the table. Her lover's fingers slid away from her backrest when Whyte maintained his standing position between her and Rushe as he handed over her glass.

"I'm showing Flick the place," Whyte said to him, and then leaned down toward her. "Rushe is a fan of the X-Lounge; he's becoming a regular already."

"Yeah," Rushe said, shooting to his feet, his focus stuck on her. He glanced at her drink and took a step away as he looked at Whyte. "She doesn't like vodka."

On those clipped words, Rushe took off in the direction of the couches, of the private dancers.

Whyte took the seat Rushe had vacated. "How does he know that—?"

"He misunderstood," she said, taking an exaggerated sip from the glass. "I told a joke. He obviously didn't understand I was kidding."

"I can get you something else if—"

"No," she said, drinking again. "No, I don't need anything else."

She didn't dare look in Rushe's direction. Frustration boiled in her gut; their altercation was unfinished. Their home had been robbed, triggering a lot of questions. Except it wasn't their home. They didn't have one.

TWENTY-SIX

A COUPLE OF HOURS later, she was still in the X-Lounge with Whyte, enjoying the music and the dancing. There she felt like Alice must have in Wonderland. The place was so bizarre, so at odds with everything she had experienced in her upbringing. Never in her life had she been anywhere like this, it was enlivening. The experience wasn't so much sexual as it was enthralling. These peculiar creatures in this alien environment captivated her.

Rushe hadn't been back to their table. He'd be watching her, probably while getting a private dance on the other side of the bar.

Whyte took her hand under the table. "How do you feel?"

The contact startled her. Fuzz hung in her head from the couple of vodkas she'd consumed, but adrenaline was mixed in there too.

"I feel good," she said.

"You like the dancers?" he asked, sweeping her hair away from her shoulder.

"They're very talented. There's energy about this place, it's so alive."

"Yeah." Whyte grinned. "Do you want to try it?"

"The dancing? Oh no, I couldn't possibly—"

"Don't worry, everyone here had to start out somewhere." Whyte leaned in and brushed her cheek. "Don't think about them… think about me."

"You want me to dance?" she asked. "You want me to dance, out here in public, for you?"

"We can go up to my suite if you want privacy."

"I'm not ready for that yet," she said, trying to withdraw her hand from his.

Whyte held on. "Okay, it's okay, we're going slow," he said. "Why don't we go and sit on the couch, just over there." He nodded past her to the seating area. "We're just going to sit there, quiet, private, but still here with everyone, okay? There's no pressure, Flick."

Indecision swirled. Technically, there was nothing wrong with his request. They were on a date, thinking about a relationship, it made sense he'd want to spend time alone with her. If she pushed away too much, he would know things weren't as they seemed. That left her with one choice, she bobbed her head in assent.

Whyte kept her hand and his smile glowed as he towed her from their table in the lit area. She followed on but felt unbalanced by the move. What would come next? Would Whyte kiss her? Would he touch her?

Damn, why couldn't she have Rushe's forethought? As she tried to reach for it, they crossed into the darkened area. Her eyes adjusted to the illumination, and the first thing they fixed on was Rushe, in an armchair, a brooding professional, no female in sight. Still Whyte guided her on. Rushe was ready to explode. She needed a way out of this. Instinct was all she could rely on.

As they were about to pass Rushe, she

deliberately twisted her foot from her heel and stumbled forward, landing on Rushe, sending his drink spilling over both of them. His arm came around her in a stabilizing embrace.

She gasped. "Oh, oh, I'm so sorry!" she yelped, and pawed at Rushe's chest. "You're all wet."

"Don't worry yourself about that, sweetheart," Rushe said.

In her mock sorrow, she glanced up to see Rushe ogling her cleavage. Her fury remained, but when she read the potency of his pride, the anger subsided a little. At that same moment, she became aware his erection was digging into her hip too. Some things, it seemed, were automatic where they were concerned.

"Did you trip?"

Whyte's voice reminded her of the executive's presence, and just in the nick of time too. Her vodka-drenched senses were only a few seconds away from seeking out Rushe's mouth with her own.

"No, I don't think so," she said and managed a giggle.

That would be in character of the naive woman Whyte assumed her to be, right? She also batted her eyelashes, just like she did for her date.

Rushe peered closer. "You got something in your eye?" he asked, tilting her head.

Whyte took hold of her waist and lifted her back to her feet.

When he let her go, she dropped onto Rushe's knee. "Oh, I think I hurt my foot," she said, bending to rub her ankle.

Sitting on Rushe was a perfectly natural thing for her, but it wouldn't look very good from Whyte's perspective.

"Is this gonna be added to my room tab?" Rushe asked Whyte.

Flick laughed. Loud. "You're funny?"

"Am I?" Rushe asked, without moving his lips, but she knew from his relaxed expression that it wasn't anger he hid. "Are you staying in the hotel?"

"Uh, yes," she said to him, then glanced at Whyte and back to Rushe. "Yes, I am."

"You are?" Whyte asked.

"I'll take you to your room," Rushe said.

As he stood up and discarded his glass, he took her under his arm, supporting her weight.

"You will not," Whyte said.

"I'm wet," Rushe said. "And she's wasted."

"Which is why you're the last person she should be alone with," Whyte asserted.

"You think I'm gonna fuck her?"

She laughed again. The act was much easier to pull off when Rushe was beside her. "I'm a virgin."

"Sure you are, sweetheart," Rushe said, the twist of amusement in his voice.

"I will accompany her."

Whyte was annoyed, Rushe was as aloof as ever.

She laughed in her supposed drunken state. "I'll be fine," she said, patting Whyte's arm. "I had a great time, thank you. I'll be here at work tomorrow."

Rushe didn't wait for anything else, he just started to move. Being that she was still connected to him, she went along as well. Eventually, they were out the hotel access door and in the elevator going up.

"What's your room number?"

"Six something," she said, leaning on him as she took her key card from her clutch.

"Six what?"

"I don't know," she said and laughed again.

"You're not that drunk," Rushe said.

"I might be."

"You're not."

"How do you know?"

"You snort when you're drunk," he said.

Her chin fell as she gasped and glared up at him. "I do not!"

"You do."

"I don't," she said. Rushe just watched the numbers. "Six twelve." She slapped the card on his chest forcing him to take it. "Here."

"You should be pissed at me," he said.

The pair of them stood, side by side, watching the floor numbers illuminate.

"I am pissed at you."

"More pissed. Why aren't you more pissed?"

"I trust you," she said and took his arm around her waist to lean on him as they left the elevator and walked down the hallway to her room. "We'll fight about it later, and I'll make you grovel, but not here like this…" They stopped at her door, she rested against it to look up at him. "I panicked, downstairs, I'm sorry. Whyte wanted to move seats, and I thought he might try to kiss me, and—"

"You did the right thing," Rushe said, taking her chin into his grasp. "You hear me? You did the right thing and I'm proud of you for thinking fast like that. I'm only happy I was there to—"

"I'd have fallen over another man if I'd needed to." She smiled, but his expression had settled into something peculiar… and enticing. "Usually when they're around, you look at me… like you don't know me. I don't like it when you look at me that way." Rushe didn't respond, but his look of interest traveled to her lips. "Whyte will be suspicious, if he thinks you're interested—"

"I want him to think I'm interested."

"What?"

Rushe leaned closer, like a man ready to swoop in for the goodnight kiss. "Whyte has a fetish."

"A fetish? I don't understand what…"

His fingertips sailed up her arm in a caress that was so gentle it was barely there. He'd never touched her like that before.

"He likes to watch."

"Watch what?" she asked. "I know he likes the dancers—"

"Sex, Kitten. He likes to watch other men having sex with his women."

His palm slithered over her shoulder to her cheek, and he tipped her head back for better access. "Don't you kiss me," she murmured, "don't you dare kiss me for them. How do you know about that?"

"Lisa told me."

"When?"

"On Monday night, after you left."

"You went to the Lounge?" she asked, and Rushe nodded once. "Did you have sex with her?"

"Kitten," he groaned.

She rested her hands on his still damp chest. "Okay, I know, I'm sorry."

"Whyte can't get it up on his own; it's how she and Joey got involved. Lisa was dating Whyte and things heated up. Galante Senior stepped up first, but then one night he was busy, so Joey did the honors. It's not a new thing. They do it regularly."

"And you want to do the honors with me?" she asked. "Rushe, I wouldn't be comfortable having an audience when we—"

"I'm not gonna share you," he said. "He doesn't know me very well. Right now, he'll feel threatened. I'm on your doorstep, which is further than he's got."

"But it would arouse him to see this, to see you with me?"

"Yeah. Trouble with Whyte's fetish is that the couple having sex figure out they don't actually need him, so Whyte is shut out."

She wanted to question Rushe about the apartment and wanted to know why he'd misled her. Instead, she stroked his chest, just happy to have her lover within reach.

"We've never…"

"No one watches me fuck you, not with a gun to my head. You're mine."

"No, I was going to say," she said, pressing her palms to his pecs. "We've never… there's a bed right through this door behind me."

"You want me to fuck you?"

"I'm saying it's odd we're not just going for it."

"You're a virgin," he said.

She sighed. "I know."

"Best cover ever."

"Not from where I'm standing."

"It's a turn on," he said.

"You're always turned on… I want to go home," she confessed, then shrugged. "I don't know where that is anymore."

"It's here. I told you we live wherever you want."

"You set up a false home under a false name," she said. "Why did you do that?"

The look of desire on his face vanished. Just like that, he'd put up the walls again. "Go to bed."

"That's your response for everything, to walk away," she said. "You can't just shut me up because I'm inconvenient for you."

"We can't argue here," he said through gritted teeth. "The cameras have eyes but no ears. They'll notice if we're fighting."

"Oh, whatever," she said, snatching her room key and spinning around to dig it into the lock.

He snatched her arm and whirled her around. "I'm trying to protect you."

"From what?" she asked but received no reply. "Why can't you tell me the truth?" Still, he said nothing. "Don't you trust me?"

"Not to screw around on me, sure."

"No qualifier, do you trust me?"

"You're reckless and—"

"Rushe!"

"What the fuck do you want me to say?" he snapped.

"I want you to answer the question, Rushe. Do you trust me?"

Out of other options, honesty was all that remained for him. "No."

Pushing for the answer might not have been the best course. If she was honest with herself, she'd expected that reply. Hearing him say it aloud was a step forward, but it wasn't one she savored. With nothing more to say, she went into her room and left Rushe standing in the corridor alone.

TWENTY-SEVEN

SHE GOT A NEW uniform before starting her shift, and Rosa didn't ask questions. Two hours later, the room had quietened to less than a dozen patrons. Rosa approached, clearly with something to say.

"I want to talk to you."

"Okay," Flick said, following Rosa to one of the couches where the women sat together. "Are you firing me?"

"No. Last night, with Evan, was everything okay?"

"Sure."

"It's just, I saw you leave with that Rushe guy, and—"

"I fell. It was embarrassing, but he only walked me to my room because I soaked him with alcohol."

"Evan brought you down here to see what you thought of the X-Lounge. You asked for the shift change, and… Monday, Tuesday, and Wednesday are different here. They tend to be quieter in the casino and in the hotel, so we have to offer something special, something extra, something exclusive."

"I understand," Flick said. "I had a lot of fun last night."

"Are you still interested in the change?"

"Of shifts?"

Rosa nodded. "We always start women on the Thursday to Sunday shift, to see if they have what it takes. Obviously, Evan thinks you do, or he wouldn't have brought you down here. I wasn't so sure of you to be honest."

"Is that why he asked me out? Why he dated me? To groom me for—"

"Oh no," Rosa said. "No, he likes you. It's a compliment actually. When he and Lisa started…"

The hostess trailed off and a few shades of color left her face.

"It's okay," Flick said, covering Rosa's hand. "I know he saw other women before he saw me. It must be problematic for him to see Lisa with Joey. Do you know what happened?"

"Joey likes to invite other women into his bed," Rosa said. "I suppose Lisa was one of those women."

She couldn't tell if Rosa believed that to be true, or if she was covering up the truth. "Wow… Lisa said you used to date her brother."

"Date is exaggerating it. We had a fling, turned out he was totally nuts though, so…"

"I'm sorry, it must be difficult for you," she said. "Your feelings for Joey's father and—"

"You been asking about me?" Rosa scowled.

"No, no, it was just what Joey said that day here in the Lounge."

"Joey doesn't know what he's talking about. You should stop talking too."

"I'm sorry," she said. "I just hoped we could be friends."

The hostess was unimpressed. "If you want to change shifts you can, that's all I wanted to tell you."

She dropped the issue. "I just want to be sure that... would I be expected to... sleep with anyone? I couldn't..."

Rosa looked left to right and relaxed. "No, you're a server. But if a guy asks for a dance, our servers would usually do that. There are women provided for sex, but... if a guy is really adamant, we would..."

"What?"

Rosa sighed out, resigned to the truth. "Some of the men like to... we don't report drug use. Sometimes if a guy needs a little something to loosen him up, we might slip something into his drink, take him upstairs to the hotel, then let him pass out in bed before... you know... let him sleep it off."

Her assumptions hadn't been far off. "So the hotel gets his money?"

"If you want to empty his wallet before you leave his room, we won't ask questions," Rosa said with a laugh.

Flick wasn't convinced that she was joking. "I've never danced for a man... like that."

"There's nothing to it," Rosa said. "Shake your ass, lean forward so he can see your breasts, he doesn't really care about the rest. You've got the body for it. Kimberly will show you."

"Kimberly?"

"She used to work that shift, switched back a couple of years ago when she had her kid."

"Kimberly has a kid?"

"Sure." Rosa stood up, Flick followed. "We'll get you a new uniform. You can finish out tonight, and then we'll see you here on Monday midnight to three. We work half shifts those days... It's a lot of extra work!"

With another laugh, Rosa walked away. Terrified

didn't begin to describe her mood. She had a fake relationship with Whyte that may or may not be depraved, and it turned out the man she loved wasn't as invested in her as she thought. The wheels were coming off the wagon, but she was already going too fast down this steep hill to stop. All she could hope for was a soft landing.

TWENTY-EIGHT

PERSISTENT KNOCKING rudely awakened her from her slumber. On coming back from her shift at the Lounge the night before, she'd hung the do not disturb sign. Yet her visitor persevered. So as much as she didn't feel like being social, and she wasn't ready to receive visitors, she rolled out of the crisp white sheets and stuck her arms in the fluffy hotel-monogrammed bathrobe.

The basic room hadn't come with extras, at least not until yesterday. Strange that she should benefit from special treatment only after Whyte discovered she was staying in the hotel. She plodded toward the door, aware that Whyte and Rushe, and possibly Rosa, were the only people who knew she was there.

Sure enough, when she peeked through the peephole, she saw Whyte. With a yawn, she unfastened the door lock and opened it with a smile.

Whyte was poised to speak but paused when he took in her features. She hadn't slept well and hadn't been up for a shower let alone pulled a brush through her hair. Clearly, her disarray bemused the businessman.

"Sorry, did I wake you?"

"No," she said on another yawn. "I was awake, I just wasn't up yet."

"Can I come in?"

She didn't have a suite, only a room with a bed and a bathroom. She didn't know where they'd sit, but there was no reason to object. Stepping aside, she held open the door to allow him in. He handed her a rolled-up newspaper.

"You brought me a newspaper?" she asked, closing the door, wondering at the unusual gift.

"No, I assumed you ordered it. It was at your door. They're delivered by the staff with breakfast each morning."

"Oh yes, of course," she said, as though she was merely forgetful.

Tossing the newspaper to the TV unit, she gestured to the fabric-upholstered chair in the corner.

"No, please, you sit," Whyte said.

She did so, on the corner of her unmade bed. "Is this important, you seem… alert."

Whyte stood so still and looked at her so intensely that she wondered at his state of mind. His suit was as immaculate as ever, but something about him wasn't as composed as usual, and his hair was mussed when usually every lock was in place.

"It won't do."

"What?" she asked. "What's the matter?"

"I want to apologize to you," Whyte said.

"Apologize for what?"

"Things haven't run smoothly, but I'm preoccupied with you."

"Preoccupied?"

"I would have come to you yesterday. I wanted to come. I was worried about alarming you."

Maybe it was sleep deprivation, or the melee of

thoughts distracting her, but it only then struck her they were alone. Something she'd told Rushe wouldn't happen. It might be the middle of the day, and they might be in a busy hotel, but alone was alone. That's what Rushe would tell her.

He'd remind her to have her guard up too, which she hadn't when she answered the door. A whisper inside her thought it might be, or maybe hoped it would be, Rushe. But Whyte shouldn't have been a complete surprise.

"Alarming me?" Her throat parched. "Why would you—"

"You told me something personal," he said. Coming to seat himself at her side, he snatched her hand. "It can't have been easy to admit your sexual naïveté. I have to know why?"

"Why what?"

"Why did you tell me?"

"I wanted to be honest."

"Is it possible… you told me because you sensed that I was… there was something significant between us?"

She hadn't had much time to sense anything by that point in their relationship. But when Whyte's hand loosened from hers and spread against the fabric of her robe on her thigh, she tensed.

"I won't hurt you," he said.

"What does that mean?"

"You have to be curious. Are you curious?"

"About what?" she asked, uncomfortable with the way he leaned closer.

"Or is it true?" Whyte probed. "Are you pure as you claim?"

"You question my honesty?" she asked, alarm bells ringing louder.

Rushe's name thumped from her head to her

heart.

"I don't think Rosa believes it," he said, casting his eyes downward as his hand slipped under her robe.

"No!" she said, trying to force his hand away and get up, but he held her in place.

"I won't hurt you," he huffed and launched himself at her, flattening her out on the bed, fumbling to loosen the robe.

She kicked out and grabbed at his hands to prevent him gaining access to her body. A searing pain in her jaw made her yelp, but she kept kicking when his mouth slobbered on her neck.

"No!" she yelled out.

Bringing up her knee, she made solid contact with his groin, presenting an opportunity to roll his body one way as she went the other.

Whyte grabbed out for her hair and caught the ends dragging a clump of strands loose. It felt like needles were piercing her skull, but on reaching the floor she pounced back to her feet and went straight for the door.

"I'm sorry!"

She spun around, her hand locking around the door handle at her back. Whyte was coming toward her; she opened the door an inch.

"I'll scream," she said. "I'll run. If you think for one second that I won't fight you…"

"I'm sorry," he said again.

When his hand moved toward her face, she recoiled. "No," she said, looking him square in the eye. "I am not afraid of you."

"I would never want you to be. I apologize, I shouldn't have… that was inappropriate."

As apologies went, Whyte sounded sincere enough, but she didn't believe a second of it. He was sorry because she fought, because she got away, because he didn't get what he wanted from her.

"You're going to walk out of here now, and I don't want to see you again."

The apologetic sincerity vanished. "This is about Rushe?"

"Rushe," she said, thrown for a loop. "What does he have to do with you attacking me?"

"I saw the way he looked at you. I saw arousal in you too. There was energy between you."

"You're jealous of him for catching me when I fell? Nothing happened between Rushe and me that night. He was a perfect gentleman."

Whyte studied her. "He entices you."

"You should go," she said, not interested in having a discussion.

She opened the door fully and stood against it, signaling that she was finished with the exchange. "I should like the chance to make amends for—"

"No," she said, and looked him in the eye again. "I no longer wish to see you socially."

The line was amiable. In fact, she had used it in the past with men she dated while living under her family's rules. Despite Whyte's attack, she was polite but didn't dither on her resolute tone.

"I should point out that you live and work—"

"I would go homeless and penniless before I would give in to a man like you. Believe that you are the center of your universe if you must, but you are not now, nor will you ever be, the center of mine."

Whyte heard her words, but he didn't react. He walked straight past her and out into the hall. She closed the door and locked it. Returning to the body of the room, she leaned over the television to check her reflection, tipping her head to examine the blood under her jaw. He'd bitten her. Asshole.

His actions were frantic. Why? Was it something

to do with what Rushe told her? Was it possible Whyte had been stimulated watching her interact with Rushe? Had he let that build up over the last day and a half until that arousal burst out of him?

She flopped away from the mirror to sit on the stool beside the unit, and her attention landed on the newspaper. She didn't read newspapers, she got news on the internet like most people these days. Her certainty she hadn't ordered it was absolute; she hadn't ordered anything.

On the chance it had been delivered to her room by mistake, she flicked through the pages, trying to find a name or room number. A smudge of blue ink caught her eye, and she fumbled through to find it again. When she did…

The newspaper hadn't been left in error, it was meant for her.

Scrawled down the outer margin was a note, "Rich Room @ seven thirty," and it was signed, "Jimmy J."

Either she was about to meet Rushe's alter ego, or someone knew more than she did. The handwriting wasn't Rushe's, she knew that for sure, it left her far too curious not to show up and find out what the author of the note had to say.

TWENTY-NINE

THE RICH ROOM was on the opposite side of town. At that time of the evening, the nightclub section wasn't open yet, it was just a bar.

She arrived and looked around the shadowy, windowless space. Only two booths were occupied. One by a party of four, clearly students, all laughing at one member of the group trying to chug a beer.

The other booth contained only one man. Because he sat angled away from her, she couldn't see his face. The proximity of the students gave her the courage to close the gap between them.

When she got closer, the man turned. Yeah, she was in the right place. "I know you," she said, sliding into the booth opposite him.

"You got my message."

"Obviously," she said. "What do you want? Why didn't you just knock on my door? Are you Eric or Scott?"

"Eric," he said.

He might be sitting down, but the man with the

sandy brown hair was built broad and thick, with a physique that would dwarf many men.

"You've been watching me."

"Rushe told me to," he said. "We've cleared out your apartment, stripped it bare."

"I don't care about the apartment. Why did you want to meet like this?"

She spread her hands on the table, observing his hunched shoulders and the bottle of beer on the cardboard coaster in front of him.

"What happened to your face?" On her descent to the seat, he must have noticed the Whyte-inflicted wound on her jaw that she'd tried to conceal with make-up.

"None of your business. Why am I here?"

"Rushe wants you out," Eric said.

"Does he? Out of where?"

"The country I'd guess, but he'll probably settle for off the job."

"I'm not walking away," she said, and began to slide out of the booth.

"You been here before?" he asked, a blaze of awareness in his gaze. "To the Rich Room?"

Flick sighed. "No."

"Me either. You know any of the staff?"

"One of the girls who used to work at the Lounge works here, Rosa told me."

"Yeah, she told me that too," Eric said. "I showed some interest in Nancy on her first night, so when she stopped showing up, I went in and asked."

"So? You came here and found her, happily ever after."

"No one here's ever heard of her."

It took her a second but... what did that mean? Why would he tell her that? Why was it significant? Most importantly, what had actually happened to Nancy?

"Did you read the newspaper?" Eric asked.

She shook her head. "No, I didn't, it's out of date. I thought its purpose was the message."

"Have you got it?"

She'd stuffed the newspaper in the front of her library bag, which currently hung across her body. Eric would have seen it sticking out. She obliged without protest and handed it to him. He opened it to the page of his note, then folded the paper front to back and then in half.

He pointed at the page. "Do you know her?"

She looked down at the small picture in the article at the bottom of the page.

"No, why would I…" Denial lodged in her throat. "Yes. Wait, yes, I do."

Eric nodded and she sat back. The picture was familiar. It showed the refined blonde woman who'd come to talk to Davis that night in the Lounge when Flick first met Whyte.

"They pulled her body out of a dumpster… we don't know where Nancy is."

"You're saying that these women are missing?"

"I'm saying that she," Eric said, stabbing his finger toward the picture, "is dead. Nancy is missing."

"You think that those crimes have something to do with Whyte? With Galante or Davis? The casino?"

"That's what we've been trying to figure out."

"But we were looking for Lisa. Someone has to tell her about this, and—"

"No one has seen her since Monday, far as we can tell Rushe is the last to have seen her… alive at least."

"Do you think Rushe has something to do with this?"

"No," Eric said. "We've been trying to get something on these guys for months."

"Nancy is missing. Lisa is missing. This other

woman is dead, and you've suspected something grievous for months…? You weren't going after Lisa, were you? She wasn't the job you wanted Rushe for."

"No."

"That night you came to the apartment," she said. "You were trying to get Rushe to do something, but he wouldn't do it."

"No, he wouldn't."

"Michael Lewis, he was genuine, looking for his sister?"

"Yeah," Eric said. "He had a relationship with Rosa, an obsession. He started stalking her, but security kept kicking his ass every time he showed up. So he paid his little sister to lie about her age and get a job so he could get information on Rosa."

"Then she started her relationship with Whyte, then Joey. But Michael…"

"Lisa likes the life," Eric said. "It was easy for them to convince her that Michael is crazy, 'cause he is."

"When you found out Michael was looking for his sister, you what? Convinced him that you would get Lisa back? That Rushe would get Lisa back?"

"Yeah. He didn't tell us about Rosa straight off," Eric said. "We thought he really lost his sister, thought he was in the same position as us. Rushe got to the bottom of that one quick."

"Position? You think there's something else going on."

"We know there's something else going on," Eric said. "We've known it since Scott's girl was hanged in that hotel."

"She was… she left him."

"No, she didn't," Eric said with a shake of his head. He clasped his hands on the table and leaned forward. "Rushe works alone, and we've always respected that. Sometimes he's helped us out. Susan went in the same way Lisa did."

"Susan is Scott's girl?"

"Was, yeah. She started working in the Lounge, Whyte sucked her in, and she went for it… She left Scott, gave up everything, but Scott fought for her, he wanted her back. We tried to get in touch with Rushe, but he was working another job, trying to find some woman who had a dumb cop boyfriend." Jansen, Flick thought, Eric was talking about the job Rushe was doing when they met. "Rushe was gonna help, but… Things got complicated, they got messy fast, and Susan died."

"You think if Rushe had been here that might not have happened? Does Scott blame him?"

"I don't know," Eric said, sitting back again. "I think Scott blames everyone, and he wants blood."

"You're not a cop?"

"No," Eric said on half a laugh. "Rushe is the good guy here, believe it or not. Scott can't go near the place. They know his face, Whyte and the others. We needed someone to get close, to find out what was going on, to decide the best way to hit back."

"Retaliation," she said. "You're out for vengeance."

"Yeah, but Galante, Davis, and Whyte are mixed up with the King Club. If those guys know what's going on, they'll protect their members."

"And if they don't?"

"Then those three men could have signed their own death warrants. Way we hear it the Club like to know about everything their members are into. Something is going on there; we have to find out what."

"So you can get your revenge?"

"Yeah, but now that you've walked into it, Rushe is all over the place. He tried to back out… he's never backed out of a job, never since I've known him… You fuck with this, and I don't know what Scott will do."

"Are you threatening me?"

"I'm telling you there are two guys here both fighting for the women they love. Rushe's woman is still alive, and he wants her to stay that way. Scott… he's a man with nothing left to lose."

"Rushe doesn't know you're here, does he?"

Eric shook his head. "I'd like it to stay that way. I don't have a steady girl, but I like my body intact." He managed half a smile, so she reciprocated. "If you don't bow out and walk away now… Rushe can't do what he does without a clear head."

Her breath quivered when she inhaled. Letting her focus fall to the table, she readied herself to make a confession. "If I can't be a part of what Rushe does, a part of his work, then I can't be a part of his life. He is what he does, it's all he has."

"He has you," Eric said. "He told me to set up that apartment, no questions asked. He never told me about you. If he's willing to walk away from the job to protect you, then he's proved you're more important to him than the job."

"What he does is important," she said, raising her head. "These women have gone through terrible things at the hands of vile men. They've lost their lives. They deserve justice."

"I don't know if we have the same idea of justice."

"You want to cause them pain, Whyte and Galante, but revealing the truth of who they are and what they do will make their carefully constructed worlds crumble."

"Do you think that's what Scott wants? A press release?"

She leaned as far across the table as she could. "I'm the closest to this, and the most vulnerable," she said. "If you want to know what these men do to women, if you want to catch them in the act, I'm the best bet you've got."

"What are you gonna do?" he asked. "Get naked with Whyte? Wait for him to bring in Galante or Joey? Then what?"

That wasn't an option from any perspective, but she quickly formed a plan of action on her own. "No."

She shuffled out of the booth.

"Where are you going?" Eric asked with a note of panic.

"No more messing around."

She didn't wait or explain and went straight for the door, out of the club and onto the street. Getting back to the hotel might take an hour in this traffic but she didn't doubt herself for a second of it.

THIRTY

"TAKE ME TO DINNER."

As much as she'd wanted to sprint straight to Rushe on returning to the hotel, she went to her room first, prettied herself up, and then knocked on Rushe's suite door, all civilized like. Getting hold of his room number had been easy when she phoned down to the front desk and spouted her employee credentials.

"What?" he asked, still holding the door in one hand and the frame in the other.

"I want you to take me to dinner," she said more slowly, enunciating each word. "Put a shirt on."

"What the fuck are you—"

She groaned and planted a hand on his chest to push him out of her way. Rushe let himself be moved, and she took the door from his grasp to throw it closed. Following him into the lounge area of his suite, they faced each other, only a foot apart, neither touching the other.

"You're going to take me to dinner. We're going to have a relationship."

"What the fuck have we been doing? If you want one of your pretty boys—"

"You're going to take me to dinner," she said, determined. "We're going downstairs to the restaurant in the lobby now, tonight. You're going to be charming, and I'm going to swoon… there's also a good chance that you'll get laid. It depends how much champagne I drink."

"Kitten, things have gotten serious, Lisa Lewis is—"

"I know… You told me that Whyte likes to watch, that all this centers around sex. I've proved I'm not going to sleep with any man other than you, and you've proved that you're not interested in other women."

"Yeah, but I've spent most of this job in a strip joint."

"You haven't had a single private dance."

"How do you know that?"

"Because I do," she said. "Because you knew exactly where the other thirty-seven men were and didn't even notice the topless women. You love me, Rushe. I know you like to push at me. I know you try to keep distance because you think it gives you perspective. And I also know that when you left me, that very first night, you planned to do this job without me."

"How did you—"

"Are you going to deny it? The deep background, the cover, you wanted me to think we were working together, but you planned to shut me out, didn't you? You've always worked alone, and you didn't plan on me.

"You wanted to take care of all the dirty work while I sat at home waiting for you, safe, secure. In a place danger was unlikely to find me. It was a safe house, wasn't it? A place unconnected to you, a place unconnected to me. The only three people in the world who knew about that apartment were you, me, and Jimmy."

His shoulders remained tight, but his confused expression hardened and then loosened. "How do you know that?"

"Eric set it up."

"He told you? When the fuck did you—"

"No," she said, shaking her head, closing in on him. "My investigative mind is green, I'm not as quick as you, but I'm new to this. I'm learning. I might not know how to scheme or predict the future, but I know you. Every time you've lied to me, you've done it to protect me. "

"When you walked into that lobby with Whyte…"

"You didn't know I was working in the Lounge?"

"No, I thought you were at home," he said. "We only visited the Lounge Monday to Wednesday. When am I gonna learn that you can't do what you're told?"

"You told me to keep poking around," she said. "I thought we were part of a team. But you never intended to change the way you worked. You turned down jobs to be with me. You didn't want me to ask questions, you didn't want either of us to get hurt."

"And that fucking little prick Lewis—"

"This isn't Michael's fault," she said. "He wants his sister back. All of you made him believe, you made me believe, that was the true motive here. You lied to me about Scott's girlfriend. She was only one of the victims, and now we know there are others."

"How do you know all this?"

"That doesn't matter," she said. "You want me to be safe, and I want to be by your side. I want to do this; I want to be your partner. But we have to be equal, Rushe. None of this would've happened if you'd been honest from the start. If I'd known what was going on, I could've been more useful. Alone, I'm vulnerable, and when I'm vulnerable, you're vulnerable."

"I can keep you safe."

"From afar?" she asked and shook her head. "You gave me a choice. You told me if I didn't want to be a part of your life, you would provide me with security and walk away. I didn't choose that. I didn't choose to live in an open prison without you in my life. But that's what you tried to put me in when you left me in that apartment."

"Almost losing you once was enough."

"But you didn't lose me," she said, sliding her hands into his pockets. "You told me if I came with you that you couldn't guarantee I wouldn't be hurt. But I came with you anyway because I love you. So now I'm giving you a choice… you accept that I love you and want to be a part of this, risks and all, and we start working as a team, together, looking out for each other, or…"

"Or?"

"Or we walk away together now. We turn our back on Lisa and all the other women who could benefit from a justice not provided elsewhere. We live selfishly together, resenting the shit out of each other… while having lots of dirty, angry sex."

It took a few seconds, then eventually the slope of his smile appeared, distant, but it was definitely there. "Neither of those options involves us walking away from each other."

"How many times am I going to have to remind you that you can't get rid of me?"

"You've fucked up this whole job," he said, "just like the last one."

"Both times I did that because you hid things from me. From here on in, we work together, side by side. If we'd done that from the beginning and I'd known what was going on, I could've told Whyte I had a boyfriend who enjoyed sexual experimentation. You could've visited me at work. Often. We'd have got inside together."

"Lisa tried it on," Rushe said, setting his hand on top of her head. "On Monday, after her tantrum, when she and Joey were in the X-Lounge, she asked me to join them in bed."

"And?"

"Don't think Joey would've liked it but… I couldn't touch another woman if I wanted to. I couldn't do it with Simone, couldn't do it with Lisa. I don't even give a fuck about the strippers shaking their tits in the X-Lounge."

"I thought fucking the right woman at the right time could convince the right people of anything."

"Looks like you're gonna have to be my sexual cover from now on."

Her lips curled upward. "Does that mean…?"

"I was trying to keep you safe, but you're not a china doll… You're a dirty little whore."

"Your dirty little whore," she said, her own smile stretched when Rushe's formed.

He stroked her hair. "That's right, my dirty little—" His words ceased when his hand met her jaw. Jabbing his thumb in the soft spot beneath he angled her head back. "What happened?"

"I broke up with Whyte."

Rushe tried to push her aside. "He—"

She planted her hands on his torso to stall him. "Whoa, cowboy. It doesn't matter because you're going to be at my side. I think you were right that he was turned on watching us together. He said there was energy between us… that you enticed me."

"Damn right, but if he thinks that he can—"

"It doesn't matter," she persisted. "I ended

things with him. But because he sensed that energy, because he knows it's there, if we start dating… It makes it all the more believable, doesn't it? You said yourself that we met through the group, so we know each other. The cameras would have seen me come up here, if anyone is checking them. Maybe I wanted to apologize for the other night, maybe I'm a timid virgin, tempted by the strong, virile, dangerous type."

He didn't look convinced but was amused. No doubt by her tendency to romanticize again.

"You gonna let me fuck you?"

She tsked and strolled toward the exit. "I thought we might go on a date first, you know, something visual for interested eyes to see."

"I'll fuck you in the lobby."

"No you won't, no one watches you fuck me. You already told me that."

"You want dinner," he said. On a nasal inhale, he rolled his shoulders. "Then I get to fuck you?"

She propped a shoulder on the wall of the entry space and watched Rushe grab the fabric at the back of his neck to tug his tee-shirt off. "It has been a while, hasn't it, Lover?" she said om a sigh, mesmerized by the shape of his body, the ripple of those muscles that were for her pleasure alone.

When he turned toward her, her breath caught in her throat. She hadn't thought it was possible to forget his delectable form, yet at times its perfection still surprised her.

Rushe was coming in her direction but went to the wall opposite hers in the narrow space. Rolling her body until her back was against the wall, the couple stood facing each other.

He shuffled down the wall slightly, until his feet were between hers, his back still against the wall.

"Come here," he said, loosening the buttons of

his jeans.

The smile on her face betrayed her feigned indignation. "Now?"

"This'll be quick."

She shimmied forward, lifting her dress to her hips to give her the room to straddle his thighs. "We're partners now, right?"

"Sure," he said, slipping his fingers under the straps of her dress to pull them down her arms and free her breasts.

"After this, the date will seem sort of redundant."

"You nervous, Virgin?"

While she laughed, she curled her fingers around him and hooked her own underwear aside. His hands skimmed up over her breasts to her jaw and he pulled her mouth to his. This was the kiss she'd craved. Sweet longing and devotion enveloped them in some of their more dire, and most intimate, moments. It hadn't escaped her that the kissing had been missing from these last few weeks. Since the case started. As much as she didn't want to admit it, they had gone back a step. Since he asked for her consent, since he left her to be the man she'd met, before he found his love for her.

Imagining the transition would be seamless had been naive. Of course there were bumps, she just hadn't realized it until after the fact. Rushe tried to do the job he did, in the way he had always done it. Intending to help, she'd dived in, without either of them communicating with the other, and managed to wade in up to her eyeballs before anyone else noticed.

They should have communicated in the beginning. This way of working, this job, would be a change for both of them. Both of them would have to alter their behavior. But they were still learning too, and ultimately the bumps would bring them closer. If they didn't kill each other first.

"Can I fuck you now?" she asked.

Rushe kissed the corner of her mouth. "You go right ahead, fill yourself full."

THIRTY-ONE

"I HEARD A RUMOR once," she said, straightening her wine glass on the restaurant tablecloth.

"Yeah? About what?" Rushe asked.

They'd already eaten, but conversation had been on the sparse side. He sat slumped back in his chair, unimpressed and uninterested in equal measure.

"I heard that you were a man of infinite patience…" she said. "Why have I never seen that side of you?"

"It takes you an hour to get from the shower to the bedroom, they're ten feet apart," he said. "I'm patient every day."

"No, you're not. This is supposed to be a first date, and you haven't looked at me for two minutes together." His eyes flashed from the restaurant entrance to her and then back again. "You hate sitting out in the open like this, don't you?"

The restaurant was the same one Whyte brought her to on their first date. Tonight it was open to the public and teeming with people.

"Is that why we never go out to eat?" she asked.

"You want fancy restaurants and flowers, I'm not your guy."

It was unlike Rushe to get irrationally defensive, but still he kept his scowl on the door. While tapping on the table, he squirmed in his seat.

"What is it?" she asked. "You're supposed to be a man trying to impress me out of my underwear."

"I'll tell them I spiked your drink."

"I don't think being considered a rapist will do anything for your street cred here," she said.

Rushe sat up to dump his forearms on the table. Pushing forward on his elbows, he glowered at her. "You want to know why we don't go out to eat? Why I hate sitting in this place? Why I won't look at you?"

"Yes, actually, I do."

With a snarl, he bit into his own lower lip as he fixated on hers. "Because when I look at you, I wanna fuck you. I wanna watch you strip out of every thread on your body, and then I wanna touch you. I wanna put my hands on your tits and brand you. I want your body to stink of me, and I want every guy who looks at you to know damn well that you're off the market. When we're out here and they're looking at you, I wanna rip out their eyes. You get it, Kitten? I don't play games. I want you naked, all the time, I wanna feast on you any time I damn well please, and I want your pussy open for business every minute of the goddamn day.

"You don't deny me. I know you want it. I know you're thinking about my cock right now. But I can't do a fucking thing about it, 'cause out here they control you... and you belong to me, you're mine. No one stands between us; no one gets between me and my woman.

"Out here it's not real, this is all bullshit. It's real when you're naked, under me, sweating and screaming as I pump your cunt full. My dick should be ramming itself far up inside you, stretching out that snug little pussy any fucking time it pleases, that's what I want, that's real… This is bullshit."

Hadn't she learned her lesson about pushing Rushe for answers? As he jolted back into his seat and returned his glare to the door, she swallowed down her urge to demand action from him there and now.

"Rushe," she whispered. "I want you."

Her voice had activated all on its own. From how his attention crept around to hers, he knew it too. The whole mission could be blown out of the water if they ran upstairs to his suite and started screwing like bunnies. But the pulse between her legs throbbed for action. Her pussy was calling to his cock. Now that he'd articulated the desire, she understood. Being out there, in public, with society, only caused division in their relationship.

They had to be civilized out there. They didn't have to be anything behind closed doors; they had all the time and freedom in the world to express their carnal urges.

Moving her hands from the edge of the table to her face, she stretched her fingers on her cheeks, let them slither down her jaw, and then tipped her head enough that they could float down to her breasts. Gliding them down then up until her fingers curled around her shoulders, she would appear to the rest of the world as a woman composing herself. But Rushe saw his hands on the path hers trekked, and his pupils dilated. He wanted them in the dark, alone, bare, and his mind was overflowing with the ideas he'd inadvertently transferred to hers.

"Please," she exhaled. "Sir."

The single word was enough to get him on his feet. She might play the submissive role in the bedroom, but her lover followed her orders too. When he came to her side of the table, he practically tipped her out of her chair to grab her arm and pull her from the restaurant. Rushe wasn't delicate, and he'd spurn the title of gentleman, but he was a man who knew what he wanted. Right now, that something was her.

"Don't we have to pay the bill?" she asked when he swung her in the direction of the elevators.

"They charge it to our room."

"Our room?" she asked, noting his bassy intonation had returned and his lips weren't moving.

They'd had quick, sloppy sex in his suite right before they came down to dinner. But the thump in her chest matched the huff of his breath. They were in for an all-nighter.

She didn't move fast enough, so he took her arm again and dragged her to the elevator bank, stabbing at the button three times. His gaze flashed to her, and she knew that look so well her body trembled in wanton response. He wanted her naked, he wanted it now. He wanted all of her, laid out and obedient, ready to receive his cock in any way he chose to give it.

"Hey!"

The slap back to reality came in the form of Joey Galante's voice. She gasped at the rude awakening from her stupor. Rushe still had a hold of her, and at the sound of another man, he yanked her closer like it was some kind of primal, caveman response to another hunter sniffing around on his turf.

"Hi," She got the word out in one sharp breath.

"You two getting acquainted, I see," Joey said.

Her body was partially in front of Rushe, and her own primeval impulse was to push back against him, to seek out the object of her desire. But they were on a mission, a case. She had to remember that they were partners on a job right now, which had to be prioritized over their copulation.

"We haven't met," Flick said to the red head on

Joey's arm. "I'm Flick."

"Yeah, this is…" Joey trailed off.

The petite redhead squeaked out a laugh. "I'm Laurie. Joey's taking me to a party."

"Is he?" Flick asked.

"Yeah, we're going over to the casino, we're meeting for poker. You should come with—"

"I don't know if that's a good idea," Flick said. "Evan and I—"

"Yeah," Joey said, losing some of his usual ease. "The guy's a piece of work…."

She might have been gratified by Joey's reaction to whatever he'd heard about her and Whyte, if it wasn't for the fact that Lisa had inexplicably vanished. The young woman's post hadn't remained vacant for long either. This clueless redhead, Laurie, had already filled it. These men all seemed to be part of something sinister.

"Thank you," she said, with no other option but to act mollified.

"Forget about him, come and join the game."

"I suppose we could come over for a while," she said and tipped her attention behind her. "Rushe?"

By all outward appearances, Rushe was the same Rushe he presented to the world. Cool and unmoved but pissed off and stern. Except psychically, she heard him cursing the elevator for not arriving on his first demand for it.

"Whatever," Rushe said.

"Great," Joey said.

Joey led them through a door on the outer edge of the hotel lobby to take them down a sloping walkway that turned on itself to go deeper into the bowels of the building. The happiness in Joey's tone made her wonder if he wanted to stir a reaction in Whyte.

If only there had been more time for her and Rushe to plan their course of action. Rushe's advice would be to remain on guard at all times. But her concern now wasn't for herself, it was for him.

Being cover was more complicated for them because their genuine feelings were involved. This wasn't a ruse, put on to convince the world of something false. On the contrary, what they had was real, and downplaying it was essential. If Rushe got too possessive, or jealous, or defensive, the others might smell something off.

So far, she hadn't explained the specifics of what went on between her and Whyte. Now she wished she had. Ensuring their stories were straight had become urgent. If the set up was the same as before, she as a female would be separated from Rushe, who would be expected to go with the men. They didn't have the time or the space to make sure they sold the same lines.

At the end of the slope was a wide hall. They went through a door, and on entering she realized they'd arrived in the room, dubbed "A," coming at it from the other side this time.

All of the usual suspects were there. In addition, there were a dozen other people. Laurie took Joey's arm and he started to introduce his date around.

Flick remained in Rushe's shadow. "I'm nervous," she whispered.

"Don't hide it," Rushe replied, then hooked her hand into his back jeans pocket.

She stayed with him, at his side, as they moved into the room.

"Rushe!" Galante came over with a beaming smile and a blonde woman half his size, and probably not far off a third of his age. "I tried to get hold of you."

"I was out."

"I didn't know you were seeing each other," Galante said. She couldn't tell if his statement was true. "I'm sorry, I don't remember your name."

Either this guy was really good, or really that uninvolved. "Flick," she said.

"I heard things didn't go well with Whyte this afternoon. He's not usually a bad person. He's just been under a lot of pressure."

"I'm sure he has."

Flick smiled. No amount of pressure could excuse Whyte's actions, but she didn't know what version of events Whyte had relayed.

"I've got to get my date a drink," Rushe said, moving away from Galante.

"Blind's at a thousand," Galante called toward the retreating couple.

Taking her to the bar, Rushe brought her all the way around it, then removed her hand from his pocket and smoothed it onto the bar. "Stay."

THIRTY-TWO

HER LOVE BYPASSED the alcohol as he poured their drinks. He made a good show, but the only thing that made it into their tumblers was the mixer.

"Listen…" he said, leaving their glasses to come up in front of her. "I'm a forward guy. I know what I want, and I take it."

She might remind him they'd met before, but her back was to the room. Only Rushe could see who was close to them, or rather who might be listening.

"Okay."

"When you're on a date with me, you belong to me. I don't know who else is interested, I don't know what shit went on with you and Whyte. But I'm being clear, you don't talk to another man unless I'm at your side, you get me?"

She nodded, and one corner of her mouth curled up. "You're a real brute, aren't you?"

"I'll show you after I separate some of these rich boys from their wads."

Despite the cushion of money in his bank

account, Rushe would never consider himself a "rich boy." Then again, it was all in the attitude, and her love certainly didn't have the attitude of a socialite.

He put her drink in her hand, hooked her other one into his back jeans pocket, and with his own drink in hand led them out from behind the bar. No one was close by. The other men were settling in around two separate poker tables. The number of women had thinned to only a few, and those that remained sat around a third table, further away, without a chip or card in sight.

A private tournament? Was it a regular feature? She wasn't sure. Rushe took her to a spot a few feet from one of the tables, unhooked her hand, and directed her to stand with her spine at the wall.

"You're gonna stay here until I need you," he said. With his back to the others, he warmed her in the shade he provided because his eyes belonged to her love, just for these few secret seconds. "You keep your eyes on me, don't look at anyone else. Don't make a sound, okay?" Familiar with this role, she nodded. "Good 4."

He stroked from the top of her head, down to her jaw, then went to take his seat, at the table in her direct line of sight.

"You've got her trained," Joey heckled. "After one date? You're a pro."

"Start as you mean to go on," Rushe said.

The men jeered and joked as the final preparations for the game were carried out. Rushe didn't look her way once, his order to look only at him had been in response to Whyte's presence. He didn't want her to look at the man who had assaulted her. Knowing the details made no difference to him, he knew her enough to know her thoughts and emotions.

He didn't want her to be hurt or uncomfortable. The words he'd spouted at the bar might have sounded detached or unfamiliar, but they served as a reminder of her role, and of his. They were there together, to help each other. They weren't there to distract one another.

Rushe conveyed the persona of a man who didn't care about anything but himself. A mean guy with a one-track mind, more interested in knocking heads together than using his. He projected a thug because that's what he was. He didn't show the heart beneath the exterior to anyone, even she lost sight of it from time to time.

But she remembered this. Remembered how her love had looked after her in the shack full of rapists and murderers who wanted to get their hands on her. Part of the way he did it, part of the way he ensured her safety, was to ensure that no one doubted his resolve. He made it damn clear to everyone he would do whatever it took to protect what was his, and to remain alpha dog. It was the same thing there.

Maybe the men in this room were richer, and portrayed class, that didn't mean they had it. An alpha was an alpha in whatever room he walked into, whether it was a room full of hounds or kings. Money wasn't why these men feared Rushe, why they resented him. They resented him because he didn't need them. He wasn't impressed and could take on any one of them and win. Somehow, other men knew it. Rushe was superior to them all because none of them impressed him, and he didn't give a damn what they thought of him.

Being so aloof came naturally to her love. While other men craved attention or adoration, Rushe just wanted to be left alone. He was a loner at heart. The only reason he stepped out of his coveted obscurity was to ensure scum like this couldn't take advantage of people who couldn't protect themselves.

Women. Women who couldn't protect themselves. In his primitive, straightforward way, that's what men did. Women weren't to be disrespected, and no one should take control over those unable to defend themselves. It wasn't the role of a man to belittle or humiliate in order to display his masculinity, his machismo, his strength as a man. It was the role of a man to stand up for, to protect, and cherish what was real. That was the proof, the sign of a real man.

After Rushe won a particularly large pot, a break was announced. Several men went to the bar, their women scurrying after them. Rushe slid back in his seat, turning his body slightly toward her.

"Come here," he said.

She put her drink aside to comply. He slung her arm around his neck as he drew her down to sit on one of his thighs, her legs nestled between his.

"How you doing?" he asked her, and she nodded. "Smile for me, Pretty." She let her lips curl, resisting the urge to coil closer.

Her love took care of that himself. His huge hand covered her waist and pulled her body tight into his. He skimmed his palm to her hip and upward until it met the side of her breast.

"You're a tiny, little thing, I'm gonna have to be careful with you."

"You don't strike me as the careful type." Galante's voice broke the verve between them.

Rushe didn't seem offended. "If I snap her in two, she won't be slinging drinks in your Lounge no more, will she?"

"Waitresses like her are a dime a dozen," Galante said, twisting a chip between his fingers.

"We go through enough of them," Joey said, returning to his seat.

Whyte was at this table too, silent at this table. She didn't seek him out, but on facing the rest of the group, she wasn't surprised to see Whyte watching her.

"You certainly do," Galante said to his son.

"Didn't get that one in the Lounge," Joey said, nodding his head backward, but he didn't bother to turn to Laurie.

"Where's Lisa?" Flick asked.

All the bodies at the table altered posture.

"Took off," Joey said.

"Better for it," Galante said. "That girl couldn't keep her mouth shut."

"Or her legs," Joey replied.

"She cheated on you?" Flick asked, with a sympathy that she hoped came off as genuine. "That's terrible."

"You get through a good number of men yourself."

The focus of the table moved from her and Rushe at one end to Whyte at the other.

"I don't think—"

"Hush," Rushe said, cutting off her words. But he wasn't looking at her, he was glaring at Whyte. "This is my girl tonight, so if you have a problem you take it up with me."

"She was my girl this morning," Whyte said.

"Way I hear it she wasn't your girl at all."

"She sell you that virginity line too?"

This was news of interest to the table, but she didn't have time to blush. "You want to get personal?" Rushe asked Whyte.

She didn't want Rushe to fight. It could get a little too real if he did.

Luckily, Galante stepped in to keep the peace. "You both have an interest in the girl, but give Flick her modesty, and let the cards talk for us."

"Whatever," Rushe said, still scowling at Whyte.

"Perhaps I should go," Flick said.

"Yes," Galante said. "That's a good idea, let's dismiss the women."

None of the other men objected.

"I'll take you to your room," Rushe said, standing up, boosting her feet.

"Hiatus, fifteen minutes," Galante said, and the men summoned their women.

Flick had things to say, questions to ask, but Rushe took her from the room so quickly that she was jogging by the time they got to the hotel elevator.

This time it came on the first call, and Rushe bundled her into it.

"Rushe—"

"In a minute."

Reasoning with Rushe was tough at the best of times, so she stayed silent.

As he dragged her down the corridor to her room, he demanded, "Key."

"If they see you coming into my room—"

"Key."

Flick didn't resist and handed it over for Rushe to stuff it in the slot. On the blink of green, he opened the door and shoved her inside.

"Give me the details," he said, the second the door clicked shut.

And she knew exactly what he was referencing. "No."

"I didn't ask you a question. Give me—"

"Why?" she asked. "If you go back downstairs angry, you'll be the one screwing up the job."

Standing up to Rushe didn't scare her. Not for herself. Not even when he barreled toward her, swept her up off her feet, and kept going until he slammed them against the opposite wall.

"Calm, Lover," she soothed, sliding her hands from his chest to his face. "Calm."

"Did he kiss you? Touch you?"

She let her head move side to side. "I fought him.

No kissing, no groping, I fought and ran."

"Good girl," he growled, baring his teeth. "I'll hurt him. I swear to you, Kitten—"

"When the time is right. We find out the truth first… You can't come to me tonight. But take me to dinner tomorrow, and on Sunday too. They have to see us together. Remember, Lover, you cannot make enemies down there. Galante wants your money, but we need to know what they do with women. You have to talk about me, about sex. They have to think you're willing to share me."

He growled again, seizing her hips. Mounting them higher, he anchored his weight to hers.

"Think," she said, stroking her hands up and down. "You turn me on, Rushe. I trust you, I love you. Lover, I—"

Stealing her mouth, he let actions speak instead of words. Strangling her arms around his neck, she tangled her tongue with his. She didn't want to release him, restraint hadn't been their strong suit. Why should they deny themselves? It felt like they'd been doing that for months.

"I want your cock."

Hurtling round, Rushe literally threw her to the bed. On her bounce landing, she tossed her hair out of the way and pushed up to her palms. Rushe was unbuttoning his jeans, bearing down upon her. Shit, she wanted this, but if they started…

She clambered up to her knees. "We can't," she said, guilty that she'd encouraged it. "I'm a virgin, and you have a game to get back to."

"Kitten—"

"I know, I know, but we're here to do a job. Partners, remember?"

"You wanted—"

"I'll always want you, Rushe. Sex isn't time

sensitive for us. I want you when you're not on a stopwatch."

In one stride, he reached the bed and clasped her chin to haul her attention in close. "Twice in one night."

She smiled. "You're regretting the working partnership already, aren't you?"

"Never again," he snarled. "My access to you is restricted by nothing but your wishes."

"Get back to your game, Lover. I'll be yours again when we have nothing but the night ahead of us."

THIRTY-THREE

THE IDEA OF HER Monday evening shift provoked anxiety. Being in her underwear in public was unsettling enough but knowing that she may be expected to dance for strange, lustful men was scarier.

Yet neither of those things were her biggest worry.

Her biggest worry brought her there, to Rushe's suite, only minutes before her shift was due to start.

When the door opened, Rushe was gulping down liquid from a sports bottle. He opened the door wide to let her in without question, or etiquette, as if he expected her arrival.

"Okay, I have two problems," she said, stopping in the center of Rushe's living room. "I know I'm not supposed to be here, and my shift starts in a few minutes, but…"

"But…?" he prompted when she stopped talking.

"I don't think I can do this," she whispered. "My body is supposed to be for you. I know a lot of the dirty talk is for effect. It's there in the moment because it's sexy… But this just feels wrong. I feel dirty and violated, and I haven't even done anything yet." She scanned around, taking in the room. "It's like I'm cheating on you, which is ridiculous because nothing physical is going to happen. There's no way I'd consent to anything, with…"

When her focus came to rest on Rushe, she was surprised to see him smiling.

"Let me see it," he said, casting the bottle aside. "I'm guessing problem number two is my reaction to what you're wearing, if I see the get-up in public."

"Yes," she said.

"Let me see it."

She'd chosen to don the knee-length wool coat again. From there all Rushe could see were the shoes, stockings, hair and make-up, all of which he'd seen before. They were the same as her original uniform.

Forcing her dry lips to part, she curled her fingers around her lapels and opened the coat to reveal the hot pants and Wonderbra.

"All the way off," he said, gobbling her figure with his eyes. Shrugging the coat from her shoulders, it fell to the floor. "Turn around, all the way, three sixty."

She did as told, worried how this usual foreplay would progress because she was due at work.

"Don't turn me on," she said. "I'm freaking out. If you try to shoehorn in sex before my shift, I'll—"

"Relax," he said. "Everything's under control."

"With the job? Yeah, sure. Don't you get other men are going to see me like this? My body, your sexual playground. Other men will—"

"Think about what you're saying, Kitten. Does that sound like something I'd let happen?"

Now that he mentioned it… "Well, no, I guess not. But I got us into this mess! I got the job and dated

Whyte, showed an interest in the Monday night shift, got myself—"

"All of that happened because we weren't working together, you were right about that, and it won't happen again."

"Okay, we've got that clear already, but look at me," she beseeched, holding her hands open and out. "Should I call in sick?"

Her love shook his head. "I've got it under control. Did you really think I'd let you out in public like that?" he asked. "I don't share my woman."

"I don't understand. What should I do?"

Rushe wasn't the type to get frantic, but his composure was unexpected. "Put on the coat and go to work."

"What if someone wants a dance, or tries to touch me, or—"

"It won't get that far," he said. "I have a plan."

"If we're a team now, shouldn't I be party to the specifics?"

"It'll work better if you're surprised," he said.

"You don't think I could act surprised?" she asked. "What if I do the wrong thing and mess up your plan?"

"You won't." He came over and picked up her coat to hang it on her shoulders. "I trust your instinct more than your acting ability."

Which, she supposed, was a compliment in itself.

"Why?" she asked him.

"Because your instinct was to come to me tonight. When things get tough, or you worry, you always come to me."

"What should I do instead?"

"Nothing," he said. "You should come to me. Your instinct is to come to me, that's why I trust it."

"Okay," she said letting him guide her to the

door. "So I go downstairs to work, and you'll take care of everything else?"

"Yeah."

"I'm confused," she said when he opened the door. "Other men are going to see your girls."

"Not on my watch," he said, stroking her hair. "Get."

Confusion joined her in the hallway as he closed the door so abruptly she was propelled the last few inches out.

Rushe didn't share her; she had no doubt about that. But if he thought another man might be thinking about touching what was his, he'd get himself into trouble. Committing murder with that many witnesses wasn't wise.

But, for maybe the first time, she was going to follow her love's instructions. Then again, under the circumstances she had little choice.

Coming from the hotel, she had to traverse the width of the X-Lounge to enter the employees room. Wrapped in her wool coat, she earned herself a few double-takes. With the hair and the stockings and the shoes, the customers would probably think she was otherwise naked beneath the coat. Though it wasn't like she was far away from it.

In the dressing room, she re-applied her lip-gloss from the tube in a drawer and looked at herself in the mirror.

"My appearance will not get Rushe killed or arrested," she murmured to her reflection, then began to unbutton her coat.

She hadn't separated the fabric when the dressing room door opened.

Rosa hurried in. "Flick!"

"What is it?" she asked her flustered boss.

"Joseph wants to see you, Joseph Galante."

Joey's father. "About what?"

Rosa took a deep breath and sighed it out. "You've been seeing that Rushe guy. Whyte's been fuming up and down, but Joseph wants this guy involved."

"Rushe?"

"Yeah, Lisa talked about him too," Rosa said. "Kimberly asked as well. He's hot, but…"

"Rushe has an intensity."

"Yeah, he's dangerous," Rosa agreed. "We need a whole new word for bad boy. He's panty-melting."

Rosa's beaming grin made her laugh. "Yeah, I suppose he is."

"He's taken an interest in you," Rosa said, returning to serious. "Joseph needs him."

"I don't understand what… if it's money Galante needs, why not let Whyte—"

"Money?" Rosa asked. "Rushe tried to buy his way in, but he doesn't have anywhere near the cash needed. Galante and Whyte, Davis, they deal in the millions."

"So why is he here if…"

Rosa moved in close, folding her arms in the process. "Flick, things around here are serious, there's serious shit going on."

"What do you mean?" she asked, playing the innocent.

"You're not stupid, Whyte trusted you enough to bring you down here. You had no problem with the gentleman's club… Why'd you break it off with Whyte?"

"He got fresh, tried to force the issue."

"You told him where to get off?"

"A knee in the 'nads helped."

Flick smiled when she noted Rosa's partially disguised admiration.

"There's something wrong with him, in his head

I mean. He's kind and gentle one minute, then boom he's a different person. Davis is worse though, he's just mean. I don't know why Eleanor puts up with him."

"You've known them all a long time."

"Yeah, unfortunately."

"How long have you known Rushe?" Flick asked despite knowing the answer.

"I guess you could say his reputation precedes him. Rushe did some work for a colleague of Joseph's a couple of years ago. Recently, that colleague introduced Rushe and Joseph."

"You're talking about Joseph Galante Senior, right? Joey's father?"

"Yeah."

"So why the introduction? If Rushe doesn't have the cash to—"

"He has other talents," Rosa said. "Rushe knows how to do things… he has useful skills."

"The dirty work?"

"Yeah, but it's nothing Rushe hasn't done before. The stories of what he's done… Joseph's very rarely impressed."

Rosa seemed awestruck, proud to be discussing the man she was sleeping with. If she needed further confirmation Rosa was still having sex with Galante, the blush in Rosa's cheeks provided it.

"So he wants Rushe working for him," Flick said. "But why does Galante want to see me?"

"He picked you, Rushe picked you."

"What for?"

"What use could Rushe have for a woman like you?" Rosa asked, arching a brow. "He doesn't want you working down here. He wants you up in his suite."

"To service him sexually," she said, understanding why her love had been so nonchalant earlier. "I'm not very experienced in—"

"I think that's why he wants you," Rosa said. "I heard about the virgin thing, I don't give a shit whether it's true or not, but you got Whyte's attention and now you've got Rushe's too. Maybe Rushe wants a rookie, or maybe he wants to piss off Whyte, I don't know. I don't care, and neither does Joseph. Whyte doesn't like how Joseph and Rushe are getting along, but he's a petulant diva at times. No one pays him any attention. Joey didn't either. He's been this way since high school."

The recognition hit her again. The yearbook. "You went to school with them, with Joey and Evan?"

"I dated Joey all through school. I was a couple of years behind him. I thought he was a rock star, a rebel. Now I know that he was a loser, like the rest of them, he just knew how to hide it better. He screwed around with every skirt in the place."

There was still some anger there. After more than a decade continually screwing her ex's father, shouldn't Rosa be over Joey's infidelity by now?

"Whyte?"

"No! He's creepy, he used to sneak around watching Joe and me have sex. He was caught peeping a dozen times. His dad got him therapy and everything."

"Watching?" She gaped in appropriate shock. "That's... I wonder when he grew out of that?"

Rosa's eyes darted up and to the side in a deliberate act of telling without saying. "Galante is waiting to talk to you."

"He thinks he can purchase me?" she asked. "I asked you if I was expected to sleep with anyone—"

"You're seeing Rushe anyway, and he's not like the sleaze balls we get in here with their grubby paws."

"So I should have sex with Rushe to persuade him to work for Galante?"

"He's already working for Galante," Rosa said, to Flick's surprise, though she tried to mask it.

"So why does Galante want to—"

"You're a perk," Rosa said, with a re-emerging smile. "He'll make it worth your while. Trust me, these guys will pay to get what they want. You might not get treated well all the time, but you'll be treated regularly."

"Perks of the work, diamonds, and flowers?"

"Totally, clothes, apartment, whatever you want. It's a compliment that Rushe picked you. You haven't been here long; I guess you make an impression."

Pre-Rushe, she'd never agree to any sort of arrangement like this. Post-Rushe, if anyone else made this suggestion her love would land them in a pine box.

Technically, Rushe was making the suggested arrangement. It gave both of them all the cover they needed.

With a short, shallow breath, she began to button her coat. "Where's Galante?"

ROSA TOOK FLICK up personally. Galante welcomed the women into his white-carpeted suite, with its faux flame open fireplace and black leather furniture. He and Rosa whispered by the door, so Flick gave them their privacy and surveyed the room. The place was modern but functional, practical. There was almost no trace of personality.

"Flick."

At the sound of her name, she turned to find herself alone with Galante. "I'm supposed to be working," she said.

"There's no need for that now," Galante said. "Rosa made you aware of our request?"

"Yes. I have to say that when I got my job at the Lounge, I didn't expect this."

"You've been seeing Rushe. He's made his feelings about you clear to us. We believe it would be a generous gesture on our part—"

"Shouldn't I be having this conversation with Rushe? If he wants things between us to become physical—"

"Presently you're an employee of my casino," Galante said. "Rushe has made it plain that he doesn't want his girlfriend working in that environment."

"You're firing me?"

"You will remain on payroll for the duration of your relationship with Rushe."

"And when he's finished with me?"

"We'll renegotiate," Galante said, making no promises. "You are free to walk out of here now. But we're not responsible for what Rushe will do in that instance."

Was that meant to scare or reassure her? "Then I think I should talk to Rushe."

"I'M A PERK," she said, pushing past him to enter the suite she'd left him in not long ago. "You used me as barter, and what exactly is it that you're doing for Galante?"

"Perks don't talk," Rushe said. "Perks also do as they're told."

The door closed and his arms came around her to unbutton the coat.

"Rosa said you'd make it worthwhile for me with diamonds and flowers."

"All you'll get from me is sex."

"Why don't you get naked," she said, when he took off her coat.

Straight away, he unhooked her bra and tossed it aside. He didn't linger to admire the costume.

"I told you I'd handle it," he said.

In his arms, she turned to unbuckle his belt.

"You do think of everything."

"I'm gonna get my money's worth out of you, Kitten."

"I told you I'd be expensive."

"All mine."

He lifted her up and she coiled her limbs around him. "You really do think of everything."

Taking her toward a door in the corner, he kicked it away to carry her into what she assumed was his bedroom. They had a lot of catching up to do.

THIRTY-FOUR

"GET DRESSED."

On coming out of the restroom, she hadn't expected to see Rushe sitting on the end of the bed they'd just shared, tying his boots. It was the middle of the night. She expected them to be inside, in bed, entwined until well after daybreak.

"Where are we going?"

"Work to do," he said. Finishing with his task, he looked up and took the time to admire her naked figure. "Never gets old."

"I'm so glad to hear it," she said. "Where are we going? I don't have any clothes—"

"Drawers," Rushe said, nodding to the unit in the corner.

Despite not knowing what to expect, she went in the direction he indicated. "You bought me clothes?"

"Brought not bought," he said when she opened the top drawer. "Everything from your room downstairs."

Everything she'd salvaged from the apartment.

"When did you do this?"

"Staff did it when you went down for your shift. I think of everything."

"If the arrangement between me and you, as some random man, was real, I'd be offended."

As it stood, she fumbled for underwear to don.

"If the arrangement was real between you and some random man, you'd have bigger things to worry about."

"Like what?"

"I'd already be dead," he said, abandoning his seat on the bed to come toward her. "At least ten other guys I'd have bribed to look after you in that eventuality would be dead too. Plus, you entered into this arrangement voluntarily. If it was real, that wouldn't happen. So you'd be injured, or drugged, or incapacitated as well."

"In recap," she said, pausing to lean against the dresser when he came into her personal space. "The love of my life is dead. There's an evil someone killing a bunch of other men, and I've been lobotomized…? Yeah, you're right, bigger things to worry about."

"I think of everything," he said, bending to grab her ass and haul her up again.

She ran her fingers into his hair. "Is this work we have to do really important?"

"It's good having you with me, Kitten. I didn't like having you out there alone. It's better I know where you are at all times. I'm taking you with me 'cause you want us to be together, but don't make a nuisance of yourself."

"We're working together now."

"Get dressed," he said.

"You'll have to put me down first," she replied.

Reluctance rang from every fiber of his body, but he did put her down, and then turned his back to walk away. The action wasn't about her modesty, this was about drought. Her love turned his back so he wouldn't have to watch her cover her naked form, in contradiction to his true desire.

Without knowing where they were going, she dressed in jeans and flats, imagining it would be a good idea to be ready for conflict.

"Done," she said, tying her hair back.

"Leave it down," Rushe said, facing her and checking out her figure.

Being short next to her love was nothing new. Having shed the X-Lounge uniform, it was nice to feel more like them again. For three months, they'd had nothing but time together, able to suit themselves. By establishing this cover, they could remain with each other throughout the rest of the mission, come what may.

Just in case she might need it later, she looped the hair band around her wrist. Rushe threaded his fingers through her loose locks and combed downward. The relaxed look on his face, the look of wonder, told her he felt the same way about being with her. Apparently, he'd missed her hair as much as the rest of her body.

"Where are we going?" she asked again, interrupting his moment of reflection.

His fingers fell from her hair to thread between hers for a moment before tucking her hand into his back jeans pocket to lead her out of the room and out of the suite.

"You're going to stay close to me," he said as they traveled down in the elevator. "And you're going to do what you're told, Flick."

"Mm hmm."

Unconvinced by her response, his glare landed on her. "Out there, when we're doing this, you've got to trust me."

"I do trust you," she said. "You're the one who denied trusting me."

"Because of this, Kit. If I tell you to go somewhere, or do something, I have to know that you'll do it. If you don't, then I can't rely on you, and we'll both end up in trouble, or dead."

"You value my life more than your own. I don't disobey you to be spiteful. I do it because I value your life more than mine. One of us has to be looking out for you, and you're too busy looking out for everyone else."

Rushe wasn't pleased, but the elevator doors opened, bringing the conversation to a halt. Still clutching his back pocket, she followed her love to a gray sedan. Opening her door, he slung her inside, then rounded to get in the driver's side.

"Where are we going?"

"We've got two stops to make," Rushe said, obviously still dwelling on what she'd said in the elevator.

A street address wouldn't actually mean anything to her, so when he didn't elaborate, she said nothing else. Brooding extended to every aspect of his life. She recalled their previous escapades in cars and deduced he liked to use his driving time for thinking. Either that or he used it to practice ignoring her.

Recalling a past car journey that hadn't ended with him ignoring her brought a smile to her lips.

Rushe pulled to a stop. "What are you smiling at?"

The back door opened and after someone slid inside, it slammed shut. "What's she doing here?"

She twisted to look over the shoulder of her chair. "Very nice to see you too, Eric," she said. "I am part of the team."

"The team?" Eric said. "There ain't no team."

"You two know each other," Rushe said, merging back into traffic.

"She didn't…" Eric glared at her. "You told him?"

"I didn't tell him anything," she said.

"You did just now," Rushe said into the rearview mirror.

Eric slumped back into the seat. "You drive all the way over here to pick me up just so you could put a bullet in me?"

"Guys punished for intercepting my woman pray for a bullet."

The men who were party to the affair that brought her and Rushe together could testify to her love's dislike of her being approached. Michael Lewis could too.

Being a part of the team meant she would have to earn the respect of those already on it. She and Eric didn't know each other very well. It was important for him to know she shouldn't be messed with.

"I shot a guy," she said to Eric, realizing the moment it came out how lame it sounded.

"Good for you," Eric said, implicitly agreeing with her assessment of the statement.

"She didn't kill him," Rushe said, then lowered his voice. "You don't announce shit like that."

Admitting to breaking the law could be bad. "But you trust him," she said to Rushe.

Eric laughed. "He doesn't trust no one. I don't care how many times he's flown up your skirt, darlin', he doesn't trust no one."

That specific issue was a sore spot at the minute. From her silence, and Rushe's too, Eric should get the unspoken message.

"Where are we going?" she asked, sick of sounding like the grumpy, whiny child on a long car journey with their parents.

"Ten minutes," Rushe responded.

"You going in the back?" Eric asked, poking his head between the seats.

"I don't skulk," Rushe said.

"Yes, you do," Flick said.

"He's scared of the dog," Rushe said by way of explanation.

"I'm not scared of a dog!"

"We went into this place a couple of years ago," Rushe said. "Pit-bull flew at him, took a chunk out of his thigh."

"A few inches over and Gracie wouldn't be around wearing her big, beautiful smile."

"You said you didn't have a woman," Flick said.

"His daughter," Rushe murmured.

"You have a kid?"

"Born after the bite, yeah, so we know everything still works…" Eric said. Had that been a genuine concern after the incident, or a male display of virility to highlight he was good stud material? "She's a smiler."

Such a simple statement changed everything. These men didn't always seem human. Eric might be a new acquaintance, but she already knew he had a weakness. Rushe had infiltrated her mind and changed her way of thinking.

"How old is she?" Flick asked.

"Don't get cute," Rushe said. "We don't give a fuck about Gracie, and you better not be carrying her picture again."

Eric disappeared into the backseat.

"You should carry a picture of me," Flick teased Rushe.

When he switched his focus to her, he took a long look over her body. "Who needs a picture?"

Rushe wasn't the kind of man who would sit staring longingly at a photograph anyway.

"What's the deal with you two?" Eric asked.

"Never known you to have a steady girl."

"Us?" she asked, twisting to look at him again. "Tell me about you two first."

"He shot me," Eric said. "We were the only two to walk out of a bloodbath."

"You didn't walk anywhere," Rushe said.

"Yeah, this bastard dragged me out of there. Place went up in smoke, didn't it? They never found out what happened there, did they?"

Eric might have been appealing for Rushe's input, but her lover was his usual stoic self.

"So you're friends?"

"Your man doesn't have friends."

"He doesn't have girlfriends either."

"Plenty of women," Eric said and paused. "I don't know why I said that. Rushe actually can kill a guy with his thumb, I've seen it."

"If you're done," Rushe said, pulling the car to a stop on a dark road that didn't have another vehicle on it.

She scanned the tall buildings and covered windows, some with light beyond. People lived there. Though there was graffiti in the alley down the block, it was quiet. She didn't see menacing youths hanging around, or any evidence of drug use or prostitution. This was a decent neighborhood.

Her love took her hand, an odd thing to do in the car—tensing, she gasped, but by the time her head came around, Rushe had linked the cuff from the wheel to her wrist.

"You're not coming in, Kitten," he said, "not this place."

Eric laughed and got out, leaving the couple alone.

"You still don't trust me," she said.

"I'll be back in under three minutes."

Rushe would never explain himself to her, but to be a part of the team she would have to encourage an improvement of his communication.

Rushe and Eric met on the sidewalk and didn't waste time talking. They went straight to a door twenty or so yards further down. Neither bothered looking back to her. Rushe wouldn't do anything so telling. So she'd wait... again.

THIRTY-FIVE

THERE WERE FIVE story buildings on each side of the road. She couldn't see a street name or fully see into the alley, just the corner of a dented metal dumpster poked out.

The window directly above that dumpster had a blue plastic daisy on the sill. Random details weren't what counted. She had to learn how to pick out what was important, give the details cohesion, gather the relevant and dismiss everything else.

Honing her skills would have to wait though because Rushe and Eric reappeared and returned to the car. Neither spoke when they got back in. Rushe unlocked the cuff from the wheel, leaving it around her wrist. She used the key he'd left in the cuff to free herself as they roared out of the street. What the hell went on in that building? She wanted to know but knew better than to question her love in front of people.

Not too long later, they dropped off a still silent Eric, and continued their drive back toward the hotel.

"Are you okay?" she asked. Blood on his

knuckles preoccupied her. "Was that work for Galante?"

She got no reply. He drove them back to the Waterside, parked the car, and took her up to his suite, all without uttering a word.

"You have to start talking to me, Rushe, what's going on?"

Snatching her hand, he led her to the couches arranged in the corner. They didn't sit, he took the hem of her top to pull it up over her head. She let him take it off but wasn't going to allow sex to take over again.

Except Rushe didn't try to take things further. He took her hand again and pulled her down to sit facing him on the couch.

"Yes, it was work for Galante, a bookie trading on his turf," he said. "I didn't take you in because fast and mean works best in those situations. You're not mean, Kitten."

So brooding and scary was what he was going for. Her presence would detract from that, she couldn't argue the opposite. Being involved was important, but she couldn't knowingly hinder the job.

Her love did have his strengths.

"I'm okay not being there for the thug stuff; you work better on your own for that. Why did you take Eric?"

"Two are more effective than one," he said.

"Not Scott? What is the deal between them?"

"They work together, partners."

"What do they do?" she asked.

"Fence stolen electronics."

Honesty was good. "What's the plan?"

"Women are disappearing," he said. "It's not only about Susie or Lisa."

"You've known something was wrong from the beginning."

"Yeah, they're involved in something, a sex game

gone wrong, or a compulsion one of them has."

Getting a chance to discuss the details, and compare notes, got her closer to her love and made her feel somehow more important in his life. This conversation proved how his own respect for her, his trust in her, had grown.

"Do they all take part in the murder?" she asked. "Or is it one of them, and the others are covering it up?"

"We don't know," he said.

"Who is involved?"

"Whyte was the first one to see Lisa, and the first to date Susan. Whyte made a move on you first too."

"Rosa said he's unhappy about this, about us."

"Why do you think I wanted you close?" Rushe said.

"She went to school with Whyte and Joey."

"Rosa?"

"I recognized her, but it took me a while to place her in the yearbook," she said. "I was looking through so much information."

"Why is she still hanging around?" Rushe muttered.

The arm he had resting along the back of the couch shifted, and his fingers spread through the ends of her hair.

Drawing her knees up, she curled toward him, relaxing her legs against his thigh. "Joey was her high school boyfriend, her first love, but he messed around on her."

"So she got back at him by screwing around with his dad. What about Whyte?"

"She never slept with him, she thinks he's creepy," she said. "But you were right about his fetish. Whyte used to watch her and Joey having sex, so it goes back a long way." Studying his eyes, she could see how he absorbed the new details. "Whyte's father got him therapy; it must have been a serious concern. Though he has no police record, at least not that I can find."

"Men like Whyte can pay for whatever they want," Rushe said. "If all he wanted to do was watch, he could pay for that."

"If it's not just watching, what—"

"It's the kick of doing something wrong, watching without getting caught by the women. They can't have known he was observing."

"Joey slept with Lisa, Galante did too, except—"

"The men knew," Rushe said. "They must have seduced the women… did Joey come on to you?"

"Yeah," she said. "But it wasn't a serious offer, it was opportunistic. He didn't have intent."

"Lisa must have known."

"Known what?"

"When she blew up at that poker game. She heard Joey was interested in you. It was exactly what happened to her," Rushe said. "She started working in the Lounge, Whyte showed interest, she ended up working in the X-Lounge, then Joey made a move on her. I don't know if she was intimate with Whyte first, I doubt it. Joey tempted Lisa, they had sex and Whyte watched somehow, so he got his rocks off."

"Do you think that's what happened with Susan?"

"I don't know," Rushe said, pushing up off of the couch to pace to the window on the far wall. "I wasn't around then."

"Because you were with me," she said. "Do you feel guilty about that?"

"No."

The reply was abrupt but adamant. Was it a little too quick? "You had no way to know what was happening here."

"I knew enough," Rushe said. "I knew she was in trouble."

He beat himself up about Susan's death. Maybe because of his issue about protecting women, or maybe it was because Scott was an acquaintance and Rushe felt he'd let him down.

"Are you okay?"

"All my life I've…" Rushe stared out past the gauze curtains, and she settled back, giving him time to decide what he wanted to say. "I've always done this. It sort of happened by accident. One job led to the next until eventually this was what I did. I've taken a lot of cases and helped a lot of women, in every walk of life. I've lost a few in the process, but… I didn't know it was like this."

"Like what?" she murmured.

"It was always about fighting against something, solving the problem, pushing back for the women who couldn't push back on their own."

"It's noble."

Rushe spun around. "What those guys did to those women was unfair. I evened the odds, made them fight someone their own size."

"Or bigger," she said.

"I never thought about the…"

"The what?"

"You make me weak."

"I know," she said.

"I never thought about those who lost. The partners and families of the women I helped, of the women I lost. I never considered them."

"You fought back against the evil," she said. "You said it yourself that it's not smart to get too invested. If you care too much and fail, you might never come back from that. Are you thinking about Scott?"

"I'm thinking about me," he said, coming two

strides closer. "What do I do if I lose you?"

The disorder of his thoughts was obvious in his manner, and her love was never muddled.

"You won't lose me," she said.

"You're not gonna leave me, but if something happens to you…"

"You'll go out and make the lives of the men who hurt me a living hell."

She meant the statement to be light-hearted, an attempt to hopefully defuse some of the futile frustration.

"Then what?" he asked, gravely serious. "I still won't have you."

Her love liked to be a few moves ahead of everyone. It was just like him to think beyond the immediate retribution.

"Rushe," she asked, rising to her feet. "Will you make love to me now?"

Appeasing him with words was impossible; he wasn't the type to be appeased. His concerns had occurred to her as well. He would've been toying with them for longer than she had. His habit was to mentally toss things around for a spell before he gave them voice.

Rushe must have sensed her thinking because he relaxed, though the chaos remained in his mind.

"Please," she said, attempting a smile.

"Take off your clothes."

"You first," she said, and his smile reciprocated.

He gathered his shirt at the back of his neck and pulled it off to let it drop. "Your turn."

She had on her jeans but went for the hook of her bra, he loved her breasts. Her bra joined his tee-shirt and she moved forward, narrowing the space between them until it was non-existent.

"You'll never lose me, Rushe," she said, tucking her hands into his pockets. "You don't need a picture;

you don't even need my body. I live here." She placed a hand by his sternum, over his heart. "Am I any less yours when I'm not standing right in front of you?"

"You talk too much."

He bent to pick her up. Ever the gentleman, he went straight for her ass and wrapped her legs around him.

"Couch?" she asked, shaking her hair down her back, pushing her breasts to his chest.

"Won't get that far," he said, and descended to his knees, laying her on the carpet, right there in the middle of the suite.

She lifted her head to kiss him, but he cut it short. He kissed her jaw and her chin while covering her breasts with his hands. Grasping them, he stroked her flesh, and when his mouth found her cleavage, she enjoyed the feel of him against her skin.

Her love wasn't the subtlest of men, and he wasn't often gentle with her. So lying there, she didn't object and let him sample his fill of her. As he salved and suckled her, he loosened her jeans and yanked them to her knees.

"Jeans off."

She kicked away the offending clothing before he lay down over her. The other breast got a quick kiss on his route down to her thighs. Instead of moving onto new pastures, his hand slid down her leg to circle that sensitive spot on her knee. He lowered until he could tickle it with his tongue, then came back up, the height of his body enveloping hers. Lying under him, her arousal pulse hotter, faster, she was wet and ready for him.

"Fuck me, Rushe," she whispered, happy to have his mouth back on hers for these few moments.

"Not tonight, Kitten," he said, tracing his lips back and forth on hers. "You're the best sex I ever had."

She'd almost forgotten the question; her impulsive grin reminded her. "I know that."

"So why did you ask?"

"To show you that I'm better for you in ways that others can't be. I'll be the best business partner you ever had too. The best sexual cover."

"Time to get into character," he said.

One of his fingers probed into her, she sighed out at the joyous intrusion. Another joined the first and withdrew to rub the length of her folds, sliding his fingers in and out of her, catching her clit in the process.

"I want you to come. I want to watch you."

"You see me all the time," she said in a rush of breath, caught in his delicious action. She sensed how slick she was, how she coated his fingers, how sweet a space her pussy was for him to slide into. It wanted his cock embedded deep, but her mind was stuck in the tumultuous ocean of endorphins he created on speeding his pace.

"Talk… God, I love to hear you talk."

"You always tell me I talk garbage," she said and smiled, unwilling and unable to open her eyes and lose the warmth of the protective shell around them.

"You do," he said. On kissing her again, his smile met hers. "It's not the words I like; it's the tone, your voice."

Whyte had said something about her voice in Rushe's company. Was that why he was saying this? Maybe he hadn't considered it until Whyte pointed it out.

"Rushe."

"That's it," he breathed, matching her husky tone. Still their lips rested together. He spoke into her mouth, feeding his words to her. "That's the word I like. Who controls the pleasure?"

"Rushe."

"Who makes you feel like this? Makes you feel

good?"

"Rushe."

"Good girl," he said. "Who's your man?"

"Rushe."

After a pause, his knuckle pressed into her clit, massaging it until she cried out. Although his form shifted, she couldn't move into the sheer indulgence he bestowed because he held her down.

When his hand left her on the brink of gratification, he parted her legs. The tickle of his hair on her thighs betrayed what would come next. He kissed her clit, sucking it in between his lips. she yelped at the plunge into orgasm, but he wasn't done yet.

Probing her entrance with his tongue, he tickled it up one side of her and down the other, bypassing the clit. Again, he tasted her intimately, and on her gratuitous whimper, he flicked her swollen bud. Once and again, working until he got her into another lather. Her feet met his shoulders and slid up until his hair tickled between her toes.

Removing her feet from his head he pressed them into the carpet, his tongue still working her clit. He let his hands glide up her shins and snatched hold of her thighs, pinning her pelvis in place for him to sample her deeper, pushing his tongue into her aching passage.

"Rushe."

The word dissolved on her lips, so she said it again, and again. Saying his name anchored her, all that was in her mind was him, he was the only thing that existed, and they had each other. Every second they had together was precious, and Flick didn't want to forget that for a single heartbeat.

On the cusp of another climax, Rushe's mouth left, and he came up upon her, smudging their mouths, treating her to the taste of herself on his lips. Linking her ankles high on his back, Rushe sheathed himself in her at a gradual, luscious pace, designed to remind them both of what was happening. Getting caught in the moment, the drive for completion, for consummation, often left the process lost. But the process was what mattered.

The orgasm might be the end goal, but that was easy; they'd proved their ability to pleasure the other. But this tender action reminded them that getting here wasn't easy, and they could still lose each other again. They could be ripped apart, and if they were, all they'd have were the memories.

Flick opened her eyes to see Rushe there above her, watching the nuance of her expression. Somehow without saying the words she knew he'd shared her thoughts.

"I love you," she whispered when he slid out and in again, taking his sumptuous time.

His smile was elusive, but he lowered some of his weight to her, rasping the stubble on his jaw into her hair. "I love you."

Flick slipped her hands up his back to take hold of his head and lift it to again meet his eyes. This union was as important as the one of their bodies. For a brief second there they'd almost lost each other, they'd almost forgotten the trust they'd forged. But now they were on the same page again. So bringing his mouth down to hers, Flick delighted in the flavor of them. Keeping their tongues woven, Rushe controlled the pace. Flick brought her hips up to meet every one of his plunges. He kicked it up when she moaned out while coiling her arms around his neck.

Rushe knew her body better than she did, and he knew exactly what he was doing to her. Their bodies had become attuned to what the other needed. Rushe always delivered right on time.

THIRTY-SIX

THE HOTEL CURTAINS let in more light than their once at home meaning she woke earlier. Which worked out pretty well given Rushe was hornier than sin and she was happy to oblige. Okay, so it had been her fault for pleasuring him awake… and she'd been the one who joined him during what turned out to be aborted shower number one. They had a lot of catching up and making up to do.

To entertain her while he went to the gym, after promising faithfully that she would not leave this suite, Rushe gave her his laptop. She worked on delving deeper searching for information that had so far eluded her. Unfortunately, success eluded her too.

Abandoning her work on the laptop, she crawled across the suite floor from where she'd been sitting and grabbed the hotel phone and requested the operator. Reinforcements were needed.

"You on the run?" Liam said, when she got through to him.

"On the run?" she asked. "Why would I be on

the run?”

“There were some guys here asking about you today. Suits. I figured you’d used your covert information-gathering skills for evil.”

“No,” she said. “When was that? When did they come over?”

“This morning.”

“What did you tell them?”

“Nothing,” Liam said. “I didn’t know any of the answers to their questions.”

“Okay, good,” she said.

Another problem to add to the list. In addition to the still unanswered question of who had broken into the apartment. If someone was looking for something, they hadn’t found it during the burglary last Tuesday. Seemed now they’d moved on to questioning Liam at the library.

“What can I do for you?” he asked. “I assume it’s not a social call. You’re still with the big scary boyfriend?”

“Yeah,” she said. “Look, I was wondering, is there any way to… if I wanted to find out about records, criminal records, which might be sealed. Can I do that?”

“You want to look at… why?”

“I can’t say,” she said, squeezing her eyes closed. “If I did, you’d only end up in trouble.”

“I could be in trouble either way,” Liam said. “That kind of hacking isn’t exactly legal.”

Most of her questions to him related to things that weren’t exactly legal, but it was different this time, the stakes were higher.

“It’s important,” she said. “But if you don’t want to help me, I understand.”

“You can’t tell me what it’s about?”

“I’m trying to help people. I’m trying to help women… Have you noticed anything in the newspapers about women turning up dead?"

"No," he said and paused. "But I might have…"

"What?"

"Been keeping an eye on the daily crime logs."

"What about them?" she asked.

That wasn't in the scope of his job description. But their matching inquisitive natures brought them together in the first place.

"Lisa Lewis, you were looking up stuff on that chick, weren't you?"

"What about her?"

She hadn't told Liam anything about the job but uncovering what she'd been researching on a terminal only a few feet from his office wouldn't be difficult for a man with his skills. Suits showing up, asking questions about her, probably prompted him to investigate whatever she'd been researching.

"OD'd, Thursday night," he said. "They found her on Friday, in an alley a few blocks from the college."

Thursday night. Her mouth parched. Whyte hadn't come to her on the Thursday, despite her falling on Rushe in the X-Lounge the previous night. He came to her frantic on the Friday morning, only a few hours after Lisa must've died. Was that the reason for his uncharacteristic behavior?

The sting in her eyes matched that in her nostrils, the tightness of her throat hindered her breathing. Falling back onto her haunches, she focused on the table. Michael Lewis had come to her. She'd made Rushe take the case. Lisa had been Joey's sexual plaything. The woman had accused Flick of trying to steal him. Lisa had love, fear, and passion in her heart, and now she was dead.

"Flick," Liam said. "Flick, are you there?"

"She's dead?"

"Yeah. Whatever it is you're doing, I'd advise you

to stop. You should get the hell away from whatever you're mixed up in. If your boyfriend—"

"He told me to stay away from it, but it was my fault. I got both of us mixed up."

"Then you should both get out of here," Liam said. "This girl is dead and now people are asking questions about you. You're not safe."

"I can't leave now," she said. "It's exactly what they want me to do. If I run scared, more women will die."

"How will you help them if you're the next one dead?"

"Rushe won't let that happen."

"He's the boyfriend?" Liam asked. "He doesn't have his head on straight if he's let you get into this."

Finding her purpose, she shook off the unhelpful despair. "How do I access sealed police records?"

"Flick—"

"Help me or don't," Flick said. "But I don't need you to give me safety advice."

Liam sighed like he was about to tell her to get lost. "Tell me what you need, and I'll find it."

"What? No, I couldn't ask you to… it's not safe."

"I don't need safety advice either," he said. "If you want the information, I'll find it."

She gave Liam the details before they ended the call, then didn't know what to do with herself. Rushe needed to know. Michael needed to know too. His family would be devastated.

As the swamp of reality almost swallowed her down, she recalled what Rushe had said about caring, about getting too close. She crawled back to her computer and kept on going. Grieving wouldn't do anyone any good, the family would have that covered. She needed to do her job.

THIRTY-SEVEN

A COUPLE OF HOURS later, there was a knock on the door. She scrambled away from her notes to answer it, remembering to peek at who it was first. Identifying Liam, she opened the door and snatched his jacket to pull him inside.

"What the—"

"Sorry," she said, patting his jacket back down when the door closed.

Allowing Liam to come there was an easy decision. He'd answered her questions, without pushing for more information. The fact he'd been visited by suits and hadn't revealed what he did know scored him points on the trust scale. The library visit also proved that if anyone had wanted to hurt the engineer, they'd had ample opportunity to do it while he wandered the streets and had failed to do so. She felt safe inviting him into what was now their home. She didn't have Rushe's aversion to asking for help.

"Do you want a drink?" she asked, as they moved into the room.

"I want to know what you're mixed up in," Liam said, marching over to where she'd been working to dump the files he'd brought.

She went to the bar to pour a couple of mineral waters. "I can't tell you."

"Why the hell are you staying here?" Liam asked. "In a hotel? What's wrong with your apartment?"

"It was robbed."

His usual easy manner was a far-flung memory because right then his frown was rigid. "Robbed? I didn't see that on the police logs."

Liam wouldn't have her address, unless he'd looked her up on the library computer, which she supposed was likely.

"I didn't report it to the cops. I got the locks changed. We're moving out of there anyway."

"Which is why you're in a hotel?"

"Sort of," she said, bringing him his drink. "Sit down."

She sat on the couch and picked up his folders.

Liam remained on his feet. "What do you need info on those guys for?"

"Background," she said.

"Joey Galante has a solicitation rap."

"I knew about that," she said. Liam chose to sit in the chair at the top of the table. He shrugged off his jacket and drank from the glass she'd given him. "I need to know what isn't a matter of public record."

"Kids' stuff."

"Whyte?" she asked, lifting her attention to him.

"There's a couple of things on there, but the guy is a saint now. This is his hotel you're sitting in. If you think he's dangerous—"

"I don't think he's dangerous," she said, scanning the papers.

"You should."

She turned toward the sound of Rushe's voice to see him throw the door back into its frame.

"Lover…"

Rushe wore his permanent scowl and did that thing where he seemed to physically grow while he intimidated people. He was always big, but when he was like this, he truly was the immovable object.

"Up," Rushe said, when he reached Liam's chair.

Liam stood up, but his height of five eleven didn't come close to matching Rushe's superior vantage point.

"Am I in your seat?" Liam asked.

"You're in my room, with my woman."

Liam glanced at her. "You weren't kidding about him, were you?"

"You can pee on me later, this is important," she said. "Rushe this is Liam, Liam meet Rushe."

"Bedroom," Rushe commanded, without taking that fixed glare from Liam.

"No," she said. "You do not need to protect me from him. Liam is here to help. He got us information on Whyte from before… he has been in trouble with the law…" Still Rushe glowered. "Look at the information, Rushe, please. If you still want to beat Liam to a bloody pulp later you can… we know where he lives."

"For crissakes, how did you…" Liam started, but Rushe turned and snatched the folder from her, skulking away to take the time to absorb the material she hadn't completely read yet.

Liam sat down again, or rather his legs gave from under him. She sat too giving the computer geek some cover for his anxiety and adrenaline fueled action.

"Is he going to beat me up?" Liam whispered. "You said big and scary, you didn't say…"

"What?" she snapped. "He's not going to beat you up unless you upset me. If you plan to be derogatory about the man I love, that might happen."

"I wasn't going to say anything derogatory, I was going to say intense. He's intense."

"Yeah," she said, half a smile curled her lips as her eyes drifted to her love, standing against the wall, reading. "He is, isn't he?"

"This cop—" Rushe lifted his head but stopped talking when he saw her looking at him. "What?"

"Nothing," she said.

"Why are you looking at me like that?"

"No reason."

"We're working," he chided.

"I wasn't thinking about sex," she said, though being the first one to use the word sort of disproved the claim.

"I feel awkward," Liam said.

She shook her head. "What about the cop?"

"In this report…" Rushe said, glancing back at the page as he moved in toward the back of the couch where she sat. "The cop said they found him in this person's house. That's risky."

"Whyte?" she asked. "Maybe he was robbing the place."

"No," Rushe said, shaking his head and scraping through the pages to find something else. "Joey's got charges for shoplifting, for stealing, they caught him trying to boost a car."

"Kids' stuff," Liam said.

"Right," Rushe agreed, and went back to the original sheet he'd been looking at.

"Joey's father, and the Galante family, had plenty of money," she said. "Why would Joey need to—"

"For fun," Rushe said. "He did it for attention, from his folks, or his peers. I don't give a fuck."

"Why is that report significant?" she asked, noting Rushe was reading it again.

"There are a few other incidents. Whyte creeping around in yards, snooping around in the places teens went to make-out and whatever. He doesn't get involved in the regular kids' stuff. No vandalism, no noise violations, no drunkenness…"

"But we knew he liked…" She trailed off and went back to her original question. "Why is that report significant?"

"Escalation," Liam said, drawing the attention of the couple. "I don't know what you guys are talking about. But a kid caught snooping in yards, or on kids in cars, that's one thing. Getting into a person's house, while they're in it, that's an escalation."

"Right," Rushe said, though it cost him to agree with Liam, but that only widened her smile.

"So he was in the house, and they caught him? What was his excuse?"

"Panty raid dare," Rushe said, closing the folder and tossing it down on the couch beside her. "But it's significant…"

"Because it's an escalation?" Liam asked.

"Because the parents weren't home," Rushe said to her. "The kid called the cops, the cops found Whyte. The kid had an empty house and he'd snuck his girlfriend in. They planned to have the house to themselves."

She opened the folder to seek the report and began to skim read it.

"Surprised they called the cops," Liam said. "The kid would have been afraid to get caught."

"Not afraid enough to confront a burglar, or to explain to his parents why their house was stripped."

"Oh my God," she breathed and looked up at Rushe, his eyebrow relaxed a fraction. "The girl."

"That's right."

"What?" Liam asked.

Rushe locked his eyes on her. For half a beat,

their conversation was psychic. That one piece of information was so crucial, they would have to revisit it together. But with their audience, that wasn't the time. Gathering up the file, she put it back on the table as Rushe strode to the door.

"You've been a great help," she said to Liam, leaving the couch to take his hand and pull him up from his seat.

"You're kicking me out?"

"I thank you so much."

"Flick, you have to think about—"

"You don't need to worry about me," she said.

When they got to the door Rushe opened it, and she went to his side, hooking her hand around him, into his back pocket.

"I am worried," Liam said, though he bristled at Rushe's proximity.

Speaking those words while clearly so nervous was ballsy.

"Rushe has got you covered on that," she said. "Take care."

Rushe closed the door on the words Liam was still trying to say. On the click of the lock, she shifted to go back to the couch but ricocheted when Rushe captured her wrist.

"Other men?" Rushe said. "Where's your guard?"

She knew what he meant, and it wasn't her fidelity. He was worried for her safety, just as she'd told Liam.

"I'm safe," she said. "I needed some help and Liam provided it."

"I don't want you alone with any man for any reason, you hear me?"

"I see Liam at the library regularly, you know that."

"That's public," Rushe said. "This isn't. They're watching the suite; I guarantee it. Now we have to explain what the dork was doing here."

She should have considered that, but news of Lisa's death had crashed into her like the seventh wave.

"They're not going to ask."

"Not outright, but it's suspicious if we don't mention it."

"Lisa's dead," she said, ripping off the Band-Aid. "What?"

"She's dead. They found her in an alley, drug overdose, on Thursday night. The night before Whyte came into my hotel room, and… she's dead, Rushe."

"You're happy with that?" His lips didn't move, but it wasn't a show of intimidation, it was a knowing gesture. She shook her head and appreciated Rushe snatching the back of her neck to haul her body against his. "I knew you would get hurt. I knew this would happen."

"I'm okay," she said. "It was just a surprise. All this time I thought we were going to find her. I thought that everything would be okay."

"Not every story has a happy ending."

"I know that now," she said. "I have to be more like you. I have to toughen up. This is the first person I've… When those women died at the side of the road, I was shocked and sad, but I didn't have time to think."

"That's usually the way it is."

"You were in trouble, I had to help you… when I thought about it at the time, I believed they were better off, free of Victor and his gang. But after… I mean since then, it's been easier not to think about it. I didn't know any of them. I didn't know their stories. But it's not like that with Lisa, she's a real person. Her brother came to me, you took this case because of me, and—"

"Hey," Rushe said, and taking hold of her arms

to separate their bodies, he walked her backwards until she hit the wall. "Lisa would be dead whether we took this case or not."

"You don't know that. No one has seen her since the night she was yelling at me. She was arguing with Joey because of something he said to me. I was the catalyst."

"Until we know what's going on, we don't know that. I was with Lisa that night too, after you were, maybe I was the catalyst."

"Joey was jealous that Lisa wanted to be intimate with you?"

"It doesn't matter," Rushe said. "You didn't pull the trigger, Flick. You didn't kill her."

Fabricated images of Lisa alone in that alley, dead after going through such an ordeal, flashed through her mind. "A drug overdose... do you think that's painless?"

"Depends on the drug," Rushe said, releasing his grip. "What do you want to do now?"

"Davis' woman, they pulled her out of a dumpster too. We have to find out about her connection, and how she died."

"I have her bio, and the police report," Rushe said. "She OD'd too, opiates in her system."

"What's her name?"

"Jeri something, I can't remember."

She had a new appreciation for Rushe's like to keep distance from the subjects. "If Jeri was a drug OD, and Lisa too, then... Nancy is missing still, isn't she?"

"Yeah, but it might be worth going through the Jane Does," he said. "I'll put Eric on it."

"But we can—"

"We don't need to know them intimately," Rushe said, most likely as a further attempt to insulate her emotionally.

"Are they addicted before their deaths?"

"It's possible. Davis and Galante, any of them,

would have the financial means to provide any sort of pleasure."

"It's mostly coke use I've seen in the Lounge, but there's plenty goes on in there I haven't seen. Maybe if I get my job—"

"I don't think so, Kitten," Rushe said. "I put my stamp on you, for every guy to see, to lower your risk. Women keep turning up dead, Flick."

"Is that what you're worried about? Pulling my body out of a dumpster? I'm not going to use drugs. I've never used drugs in my life. I've never even smoked a cigarette."

"We don't know if it's done by choice."

"Choice," she said, considering the alternative. If the women weren't hooked on drugs and the overdoses weren't, as they suspected, accidental, then she would be at risk. "Okay, I'm sticking with you. So what do you want to do next?"

"Dinner."

She wasn't used to two syllable responses. "What?"

Rushe headed toward the bedroom. "I'm taking you to dinner, then there's a party downstairs."

"Oh no, I'm not..." she said, and he paused. "I can't be in the room with these guys. They'll sit there with their cards, drinking their expensive liquor in—"

"I didn't ask you a question. I told you what was happening. Get changed. Wear something..."

A shudder went through his body when he paused, and he cringed, averting his attention. All very un-Rushe like.

She got to his side and took hold of his jeans pocket. "What's the matter?"

"Concealing," he said. "Wear something that covers..." His open hands moved in front of her breasts.

"My décolletage?"

"Yeah, whatever, show as little skin as possible."

"That's not what you were going to say." She smiled. "Is it?"

"No," he admitted. "But I can't tell you to wear something showcasing my girls."

"You told me to put them on show once," she called after him when he disappeared into the bedroom.

"Yeah," Rushe called back. "The dogs can pant from far away."

He'd said that in the midst of sex talk, before they'd declared their love, and realized a real relationship between them was viable.

"I could wear your clothes," she said, wandering into the huge brown and bland bedroom. "They cover me up."

"No, makes me think of sex."

"Does anything make you not think of sex?"

He scanned her figure. "No."

"Why were you going to tell me to dress skimpy?"

"This is about sex."

"So you're going to share me in a sex game?" He slammed a drawer and scowled at her. She held her hands in surrender. "I didn't mean really, I meant that was what you wanted to imply."

"Whyte likes to watch."

"Do you want to make him an offer?" she asked. "I am technically his ex now."

"He's had his share of hookers too."

"He has sex with hookers?"

"He pays hookers to have sex with Joey," Rushe said. "Two and three at a time sometimes."

"I wonder what makes the hookers different."

"We'll find out."

"How?"

"By going to dinner and this party," Rushe said.

"Hurry up, I made a reservation." Her expression must have conveyed her surprise. "I saw a guy do it in a movie."

As usual the crisp line was delivered without nuance, but she laughed. Her love could be hilarious when he wanted to be.

THIRTY-EIGHT

DECIDING, in the end, on a square neck midnight blue satin dress with wide straps that hugged her waist and then flared to her knee, Rushe had appreciated the view of her figure. But he wasn't wild about sharing it.

His mood had soured further by the time they were finished with dinner. Rushe went to the extreme of ordering dessert that neither of them wanted and ordering coffee too. Usually, like over the last few days, when they came to the restaurant, he wanted out as quickly as possible. That night he was stalling.

"You've played poker with these guys before," she said. "What's different tonight?"

"It's not a poker party."

"Then I don't understand what… where is it?"

"The X-Lounge," he said.

Just like that, she understood his hesitation. "They're all going down there? Are you supposed to bring a date?"

"That's what they said."

She couldn't imagine Eleanor there with the

topless dancers. "A date for just tonight, or your wife and long term partner kind of date?"

"I don't know," he said. "But I singled you out."

"You think they're curious as to why you did?"

"I think if I show up with another woman, they'll question my motivation for wanting you."

"Maybe you wanted to strike out at Whyte?" she asked. "Challenge him for dominance?"

"We're not in the Serengeti."

"Sometimes the way you men behave, it feels like it."

"Am I the same as them?" Rushe asked.

"No. You're right, I'm sorry. Okay, let's go to the party."

"Rules," he said, before she could leave the table. "No man touches you. I don't care if he so much as hands you a napkin, you are not to be touched."

"I know that," she said, unsure if this was about them or their cover.

"You stay beside me at all times… I'll watch you piss if I have to." It wouldn't be the first time, she nodded again. "Do not drink anything, not a thing. I don't care how thirsty you get, and I don't care how many times they offer."

"Okay," she said. "You think they might spike my drink?"

"I don't know," Rushe said.

"Which is what makes you uneasy." She was getting better at reading his mind. From the way his jaw worked at grinding his teeth, something else was bothering him. "What?"

With a nasal inhale, he leaned forward. "If I have to touch you…" he growled without moving his lips.

"It's okay," she said, reaching over to slip her hand under his. "I trust you, Lover. You have my consent."

"In front of those guys, I won't—"

"I know you won't," she said, letting her smile spread. "I trust you. Your boundaries are my boundaries. I don't want to have sex in front of them, but I know you don't either, so we're fine. I trust you. If you've got to grab my ass, or touch my boobs, who cares? You would do that anyway. You touch me up all the time in public. You made me come in the movie theatre… twice."

"That's not the same fucking thing."

"I know it's not, because it's still private, and in its own way, it's a secret," she said. "You're reluctant because you don't want these men to think I'm only a sex object to you. But it's our cover, Rushe. They have to think you want me sexually, and not want me sexually like you've already been there a thousand times. We're going to be the only two people who know that you have."

"You are my woman," he snarled.

Rage built up behind his façade, the sentiment was touching. His turmoil romanced her in a way only Rushe could pull off.

"We're going down there together. We'll watch a few half-naked women shake their asses, you make some chauvinist comments, then we'll go upstairs to bed."

"I will not share you or let you dance for them."

"I couldn't even if I wanted to," she said. "But you've made your views on that clear, Rosa told me. I'll do what I'm told, Rushe, because it fits with our cover, and because I trust you. I don't want to be out of your eye line. I'm not interested in chatting it up at the bar or getting drunk. If things get tough, use me as your out." Rushe's head tilted. "Tell them I'm jealous of other women, or insecure about my lack of sexual expertise, or hungry for your cock. You've used that one before."

"Yeah."

"Has the added benefit of being true."

"You sure you want to do this?" Rushe asked her and she nodded. "I can tell them you ran off, get Eric to come and pick you up."

"Are you going to try scaring me off every time a job gets tough?"

"Probably."

"Okay." She smiled at his honesty. "Come on."

Though she'd said the words, it was him who took her from the table. Without losing hold of her hand, he tucked the one closest to him into his back pocket and took her other one across her body to hold it in his. His arms were long, so their joined digits hung in front of her frame. The double connection was unusual, but her love didn't like walking into unknown situations alone. With her at his side, he'd hate it even more.

The elevator journey was short. By the time they got to the X-Lounge door, Rushe had his game face on. She wouldn't distract him and knew her role. They wanted information about what went on with the now dead women. Shouting about it wouldn't get them any answers. Her role was to be Rushe's woman, to let her man work.

Finding her feet with the investigation had been okay at the beginning, at the paper end of things. But when working the Lounge alone, or with Whyte, apprehension always joined her. Now Rushe had her arm, and her back, her confidence soared.

The noise level and setup were the same as when Whyte took her there. The number of men was higher, maybe the number of dancers too. What was struck her first... the men they expected to see were not here.

Where were they? Rushe stayed still scanning the space. Did he know where they were? Clandestine conversation was unfeasible with the noise level, so she just waited, ready to follow Rushe's lead.

Part of her hoped that they would give up and

walk out, plead ignorant with the others if their absence was noted. Except they had to do this. Avoiding it was only putting off the inevitable.

"Hey!"

Rosa came from the other side of the bar and greeted her with a warm hug. For the time being, it seemed, she was part of the club. Being on Rushe's arm definitely helped.

"They're in the private room," Rosa said without further explanation.

The hostess directed them to a narrow corridor in the corner behind a sheer curtain that she'd assumed was for show. A few feet later was a door. Rosa produced a small fob from her cleavage, which she scanned to pop it open.

"Enjoy," Rosa said

She didn't sense genuine amity from Rosa, but the hostess disappeared, leaving Rushe holding the door. Her love didn't look at her, he wouldn't want to lose his mask. He also didn't hold the door for her to enter first as would be traditional. Rushe went in, tucking her hand into his back pocket as he went.

The room was small. In the corner was a podium with a single pole. Another pole stood in the center of the room on another table. Currently, neither were occupied.

Joey sat on one of the couches arranged around the center pole, the same little redhead they'd met before at his side, Laurie. The redhead smiled, her dress had been pulled down, exposing both breasts, yet Laurie seemed unaware of the fact. Maybe she had no inhibitions, maybe she'd done this before, or perhaps she was on drugs.

Still, knowing now how the others had died, maybe she only saw what she wanted to. The power of suggestion could be potent, it was difficult not to jump to conclusions.

"Hey!" Joey said, in his usual jovial tone. "The others will be here soon. Take a seat, make yourselves at home."

Rushe's arm came around her as Joey picked up his drink and downed the rest of its contents. When it was empty of liquid, Joey brushed the condensation from the heavy-based tumbler across one of Laurie's nipples, wringing a giggle from the woman. As Joey ducked to lick up the liquid with his mouth, he moved the glass to the other breast.

Her emerging confidence flagged. Rushe took her to the couch opposite Joey and Laurie's and pulled her into his lap as he sat. Joey had moved on to the ice cubes from the glass. He covered Laurie's breast with the quickly melting water before his hand changed. Still with the ice cube in his grasp, the playboy's hand went under Laurie's skirt.

Joey was too interested in watching Laurie's face when he slipped the ice cube inside her to care about spectators. That was the only thing he could have done because Laurie gasped and Joey laughed, while pulling her legs apart with his now empty hand.

"This what you call a private party?" Rushe bellowed, far louder than he had to, though the bass from the X-Lounge did thump through the walls. "You need an audience, Joey?"

"No!" Joey laughed and abandoned Laurie, though his arm remained around her. "Unless you want me to do your girl, switch it up, whatever you want. There's rubbers under the table, get busy."

"Thanks," Rushe said, tightening his grip, drawing her body in close against his until no atom of space existed between them. "But you said it yourself, this one's mine."

Joey shrugged and went back to Laurie's nipples.

Flick tipped her head back while slipping off her shoes and bringing her feet onto the couch to twist her form into her love's.

"We never considered that we'd have to watch," she said, tucking her head under his chin and curling her arms in close.

"Just close your eyes," Rushe whispered into her hair.

THIRTY-NINE

THE NEXT SECOND, the door opened, and Joey straightened up again. From there they couldn't see it, but only a couple of heartbeats went by before Joseph Galante came into view. Unusually, Rosa was with him, and Whyte too, but the latter was conspicuously alone.

"Everybody's here," Joey exclaimed.

What substances was he using?

"I see that," Galante said, ignoring his son's salivating on the breasts of the doped-up woman at his side. "There's been a development that's got us slightly worried."

"What kind of development?" Rushe asked, the vibration from his chest rumbled against her.

"One I don't think you'll like," Galante said.

Whyte came further into the room and sat on the couch closest to her and Rushe. His proximity was unsettling. Her love must've thought so too because he held her closer. No, maybe he wasn't as concerned about Galante, maybe it was another man. Whyte was watching Joey and Laurie kissing as Joey fondled Laurie's breasts.

"Rushe, perhaps we should talk with you alone."

"You want to leave me alone in here?" she asked aloud.

Maybe it wasn't in character, and maybe it wasn't appropriate, but Joey and Laurie were going at it, while Whyte sat in the chair next to hers, intent in his eyes. Her anxiety wasn't easy to mask.

"I'll stay with you," Rosa said.

Rushe shook his head. "You can talk in front of her, what is it?"

"It would be better if we—"

"Would you like me to leave?" Flick asked.

Rushe's hand clamped onto her thigh. "You stay put. Whatever the fuck is going—"

"It's about her," Galante said, nodding at Flick but looking only at Rushe. "We'd rather not discuss the matter with her present."

"About me," Flick said. Her love let her move enough to sit up straight, though she remained in his lap. "What about me?"

"Don't freak out," Rosa said, shimmering with conceit. "If you haven't done anything wrong, there's nothing to worry about, is there?"

The trouble was the definition of wrong varied between the factions. "Am I on trial? What are you accusing me of?"

"Asking questions," Galante said.

"Oh well, I'm so sorry. Would you like another drink? Oh look, I've done it again."

"Sassy," Rosa said, her gaze trained on Flick. "I knew there was more to you than met the eye. I told you."

Her last three words were for Galante, who held up his hand. "Okay, yes."

"I told you!" Rosa shouted, leaning to the side, clearly trying to rouse Whyte's attention, but it remained elsewhere.

"Rosie, come on," Galante said. His awareness remained on Flick while he spoke over his shoulder. "What do we do now? Joe! Joey!"

With a sputter and a mutter, Joey came up for air and huffed at his father like a teenager. "Dad, give me ten minutes."

"Now," Galante said.

"Fine," Joey said and shoved Laurie off the couch.

The laughing redhead clattered to the floor, all arms and legs. Joey threw her over his shoulder, breasts still out, and went for the door. Rosa grunted in protest but went with Joey, presumably to unlock the door or put the redhead back together.

"You gonna tell me what the fuck is going on?" Rushe asked.

"We think you're being played."

If it wasn't for the terror, she would've smiled. Rushe being played by her was laughable. Rushe being played at all was unlikely. But at least the accusation meant Rushe's position wasn't being questioned. She could handle her own credibility being called into doubt, so long as Rushe was safe. Rushe was used to sitting at the big boys' table. He could control this.

"Played?"

"We want to know what your deal is," Galante said, directing his gaze at Flick. "What's your history, Felicity Hughes?"

They couldn't have linked her to her family. She hadn't used her middle name and they didn't live close to her parents. The Hughes family home was hundreds of miles away. Any search on her wouldn't bring up much given she'd used the false social security number Rushe gave her to use at the library.

In the past, they'd been burned when people

discovered her family's wealth; they didn't want that to happen again. Especially since the last time Rushe had to cover the ransom that her father wouldn't.

Joey and Rosa returned to the room, coming in at Galante's back. With no more to watch, Whyte left his seat and came around to stand with the others.

From what they knew, the only two things this group knew about her were where she lived, and that she had a library membership.

"It was you," Flick said. "You broke into my apartment, you trashed the place."

Rosa smirked. "You think Joseph dirties his hands?"

"Not him specifically," Flick said. "You were the one who ordered it. Why did you do that?"

"We like to know the associations of our employees," Galante said.

"What business is it of yours what I do or where I came from? I came here for a job, to serve drinks."

"But ended up in a relationship."

She glanced at Whyte. "You were checking up on me, because of him?"

Being with Whyte meant they assumed she would die at their hands. Checking that nobody would notice or question her death must be par for the course. Did Scott's reaction to Whyte's relationship with Susan have anything to do with their vigilance?

You had information on the history of our businesses in your apartment."

"I was coming for a job. I wanted to know what I was getting myself into and to be knowledgeable if I was asked anything. Google didn't warn me about this."

"We weren't overly concerned," Galante said.

Thank God she'd had her library bag on her person during the break-in. It contained the more sensitive information and her computer files.

"We socialized together on Monday night," Flick said. "Lisa threw a tantrum and stormed away. Why did you violate my home the following night?"

"We had a conversation," Whyte said. "Galante and I. I told him a relationship between us was likely."

So Flick had been chosen as the next victim, since Lisa's card was marked by that point. Unbeknownst to them at that time, the poor girl had less than three days to live. The burglary was orchestrated for the Tuesday night to ensure Flick could be disappeared without much fuss. By the Wednesday, and her date with Whyte in the X-Lounge, they would've known all they needed to about her.

Then she had fallen over Rushe, riled Whyte, and left early. Screwing up their plans. Lisa died on the Thursday night, setting the ball in motion and bringing them to that moment.

"Investigating the details of your life gave us the chance to ensure Evan was safe from anything… unsavory," Galante said.

That was rich. "You didn't have to trash the place so thoroughly," Flick grumbled.

"A scared girl is a horny girl," Joey said.

With his glimpse of a smile, he confirmed his complicity in these incidents. He didn't seem to take a very active role, other than the seductions, and wasn't quite as daunting as the others in the clique. Still, Joey was determined. From where his focus had been not so long ago, the turnaround was impressive.

"The library too, you were the one who sent those men to question Liam?"

"He wasn't very helpful," Galante said, wearing a bold, practiced smile.

"But why? Evan and I had already broken up," she said.

"Your interest switched to Rushe very quickly,

which intrigued us," Galante said. "We knew then there had to be more going on than it first appeared."

"Why are you all so paranoid?" she asked, taking the chance to turn the tables. "What do you think I know?"

"We know you lied. Your chastity was clearly a fabrication. There was evidence of male companionship at your apartment. We initially assumed the falsehood was meant to entice. Such a startling revelation would tempt men, as it did Evan."

"So you broke into my apartment, assumed I was a liar, but let it go?"

"You wouldn't be the first woman to lie to gain the favor of a man, especially one with means as extensive as Evan's."

"But you no longer believe it's minor?" she asked.

"Not after what happened today," Rosa said.

The group remained intent on her, and she was beginning to feel the pressure of being so closely scrutinized.

"Your visit from the man we questioned concerned us enough to probe further. Now we wonder if your claim of chastity was cover used to guarantee you wouldn't have to get intimate at all."

"You didn't want things to get sexual," Rosa said. "Why would a woman come here, and start dating rich men, but be unwilling to sleep with them?"

"You wanted to close the door on the possibility of sex completely."

"Meaning…?" Flick asked, looking at each individual face. "What?"

"Are you a cop?"

Laughter burst out of her. Talk about déjà vu. Rushe had been accused of the same in the past. With the shoe on her foot, she realized how ridiculous it felt.

"You think I used the virginity cover so I didn't have to sleep with any of you, but I could still get close? Was I supposed to make you feel sorry for me?"

"It makes sense that your focus would shift when Rushe got involved," Galante said. "He, I'm sure, has pertinent associations and access to a vast amount of criminal knowledge, certainly far more than we would."

"Which brings us to the question…" she said. "What have you all been doing wrong that the cops would want to investigate you for in the first place?"

She herself had thought how interested a vice cop would be in monitoring the Lounge. She hadn't for a second considered the possibility it might be an accusation laid at her door.

"We have a close relationship with the police department," Galante said. "We keep them informed of any misdeeds that we witness or have proof of."

"Then," Flick said, feeling somewhat triumphant, "as Rosa said, if you haven't done anything wrong, there's nothing to worry about, is there?"

"We worried when you had another man in Rushe's suite today," Galante said, arching his eyebrow.

"This is about trying to separate me from Rushe? If he believes I've been messing around on him, and he joins your side, what next? He's supposed to do your dirty work for you? What are we talking about? A beating? Rape?"

"You don't seem concerned," Joey said.

"I haven't done anything wrong," Flick replied, reaching to the floor to hook her feet back into her shoes. "You people, on the other hand, obviously have. You talk of police and committing criminal acts."

She stood up with all the indignation required to leave, hopeful that Rushe would follow her lead. But as soon as she had her weight, Galante's group moved in closer, evidently not willing to let her go anywhere. They blocked her forward exit. Rushe's legs were in the way of a backward exit, not that it mattered. If she got around Rushe, she'd still have to double back because the only door was the one out to the X-Lounge, behind the odious group.

FORTY

"YOU CAN'T GO," Rosa said.

"Are you holding me hostage?"

Hostage would be preferable, if the smirk that spread on Whyte's face was anything to go by.

"Crazy fuckers," Rushe muttered, filling her with gratitude when he rose to his feet behind her. "We're out of here."

With a hand on the back of her neck, Rushe began to move forward. Except the crowd didn't budge out of the way.

"Excuse us," Flick said.

"We can't let her go until we know what she knows," Galante said. "She had another man in your suite today."

"I threw him out," Rushe said.

"We saw that."

From what the cameras in the corridor would show, Rushe was the one at the suite entrance, slamming the door on Liam. She wouldn't have been visible.

"Am I not allowed to have a friend?" Flick asked.

She had no idea they'd be interested in something so mundane, or in her life at all for that matter. As far as she could perceive, none of these people had any reason to be monitoring her, and there was no history of this group tracking anyone.

Her role was as a distraction, a plaything meant to entertain a man in their alliance. It wasn't as though she and Liam had been alone in the suite for long enough to get naked.

"Is he the fuck buddy?" Rosa said. "The one you were screwing at your apartment?"

"No," Flick answered.

"A cop?"

"No, he's not. He works in a library, you found him there yourselves."

"He works with information," Galante said. "Perhaps he may be useful for finding out things people don't want known. Was he part of your snooping?"

"I've fucked the bitch, she's nothing but a dumb 'ho," Rushe said. "You telling me she's a criminal mastermind?"

"We've got enemies," Galante said. "She fooled us all."

"I knew there was something off," Rosa said. "That's why I never let her in on the deal."

"The deal?" Flick asked.

"We've heard the rumors and conducted our own investigations," Galante said. "None of our employees have acted inappropriately."

"What rumors?"

"About guys waking up in rooms they never booked with empty pockets," Joey said.

Rosa tsked and hit him in the ribs. Galante and Whyte maintained their focus.

"You think this is about a few empty wallets?" Flick said.

Rosa had alluded to such a thing. Seeing the truth of the people in front of her, it didn't come as a surprise that Rosa was running such a racquet. The hostess had to be the leader. None of the men had the ability to access and charm patrons in the way Rosa would.

Her particular charisma would be required to drug vulnerable men, lure them to their rooms on the promise of sex, and rob them. It was one of the oldest cons in the world.

"If not about that, then let us find out what your motive is," Galante said.

For the first time he glanced backward. Something went unsaid between him and his mistress, and Rosa left.

"We're going too," Rushe said and again he tried to direct her out.

The men remained in their path.

"You're not concerned by this?" Galante asked Rushe. "If she's a cop—"

"If she's a cop, what's she doing riding my cock like a pro?" Rushe said.

"That guy today could be her handler or something," Joey said.

"More like a lovesick puppy," Rushe replied. "Pathetic."

"So if she doesn't want Evan's money, and she's not a cop," Galante said, narrowing his gaze on her with laser precision. "Who are you working for? Davis? Johnson?"

"You think I'm working for one of your competitors?" she asked.

Her impression of Davis was that he was a friend to Galante, that he belonged there. Though, his absence for this intervention was revealing.

"Industrial espionage is not a new thing," Galante said. "You better tell us."

"I don't have to tell you anything," she said, pleased that Rushe's hand remained on her neck. "Unless you plan to kill me, you'll have to let me leave eventually. Sooner is better than later. You've shown your true colors; you're all sick and twisted."

The group tightened their ranks, obstructing her when she tried to walk. She regretted her choice of words. By not letting her go, they confirmed their intentions.

"No one's killing anyone," Rushe said. "What the fuck—"

"We can handle this, Rushe. If you want to walk out the door, you may. I didn't have you pegged as the weak stomach type."

"You want to murder an innocent woman."

"We don't know if she's innocent," Galante said.

"You'd prefer to murder her than give her the benefit of the doubt?" Rushe asked. "No, we don't want that heat on us."

Rushe drew her back, placing his body between her and Galante at the head of the knot barricading their escape route.

"Rushe," she said, resting a hand on his back, but her love didn't flinch.

Her own fingers shook even with his mass to steady them on. Circumstances had changed in a heartbeat, something she should get used to. Not that she would have the time if Galante got his way.

"She was never walking away from this," Galante said. "You're a part of our group now. As soon as you chose her, you sealed her fate."

No, she didn't want Rushe thinking any of this was his fault.

"I chose her for sex."

"We visited her colleague in the library today to verify her identity for your security, Rushe. Despite her dealings with Evan, we allowed you to stake your claim on the girl. It was important to us to show you that respect."

"You could've come to me."

"That was our intention tonight. We believed we were anticipating your concerns… it may have been ahead of schedule, but Flick gave us the chance to bring you to the inside of our group."

No doubt Whyte still wanted to watch her having sex, and Joey probably wanted to indulge with her too. If Rushe took his place as a part of their sex games, they would all get to play with her, as they had believed they would through her relationship with Whyte. They weren't easily thwarted.

In picking her out, affirming his interest, Rushe gave this gang a vessel. She was a tool they could use to test him to see if he would be open to playing along.

"Doesn't seem new members of your group last long," Rushe said.

"You are of the male variety, women tend to be more fickle," Galante said.

Joey snickered while Whyte's sinister enjoyment only increased.

"I noticed. Lisa's gone, Jeri too," Rushe said. Jeri was the woman Flick had seen talking to Davis in the club. The woman pulled from the dumpster in the newspaper article Eric showed her. Rushe must have encountered Jeri previous to her knowledge of his involvement. "You've lost at least one server since I've been around…"

"High turnaround," Galante said without any good humor.

"Been doing some investigating of your own?" Joey asked.

"Maybe," Rushe said. "If you knew my history, you'd know that's not unusual. They pulled Jeri out a dumpster, I saw that in the paper. Nancy never made it to the Rich Room."

Why was he being so open? Why was he revealing details of their investigation?

"You know a lot about it," Galante said.

Goddamnit, her lover's revelations were his way of diverting the focus of suspicion.

"Stop talking, all of you," Flick said. "I just want to get out of here."

"I don't give a fuck what you did to those bitches," Rushe said. "But you're not touching my woman. No one touches what's mine."

Rushe's fist came up so fast that Flick never saw it. Blood exploded on Whyte's face, and he howled, doubling his body as he clutched for his shattered nose. Somehow, she knew Rushe had been eager for a chance to injure the man who'd wounded her. The snarling gratification that spread on Rushe's expression confirmed it.

"Got that off your chest?"

Everyone swung around to see Rosa enter from the other side of the room. The narrow entrance she'd used was hidden, an optical illusion of the walls behind the corner podium. The hostess had a package tucked under one arm. In her other hand was a gun trained on them.

Rushe growled and her hand found his pocket. They were surrounded.

FORTY-ONE

"OVER HERE!" Rosa demanded. Both she and Rushe began to move, but Rosa spoke again. "Not you, just her."

She stepped away, but Rushe caught her hand, causing her to look back. Though his mask remained in place, a turmoil of rage churned behind it. All she could offer was a small smile. Her love squeezed her fingers, neither had a choice in their physical separation.

"You think about hitting anyone else, and I'll shoot the sexy girl you're so committed to rescuing."

Rushe remained in the middle of the room. Flick went to the corner podium. Averse to the idea of anyone else sneaking up on her, she kept her back to the wall.

"What you got?" Galante asked.

"You go over there," Rosa ordered Rushe, nodding to the opposite wall, near the door to the X-Lounge. When Rushe complied, Rosa tossed the bundle to the table. Joey and Galante went to look at it. Whyte was still concerned with his nosebleed.

"What is it?" Galante asked.

"Plenty of sex going on up there," Rosa said. "No rubbers, suggests a commitment."

Rosa had been snooping in their bedroom? She shouldn't be surprised, yet outrage was impossible to quash.

Galante unwrapped the fabric from the bundle to reveal two things: the folder Liam had brought to her that day, containing the information on the sealed records and an already filled syringe. Whatever drug was in it was ready to go. Rosa had rummaged through their room and prepared Flick's lethal injection.

Galante and Joey read through the file. When their attention rose, it didn't land on her, Rushe got the honor.

"You knew about this?" Galante asked. Rushe remained silent. "Knowing your enemy?"

"If I can find it, someone else can," Rushe said.

"Protecting a friend, are you?" Galante said, though he evidently didn't know what to make of the unexpected revelation.

"I don't give a fuck what you do," Rushe said. "I like to know what I'm dealing with. He's a sick fuck." Rushe nodded toward Whyte, who took enough notice to snatch for the file.

"You can be bought," Galante said to Rushe, relaxing back on the couch. "You can't go to the law; you don't work under the protection of it. You don't testify; you never have."

"Right," Rushe said.

"We don't know enough about you," Galante said, his attention returning to her.

While going to take position at the back of the couch, behind Galante, Rosa kept the gun trained on her. The hostess slid her other hand onto Galante's shoulder, he took hold of it to kiss her palm.

"I know, Rosie," Galante said, still kissing her

hand.

Flick hadn't seen him so dedicated, or affectionate, with anyone. Galante wasn't warm toward his child, she'd never seen him so much as talk to a date. But now he was enraptured.

"Let Rosie have her fun," Joey said, sitting back to address his father, who rubbed his face on the back of Rosie's hand as he spoke. "We were gonna off her anyway… gives me more time to play with Laurie."

Laurie must have been the next tagged victim. This new development altered their plans, and their new intention was for Flick to be the next body discovered in an alley. Would she be another woman with an overdose reported in the newspaper tomorrow?

"You want to drug me," Flick said.

Her eyes flared when they landed on the syringe on the table. She'd never taken drugs and didn't know what substance was in that vial. Would it hurt? These thoughts darted through her head at the same time she looked to the scowling Rushe.

Rosa grinned like a smug, spoiled child while Galante caressed her hand with his mouth. Joey watched the couple with an indistinct expression. Whyte was ignoring his bleeding nose to read the horrific details of his past. Ones he'd tried to hide and deny for all these years, and that were now out there, in the public domain.

"Is this what you did to Lisa?" Flick asked, trying to swallow away her own fear.

"Lisa was asking for it," Rosa snapped. "That girl thought she could be part of our family."

"Your family," Flick said, three men, one woman. "You don't want there to be other women, do you? It's you. You're the one who doesn't want these men forming attachments. You thought you could bring Rushe in, is that it?"

"Rushe would have joined us anyway, but if you

stayed with Whyte then moved onto Joey like every other…" Rosa forced herself to stop and take a breath. "Once he has joined us in this, then he will be part of our family."

"And you'll have another man at your beck and call," Flick said. "You've got father and son, what about Whyte? Why is he here?"

"You don't know what you're talking about," Whyte barked. "Someone shut her up, do it already."

Whyte slapped the folder closed but kept it nearest him on the table. No doubt that information would be burned before the night was over.

Galante took the gun from Rosa, who rounded the table to retrieve the syringe.

"I'm not going to tell anyone anything," Flick said. "You can let me walk out of here, and I promise I'll never—"

"Don't need your promise," Rosa said. "One little prick, and our problem will go away."

"This is what you do when the women get too close, or when the men are bored with them," Flick said. "You drug them and dump their bodies, that's why they show up dead in the alleys."

Flick was the problem that Rosa alluded to, and this group wanted to erase her. Once they injected her, she was as good as dead. Her options were gone. Rushe was stuck between the devil and the deep blue sea. If he tried to rush any of them, Galante would shoot, and she would be dead anyway.

Whyte got to his feet as Rosa inched closer, Joey stood too, and they spread out, eager to witness what was about to happen. This wasn't a game, it wasn't prolonged; someone had the fetish, someone was out of control. Murder was the ultimate control, the power over life and death, and someone enjoyed exercising that power.

Rosa had these men behind her; Rosa held the needle. Flick hadn't considered the possibility, until now. It wasn't the men doing the deed. The men were covering it up for Rosa's sake.

"Please, you don't have to do this," Flick said, as they closed in around her.

Rushe could walk out of there right now if he wanted to. No one was watching him, but with security features on the doors, he'd never be able to come back in, so she would be left alone.

The distance between Rushe and the group bent on violating her was too great for him to be physically effective. He'd never get all the way across the space to her position without the others noticing, and right now there was a gun and a syringe headed in her direction. They'd kill her before he got within arm's reach.

"Give it to me."

All the faces in the room turned to Rushe.

"Why would we do that?" Galante asked.

"How do you think I'm going to react when you kill my woman? There's only one threat to any of you in this room, and it's not Flick."

Rushe's question gave the cult something new to consider. As they did, the cruel ice of panic spread in her chest. The deep fingers of dread reached her throat. Her sinuses didn't get the chance to burn, tears were already streaming from her ducts.

"No," she said and tried to move toward her lover but the bodies between them prevented her. "No, I won't let you do it."

"Rosa, you want the women to die to maintain order in your pack, to maintain superiority," Rushe said. "Flick never threatened that, she left Whyte, and she didn't touch Joey or Galante."

The hostess relaxed in a way that suggested she was considering Rushe's words. "But she knows now,"

Rosa said. "She knows what we have done."

"No one will believe her, what's she gonna do?" Rushe asked. "She has no connections, no money, nothing. You checked her out for yourself. You didn't turn up anything threatening."

She'd never asked Rushe of the history connected to that social security number. Knowing him as she did, it wouldn't surprise her to learn there was a false credit history, or even a faux family tree, traceable through it. He'd go to any lengths to ensure her safety; he was nothing if not thorough.

"You can be a part of our family," Rosa said with an emerging seductive intonation.

"You want to have control over these men. They keep your secret proving their loyalty to you, but I won't be loyal to you. I will not be a part of your family, I'll destroy it."

"No," Galante said. "We can still work together."

"Work?" Rushe growled, lowering his chin. The storm clouds around him echoed with thunder. "If you hurt her, I swear I'll make every single one of you pay. You'll die slow and it'll hurt. I promise you."

"No," Flick said again.

Galante stepped up. "I know your reputation," he said to Rushe. "I know how dangerous you are."

"It's why you wanted me on your team. You told me that being on the receiving end of my talents would be worse than dining with the devil at your last supper."

"Yes," Galante said and glanced from Whyte to Rosa. "Have you been in cahoots this entire time, or has she seduced you in these last few days?"

"It doesn't matter," Rushe said. "She's useless on her own… I'm not… You hurt my woman, what do you think I'll do to yours?"

"Fine," Galante said. "We'll let her go."

"No!" Flick exclaimed.

"If he refuses to join us…" Rosa said, "we kill them both."

Galante looked Rushe square in the eye, recognizing a kindred spirit. "You would sacrifice yourself for this woman?"

"As you would for yours," Rushe replied.

"No! Rushe!" She tried to run to her love, but Whyte lifted her from her feet. Kicking free, she heard Joey curse as she barged her way through the others. Rosa got between her and Rushe in the last few feet. "I won't let you do this," Flick wailed. "I don't want you to do this!"

"There's nothing you can do to stop me," Rushe said. "Do as you're told, Kitten."

She shook her head and tried to shove Rosa aside, but the woman fought back. The edge of the capped needle made contact with her skin, reminding her of the threat at the same time Joey hooked his arms around hers to pull her away from Rosa and up off her feet.

"Enough!" Rushe bellowed, stalling everyone. Joey relaxed enough to let her stand. "Go on, Kitten, get."

"No! I will not let you hurt me like this! You would never hurt me! I need you!"

"Turn around and walk away," Rushe said. "Do not look back."

FORTY-TWO

THIS COULDN'T be real. Rushe would stand there and let these crooks do anything they damn well pleased to him, just to save her.

"Stockholm," she whispered. Rushe's chin came up slightly. "I want you to stop what you're doing. I don't consent to this."

The fervor of the moment tumbled down her cheeks in constant, unyielding tears, a flicker of pain crossed her love's expression. Nevertheless, the use of their sexual safe word didn't change things. He couldn't get them both out of this, and neither could she. Only one of them had the chance to walk away, and Rushe was making that choice for both of them.

Rushe's hand came up to the top of her head, and he stroked downward once. Walking away from him had never been easy for her. In the past, when she objected to his command to do so, he'd often been cruel in pointing out that she was embarrassing herself. But it wasn't like that anymore.

Joey pulled her backward, then suddenly Rushe

lunged out. Rosa screamed when he got a hold of her, and everyone in the room pounced to attention. All focus landed on Rushe's arms around Rosa, her back to his front, as one of his forearms squeezed around her throat.

"Let her go!" Galante demanded, taking a stride toward Flick. "I'll shoot her now."

"And I'll snap her neck," Rushe growled. "I lose my woman, you'll lose yours. I told you not to cross me. I warned you."

"Shoot her!" Joey demanded, hauling Flick toward his father.

"He'll kill Rosie!"

The stalemate wouldn't be easily broken. She struggled in an attempt to liberate herself from Joey, but Whyte came over to do his part in restraining her.

"Enough!" Rushe declared. "You let her go."

"Release Rosa."

"I let go of this bitch, and you'll kill us both."

"We'll kill you anyway," Rosa said, trying to wriggle, but Rushe used the motion to get his back to the wall, and he began to move toward the club door.

"No, no," Galante said. "We'll let her go, we'll let Felicity go, you have my word."

"Means squat to me," Rushe said. "Empty the gun."

"But—"

"You empty it now!"

Her whole body trembled like she was coated with frost that radiated from her core. Galante fumbled with the gun, and Joey yanked her back, tight. Whyte stood against her feet, keeping her immobilized. That black veil around Rushe was in place to keep him cool, it was the same reason he wouldn't look at her.

She wanted to scream, she wanted reassurance, she wanted to reach out to him. It might appear to all the world as though he was in control, but this was why he resented their love. Because in his mind this wasn't control, this was desperation.

Two factions, two women, each side had something the other wanted, and Rushe wouldn't relent; he'd do anything for her. But the idea of hurting a woman to achieve his goal would pose an impossible dilemma for him.

Bullets scattered across the floor when Galante popped them from the weapon. They rolled toward the center of the room, under the couch, and into the air vents. When the clatter of metal in the passages ceased, everyone looked to Rushe.

"The one in the chamber too," Rushe growled. Galante sagged but complied. "Send her out."

"No!"

"Get her out of here," Rushe said, nodding toward her.

"No!" Flick exclaimed.

"Be a good girl… get," Rushe said without looking at her.

Unable to walk out of there, she wouldn't leave the man she loved and couldn't endure his noble betrayal. Rushe was using his life to prolong hers. It was wrong. But the decision was taken from her when Joey picked her up. This time he raised her high enough that Whyte could grab her legs and the two of them carried her toward the door.

"No!" Flick exclaimed, still trying to fight. "No, Rushe! Please, baby! Please! I love you!"

Something plastic popped. Rosa had managed to work the cap off the needle without breaking it. Just at that, Rosa lifted her arm and stabbed the needle back into Rushe's thigh and drove in the plunger, sending the liquid coursing into his veins.

"No!" Flick wailed.

The imitation ice that flooded her followed the same path that the poison would in her love's body. The atmosphere around the hostess sparkled with subdued glee, but it wasn't sustained. Whether Rushe was startled or not, he didn't show it, he remained rigid. The tension in his arm increased the pressure around Rosa's neck so suddenly that his muscles strained and the hostess squawked.

"Get Flick out of here!" Rushe roared.

"Let her go!" Galante pleaded. "Let Rosie go, please!"

She didn't know anything about drugs, but if what Rosa had just administered was enough to kill him, Rushe was acting on borrowed time. And, of course, the stubborn jerk was using his last minutes of strength to fight for her life instead of his own.

"Get my woman out of here now, Galante!"

Rosa dropped the needle to claw at Rushe's corded arm, the color in her face changing rapidly.

"Yes," Galante said, sweeping his hands toward Joey, who, along with Whyte, still carried her. "Get her out of here! Let her go! We'll release her! You release Rosie!"

Rushe had enough time left to end the life of Rosa Vallario, the murderess, and Galante loved the felon too much to take that risk. But Flick didn't want to abandon Rushe. Whyte and Joey lugged her toward the door Rosa had emerged from. She screamed for Rushe, but he maintained his stare on Galante.

"Rushe!" she cried out. "I love you! Rushe!"

Rushe's form faded from her line of sight when they took her into the dark and the door shut behind them.

"Give her something," Whyte said. "What have we got?"

"These, I got these," Joey said. "There's not

enough to kill her, but it's all I got!"

"Just give it to her and get her the fuck out of here!" Whyte replied. "We've got to go and get rid of that asshole's body."

After a brief tussle, they got her down to her back on a high, flat surface. Something was pressed into her mouth. Instinct wanted to spit out the plastic capsules, but Whyte was on her, his hand over her mouth and nose. Pinned down, she had no way to fight. Then another body landed on her, and someone stroked her throat.

"You swallow those down or you'll be dead quicker than your boyfriend in there."

Without oxygen, she had to swallow but the pressure didn't leave her face when she did.

"I should just finish her," Whyte snarled.

"Yeah," Joey said but got up and moved away, apparently unwilling to get his hands dirty for Whyte. "I've got to check Rosie."

When Joey disappeared, she kicked out against the hatred Whyte choked her with. The wimp of a man tried to persist, but she wrestled with Rushe, who was twice Whyte's size, for fun. So thrusting upward, she bowled him to the floor and leaped to her feet.

The darkness made educated purpose impossible, and she tried to run, but Whyte snatched for her ankle and sent her to her face. Smacking her head on something blunt but solid, nausea burst in her gut, and the agonizing explosion of pain behind her eye made her call out.

She couldn't give into the threatening unconsciousness. Flipping to her back, she brought up her foot and slammed her heel down into his wrist, granting her immediate release and causing Whyte to howl in a pain that satisfied her.

Scrabbling up, she ran with her hands out,

wobbling on her feet, she searched the wall until she found a door. On opening it, she met light and rushed forward, getting half a dozen steps in before she recognized her location as the staff dressing area. Snapping around, she returned to her entry point only to find it had locked behind her. She couldn't go back; she couldn't get to Rushe.

Her eyes unfocused and she lost her footing. Stumbling against the wall, she had to get out of this private space. If she didn't and she passed out, they could have her, they could do what they wanted. They'd have her, and they'd have Rushe too.

Getting out of the staff room, she bypassed security and headed for the exit. Perhaps stumbling women came out of this place all the time because they didn't seem fazed.

She couldn't run, and every stair was steeper, higher, more difficult to climb than the last. She thought about Rushe, about how to help him, about how to get back there. By the time she got into the alley, the world was spinning, and she couldn't walk straight. But she had to, she had to keep going, she had to get away from this place, away from these people.

Rushe had been injected with a drug designed to kill. The man she loved was dead or dying while she struggled to keep herself upright. Stars floated in front of her when she got onto the sidewalk and the bright lights dazzled her, but someone grabbed hold of her. She braced to scream but no sound came out. Her legs went from under her when she recognized the blurred faces of security.

"Get her in a cab and get her out of here," one of the security guys said.

"Should we send her to the hospital?"

"No, this bitch is out of it. We pay the cab driver to take her out of our precinct. We get the mess off our own doorstep, that's procedure."

She opened her mouth to tell them what had happened, to ask for help, but the words were too heavy, and faded to nothing, just like the rest of her world.

FORTY-THREE

SHE COULD HEAR something she couldn't quite identify. A voice maybe, or perhaps an animal. There was movement, and the muffled sounds of vehicle engines. Paper shuffled, a phone rang, a siren blasted.

She opened her eyes.

Daylight.

Beyond the end of the tunnel, she could see blazing sunshine. Daylight. Rushe. She tried to leap up but the weight all over her body pinned her down. Though her head hadn't moved at all, a searing pain fired through it.

She didn't think she'd made a sound, but someone came over and touched her hand. She opened her eyes again and tried to see the point of contact but couldn't move her head.

"Take it easy," someone said. "You're in the hospital. Can you tell me your name?"

"Rushe," she said, trying to sit up again.

The person next to her guided her back down. "Your name is Rushe?"

"No," she said, licking her cracked lips. "You have to find him. You have to help him."

"Let's worry about helping you."

"No," she said. "You don't understand. They'll kill him. You said this is a hospital, he could be here. Is he here?"

"No one by that name has—"

"He's six four, broad. He's striking, you would have noticed him, dark hair and eyes. He has a scar on the back of his neck and on his shoulder. There's one on his right temple from—"

"No one by that description has been brought in," the doctor said.

She hadn't even processed whether the caregiver was male or female so took the time to blink and orient herself.

"Where am I?"

"You're in a hospital, I told you that."

"She awake?"

This was a second voice, and a dark figure came into her peripheral vision. Concentrating enough to focus, she found she was in a curtained-off area. The doctor was a female, her hair drawn up in a blonde chignon. The second voice and the dark form appeared to be a man in a police uniform.

"I need help," she appealed to them, managing to push her weight onto her fists.

"I would say so," the cop said, coming over to her. The doctor remained in the background. "Your tox screen was concerning. Those weren't regular street drugs in your system. Do you want to tell me where you got them?"

"You go straight to that?" the doctor said, approaching the cop's side. "She was abandoned in the middle of the street. We have to do a pelvic and—"

"I need to go..." She remembered having

consensual sex the day before, but that only reminded her of her pain. She snatched for the cop. "You have to go to the Waterside. You have to arrest them."

"Arrest who?"

"They're killing them! The women, and now Rushe, and—"

"She's hysterical," the cop said with more than a modicum of impatience. "Can you give her something?"

"We're trying to get the drugs out of her system," the doctor said.

"Tell us what happened," the cop said.

"You have to find Rushe! You have to get to him; they're going to kill him."

"This your boyfriend? Your brother? What?"

"My boyfriend," Flick said. "They were going to kill me, but he told them not to. He said if they killed me there would be payback."

"Right," the cop said, then leaned back to talk to the doctor. "Talk about a bad trip."

"I am not tripping," Flick said, though she wouldn't know if she were.

She opened her mouth to tell the cop everything and then remembered that there was a chance some cops somewhere wanted to talk to her and Rushe too. Jansen's words about corrupt cops came back to her, and the memory of human traffickers out there somewhere, who may still be looking for her and their money.

Considering her options, she kept her mouth closed. Rushe was out there, dead or alive. She wouldn't believe the former until she saw a body. Rushe was a fighter and could get out of anything, she believed it. She had to believe it.

Grieving was premature, she wouldn't give it credence. Women would continue to die as long as this gang got their way. Rushe was somewhere in the world, possibly in pain, in need. Time was of the essence

Flick took a deep breath. "It was some guy in a club," she said. "Never seen him before."

"Description?"

She'd do her best to keep things vague. There was no way these people would believe her real story. She also couldn't admit Rushe's role in last night's events for fear of incriminating him too, since he had threatened Rosa's life.

Even if the cop believed enough of her tale to go to the Waterside and ask questions, that would cause more problems for her, for Laurie, and for any other oblivious could-be victims out there walking the street.

FORTY-FOUR

THE DOCTOR WANTED to keep her overnight for observation, but an hour was her limit. It took five minutes to find her clothes in a bag under the bed. Though her movements were still sluggish, she kept working on getting herself dressed.

Peeking around the curtain, she was ready to make a break for it when she noticed the clock. It was four thirty in the afternoon. What the hell? The late hour alarmed her so much that she started moving without thinking.

Quickly out of the ER, she went for the sidewalk and just kept walking. She doubted the cops would chase her, or the doctors for that matter. But enough time had been wasted already.

Unlike the last time Rushe was in trouble, she had no one to back her up. Her first idea was to go to Liam. He would be in the library, and she didn't know who would be watching and had to be careful.

Stealing wasn't something she'd thought herself capable of. But, at that moment, she had no other choice.

At least that was what she told herself when she swiped the coat of a woman enjoying a drink outside a coffeeshop. The woman was yammering on the phone and couldn't have cared less about her coat hanging over the guardrail cordoning off the external seating area.

Donning, then buttoning the stolen apparel, she hooked the hood up over her head and went toward the library, a dozen blocks away.

Liam usually went for his dinner at The Grill at around five, so she didn't have to wait long. Ideally, if she'd had the first inclination how to find them, she would have gone to Eric or Scott. Wasting half the evening trying to locate them herself would be ridiculous given how quickly Liam gathered the information on Whyte.

At almost quarter past five, she spotted Liam coming out of the library and running down the stairs to cross the street. She'd been watching from the alley opposite, and there were enough people leaving work and filling the streets that she felt comfortable enough to break onto the pavement and beat a path toward Liam. She gave him the space to enter The Grill and order as he normally would, all the while hanging back near the restroom so as not to attract suspicion.

When Liam was finished, he went to his regular booth in the far corner and flipped around a discarded newspaper left on the table. She gave it five seconds, then willed herself to go over. People could be out to get her. His position in the window made her feel exposed, and there was no illusion that Rushe was watching over her anymore.

She gathered her courage and kept her head down as she made a beeline across the room into Liam's booth. She didn't remove her hood, his inhale was probably a prelude to a joke, but the moment she lifted her head and met his eyes, he froze.

His ease became panic. "Flick, for crissakes," he gasped and lunged across the table to seize her hand. "What happened to you?"

Vanity was the furthest thing from her mind. She hadn't showered since yesterday and was fighting the worst hangover of her life. No doubt her eyes were sunken and shadowed, her skin would be pale and sticky. If the way her head thumped was anything to go by, she'd be parading a nasty bruise on her forehead, showing through her dank hair too. But those things were insignificant.

"I don't have time to talk about it. I need you to find someone."

"Flick, whatever this is—"

"They've hurt Rushe," she said. "I don't know, maybe he's already dead, but—"

"Rushe is a guy who can take care of himself. You should worry about—"

"Myself?" she snapped. "He used his own life to save mine. Do you think I should just walk away from that?"

"I think if he lost his life to protect yours, then he loved you very much. I also think you going and getting yourself killed would defeat his objective."

"I didn't come to ask your advice. I know what I'm going to do." Despite knowing Rushe would be furious about her plan. But he would admire her single-minded determination. "I need you to help me find someone. After that, you can walk away and never have to see me again. I won't bring any more trouble to you. I apologize you've been involved in this. I didn't know… I'm sorry."

"Who is this person you want to find?"

"An associate of Rushe's," she said. "I only know him as Eric, I don't know his last name, and I don't know where he lives. He's Caucasian. He makes money fencing stolen electronics, but I don't know if he has a shop or a business. He has a little girl called Gracie, but that's sensitive information. If you—"

Liam held up a hand. "I'm not interested in hurting anyone."

"She was born at some point within the last two years. Somewhere in that same sort of time frame, Eric was bitten on his thigh by a dog. There might be medical records, or an identifying scar."

"Got it."

In recounting the details to Liam, she realized Rushe had done it again. The car ride with Eric was a setup. Taking her out of that hotel suite, out of the bed they shared on the night she became his perk, on that job with Eric… it was for a purpose. This. Yes, Rushe confirmed his suspicion she and Eric had already met, but taking her on that ride-along, showed her who to turn to in the event Rushe was not available. Chances were that Rushe didn't need a second man for the task at all. He'd taken Eric on the Galante job to get the two of them in the same space with him.

He'd done it with Jansen on their last mission too, setting it up so she got a full view of Jansen, who ended up being her back up. The only reason she trusted him at all was because she'd witnessed the exchange of the two men. This time she'd had the chance to ask questions, to garner information from Eric. Rushe had trusted her to ferret away the details for future use. Would he be proud of her for understanding and following the lead he provided her?

"They might be watching you," she said to Liam, trying not to focus too heavily on thoughts of her love while there was work to do. "You'll have to be careful."

Liam frowned. "Why would they watch me?"

"The people who hurt Rushe, they have associations with the King Club, who are serious people," she said. "This is important… do not discuss me, or Rushe, or any of what you've heard or seen here with any of your colleagues or friends. You cannot go to the cops either, do you hear me? Do not contact the police. When the time is right, I'll give you instructions, but you can't go to them now."

"They may be able to help if—"

"It's important, Liam," she said. "I need your word."

"Are you on the run?" Her eyes darted away from his. The gesture would be telling but had been automatic. "Jeez, Flick, are you a fugitive?"

"It's complicated."

"Is it Rushe?"

"No," she said. "There are people who would like to know where I am, that's all."

She wouldn't disrespect Rushe's name and didn't want anyone to think less of him. Especially not while there was a question mark over his condition, and he wasn't around to defend himself.

"Okay," Liam said. "I'll see what I can do, give me an hour?"

She nodded. "Bring it to the north alley, down the block. I can't come into the library, they might be expecting me."

"Where are you going to go?"

"There's one piece on the board I haven't accounted for yet," she said. "I need to find out if he'll be useful… If I'm not at the alley in an hour, get in touch with Eric and tell him what you know. Only tell Eric, tell no one else. Give him the information, then forget you laid eyes on any of us."

"Flick," Liam said, keeping her hand when she tried to slide out. "This'll make a helluva book."

Liam's smile was unexpected but appreciated. Maybe he wanted to say something else, and a joke was the only way he could express it.

"I'll go to any lengths for a good story." In half a beat of silence, she snapped back to it. "Can I borrow Siri?"

Liam didn't second guess her anymore. He took his iPhone from his pocket and slid it across to her. She shuffled down and out of the booth before Liam could say another word. There had been too many delays, now she had to get the job done.

FORTY-FIVE

GETTING TO WHERE she wanted to go took nearly twenty minutes. An internet search gave her the required details, including directions. One quick call to her target's assistant gave her the last of the information.

If he'd been home, getting there and back in time would be impossible. And isolating herself in his private residence wouldn't be smart. Learning her target was still at his office worked out for the best. For her anyway. Maybe not so much for him.

Any hope of Rushe being alive was dwindling by the second, focusing on the job kept her distracted.

Ascending in the elevator alone, she took advantage of the precious few seconds to steel herself. The doors clunked open, and she stepped into a lavish reception area with a broad metal reception desk and muted lighting. No doubt it was some attempt at post-modern but, to her, it was just cold, which didn't bode well for what was to come.

At that hour of the evening, no one staffed the reception desk. She went straight past, looking around for the office of the man she sought. Only the furthest office still had its lights on. In the open plan space between her and it, a few members of staff still worked.

The trick to getting to where you needed to go without interference was to act as if you belonged. Hadn't Rushe said something to that effect? Her father walked everywhere like he was already late. Rushe didn't have to walk fast; his stride was long enough to get anywhere quickly. So paying no attention to the employees, she fixed her sights on that office, and got there as fast as possible.

A woman at the desk next to the office door stood up, but she didn't wait to be announced. If she did, she could be ejected, and this step was too vital to take that risk. Ignoring the pleas of the woman, she grabbed the office door handle and walked straight in.

The man she was looking for stood at the window, on the phone. Her abrupt entry caused him to turn, despite sensing someone on her heels, she maintained her focus on the man cropped in the tall window.

"I'm sorry, Mr. Davis, she came straight in—"

"That's okay," Davis said to the assistant standing behind her, then spoke into the phone. "I'll call you back."

Davis disconnected the line, and the office door closed, trapping them alone.

"Do you know who I am?"

"No," Davis said, most probably trawling through his memories, trying to place her familiar face. "I should though, shouldn't I?"

"The Lounge, Galante's Waterside Casino."

Davis sighed. "One of Joey's girls?"

"No," she said. "Actually, you probably know me as Evan Whyte's girl… former."

A tremor of comprehension floated over Davis.

Her statement had an impact, but she couldn't read its exact nature. He could be surprised, or maybe he now recalled her. Maybe he knew something about Whyte's fetish. Maybe he had been on the phone to one of last night's assailants when she entered his office.

"Why are you here?" he asked, strolling back to the desk to replace the phone handset in its cradle.

"I'm here for answers," she said, awaking Davis' interest. "Something happened last night. Something that—"

"I don't want to know," Davis said, shaking his head.

"Why not?" she asked, her curiosity piqued. "You know, don't you? You know what they do."

"I do not know anything," Davis said too abruptly for the statement to be true.

"I had an interesting conversation with your wife the night we met," she said, straightening Davis's posture. "Eleanor's an approachable woman, easy to talk to. But you know that, you've been married for fifteen years…"

"Leave my wife out of this."

She'd never threatened anyone, not without provocation. Rushe had to be watching over her, rooting for her, inspiring her with confidence. She sauntered further into the room, admiring her surroundings as she went.

"Your wife thinks your friends are animals, doesn't she?" That was obvious from the way Eleanor snubbed them. "She's very perceptive."

"I love my wife very much. If you think—"

"Does she know about Jeri?"

The word, the name, made Davis blanch. "I had nothing to do with that."

"Really?" she asked. "Because you just said you didn't know anything. Yet you immediately know who

I'm referring to."

"Jeri worked at the Rich Room before she moved to the X-Lounge. She was a valued employee. I read in the newspaper about what happened to her… it was very tragic. A lot of young people these days are involved in dangerous social behaviors."

"Were you intimate with her? I saw Jeri come into the Lounge to talk to you. How would Eleanor feel about that?"

"I have always been faithful," Davis said.

Considering present circumstances, Davis had got himself riled in a hurry. He should have the advantage on his home turf. And she was a tiny little thing, no immediate physical threat. Sweat broke out on Davis's brow. Though he still met her eye, she sensed a cornered animal.

"You know what they do to women, don't you? Are you a part of it?" she asked. "How many women have you seduced, only to watch them die?"

"I have never seduced anyone! I will not be a part of it. I love my wife!"

This was a man afraid, despite being powerful, rich, and intimidating in himself. He was happy to socialize with Whyte and with Galante and had flirted with her as well. When she appeared at his office, he hadn't been uneasy, but she saw it in him now. His reaction to her implication was visceral.

"How long has it been going on?" she asked. "When did it start, Mr. Davis? May I call you Richard?" He didn't speak. "Does your business partner, Johnson, know? I've never met him, but I know your two families have worked together for generations. Why are you in financial trouble now? Why did Evan Whyte have to bail you out?"

"He did not."

"Why did he give you money? To silence you,

perhaps?"

"What is it you want?"

"I want to know what they did last night," she said.

"I wasn't with Evan Whyte last night," Davis said.

"Tell me when it started... I know Whyte gave you money, he told me he did. No doubt he believed he could give out that sort of information, any information, to a woman he believed would be dead soon... Should I get in touch with Johnson and ask him about the money?"

"You don't know what you're talking about."

"I do," she said. "I know what they do to women. I know about Galante and about Joey having sex with Evan Whyte's women. I know he likes to watch them do it. I know the women are oblivious, the first time at least. It's sordid, and as far as I know you're a key player; you're compliant if nothing else. What would headlines about this do to your clubs? What would they do to your marriage?"

"You threaten me with no regard for your own safety," Davis said. "If they find out you're asking—"

"Answer my questions, or I'll make sure Eleanor, and Johnson, know all about your role in this depravity."

"This is nothing to do with me. I'm no part of it. Rosa makes the rules for them, Galante and Joey, Whyte too. They're all bound to her."

"Why?"

"It's none of your business."

"You should worry less about protecting the honor of murderers, and more about the safety of your precious wife. Do you think I'm working alone?" she said with ferocious, if unfounded, sincerity. "Would you like Eleanor to hear the sickening truth of how Jeri died? Tell me why Rosa controls them, how she controls them.

Give me the details and I'll leave you both alone."

"The relationship between them all goes back more than a decade. They're like family, but… Rosa was abused by her own father, and since the breakdown of her relationship with Joey… That girl didn't have a chance to make a decent life for herself."

"We're supposed to feel sorry for her?"

"No." Davis sighed and sank down into his chair. "She is out of hand, but it's been coming for years, ever since the three of them went to school together, Rosa, Evan and Joey. She and Joey were high school sweethearts, but she was caught with another man, alone in his parents' house. They were only found out because the police were called and…"

"Whyte was caught watching them," she said, settling herself in the guest seat at his desk.

Rosa's name was the one in the police report of Whyte's arrest. She had been stepping out on Joey when Whyte broke in to watch. The boy Rosa was fooling around with was panicked by the intruder and called the cops. After that, the truth of Rosa's infidelity would have been revealed, and the truth of Whyte's vice too.

"Whyte's father put him in a rehabilitation facility for a while. I suppose it didn't stick. Joey went off the rails after her betrayal, he got involved in drugs and sex."

Rosa had accused Joey of cheating first. It seemed now that wasn't the case. "When did she start sleeping with Galante Senior?"

"She too has unsavory sexual tastes. Joey's wild behavior unsettled her. Galante stepped in as a father figure, to silence her about Whyte's arrest because he was showing promise and a drive for business. Whyte was already making money, not enough to take care of the Rosa problem alone, and his family is not particularly wealthy. The boy had been easily paid off, and he didn't know who Whyte was anyway. Eventually Rosa agreed to keep quiet for Galante, she got paid… and she got sex too."

"From Galante? To punish Joey?"

"That was when the relationship began," Davis said. "That is all I know."

FORTY-SIX

"BUT HE WOULDN'T commit to her, that's what Rosa wanted."

"No, no, no," Davis said, dropping into his chair. "You've got it backwards, she bewitched him from the start. Her untamed ways beguiled him. Rosa wouldn't commit to Galante. He's a man in love, he's asked her to marry him dozens of times."

"She refused, why?"

"Joey got clean, the two of them…"

"They started sleeping together again?" she asked. "Both of the Galante men love Rosa, that's why they keep quiet about this. But Whyte…?"

"He couldn't let her reveal what she knew. Through the years as his fortunes have increased, so have Rosa's. If he tried to cut her off, she made damn sure he knew she'd damage his prosperity too. A large part of his success is predicated on his credibility," Davis said. "He's known for his generosity, and for his clean living. He's seen as reliable and altruistic. Whyte the man is as much a part of the brand he sells as any of his hotels. To have the truth come out, his reputation would be ruined, he would be a joke."

"So Rosa got anything she wanted as long as she kept quiet," Flick said.

"She's the reason he built the Waterside Hotel with the casino for Galante."

"All this time she's been blackmailing him," she murmured. "But if she had all the money she wanted, why run the racquet out of the Lounge? Why drug and rob men?"

"Oh, that's a silly game," Davis barked. "The girl has no sense. She enjoys making fools of those idiots. Getting them into such positions and taking advantage is entertainment."

If Rosa had been abused and spent her life having promiscuous sex, it stood to reason she enjoyed taking advantage of men, who may have at one time taken advantage of her.

"It started to get her into trouble. She wasn't going to get away with it forever."

"No," Davis said. "Whyte threatened to inform the police. I think he saw it as his chance to get rid of Rosa."

"Galante and Joey wouldn't let that happen."

"No, this was when they began to…"

"To what?"

"Whyte tried to get his kicks with prostitutes, but their knowledge of his observation lessened his gratification."

"To keep Whyte quiet about Rosa's criminality, they began seducing Whyte's girlfriends and allowing him to watch, without the women's knowledge?"

Davis answered with a single nod and closed his eyes. "It went on for years. The blackmail and sex was one thing, making fools of those men for sport was another, an escalation."

"To murder?"

"I will not comment on that ridiculous fantasy."

"Will the cops see it that way?"

"If you had something worthy of police attention," Davis said, "you would be there."

"I know that Jeri was found dead. I know my former co-worker, Nancy, is missing. I know that Lisa Lewis is dead. It seems to me that all women connected with that Lounge end up dead… like Susan did."

"You have done your homework," Davis said. "But I fail to see what this has to do with me, or what it has to do with you. You're sitting here perfectly healthy, though you're somewhat tattered and worn around the edges, if you'll excuse my saying so."

Davis was enigmatic. Had she jumped to conclusions in her assumption he'd be a sleaze? If he claimed to be faithful to Eleanor, she had no evidence to refute that. Jeri had spoken to Davis in the Lounge, but she couldn't testify as to what their conversation was about.

His apology for his comment reminded her of her own father, Charles Hughes, the epitome of perfect breeding yet somehow, lacking.

"I had a bad night and woke up in a hospital."

"That is a bad night."

"It was worse for the man I love," she said. "They murdered him."

Her aim was to commit every detail of Davis' reaction to memory. It might have been his intention to conceal how he felt about it, but she was used to reading the nuance of Rushe's subtle expressions. Davis was shocked but concerned, she would guess more for his own wellbeing than hers.

"That's unfortunate."

"Who reacts to the news of a murder like that?" she said. "I'm accusing your friends of murder. They were all there, Joseph Galante Senior and Joseph Galante Junior, Evan Whyte was there, and Rosa Vallario, the Lounge hostess."

"I'm not sure what you want me to say, do you wish me to be shocked, or outraged? I am outraged at your accusation, but I don't see a shred of proof."

"You don't want to know how they did it or what their motive was?" she asked. "I think that tells me all I need to know."

"Good."

"I had hoped you would be a decent enough person to want to help. To want these senseless deaths to end." She stood and began to head for the door. "We'll see what the cops think."

"No!"

When she turned back, Davis was on his feet with a hand on the desk to support him as he leaned toward her. That sweat on his brow had returned. She sauntered toward him. "Why are you worried? Do you think they'll turn on you?"

"The police will never believe you. Whyte has many of them in his pocket. Those he doesn't, he can easily extort. But the King Club…"

"I don't have anything left to lose Mr. Davis. I'm interested in knowing the truth, where it started, what everyone's link is." Depositing her hands on the desk, on either side of Davis's, she leaned in close. "I'm looking for a soft spot to squeeze, and if that soft spot turns out to be you… I hope your wife can handle the pressure."

"Eleanor is—"

The office door opened, she and Davis turned to see the assistant from the outer desk. The tall brunette with the small oval glasses took a few seconds to say anything.

"Sir, I'm sorry to interrupt but we've had a call and…"

"What is it?" Davis demanded. "Is it Eleanor?"

Good. He was paranoid. All the better for her cause.

"No," the brunette said. "Evan Whyte and Joseph Galante are missing."

"Missing?"

"Carjacked," the assistant said. "The driver was shot on site. There were reports of other gunshots, but… whoever did it got in the car and took off with the two men still in the vehicle."

Her smile spread as she slowly looked back to Davis. "Feeling squeezed yet, Richard?"

"Leave us!" Davis demanded and the assistant scurried away. Panic was beginning to build in the businessman, pushing him toward his breaking point. "Where are they?"

"You expect me to give you information when you've given me none?"

She had no idea what had happened with the carjacking, and she had no idea where Galante or Whyte were. But the timing of the incident, and its announcement to Davis, couldn't have worked out more in her favor.

"What do you want from me?"

"Tell me how it started," she demanded, raising her voice. "Why do they do it? How did it start? Tell me!"

The increase in volume did have an effect on him, but there was a limit. She had to be careful of outside ears listening in. Davis may be the only link she had to finding out Rushe's fate, rousing security wouldn't serve her interest.

"The first death was accidental," he said. "They have parties, sex parties, I don't know what you'd call them, partner swapping and group… activities."

He made it sound like an arts and crafts workshop. "They were all involved?"

"Yes," Davis said. "Whyte was allowed to freely indulge, they all were… One of the girls had drugs, she brought drugs, I don't know… Rosa and Joey were having sex with this woman, and Rosa had her by the throat… next thing, the woman was dead."

"Strangled?"

"I don't know," Davis said.

"You were there?"

He straightened again. "I was there talking to Galante, we weren't taking part in… The point is, a woman was dead, possibly murdered."

"They were all in it, all present, all responsible."

"Galante and Joey were never going to implicate Rosa, they love her," he said. "Whyte wasn't free and clear either, he was watching, and turns out the death only enhanced his pleasure. I was paid to keep quiet, and that was the last of it. I wasn't going to take on the King Club. Both Whyte and Galante are valued members, and murder is the least of the crimes that group cover up."

"The last? It wasn't the last, women are still dying! The man I love is dead!"

The office door opened again, breaking the seal of pressure, though she could still feel her hammering heart pulsing in her eardrums.

"Am I interrupting?"

The new voice drew her attention.

Eleanor stood inside the room, the door already closed behind her.

"Actually, yes," Flick said.

"No," Davis said. "No, you're not. I think I've said all I have to."

"I think there's a lot you still have to say," Flick said, trailing her focus back to Davis.

He met her eye and they stared, neither willing to blink.

"What is going on?" Eleanor asked. "I heard

about Joseph; this is terrible. I was in the city, and I came straight here."

"I'd be more worried about yourself, Mrs. Davis," Flick said. "And the things your husband is mixed up in."

"I've said enough. If I was you, I would keep running, or they will catch up with you."

"What is going on here, Richard?" Eleanor demanded. "Why are you threatening each other?"

"My lover was murdered last night by your husband's friends, Eleanor," Flick said. There was no reason not to talk to Eleanor; it was possible she could help. "I want to know exactly what happened to him, about what they did with him. I came here to ask Mr. Davis for help."

"This is about Evan Whyte and Joseph, isn't it? Is this why they were taken?" Eleanor asked. "Richard, call the police."

"He won't do that." Flick smiled. "He's in up to his neck. To implicate them, or to implicate me, he has to first implicate himself, because he knows all the details and he's kept quiet... That decision has cost lives."

"Is it true?" Eleanor asked. "What do you know?"

"Nothing," Davis said. "This is an ex-girlfriend of Evan Whyte's."

"I know who she is, we met. Are you saying she's orchestrating this out of some kind of revenge?"

"I broke up with Evan Whyte," Flick said. "I wasn't interested in playing his debauched games."

"I would assume Joey made a sexual advance, or perhaps his father, Galante?"

Eleanor's assumption was intriguing. "Why would you think that?"

"Those two men would do anything to protect Rosa. They are both very much in love with her. Whyte has foul sexual tastes. He likes to witness the act, not to take part himself."

Was there anyone in their group who didn't know? "What has that got to do with Rosa?"

"Rosa has been conning the men who come into the Lounge for years. Tainting drinks and emptying wallets. The next day everyone denies all knowledge."

"Right," Davis asserted. "Eleanor, don't say anything else."

"Why is Kimberly different," Flick asked. "Other women come and go, but not her."

"She is the mother of Joey's only child," Eleanor said. "She had the boy two years ago and is paid well to keep quiet about the fact. Rosa keeps her close to prevent the secret getting out."

"Joey got her pregnant," Flick murmured.

"I believe murder is a step beyond even their loose morals. If you are in anyway involved with what has happened to Joseph and—"

"Me?" Flick said. "I was with your husband the whole time, Mrs. Davis, and I have at least a dozen witnesses to that fact." She wanted to make a casual exit but glancing at the clock told her she needed to make one last request. "Give me some money."

"What? Why?"

"I need to get a cab. If I don't make my rendezvous, my associate will presume foul-play and come after you himself. Is that what you want?"

Davis fumbled for his wallet and pulled out a stack of bills, she snatched them before he could count it.

"You've been helpful but keep checking over your shoulder. You never know when I might pop up again."

Was she trying to be profound, or to scare Davis? Right then, she had no time to analyze her motives. She needed to get out of the building, into a cab, and back to meet Liam in the alley. She moved fast, praying Liam had the details she needed.

FORTY-SEVEN

ENTERING THE ALLEY right on time, she noted Liam's absence. Back up options were minimal. As the minutes passed, her anxiety increased. It would be bad enough if Liam bailed on her without having the guts to refuse her request to her face. That, however, was still the preferable option.

The other was that he'd been intercepted. If members of the King Club had spotted their meeting and united that with the details of what had happened last night, it was possible they'd identified him as a threat. Would they eliminate that threat? She didn't want to be responsible for a death, or rather for another death.

Leaning back against the coarse surface of the wall, the concrete closed in around her. During the last few hours, she'd worked on the assumption Rushe was alive, that she was still part of their duo.

But relying on that was ignoring one pertinent fact: if Rushe was alive, and they were both in trouble, he would do anything to get to her and keep her safe. In short, Rushe would've found her by now.

Avoiding the obvious was becoming more difficult. Rushe had made a commitment to saving her life. The contents of that syringe had gone into his body; she'd witnessed the injection. Denying the truth any longer was impossible.

Her ribs constricted so suddenly that her voice gasped for air. Clamping both hands over her mouth, she tried to steady her breathing but failed. Each inhale was quicker than the previous; the short, stabbing breaths caused a sharp spear of pain to impale her each time she wheezed in.

Her windpipe convulsed and although she tried to gulp for oxygen, it was useless. When her hands fell from her face, her body followed, until she collapsed onto the dirty asphalt. The thick soup of humid air closed in, and spots whirled across her vision. She curled on her side, gagging on the truth. Rushe was dead. The only man to see her, the man she loved. He had been cruelly snatched away.

The scratching noose around her neck was welcome. She didn't want to fight for breath; she didn't deserve the oxygen meant for him. She was the one they'd wanted to kill, but he took her place.

"Oh my God, Flick!"

Though she was conscious of being moved, she had difficulty swallowing and couldn't focus. She was helped to a seated position and despite recognizing Liam, she was unable to regulate her breathing.

"He—he—"

"It's okay, okay? Just try to take deep breaths," Liam said, inhaling deeply and blowing out the air. "Like this see, copy me."

She did her best. Although she babbled through her quivering lungs, she did eventually begin to breathe more regularly.

"You scared me," Liam said, stroking her hair

from her face.

She recoiled from his touch. "Don't do that!"

It was on the tip of her tongue to warn him how Rushe felt about other men touching his woman. But the reminder had her head growing heavy again.

"Sorry," Liam said, still crouched in front of her. "What happened? What upset you?"

"They killed him," she muttered.

"You're worried about Rushe?"

"They killed him! Rushe saved my life! The idiot! He always does this!" Turning her distress into anger, she pounced to her feet. "He does what's best! He takes over! He makes the decisions!"

"What happened?" he asked.

"He's dead! He's dead, and I want to yell at him! What the hell am I supposed to do without him? Asshole!"

Stumbling forward a step, she found herself in Liam's arms. "You've always been strong. I don't understand why—"

"Did you get it?" she asked, shoving out of Liam's embrace, trying to screw her head back on.

Rushe's number one rule was to keep her guard up; she had no intention of letting him down now.

Liam may have sensed her shutters going up, or maybe he knew there wasn't time to waste. He handed her an envelope. "Only two Erics listed as a father on birth certificates of Gracies within the last two years. One African American, one Caucasian, I cross-referenced. The first is forty-three has six kids, is happily married, and makes his living in real estate. No hospital admissions since his appendix burst ten years ago."

"And this is the other one?" she asked, ripping open the envelope. "Thanks."

She was about to walk away when Liam seized her arm. "This is dangerous. You could get hurt. If you need me—"

"I work alone," she said, yanking her arm free and going back out the way she entered.

Eric was her last and only hope. Rushe's time might have run out, but that didn't mean those who hurt him would get away with it.

Revenge had never been a life goal… until now.

FORTY-EIGHT

GOING BACK UP TO their apartment was not viable, but at the pedestrian access to the parking garage of their complex, she keyed in their private code and gained access. After retrieving the car key from Rushe's hidey-hole, she got inside, activated the engine, and exhaled a sigh of relief. Rushe's forethought had rescued her again.

With a shaky breath, she put the car in gear and got moving. Advising herself this wasn't the time to think of what she'd lost, she resolved her determination with the reminder she had nothing left to lose and only one goal. She would complete this next task and use Liam's research to locate Eric and finish the job.

Finding out what happened to Rushe wouldn't be easy if someone was clearing the players from the board. The carjacking was something she hadn't accounted for. Not knowing who was responsible cranked up the pressure.

Galante and Whyte were not viable targets. Tracing them would be next to impossible unless Eric or Scott could aid her in the pursuit, and she didn't have time to locate Eric and convince him of that undertaking. It wouldn't be as easy as strolling up to the address Liam had found and knocking on Eric's door. At least she couldn't take the risk of assuming it would be. She would get around to that later. After she had secured a source of information, a token of barter, for herself.

She drove a few blocks before pulling over to stop and retrieve what she needed. In the trunk was a backpack Rushe had told her was filled with essentials. She upended the sack and swept aside the survival gear. Rushe's pocketknife was always useful, so she picked it out, along with the jeans he'd stashed for her and his dark blue flannel shirt.

Slipping out of her heels, she stepped into the jeans and tucked in her dress, buttoning the shirt over the top. She shouldn't be surprised that Rushe had gone so far as to pack boots for her; he thought of everything. Wrapping herself in his scent, she was consoled to know he was looking after her from beyond this mortal coil.

Fresh moisture pooled in her eyes. After this, if she was still alive, she would have time to grieve, but she couldn't leave this job unfinished.

In her clothes and boots, she slid the knife into her pocket, retrieved the cuffs and duct tape, and stared down at the last item she needed. Picking up the gun, she recalled the first time she'd shot a man. Back then, she'd never have imagined being in this kind of predicament.

Her first thought wasn't for her safety or for her freedom. If she lost her life or went to jail, so be it. Her only remaining concern was her aim. She had no trouble pulling the trigger, she just had to ensure she hit the intended target.

Hiding the firearm under her shirt, she slammed the trunk and went back to the driving seat. The natural light had faded, only to be replaced by the artificial. Her world felt surreal. The overdose of adrenaline made her lightheaded but fueled her determination. By the time the night was over, she would have her answers, but not her love. She would never have him again.

AS SOON AS she reversed into the alley to lie in wait, the rain began to cascade down. The shift was due to start, but no one paid attention to the dank back alley. The fun was happening on the boardwalk at the other side of the structure.

She didn't kill the engine, just the lights. Activity from the city masked the noise of the car, and without streetlights, she could rely on the shroud of black that held her in secret.

Rushe was in this night; he was the dark embracing her. His voice echoed in her head reminding her to stay on guard, be aware, remember the details, filter the important, discard the irrelevant.

Yet, as she reminded herself of those words, the tickle of his breath in her ear prickled her neck and his whispering love fortified her. He'd died for her, but that wouldn't be the end of the story. She would make them rue the day they crossed the obelisk of dark virtue that was Rushe, the man she loved.

Every breath she took on every day would be dedicated to hunting down every soul that his murderers ever cared about. She'd be bitter but relentless. Her life had a singular purpose. The ambrosia of hatred poisoned her throat and it tasted sweet.

On lifting her focus, her target entered the alley. She'd give time to ensure success, no need to hurry the operation. She'd take her time and get this right.

The target was only a few feet away when she spotted the car. Flick gave her no time to think about it, or to register its meaning. She leaped out and pointed the gun at Rosa.

"What are you doing here?" Rosa asked. News of the carjacking must have reached her. Such an act would've shaken her up. "I'll scream."

"Go ahead, no one's listening. The sound of your club plugs their ears."

"What do you want?" Rosa asked, taking a step backward.

"Ah, ah," Flick said. "Shooting you now would deprive me of my fun. I know you understand how disappointing that would be for me."

"He's dead, so whatever you want from Joey or—"

"I'm not here for Joey," she said, moving closer to an ever-tensing Rosa. "I'm here for you."

She raised the gun and swung the butt around to Rosa's temple, knocking the hostess to the ground. The prone woman remained motionless, but she kept the gun trained on her. Nudging her body to roll it back, she registered the blood and Rosa's closed eyes. Crouching, she quickly attached the cuffs and put the gun on her lap to wind tape around Rosa's ankles.

Anyone could happen upon them, and Rosa could regain consciousness at any time. Flick stuffed the gun into the back of her jeans, took Rosa's shoes off her feet, and threw everything into the backseat. On the crest of adrenaline, she dragged Rosa around to the back of the car.

Motivated by the honor of her purpose, anxiety gave her the strength to get Rosa into the trunk where she stuck a strip of tape over the hostess' mouth. This woman had tortured and tormented innocent women for her own sick satisfaction. She felt no guilt over her actions. Driving away from the water, her destination was firm. She needed answers, and hoped she had the stomach to see this all the way through. No matter what it took, she would do what was right. She would act as

Rushe would in this situation and would be just as thorough.

DRIVING THROUGH the long abandoned streets of the unloved part of town, she didn't have time to absorb the dereliction or the deprivation caused by industry up and leaving the area.

The last sign of life she'd seen was in one of the deserted factories. From what she could gather, the graffiti-decorated hollowed out building housed the unhoused. Those souls had no more or less right to be there than she did. Neither would be divulging the other's presence.

Slowing the car, she dipped her head to squint through the lashing rain, seeking her turn. The dazzle of headlights struck her suddenly. Gasping, she slammed on the brakes in an attempt to prevent her vehicle from colliding with this surprise company. In the last heartbeat, the assailant swerved to avoid impact but blocked her path, leaving her no way out.

Her car came to a lurching halt, and she forced it into reverse, except a wide metal pole prevented her from backing up. Adrenaline from the near miss had her heart battering her ribs, it took a few seconds to recalibrate her mind. No one should know she was there. The notes she'd made on this building had only been in one place, in one file…

Thunder crashed, but her body loosened. Through the sheets of rain pounding the hood, she watched the driver's door of the other vehicle open, giving rise to a threatening silhouette… one she'd feared in the past. The glimpse of him mirrored her first experience with the beast who'd occupied a doorway, blocking her exit then as he did now. Now, there was only one place to run.

FORTY-NINE

SHE WASN'T CONSCIOUS of leaving the car. Didn't feel the rain or the cold. One stride followed another, then she launched herself up into his arms. His embrace clamped around her, crushing her ribs, squeezing her heart and the life from her into him. When her mouth struck his, she sucked in the welcome breath his body expelled.

"Rushe! Oh, Lover!" She wrapped her legs around his waist, locking her ankles; she didn't want to ever pry her body from his. "Rushe." She caught his tongue in her teeth, and with a gasp, released him and screamed out. "You bastard! You fucking bastard!"

"What the fuck are you doing out here? What the fuck do—"

"You're alive!" she shouted. "I really thought…"

"I ain't never getting rid of you, Kitten."

"Not even in death!"

"What the hell are you doing out here?" he asked. "Where are you going? What is your plan? How did—"

"Shut up," she said. "Oh, Rushe, kiss me. Please,

oh, baby, don't ever stop kissing me."

Again, she pressed her mouth to his, the wetness of him merging with her in the mire of torrential rain that swept her woes away in the wash.

Just as she believed him lost, just as she was giving up hope, there he was. She didn't care if she was dead. She didn't care if she'd somehow joined him on the other side. Their location was miserable, and the weather vicious, but she would live there forever in this horrible place, so long as it was with him. If it was a choice to live without him, or there for the rest of her existence, she'd take the latter in a heartbeat. Life burned through her body, through his, through the alliance of their mouths.

"It's not safe here, Kitten," he said. "Why are you out here?"

Reluctantly, she slithered down his body and took his hand to maintain their contact. "I'll show you."

She guided him around her car and popped open the trunk. With a quashed scream, Rosa tried to kick and move, but her bindings kept her under control. Rushe examined the captive, and then his attention gradually rose. She braced for his response.

"What the fuck did I do to you, Kitten?"

He'd said that to her before, but instead of the shock she'd read when he first uttered the words, pride shone from his expression. He seized the back of her neck and pulled her against him. Meeting his mouth unleashed an explosion of grief and delight. Locking her arms around his neck, she pulled back enough to snag his lower lip with her teeth.

Rushe smiled, unusual for the scenario, but she growled. "I'm gonna fucking kill you for scaring me like that," she snarled.

The role reversal would have tickled her if it wasn't for the groan that sounded from the still open trunk beside them.

"We have business to take care of," Rushe said.

"Then I'm gonna fuck you 'til you beg for mercy."

Rushe bared his teeth. Swooping down, he hooked his forearm under her ass and hauled her up against the hard want in his jeans. "Think you can break me, Kitten?"

"Nothing but bareback from now on. You're mine and only mine," she said, launching in to consume him again.

Their battling tongues were ready to wage war. Rushe twisted their entwined frames to lean on the dimmed brake light. She could have him there. She'd mount him in that public place without a care... if it wasn't for the bound body next to them.

"Business first," she said, steadying herself against the stability of his unyielding form. "Pleasure comes next... I'll fuck you back from the dead."

"Good girl."

She didn't know his plan, or why he was there, but she didn't care. Her heart screamed so loud that her ears heard the song. Rushe took her to the passenger seat of his car, and then transferred Rosa from her trunk to his. The hostess thrashed around, not that it made any difference. Was that the same picture they painted when he was manhandling her?

A few seconds later, he was back in the driver's seat. "What about our—"

"That car is linked to our previous address," Rushe said, taking them around in an arc to continue the drive she'd assumed she would be taking alone. "Eric will get rid of it."

"Eric? But I... what are you doing out here?"

"Put your seatbelt on."

By the time she fastened the restraint, they were slowing to pull into a narrow alleyway. His request for safety had clearly been a ruse meant to distract her. The alley widened by a few feet when they reached a vehicle-sized entrance. Rushe drove into the middle of the gloomy place and turned off the car.

"This is it, isn't it? The Rosebud Ballroom."

"This facility is built on the footprint of the original building, yeah. This area has undergone a few transformations over the years."

"You read about it in my notes."

"Yeah," Rushe said. "Why did you snatch her?"

"She hurt you," she said. "Without you, I had nothing to lose. I had to know where you were, what they did to you. If there was any way I could've helped you… and I couldn't let them continue to get away with killing women. Last night couldn't have just been the end of it for them, or for me. We went into this job to help one woman. She might be lost, but that doesn't mean we should forget the others who could be at risk. You wouldn't have left it undone."

"I know what I'm doing."

"I've been doing okay so far," she said, and lifted her hips to take the phone from her back pocket and toss it into his lap.

"What's this?"

"Richard Davis, and his wife, admitting to what goes on there. They laid out the full story."

Rushe frowned. "How did you get this?"

"That's not important," she said. "I sent a copy of the audio to Liam's computer, with instructions if I didn't contact him within twenty-four hours, he should send it to the police."

"You'll implicate yourself and me and—"

"I didn't use our names," she said with a smile. "I made sure to use his, and the full names and details of everyone else. One way or another, there's going to be pressure on the Waterside now. At least that was the idea.

I heard about the carjacking and—"

"Come on," he said.

Rushe got out of the vehicle, forcing her to do the same. She expected them to retrieve their prisoner, but her love strode forward. She snagged his back pocket and scuttled on behind until they reached a passage. Rushe opened a door and she passed him to enter but quickly came up short.

In the center of the otherwise bare room were Joseph Galante Senior and Evan Whyte, tied to chairs, back-to-back, bound, gagged and rightfully terrified.

"You did this?" she asked Rushe when his forearm came around to rest on her upper chest.

A splice of light appeared in the corner, she watched it widen. Eric appeared in the opening with Scott in tow. She examined the whole scene again.

"What's going on?" Eric asked.

"We need another chair," Rushe said, pinning the captive men under his triumphant glare.

FIFTY

RUSHE USHERED HER across to Eric and Scott. Once inside the other room, he spoke to his colleagues quietly and then they left, closing the door, sealing her in with her lover.

"What is going on?" she asked, scanning the oblong space.

The worn yellow walls oozed mold, a foam mattress lay on the floor in the corner, and a threadbare couch in the center of the space was aimed at a small portable TV on a stack of boxes.

"Hijacking the car got those bastards here tonight, quick and clean."

"That's it?" she asked, facing her love. "What happened to you? I saw you there, she injected you…" With a slow inhale, she looked at him properly for the first time. His skin was clammy and his eyes heavy. He didn't quite have his wits about him in the obvious way he usually did. Her volume dropped to a whisper, "What did they do to you?"

She reached up to stroke her fingers through his

damp hair.

"What was your plan?" Rushe asked, not reacting to her fawning.

Apparently, he didn't think this was the time or place for an intimate reunion.

"Rosa was the ringleader. She kept those men on their knees. Not one of them stood up to her."

"She manipulated them all."

"It wasn't right," she said. "None of those women would've died if it wasn't for her."

"She gets off on the power."

Putting the pieces together, the two of them working together, was a great buzz. But it was nothing to the high of being in the company of this man, her love, whom she thought she would never share space with again.

"She killed the women because she wanted the three men to herself," she said. "She controlled them all, the Galantes with love, and Whyte through blackmail. But if she was faithful—"

"She was never faithful to either of them. Rosa loves the attention of men."

"Hence Michael Lewis," she said. "Was he one in a string of relationships?"

"Looks like it," Rushe said. "We've turned up evidence of her affairs with dozens of men."

"She wanted you too," she said. "When you told her you wouldn't be loyal… how could you do that to me, Rushe?"

He took her hand out of his hair, but it was her who withdrew and stepped back.

"I saved your life."

"At the expense of yours," she said. "You left me alone… Without you, I'm all alone."

"I took a risk, a calculated risk. I'd do it again."

"I know," she said. "That's what scares the hell

out of me. How did you get out of there? How could you think that was calculated?"

"That needle was meant for you, the dose was meant for you."

"To overdose me!"

"They want it to look like an accident," Rushe said. "It wouldn't look like an accidental OD if the dose was off the charts."

"But Rosa… when she…"

"It's okay," he said, curling his fingers into her dripping hair. "I was willing to take the dose, ready to take it. Getting you out of there was all that mattered."

"They could've killed you," she said. "I don't understand how you could take that drug, how you could be willing to take the risk of having it in your system. You told them to give it to you. You couldn't have known that Rosa would approach you, that you would be able to get hold of her."

"You did that for me, Kitten," he said. "I told you I trusted your instinct."

"To come to you," she murmured, inching in closer as steam rose from their rain-drenched clothes.

"To stick me she had to get close, but I knew if you thought…"

"That I would come to you," she said on an exhale, closing her eyes to press her face to his chest.

"Thanks for that."

"Don't thank me," she said, pounding the side of her fist to his chest, as his other hand found her crown and stroked downward. "I left you there. I ran and I… I couldn't get back in."

"You did what you were supposed to do," he said.

Tears bled from her eyes into the fabric of his tee-shirt, but she wouldn't separate them, not even by an inch. "They drugged me, and I… I thought I'd lost you."

"I'd have murdered every man there to get you out."

"I know," she whispered, rubbing her face side to side slowly.

The swallow in his throat was audible. His fingers untangled from her hair to curl around her breast, while the other cradled the back of her head to hold her forehead to his heartbeat.

"I had to get rid of the threats to you, the gun and the drugs. Once that syringe was empty… all I knew was there was no way that liquid was going into you. You're a tiny thing, Kitten. I wouldn't watch what that would do to you."

"But I was expected to watch it in you?"

Pushing against his cradling hand, she looked up at him, aware the ache in his eyes was caused by the wetness brimming her eyelashes. "I knew Eric was close by," he said. "We knew drugs were involved, we'd discussed that already and had a plan. Naloxone is easy to get your hands on. It counteracts the effects of an OD."

"You let them dose you, on the hope Eric would be able to get to you in time?" she asked. "That he would know you needed help?"

"They panicked. Nothing last night went the way they thought it would. After they took you out, Joey came back in, and… I heard Whyte holler. You hurt him." She nodded and his expression relaxed. "Good girl."

"I couldn't see, and… I hit my head, and—"

"You did what you were supposed to," Rushe said. "I know now that Scott had already followed you to the hospital. I told them to stay put inside, Rosa gave me cover out as far as the alley. Outside I went down, and I was out. She ran, and Eric picked me up…"

"You could've died," she murmured.

"The dose would never have killed me, Kitten."

"Then you left me out there, alone. I was sure that... if you were alive, you'd have come to find me."

"You were meant to be in the hospital," he said, lowering his tone to a gnarly grump. "The notes said you were to be kept in overnight."

"You came to the hospital? And left me there?"

Rushe shook his head. "Eric and Scott dealt with that, and the carjacking too," he said, and nodded toward the mattress. "I spent most of my day over there. I only got up when..."

"When what?" she asked, letting her hands drift upward.

"We heard you split from the hospital. Where do you think I was driving to right now? You were supposed to stay there safe until we were done here."

She relaxed. "You were coming to find me? You were leaving Eric and Scott alone to deal with those guys, and... you were coming to find me?"

"I should've known better than to assume you'd do what you're told," he said, laying his palm flat on the top of her head. Instead of the usual affectionate gesture, this one seemed to steady his balance too.

"It's my instinct to come to you."

"You were safe in the hospital," he said. "I didn't want you to be a part of this. You don't need to see any of this."

"I need to be with you. We're doing what is right."

"I can't believe you snatched Rosa."

"She hurt you," she said again. When her lips parted, she craved their intimate reunion, though with his compromised system it could probably be viewed as taking advantage. Rushe would never touch her while there were drugs in her system. "I planned to hurt her right back. I'd have found Eric to deal with Whyte and

Galante, but I was with Davis when I heard about the carjacking. I couldn't figure that one out, but I kept working. I wasn't going to give up."

"We know the story. All that's left is for them to tell us about Susan… then we fulfill the initial goal of the mission."

From the way he monitored her expression, he was judging her reaction to what may occur. Until it happened, she couldn't say how she would react. All she knew was that those people out there, their prisoners, had caused pain to people who didn't deserve it, and they'd believed it was their right to do so. Rushe wasn't a man who would stand for that.

Eric came in alone. "Rosa's set up. I sent Scott for the car. He's ready, Rushe."

"Not yet," Rushe said.

"You can't ask him to hold off," Eric said. "Do you know how long he's been waiting for this?"

She stayed against Rushe but surveyed the room. A pizza box lay in a corner. Open Chinese food containers sat on the floor around the couch with beer bottles intermingled. A canvas sheet covered what she assumed from the odd sizes and shapes were a pile of various different items.

"They killed his woman," Eric said.

"And threatened mine," Rushe said. "If anything happened to her, they wouldn't be the only ones tied to chairs out there."

"What do you plan to do?" Flick asked, chiming in.

"We do things my way," Rushe said.

She saw a glimmer of something in him she didn't recognize. His rumpled clothes and dazed appearance might not be quite the Rushe she knew, but that awareness within him was all aimed at her.

"What way is that?"

"We wait," Rushe said.

"Let them torture themselves," she said.

"That's right."

"She really is your girl," Eric said.

"Yes," Rushe said with an abnormal glow of admiration. "She really is."

"Is there a restroom?" she asked, struggling to tear her gaze away from her love's.

"I'll show you," Eric said. "The water runs cold, but at least it runs."

Taking a few minutes to herself to wash up and mentally regroup was required, but Rushe was her comfort, her rock. She wouldn't be parted from him for long.

FIFTY-ONE

SCOTT RETURNED an hour later. They all drank beer and watched TV saying very little to each other. The three men sat on the couch, and she hadn't objected when Rushe took her hand and pulled her into his lap. Now she had him back, she could let herself think about what had happened or what might have happened.

Any anger she had left over his abandonment of her, or his risk-taking, was quelled by his actions now, or rather his lack of them. Since before they were together, when they were putting on a show for the criminals in that shack, every time she was in Rushe's lap he touched her and fondled her with entitlement. Not that night.

Nobody said a word. They stared at the screen, but none of them watched. Jokes prompted no laughter or communication. Not one of them made any attempt at conversation. They simply sat and stared.

Scott's fidgeting increased until he cursed under his breath. Eric moved to appease, but Rushe stood, causing her to find her feet.

"Okay," Rushe said, crossing to turn off the

television.

"Now?"

Rushe nodded to Eric once. "I'll get the story straight."

"Who gives a fuck about the story?" Scott barked.

Eric glanced at her, she felt Rushe's eyes on her too. "Do you boys need me to leave the room?" she asked without any intention of going anywhere.

"You're the reason," Scott sneered, and started toward her.

Rushe swooped in to intercept him. "Where the fuck do you think you're going?" he snarled.

Despite only having a view of Rushe's back, she knew the glare he wore. Him standing between her and trouble reminded her of that room in the X-Lounge, and it wasn't a pleasant memory.

"We had a deal," Scott said.

"I gave you the tools. I told you how to do it," Rushe said. "I held up my end."

"You have more experience. I wanna cause them pain."

Shorter and skinnier than both Rushe and Eric, Scott didn't have the bulk to take on the other men. Though the venom he had could drive him toward such a foolish attempt.

"You'll get your pound of flesh," Rushe grumbled. "You do it like I showed you."

"Everybody chill out," Eric said. Her view was still blocked by Rushe. "You wanna know what happened to Susie, you do, Scott. Let Rushe work."

In the instant Rushe was about to move, she tucked her hand into his back pocket. He stopped. It wasn't like Rushe to hesitate. Though it was barely perceptible, he definitely did before he turned to remove her hand from his pocket.

"No," he said, still with a hold of her hand. "Stay."

"We're partners."

"Not for the thug stuff, Kitten."

She wanted to argue because she'd just got him back. That made her reluctant to take the risk of letting him go again. But she wasn't menacing and mean. Whatever was about to happen, she needed to let him go. A part of Rushe would always work alone.

With his eyes fixated on her mouth, he stroked her hair. Then he raised the shutters and stormed straight past, snatching up a tool bag, and striding on out to their trio of captives.

Scott crossed to the door and opened it a crack, presumably to listen in.

"You thought you lost him, huh?" Eric asked.

"He let them…" she said. "They could have killed him."

"It's not the first time Rushe has come back from the dead."

"That doesn't make me feel better."

"Which is worse," Eric asked. "That you thought he was dead, or that you were the one who caused it?"

She wrapped her arms around herself and skirted the couch to lean against the back. "I don't know," she whispered.

Eric took up a perch beside her. "We always knew it would come to this. We brought in the furniture and the supplies, hooked up the TV two weeks ago."

"What does that have to do with—"

"We all knew it would come to this. We were prepared… Rushe was prepared."

For death, she understood, but it didn't make her feel better. "Do you think Scott was prepared for what happened to Susan?"

"Guys like us know the risks, but Susan didn't.

She saw only what Whyte wanted her to see."

"So Scott wants to take revenge, why? Because those three people contributed to Susan's death, or because Whyte seduced his girlfriend?"

"Scott loved Susan, always did, but she was… she saw the best in everyone. I guess he felt he should protect her, like Rushe wants to protect you."

"You say that as though it's so straightforward. Like it's a given, it's so obvious. But you don't know what the view's like from the other side."

Scott stumbled back when the door flew open and Rushe stormed in, sending the door ricocheting back into its frame. Her love stalked an invisible infuriation around the room, making it impossible for Scott or Eric to approach him, as they wanted to.

"What?" Eric asked. "What happened?"

Eric's confusion and Scott's wide eyes betrayed this wasn't standard operating procedure.

"Lover?" she asked, crossing toward Rushe.

He grabbed her lower jaw and rushed her back against the wall. In a crouch, his whole body cloaked her as he laid siege to her mouth, probing his tongue in around hers. With a feral grunt, he pried them apart and forced her chin up, locking his eyes on hers.

"My woman."

"Yes, Lover, I'm here," she inhaled, grasping his shoulders.

"He hurt you, now, now is the time."

To punish the man complicit in murder. "Yes."

Astounded that Rushe would take the time to seek her permission for anything, she remained flat on the wall when he strode from the room as intently as he'd entered it.

"Maybe you're an asset after all," Eric said. "What else can you make him do?"

FIFTY-TWO

A SOURING MASCULINE shriek pierced the air. She couldn't imagine what would cause such a sound. A female scream followed. When Eric and Scott huddled near the door, she was right there with them.

"No, no! Stop, please!" The hurried speech was that of Joseph Galante. "Stop whatever you're doing to Evan!"

She edged closer to the door and peered through the gap. The three chairs were arranged in a triangle with their backs to each other so the detainees couldn't see one another. The captives couldn't see in her direction either, leaving her free to observe. A slumped Whyte whimpered. Underneath his chair was a wet puddle and though the color was difficult to distinguish on the mildew-stained floor, she assumed the liquid was blood.

"You don't give a fuck about him," Rushe's voice rumbled through, that savage snarl plumbed from his dusky soul. "He hurt my woman."

"She is mine," Galante said. "Rosa is mine, and you're going to—"

"She's not your woman," Rushe said, strolling to a chair situated to be visible from Galante and Rosa's positions. "She'll take any cock that tips her way." He opened the bag on the floor at his side and produced a coiled length of rope. "How many guys did she fuck in that lounge while you were paying her?"

"You shut up," Rosa yelled.

Rushe began to uncoil the rope very deliberately, letting the length spread on the floor around him. "You wanted it, sweetheart," he drawled. "You were begging me for it, handing it out for free with coupons for a lifetime supply."

"You wanted it," Rosa sniped.

He leaned forward to take a knife from the bag. "My girl would slice you open."

Rosa didn't respond to Rushe's smug retort. Whyte still whimpered and gurgled but didn't speak. Rushe bowed the rope over the knife and sawed it apart.

"What is that for?" Galante asked.

They were already attached to the chairs. What else would he need rope for? He cast the length he'd cut aside and began to loosen another strip.

"We know about the racquet you were running, Rosa. We know you were blackmailing Evan Whyte. You kept quiet and he kept you around. When did the murders start?"

"What do you care?" Rosa asked.

"I wanna know what happened to Susan. Why was she different?"

A few seconds of silence became a minute. Her love tossed the rope aside and was on his feet with the knife.

"No, no!" Galante called out before Rushe reached him. "We didn't kill Susan!"

"Don't believe you," Rushe said, admiring the blade of his knife, then pointing it toward Rosa.

"Believe what you want," Galante said. "It's true. The first girl died two years ago, but that was an accident. Please, you have to believe us!"

"I don't gotta believe shit," Rushe said, returning to his chair and picking up the first length of rope. Two years ago was when Kimberly gave birth to Joey's baby. Was that it? The catalyst that started it? Rosa's breaking point? "So your woman got a taste for the snuff?"

"It was interesting," Rosa said. "I'm not a psycho. As long as the boys didn't get attached, I let them screw whoever they wanted to."

"It was just an accident," Galante said, a quiver in his voice.

Her fascination with Rushe's actions yielded results. He was twining the rope into a noose.

"But it wasn't just her."

"No," Galante admitted. "Rosa… Evan enjoyed it." Galante was trying to protect the woman he loved by transferring the evil doing onto Whyte. "We did it again, we used the drugs, it's clean."

"Then you did it again," Rushe said, finishing with one noose he threw it toward Galante. It landed on the floor a few inches from his feet.

"Once, a couple of months later, and then a few months after that…"

"The more you got away with, the more risks you took," Rushe said. "Your woman's into some kinky shit."

"We gave them drugs, and we had sex, and—"

"It was a party," Rosa said. "They couldn't keep up, that's all."

"Susan heard us talking," Galante said when Rushe picked up the next stretch of rope and began to tie it. "I think Evan cared for her… she might have been different."

"Bitch couldn't handle it," Rosa said. "We tried to talk to her, lots, they wanted to bring her in, wanted her to be part of it. She didn't get it… I knew she wouldn't. There was no room for her in our family."

"Her death was tragic, and needless," Galante said. "But by her own hand."

The intensity of Rushe's eyes climbed and zeroed in on Rosa, scrutinizing every detail of her countenance. Again, cruel silence reigned, but her love didn't flinch for a second.

"Your woman doesn't believe it."

Rushe's words were heavy, but they stung in the air, drifting toward the restrained bodies.

"She did it," Whyte croaked out when his head rose a fraction. "She drugged her and set her up, made it look good, she told me. Rosa killed Susan, just like she killed Jeri and Lisa, and all the others."

"Whyte!" Galante shouted.

"Rosa Vallario," Rushe said.

"Susan knew what she did," Whyte said. "She saw Rosa for the twisted individual she is."

"Rosa," Galante said. "Rosa didn't, it was me—"

"When are you going to stop defending her?" Whyte asked. "She's sick."

"And what are you?" Rosa spat.

"Enough!" Rushe silenced them all.

"What are you going to do with us?" Rosa asked.

"Don't worry," Galante said, when Rosa didn't get an answer. "He said he wasn't going to kill us."

"Hanging can be framed to look like suicide," Rosa said.

"You would know," Rushe said. "And I said I wasn't gonna kill you, Galante, but I made no promises about anyone else." He got up and moved to the edge of the room, out of her view. "And I'm not the only one here who can cause you harm."

When Rushe came back into view, he had a

bottle in his pocket and a syringe in his hand. He held it up, pocketed the cap then crouched in front of Rosa.

"You're it."

"I can be useful to you," Rosa said, panicked. "I know where the money is. You can have it. We can have it."

"I already got me all the woman I need," Rushe said.

On Rosa's struggling scream, he injected her with the contents of the needle.

She'd always known her love was capable of anything, and Rosa was a murderer. Standing there, watching her lover take a life in this way, caused a strange sensation to float through her. Seizing Rosa from the street had been only the first step of her plan, the end result would have been the same.

"What are you doing?" Galante asked, trying to see over his shoulder. "Rosa? Rosie, speak to me, are you okay?"

Rosa slumped forward as Rushe stood up with the needle loose in his hand. When Whyte saw the instrument, he jerked, drawing Rushe's attention. With his free hand, her love delivered a swift punch to the side of Whyte's head, knocking him out cold.

Galante was gibbering, but Rushe paid no attention. He strode back to their little room, sending her and the other men scampering backward.

"We're out of here," Rushe said to Eric, who held open a bag for the needle. With it wrapped up, her love grabbed his jacket from the back of the couch and stuffed the evidence into it. He then took the bottle from his pocket and tossed it to Scott. "Be very careful with that."

"Thanks man," Eric said.

"Whatever," Rushe said, taking hold of her shoulder.

Scott didn't say anything, but Rushe didn't appear to expect it. He swung open the door and dragged her out, past the captives and back into the room with his car. He flung her into the passenger side.

"Wait," she said, before he closed the door. "Lover…"

Maybe she hadn't expected him to stop because when he did, she didn't know what to say.

"Later," grumbled the burdened man when she said nothing.

She'd expected him to get in the driver's seat, but he didn't. He went back through their exit door. How long should she wait? And what was she waiting for?

Rushe re-emerged with Rosa's motionless body over his shoulder.

The last time she'd seen a similar picture, Rosa had kicked and screamed. Her stomach roiled at the understanding of her role in the woman's demise. Rushe tossed the body in the trunk, adopted his place in the driving seat, and drove them out into the night.

"What was in the bottle?" she asked after they'd been driving quietly for more than a few minutes.

"Lye."

The effects a substance like that could have in the hands of a man like Scott on men like Galante and Whyte would be devastating.

"What do we do now?" she asked. "I've never disposed of a dead body before."

Rushe looked from her to the road, and then took a longer look at her. "You think she's dead? You think I killed her?"

"The needle, I…"

"Shit," he exhaled.

"She's not?"

"Taste of her own medicine. She murdered Susan, and Scott will make me pay for this."

"He wanted her dead. I know Rosa was a bad person."

"I don't argue with women," Rushe said. "You think I'd murder one?"

"I don't understand… she's not dead?"

"Tranquilizer," Rushe said. "We'll toss her out somewhere she'll be found, but we won't be spotted." He reared up and put his hand in his back jeans pocket to produce Liam's phone, which he flung to her lap. "Get that to your guy."

"It's recording?"

"Turned it off before I got the needle."

She played the recording to hear Whyte admit Rosa killed them.

A smile formed as she looked up at her grumbling lover. "Should I tell him to send this and the Davis recording to the cops?"

"No," Rushe said. "The cops can have Rosa, but those files will reap more justice in different hands."

"I don't understand," she said. "Whose?"

His grip on the steering wheel increased. "We've found a contact… in the King Club. Have him keep hold of it, I'll tell Eric to be in touch."

She recognized the growl and the slices of resolve that enclosed around him. With her own comprehension, tenacity swept across her too. Whyte and Galante, Joey too, all of them had played a dangerous game, which Davis had known about as well. If the King Club did not sanction the action, if they'd been oblivious to events that transpired in the Waterside, they could be very unhappy about what the risk of exposure would do to their own serious endeavors.

Rushe began to grumble, and she noticed his obstinate brow.

"What?" she asked.

"If I'd known you were okay with murder, I'd

have…”

“I think Whyte was bleeding enough. What will happen to them?”

“Not our business,” Rushe said.

“We get rid of Rosa, and of the evidence… then what?”

“Sex.”

FIFTY-THREE

MORE THAN TWO hours had passed by the time Rushe drove off the interstate to a roadside motel. They had dropped Rosa off and got rid of the evidence, then Rushe just drove. Processing everything that had happened would take time for both of them, and she didn't mind having quiet time to reflect.

"Get naked," he said, hurling the bag of their things to the floor when they entered the motel room.

It wasn't much, just whatever had been transferred out of the trunk of their car that Scott had got rid of, though she didn't know what was left in the trunk of the vehicle they had downstairs.

"Shouldn't we talk? If there are still drugs in your system, or you're not strong enough—"

Spinning around, his hand landed on her upper chest, slamming her back against the wall, his power pinning her in place.

"My woman, my body."

The shade of murk in his eyes wasn't one to be messed with. After what they'd been through these last few days, she couldn't deny him. Rushe needed to connect with her body, and she wanted to be a part of his. She unzipped her jeans and forced them down her hips, but while Rushe held her there, she couldn't bend, so she unbuttoned the shirt and parted the fabric.

Rushe knew their sexual safe word, but he wouldn't use it tonight. Any doubts she had about his senses, about him having his wits, were erased when she witnessed the methodical skill he'd displayed that night.

As his eyes coasted downward, some of the gloom faded. She was wearing the same dress she'd worn when he died. That night, in that hotel, neither of them had expected events to transpire as they did. Her love had died for her. She would never be able to convey to him what his sacrifice meant to her.

She swallowed away her dismay. Rushe's attention darted back up. "I love you," she murmured.

The fog gave way to a pain in him that she would never be able to heal. He lunged in and took her off her feet, urging his mouth over hers as they landed on the bed.

"My woman," he muttered, kissing his way down her throat and back up to her mouth.

This kiss was forever. The sweet texture of his lips coupling with hers was a home she had missed. Her craving for him intensified with every second she existed. More than once when she'd asked him to make love to her, he'd refused when he didn't want to reinforce her fears.

The evil had been dispensed with, so he may think there was nothing more to be afraid of. But she had never been more terrified. Losing him, believing him dead, had thrown her into a hell worse than anything she could have conceived without living the anguish firsthand.

"Rushe," she said, when he trailed his mouth

toward her ear.

"I love you, Kitten."

"Please don't ever leave me again."

His focus came up and he gazed into her, not just her eyes, but to her own buried torture. "You are my woman."

"Yes."

"You belong to me."

"Yes."

"I'll never leave you, Flick," he said. "You're the only evidence that I exist at all."

When he dropped his mouth on hers again, she parted her lips and sucked his tongue into her mouth, coating herself with the taste of him. Rushe wouldn't hesitate to protect her. That was who he was, she couldn't change that. He was a part of her; he lived in her heart. Just like she'd said to him about his own.

Her body chilled when his rose from the bed. Rushe pulled off her jeans as she shirked the shirt and pulled the dress over her head, exposing herself to him.

He offered no commands, so she shuffled to the edge of the bed and unbuckled his jeans. Pushing them downward, she dipped her head forward and kissed his shaft. Curling her tongue around the heavy organ, she tasted the weight of him, the mass that wanted to take refuge in her body.

"Every inch of you belongs to me," he growled. "Those hot tits and that tight pussy. Mine. Your hair, your hands, your heart. Every fucking part of you. Mine, every inch."

"Yes," she breathed on him, looping her lips around his head.

He got hold of her hair and tugged her head back, forcing her to look up at him. "You're getting dangerous, Kitten."

"I learned from you," she said. "I'd have made

them pay, and I'd have made you proud."

"I am proud."

She heard it in the way he spoke to her, in the things he said to Rosa and the others when referencing her. Living up to her own ideal of what Rushe's woman should be was almost impossible. He deserved the world, and she needed the strength to deliver for him.

"I am your servant," she said, sticking out her tongue, trying to taste him, but he held his hips away.

Loosening his grip, he directed her face forward. "Look at it… Look at my cock. You see what you do to me?"

His magnificence made her want to smile, to grin like a giddy schoolgirl with a new toy. The heavy length of him jutted up, proudly ready to serve her, it sent shivers from her shoulders to her neck, to her nipples, and further south.

"I need him."

Of their own accord her hands came up, but her love dipped away when she tried to clasp for his member.

"I told you to look, not touch, whore. You look at it, you think about what it feels like to have that inside you. My dick, in your cunt, filling you up full. You're empty without it, Kitten. That space was meant for me. Without my cock in you you're incomplete. You need it."

"Yes."

"You need me to fuck you."

"Yes," she exhaled, trying again to move forward.

His fist held her in place. "No man comes after me. No other dick's gonna get near my pussy, no one touches what's mine. Kiss it." He gave her just enough room to trace her lips against the ridge running the length of him. "Lick."

This time he held himself up and angled her face in against his balls. Rubbing her face in deep, she opened her mouth, releasing the saliva that had built up while she admired him. Rushe's groan was coupled with him dragging her mouth down him, forcing his cock inside as he went. Pulling back a little, he pressed himself into her cheek until the corner of her mouth burned.

"Eyes," he said, and she let hers flick up to meet his. "You serve my pleasure."

When she nodded, the friction made him moan, just as she'd known it would. On her smile, his eyes narrowed. Despite their position, she still had the upper hand.

Tossing her to the mattress, Rushe said nothing as he swooped forward, pushing her back with his body, until he lay atop her. His finger invaded her center, and she groaned. Her legs parted around him, and she tried to move, but he kept her still.

"Why are you so wet, Kitten?" he asked, kissing her once.

"I want you," she answered, and he kissed her again.

Drawing his finger out, he pushed it back in, undulating it within her then twisting it into the cushion inside her. Her ragged inhale was fired by the scorching pleasure he already imparted.

"That feels better, doesn't it? You feel better when I pamper your pussy, don't you, Kitten?"

She could barely manage to nod. His finger pulsed in and out, moving faster to build the pressure of wanton release.

"Open wide."

She spread her legs wide, letting her knees hang loose in the air and his finger slid out. She wriggled up against the solid length between them, but he lifted his hips, letting his head kiss her opening. She whined, and he touched the finger that had been inside her to her lip. She opened to receive it, but he stole it into his own mouth.

"You get only what I give you," he murmured, and traced her lips with the tip of his tongue, stealing the last of her taste.

His tongue slid into her mouth, and with the uniting kiss, her legs locked around him. Her love surged forward, and his cock found its home.

Flick's head went back, breaking the kiss, and she gasped. "Yes! Rushe!"

Biting her lips, trying to contain some of the aching release this joining burst within her, did nothing to lessen the rush of feeling that she had thought forever lost.

"What a good little Kitten you are."

"Fuck me, Rushe," she demanded in a growl to rival her lover's own.

Slowly, he shook his head and let himself smile. "Not tonight."

Dragging his member out, he almost unsheathed himself but filled her again. The pace was so delicious that she took his face and sought his mouth again. Her love was there. Her love was safe. Her love was back where he belonged.

WHEN SHE AWOKE in the dark later that night, she sensed straight away that Rushe wasn't asleep. Trailing her toes down his shins as she stretched, her legs parted so she could sit up on him.

He made no secret of the fact he was awake. The glint in his open eyes reflected the artificial light from beyond the curtains. Walking her fingertips up his sternum, she touched his jaw and his lip while shimmying up until her knees rested outside his elbows.

Leaning down, she dangled her nipple close to his mouth, watching his eyes as she let it drift nearer until the soft tip met the rough texture of his upper lip. The act meant to tease him sent a frisson of heat through her, and on a sigh her body relaxed. Her love took the opportunity to boost his head and nip the point in his teeth. When he sucked hard, she whimpered out, and he took the other nipple between two knuckles and squeezed.

"I'm meant to be making you feel better," she confessed on a smile.

In a snap, his elbows locked behind her knees. Her whole body was hefted up so quickly that she had to slap her hands on the wall to prevent it from making contact with her skull.

"Now I feel better," he said, drawing his tongue around her clit. He'd hiked her so high that her knees were now above his shoulders. She was literally sitting on his face, but he kept control of her weight with his arms wound around her legs.

"Are you going to Rushe me?" she teased.

His mouth stopped long enough for her to feel the curve of his smile around her. "How long have you been holding onto that one?" he asked, swirling his tongue, going back to the job at hand.

"You've never been one for breakfast in bed," she said, curling her fingers around her breasts.

"I've missed a few meals," he said, lapping the juice from her opening.

This intent attention was becoming too much. He would use that wonderfully talented mouth to bring her to climax after climax without ever thinking of himself.

"I don't want you to overexert yourself," she said, dropping her hand into his hair to direct his head back so he could look up at her.

"Okay," he said, and sat up, sending her slithering the length of his torso until her back hit his drawn-up thighs. "You do it then."

His cock was already hard between her folds, and she shifted to put her shins on the bed, but he took hold of them, preventing her from seating herself astride him. Running his palms down her legs, Rushe pushed the soles of her feet to his external obliques.

"Are you in pain?" she asked, suddenly aware that all of her weight was on his.

Normally, that wouldn't bother her, but he'd never put her in this position before. After everything he'd been through in the last thirty-six hours, she didn't want to sap the last of his energy.

"Make yourself come."

That intensity in his eyes wasn't torture, it was mischief. Nothing could bring this towering pillar down. His strength and virility were as they ever had been. Her worry may be unnecessary, but that didn't mean he wouldn't take full advantage of it.

"Can I fuck myself?" He shook his head, and the slope of his lips calmed her. "You want me to sit here on your cock and pleasure myself, but I'm not allowed to use it?"

"Wriggle all you want," he said.

This deep night and penetrating man were the only home that she would ever need. "I love you, Rushe."

"Won't help you now," he said. "Do it."

Watching him enjoy this, enjoy her, made her grin. She curled her toes in against him while resting all her weight on his thighs and letting her knees drop apart.

"Like this?"

"Good start," he said, fixating on that space at the top of her thighs.

"Did you miss me?" she whispered.

His eyes came up to meet hers. She didn't mean while they were parted over the last couple of days. She didn't even mean on the job. She meant this. The fun they could have, the teasing and the intimacy that they'd cultivated together. None of this was easy for him. He still struggled to trust her, and she still struggled to see what such a force of man could want with her.

But they had each other back. No job. No cover. Just the bare, inconvenient truth of their love. Resent it or not, want it or not, they were both stuck with it. There wasn't anything that would take her from Rushe. They'd become a part of each other.

"Yeah," he said. Lifting her foot to his mouth, he kissed her instep. "Now quit stalling, this might be the only chance I give you to play with my pussy."

"You are rather possessive," she said, grasping her breasts.

"I didn't tell you to touch those. My girls are gonna get all the love they want tonight, but only from me."

"What if he feels neglected?" she asked, elevating her hips enough to whorl a finger around his dick and pluck him out from under her, wriggling until he poked up against her pubis.

"He'll let you know about it in a hurry," Rushe said.

Pressuring her palm against his shaft, she squashed him against her and tilted her hips to slide up and down, effectively fucking him from the outside.

"That's bending the rules," he groaned when she pushed onto her feet and took her pelvis from his to prod his head against her clit.

She stimulated them both then slithered down his length and up again, using her palm on the other side to keep him enclosed.

"What else are rules for?" she whispered.

She was prepared to take her time and would certainly ensure her orgasm, but she'd guarantee his too.

After all the external negativity they'd been exposed to, they both deserved some internal positive reinforcement.

Their mettle may have been tested, but their love had endured. She hadn't known herself capable of the actions she'd undertaken. She wouldn't have been until Rushe. He had changed her, enhanced her, improved her. Being with him had caused her to grow into someone stronger. His infinite capability made her strive to reach a parallel of his integrity. Her love had been alone in life for too long. She would keep pushing until he understood her unerring devotion knew no limit.

EPILOGUE

THEIR NIGHT had been long, but she savored every minute of it. The peril they'd been in before didn't compare to this experience. The depth of such extreme emotions was no doubt intensified by their love. Every day she loved Rushe more, which meant every day her fear of losing him increased. This time around, for a minute, she had actually lost him. No way she'd make that mistake again.

Rushe disappeared from their room in the morning and returned with clothes and other supplies. She didn't ask questions just got dressed, they ate, and then they were on the road again.

"Where are we going?" she asked.

"There's a decent hotel about an hour down the road. We'll set up there. I'll call in a couple of favors."

"For what?" she asked. "Shouldn't we just go to your house? Do you still not trust me? Do you still think I'll—"

"I don't have a house."

"What?"

"Never needed one. I'm a drifter, Kitten. I make camp wherever I happen to be until the next job comes along."

"But you said you had an apartment," she said.

"I did. The one Eric got for me, where we lived."

"That wasn't your real home," she said, examining his stony profile. "You set that up for us, so no one would come looking."

"There's always someone looking," he said. "I stay in a hotel, or an apartment, or wherever I want. I move on when I need to. It doesn't pay to have ties, doesn't pay to get attached. If I leave a trail—"

"Weakness, I know, you told me already. You really don't have a home?"

"Never have," he said on a shrug, and glanced at her then back to the road. "I'm not gonna leave a base full of information for anyone to find."

He'd done it deliberately, made a conscious decision to never establish himself anywhere. The only place in the world he left a trace of himself was in her body.

For the rest of the journey, she thought about the nomadic lifestyle that lay ahead. If Rushe was so dead against setting up a home, it would be one meaningless apartment to the next, or one hotel to the next. Traditional life wasn't something she would ever have with Rushe. The more she found out, the more curious she got about his past, and about the future they would have together.

As time went on, she would learn more about her love. If she pushed too hard all at once, he would push back. That would never end well. So she would be patient and work to his schedule.

In the three months they were without work, she'd gained ground. Now they would have time to get back to that state of co-habitation. Rushe would remember their connection, and she could inch just a little closer.

She stayed in the car while he checked into the hotel room. While the hotel was decent, it wasn't on the same level as the Waterside. Thank God. She didn't want to recall what it was like to live there.

They had a two-room suite with a living space, bedroom, and a shower room. Nothing more or less than what they needed.

She went straight into the shower while Rushe made his phone calls. When she got out, there was a laptop on the desk.

"You got a computer?"

"You should tell your friend you're safe," he said.

Their belongings were laid out on the bed. Rushe picked up each item in turn to inspect it. Most of it was from the emergency kit, but there were some unfamiliar additions.

"Do we have another job?" she asked, sliding into the chair at the desk.

"I'm waiting for a call."

"Okay," she said. He hadn't looked at her, and tension rode his shoulders, more than had been there on their arrival. "Should we talk?"

Rushe picked up a gun and popped out the clip. "About what?"

Something was eating at him. "Are you upset with me about something?"

"No," he ground out. "I'm not."

"So what's the problem?"

He whipped around so fast she anticipated a brusque response, but the phone rang, diverting his attention. He snatched it up and disappeared into the bedroom.

Oh, well, while waiting, she logged into her email and deleted the junk. Liam had already sent her a message; she responded to let him know they were okay. The light on the phone base went off indicating the call was over, but her love stayed in the bedroom.

To her surprise, she came across an email from her sister.

"I got an email from my sister Lucia," she called out, hoping to prompt Rushe back into the room. "She and Vivian are having a joint anniversary party weekend. They want us to go… Look at that, Lucia was married on the twenty-second and Vivian married on the twenty-fourth of the same month, I didn't know that… in different years, of course. Does that mean we have to get married on the twenty-third?" She didn't hear him, but felt him approach so looked over her shoulder, his stern expression made her groan. "I was kidding. Why would I want to marry you?" He didn't respond to her quip. "What?" She got up out of her chair to slip her hands in his pockets. "Rushe, you're scaring me. What is it?"

"Jansen's in the hospital. His condition is critical."

"Jansen…? The undercover cop who saved our asses from the human traffickers, from Victor and Simone, that Jansen?"

"Yeah."

"This is it, isn't it?" she asked. "The danger has come to find us, just like you said it would."

"Yeah, Kitten, we have to go back to the beginning."

TO BE CONTINUED…

Thank you for reading this tale!
If you can, please take the time to review.

~

Ask your local library for more Scarlett Finn novels!

~

For all things Scarlett Finn
check out:

www.scarlettfinn.com

BOOK THREE

EXPLICIT MEMORY

SCARLETT FINN

OUT NOW!

www.ingramcontent.com/pod-product-compliance
Lightning Source LLC
Chambersburg PA
CBHW060728190726
48285CB00001B/118